Sorry,
Bro

Sorry, Bro

TALEEN VOSKUNI

Berkley Romance
New York

BERKLEY ROMANCE
Published by Berkley
An imprint of Penguin Random House LLC
penguinrandomhouse.com

Copyright © 2023 by Taleen Voskuni
Excerpt from *Lavash at First Sight* copyright © 2023 by Taleen Voskuni
Penguin Random House supports copyright. Copyright fuels creativity, encourages
diverse voices, promotes free speech, and creates a vibrant culture. Thank you for buying
an authorized edition of this book and for complying with copyright laws by not
reproducing, scanning, or distributing any part of it in any form without permission. You
are supporting writers and allowing Penguin Random House to continue to publish books
for every reader.

BERKLEY is a registered trademark and Berkley Romance with B colophon is
a trademark of Penguin Random House LLC.

Library of Congress Cataloging-in-Publication Data

Names: Voskuni, Taleen, author.
Title: Sorry, bro / Taleen Voskuni.
Description: First edition. | New York : Berkley Romance, 2023.
Identifiers: LCCN 2022021260 (print) | LCCN 2022021261 (ebook) |
ISBN 9780593547304 (trade paperback) | ISBN 9780593547311 (ebook)
Subjects: LCSH: Armenian Americans--Fiction. | LCGFT: Bisexual fiction. |
Romance fiction. | Novels.
Classification: LCC PS3622.O84 S67 2023 (print) | LCC PS3622.O84 (ebook) |
DDC 813/.6—dc23/eng/20220506
LC record available at https://lccn.loc.gov/2022021260
LC ebook record available at https://lccn.loc.gov/2022021261

First Edition: January 2023

Printed in the United States of America
1st Printing

Interior art: Pomegranate frame © Saltoli / Shutterstock
Book design by Alison Cnockaert

For my sister, my mother, and my homeland.

Sorry, Bro

A good girl is worth more than seven boys.

Լաւ աղջիկը եօթը տղի համ կուտայ:

—Armenian Proverb

1

Arrows, like words, once darted, do not return.

Նետն ու խօսքը դուրս թռչելէն վերջ ալ ետ չեն դառնար։

—*Armenian Proverb*

I squeeze past a group of rowdy tech boys and a waitress dressed in a traditional German folk costume, similar to the one I own, thanks to a gift from my boyfriend, Trevor, and the beer maiden fetish he won't admit he has. Polka music blasts through the speakers. Patrons are pounding on tables and singing. The stuffiness in this restaurant is second only to sitting in a hot car with all the doors and windows shut.

I'm late to meet Trevor, but what else is new? It's hard to pull away from my family and the bonds of duty (in this case, setting up for my cousin Diana's bridal shower). My hands are aching from handling bushels of thorny crinkle roses and darting them into flower arrangements. I rub them together, hoping for some relief.

I spot Trevor. He's tapping wildly at his phone, wearing his work-concentration face, which is impressive because we are in the midst of a sausage-fest polka party. He's sporting his usual precision *American Psycho* hair (his words, not mine) and is wearing a quarter-zip pullover even though it's a million degrees. He looks every part the hot evil San Francisco tech lawyer he is, minus the evil, because Trevor is a teddy bear who just happens to enjoy following the letter of the law of patents. I slam into the seat opposite him and immediately shout my apologies.

His face lights up, and for some reason, that makes this guilt sit in my gut.

"Schatzie! You are sizzling. Total smokeshow. Glad you remembered to dress up."

I don't remember him asking me to dress up, but luckily I put on my red power dress earlier today in an attempt to impress my boss and pitch him a serious story instead of the usual fluff I'm assigned. I ended up filming the following news segment: "Ingrown Toenails: A Silent Killer? Local Doctor Weighs In." So yeah, the outfit didn't work. The memory of my boss publicly shooting down my pitch with such casual cruelty sets my nerves on edge.

I scoot the clunky wooden chair close to the table. "You know how the family is. Can't get down to business. Have to gossip and nag for an hour before anything can get done."

I don't know why I'm ragging on them. Sure, Mom kept bugging me about going to some super-important Armenian event happening this month (eye roll), and Tantig Sona could not stop complaining about the heat, but there was a moment—when the late-afternoon June light hit the room and everything and everyone glowed yellow under it, the flora filling the space with the scent of buttercream cake—when I felt peaceful. We finished the arrangements, but there was still so much more setup, and I felt terrible for leaving them and feel terrible for being so late to this date.

"Oh, I know. Your crazy Armenian family. Loudest group of women in the continental US. That shower tomorrow—what are the little gifts you give out to people?"

I half smile because it's not his fault; I talk smack on them constantly, so that's what he internalizes. But also, how can he joke about loudness when this restaurant is his favorite one in the city? A cowbell rings over and over, and a flock of beer maidens parade out from the back, holding boots of beer for another techie group in the corner.

Trevor gazes at the display fondly, and I hope he's not about to recount the hijinks of Oktoberfest 2009 again.

Before he gets a chance, I quickly answer, "The favors."

"Favors. You're giving out bedazzled earplugs to everyone, right?"

He chuckles to himself, and it jarringly reminds me of my work nemesis, Mark. Yuck, no. Trevor is nothing like Mark, who strong-arms his way into getting any piece with real merit, then smiles at the newsroom all self-satisfied. On camera, he'll ask rude invasive questions to people who've experienced trauma, but the boss seems to eat it up. To distract myself from the thought of Trevor being anything like him, I scan the menu. "So, I'm thinking the jäger chicken—"

"I already ordered for us—the two-person sausage extravaganza. And a surprise."

I hate surprises. My hope is that he's referring to the apple strudel on the dessert menu, a huge departure from his usual lingonberry tart. Or maybe he bought one of the deer heads on the wall. They're cool, if sad, and he's been talking about making an offer on one. I give him a wan smile and start fanning myself with the menu like Tantig Sona.

"It feels special that we're at Diekkengräber's tonight, ja?" Trevor's only a quarter German, and his last name, Milken, is Irish, but he was a German major, studied in Munich, and is still fluent. So naturally he pronounces the restaurant name with a perfect accent and not how I pronounce it, which is a variant of "dick grabber."

"Ja," I respond, trying to smile, assuming he means because he's headed off on a twelve-hour flight to Germany tomorrow. He's assisting one of the partners on this patent litigation case with an electric bike manufacturer. It's a big deal for him. I need to pull myself together for his sake. I'm exhausted from a full day of shooting and editing—despite the uninspiring material—then dashing over to help with the shower, then navigating an hour of hair-pulling traffic to make it to the city. But he's been talking up our dick grabber date for weeks, and I am wearing my red dress, and it's Friday, and I'm only twenty-seven, so I should have the energy for this.

"I'm going to miss you so much, schatzie," he says, his voice icky-sweet. Under the table, his hand squeezes my knee a little too hard. I don't wince.

The pet name means "treasure" in German, which is cute, but he's stopped saying my real name, Nareh, or even my nickname, Nar.

"Me, too," I say, conscious of how I sound, trying to match his tone. "But you'll be back soon."

"Three weeks," he says, shaken.

The rest of June and into early July. It should seem long, but I have this feeling that almost a month of being away from him is going to fly by.

"I keep pretending it's shorter," I say. I don't know why I lie. I guess I want to make him happy.

A waitress sets a bottle of champagne and two glasses in front of us. The label says Cristal 2010, and I feel like the heat is getting to me, because that would be, like, a $500 bottle. Christ, it's five years old; it might be pricier. Then I see the Cheshire grin on Trevor's face.

"Are we celebrating your trip? That's an"—I stumble over the words—"extravagant goodbye gesture."

Looking sly as hell, he says, "Oh, we're celebrating something all right."

He stands up and wedges himself between our table and our neighbor's, his butt knocking over a beer stein, which he doesn't notice because it's deafening in here, and then he's in front of me, kneeling down. And oh my God, he pulls out a dark blue box, and my blood is rushing in my ears. I'm gripping the seat of my chair like it's the only thing keeping me from slipping to the floor. He opens the box, and the woman at the table next to us gasps because the diamond is fucking huge—no other way to say it—and I know he's done something stupid, like taken the three months' salary rule too literally, because he makes a lot pre-tax, but he owes a wild amount of student debt, and that makes me think of my dad and the secret second mortgage he left us with when he died, and I don't want to be thinking about that right now.

Trevor is beaming. "Nareh Bedrossian." He spits out my last name like it's been through a wood chipper. "Will you be my wife? Will you be Nareh Milken?"

Half the restaurant is staring at me, and the other half is still partying and scream-laughing and shoving each other. Milken. Oh God, there are going to be even more jokes about my boobs for the rest of my life. Or I can get a breast-reduction surgery. No, Mom would kill me.

"Does—did you tell my mom already?"

His smile falters a bit, but he keeps it up. "No, I didn't want your mom to get in the way of this beautiful thing. Our union."

Then he swivels around and makes some kind of "come here" arm gesture, and now the heat is definitely making me hallucinate because I swear I see Mark H. Shephard, my number one work nemesis, shoving patrons out of the way with his KTVA mic and a cameraman with the massive camera setup they usually reserve for the big stories, and he's charging toward me and smears the mic across my face so that I get my berry lipstick all over it. Trevor and Mark high-five each other, which makes my stomach roil, and Trevor presses his forehead to mine and asks, "What do you say, schatzie?"

The antlered dead deer face stares at me, and I wish I were suspended above everything like him. No more decisions, no more failures, no more disappointing people, no more . . .

I'm slipping down, down, and the last thing I feel is a dead weight against the back of my skull.

Trevor's face is in front of mine, and he is wide-eyed and panicking and spitting as he talks, and oh God, it's all coming back to me when I see Mark hovering in the background. He's actually laughing while strangers press against one another to get a look at the girl who fainted.

"We have to go," I whisper to Trevor.

Trevor lifts me off the ground and my vision momentarily blurs. People I've never met are asking if I'm okay, and I give them a TV smile and tell them I'm fine, thank you. My head clears, and I squeeze my way out of the restaurant, making sure to slam specifically into Mark and not say a word to him when he shouts, "Hey!" Because really? I'm pissed. And not just at Mark for laughing at me, but at Trevor and his idea of a romantic proposal—at this restaurant, with all its drunk patrons—and partly at myself for . . . for . . . I don't know what for! But I did something wrong, and I'll figure it out, and there will be punishment.

I'm outside and it's instantly cold. The fog washes over everything, layer after layer engulfing us like waves. Somewhere in the Marina a horn blows long and deep. It may be an idyllic warm June in the rest of the United States, but this is San Francisco, where summer means unrelenting fog and misty winds. Trevor is behind me, the front door of the restaurant jingling behind him. I have to get to one of our cars before the humidity ruins my blowout. On the way in I brought a scarf to wrap around my hair, but there's no way in hell I'm going back into that restaurant right now. It'll be in the lost and found tomorrow.

Trevor is tracking me. I hear the *pound-pound* of his feet, but I don't look back, not yet. "Schatzie! Talk to me."

I reach my car, swing open my door, and turn to him. "Get in." The fog and streetlights have colored everything a grayish yellow.

As he shifts inside, I see he's holding the champagne bottle. Priorities.

This is Trevor, my boyfriend of five years—four and a half, more precisely—who has been a source of such kindness in my life, who I'm about to hurt so badly. But inside, I'm screaming. I have to.

"You're leaving tomorrow for almost a month and you spring this on me?"

He seems relieved. "I couldn't wait until I got back," he says, grasping my hand. It's warm and sweaty. "I'm too excited about us, our future. And it's a little romantic—your fiancé's abroad, you're back home, awaiting his return."

While I am totally into romance, something about that seems gross. He has this idea that I'm going to be pining for him while he's gallivanting around. God, the whole thing. The way he proposed, bringing Mark into it, the cameras, that awful restaurant. And now, him thinking this was romantic. Before I can think, my mouth spits out, plainly, also terrifyingly without emotion, "Maybe it's good you're going to be gone for a month."

His index finger runs up and down the neck of the bottle. I realize the year he chose, 2010, is when we first started dating. His voice is uncertain. "Absence makes the heart grow fonder. You get it."

That's the problem: I don't get it. And he doesn't get me. There have been moments of connection, though, right? Like that time I caught an eye disease from TechCrunch Disrupt and he sent me a bouquet of irises so I could feel better about not being able to work until my eye stopped resembling a bloody murder scene. That was nice. But what else? His disaster of a proposal is making me rethink everything. I have been happy with him. I have. I mean, it's true, I recently started watching reruns of *Big Love*, the Mormon polygamist show, because the wives' obsession with their husband inspired me to be a better girlfriend. I never stopped to think that was probably a cry for help. I need to tell him no. Everything in me is shouting no, one giant chorus of no.

But I'm scared to voice it. I can't bear to look at his face, his cute ski slope nose, his eyes tired from casework. His beautiful features always pull me back in. His face has this innocence about it that always makes me trust that he's acting from a genuine place of care.

Then I open my mouth. "No." I glance down at my fingernails, my just-chipping manicure. I'm going to have to touch it up before the bridal shower tomorrow. "No, I mean—I need that time to think. About this, and us."

I'm actually doing this. Part of me is like, *What the hell is wrong with you? He's sweet and smart and loyal and adores you.* But there's a *but* that I can't quite articulate, and it has something to do with him not telling my mom, about her *getting in the way*, as he said.

He's frozen. "Are you serious?"

I nod, then he covers his eyes, and he might be crying or trying not to cry, but I'm not going to say anything about it. The night is reverent in this momentary silence, only the streetlamps and blurry red taillights in the distance. I hold my breath, waiting for him.

At once he uncovers his face, sniffs loudly like he snuffed out his crying. "This is all my fault. I should have talked to you about it. I wanted to make it this huge thing. Katie told me I should take you out to a restaurant that means something to us, do a grand gesture, something unforgettable that would make a great story." He pauses. "I guess we got the story part down."

Of course Katie had something to do with this. Katie is the law librarian at his firm and happens to be his work bestie, and I've been to enough firm-sponsored baseball games with them to know she's completely in love with Trevor (but he brushes me off whenever I mention it, saying she's just friendly). I sort of hate her but also don't at all. She's super smart, snide, and unabashedly dorky, and I trust Trevor. That trust, it should be enough for a marriage. But thinking the word *marriage* turns my stomach.

"That's what *Katie* wants for her proposal," I say.

I shiver, the coldness inside the car finally hitting me. I want to turn it on, but that feels rude.

"You really mean this. I'm leaving. Three weeks is a long time off. That's calling it quits."

"No," I say quickly. The thought of being alone, actually alone, is terrifying. Neither of us wants that. "I need to figure some things out, and I promise it's not you."

I shouldn't have been so emphatic about the *it's not you* part, because he definitely has something to do with it. He pulls out the dark blue box again, doesn't open it. His voice is low. "Do you have any idea how much I spent on this ring? I did this for you. I want you to be happy."

But I never asked for that. There's the memory of my dad again, always trying to keep up with the white guys at the country club and saddling us with debt that we only discovered after he passed. God, no. He pries out the ring, reaches for my hand, and I want to pull it away, but it happens so fast, his bony fingers already vising my hand, and he slides the ring up to the knuckle, where it doesn't budge. Out of pure instinct, I pull the ring over the hump; like, I can't let it flop off my finger, and I don't want Trevor to ram it on. I'm shocked at how perfectly it fits. It is stunning, honestly. But . . .

Then—oh no—Trevor wraps me into a hug, as if my fitting on the ring was some type of agreement. But his hug is gentle. His neatly shorn neck hairs prickle my nose. He smells like man soap, cool pine mountains, and I'm remembering why we've survived all these years. Maybe I'm being unfair. I know what the judges on Reddit would say: "Off to the relationship dungeon with you." But Reddit, ugh, the only time I posted there I asked for diet and exercise advice along with a faceless photo and got "If she lost 20–30 pounds I'd consider hitting it." That shouldn't be my moral compass. Still, I want to give Trevor an out. With my right hand, I play with the ring's band. "If this is too much to ask, you can break it off with me now," I say. "But I'd like this time to think while you're abroad. Then we can, uh, reconvene."

"This isn't Model UN." At once he grabs the champagne bottle and pops the cork with a practiced hand. I jump at the bang of it. The bottle steams, and he doesn't wait for it to subside before he raises it and takes an uncouth gulp, then another. He doesn't offer me any, not that I would take it right now. "Damn it. What did I do wrong? Just the timing?"

I can't help myself. "Bringing Mark into this, for one. I despise Mark."

"You talk about him all the time. Figured he was your Katie."

A flare of envy sparks in me at the familiar way he talks about her. Followed by annoyance. I can't believe he doesn't see it. The way she leans her head toward him when she's speaking. The eye contact she never breaks with him, only him. The lavish Christmas gifts she always buys him, I remember, spying the Fitbit on his wrist. "Katie is in love with you," I mutter.

He takes another swig from the bottle, and I smell it now, the fermented grapes rotting in there for five years. The car door clacks open then, and he's halfway out of the car.

"Jealousy doesn't look good on you. And you know what? You want your freedom, you got it. You don't get to break up with me. I'm breaking up with *you*," he barks, but as soon as it's out, his face falters, like he didn't plan his words and is shocked by the sentiment. He adds, less fervently, "You know, for a month anyway." He doesn't leave, suspended like he wants to see how I'll react. I lean toward him and strain a muscle on my side, like a cord snapped. I massage it vigorously and am about to plead or rant or get some more clarification, but all I sputter is an "Uh" before he interrupts me. "This champagne is amazing by the way. You missed out."

He shuts the car door with some measure of grace. I look down at my finger. The ring is still there, dull, unshining in the fog.

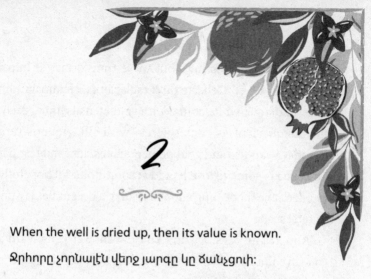

2

When the well is dried up, then its value is known.

Ջրհորը չորնալէն վերջ յարգը կը ճանչցուի:

—*Armenian Proverb*

"Nareh! You missed this entire table." My mom's voice crashes into me, breaking my reverie.

It's the morning after Trevor's proposal, and I'm at the country club, setting up for Diana's shower. I'd normally be snapping photos of the setup, posting the perfectly curated photos to Instagram (my thirty thousand followers *love* flower content), but instead I've been letting my mom freely boss me around. My mind is wading through the vast, chaotic waters of last night, trying to make sense of everything. What I said that couldn't be unsaid. Why I didn't shout yes and press Trevor into a tight hug. What it means, particularly in terms of my relationship status. How the only thing grounding me is how bone-tight my dress is. Anything with a zipper is just hell on me; why do I do this to myself?

But in a way I'm grateful for the distraction. My mom and I have created something artistic and compelling. An hour ago, this was a husk of a room (okay, a naturally beautiful husk with clas-

sic full-panel wainscoting), but we've transformed it into an in-
door garden party. Delicate pink tablecloths, champagne charger
plates, and bone-white china, with gold utensils lining each table.
Our bouquets sit as centerpieces, with silk ribbons tumbling
around tea candles and gold pomegranates. It's Pinterest paradise
and Diana is going to love it (and at some point I'll hopefully snap
out of zombie mode long enough to take a decent flat lay photo of
the tablescape).

"And," Mom says, waving a bridal shower game card at me,
"you gave doubles all over the place. Where is your head?"

Guests are going to be arriving soon, so I'm not surprised my
mom's patience is fraying. Even in her frustration, she's so pretty.
She's wearing a turquoise shift dress with a long gold necklace.
Anytime my mom's in bright blue and gold she seems like Cleopatra to me. Her hair's the same as always, dyed dark brown, parted
down the middle, stick-straight, fighting against its wavy curls,
voluminous on top and slicked back behind her ears with TRE-
Semmé Level 4 spray. Mine's similar, but longer, and I curl mine
after straightening it. Hair occupies a lot of our lives.

My darling grandma Nene is here, too, in a green floral dress.
She's been looking bored as hell because she refuses to help with
activities as frivolous as decorating (lucky). Hearing my mom
chastise me, she perks up and holds my hand for a moment. It's
cool and wrinkle-soft. Then she relaxes back into her seat, where
she's reading Proust in the original French—God, I wish I had
one ounce of her class.

I need to tell my mom about Trevor. I should have brought it
up earlier, but I needed to process it myself first. Still, I'm getting
nowhere on my own. I keep my voice casual, as if the situation is
entirely hypothetical.

"What would you say if I told you Trevor proposed to me?"

"Proposed?" she says with a sharp burst of an *R* trill. She sets the cards down on the table. "When did this . . . ? You're telling me now?"

Nene glances up from her book at my mom's outburst, then settles back into it. I dust some lint off the tablecloth. "Last night, when we went out."

"You've had this secret all morning? Kept it from me? It is unbelievable." She picks the cards back up, sets them down. Then, she stares at my hands. "Where's your ring?"

Without thinking, I touch my ring finger. I left the ring at home, but it feels more circumstantial, like I happened to be wearing it when he stormed off. I texted Trevor this morning before he took off, and he never responded. I guess we're definitely on a break. I mean, I didn't accept the man's proposal. I can't blame him for dumping me, temporarily or not.

"I took it off because I didn't want to take the spotlight away from Diana, but also mostly because I didn't say yes."

She waits a beat, absorbing my final words, then all her features lighten. She crosses herself twice and says, "Thanks to God. He was not right for you, my hokees."

Then, as if nothing happened, she starts placing the rest of the game cards on the final table. I trail after her, almost indignant.

"Well I didn't say no. And Dad always liked him."

That's an understatement. Dad fawned over Trevor. Thought he was exactly the type of guy I should be with, a real all-American boy who had a regular barber and wore boat shoes. And Trevor was with me the night Dad died. He saw me entirely undone and showed me so much kindness many months later when I was tired of holding up my glossy facade all day. Remembering that makes my stomach feel tight. That's what a person should want out of a relationship. Right?

My mom sighs. "Trevor grew up how your Dad wanted to grow up. He wished he was Trevor, tall and American with university degrees." Early on, Dad took to him so quickly. He would clap Trevor on the back twice and call him "my boy," and every part of his face would swell, his moustache spreading wide across his mouth. I miss that expression of his—the pride in me for choosing so well. My stomach turns at what Dad would think now.

She continues. "Anyway, it is your life. I'm not trying to tell you what to do. I'm only saying my opinion about you together." Then she walks over to the dessert table to straighten out the cupcakes I previously arranged.

In other words, because she agrees with my decision not to accept Trevor's proposal, she's not going to launch into the usual *opinions*. Nothing's stopped her before: lamenting how he joked that her sarmas looked like deep-sea slugs, or how she always wanted me to be with a classy man, or how some people just didn't look like a couple. She would also pull some random guys' names out of thin air, like a Sako Berberian or a Armen Shamlian, and say how they were impressive young men whose parents were pharmacists or professors, and wow, they were still bachelors; how lucky a girl would be to bag one of them. She's never outright tried to stop me from being with Trevor, because he is handsome, with a promising career, and those virtues go a long way in my mom's book. But she's always been passive-aggressive about him.

Then I wonder if my mom's thoughts on Trevor did secretly sink their hooks into me. If that was the real reason I turned him down last night. She's always been there, hovering around my every decision, but with Trevor, I thought I blocked her out. A white guy, an odar; talk about him all you want, it's not going to change my mind. But God, of course she got into my head. There it is again—this party dress feels suffocating.

My mom spins around all of a sudden. "Wait. Is he not in Denmark right now?"

"Germany." His first love.

"He works hard, and he'll get far. That's one good thing about him." She's giving me whiplash with her Trevor takes, but that's Mom. She straightens out the ribbons on a nearby table. "So what are you going to do during this time? Make a pro and con list like in that show? You know, with the blond woman. Tall? Sometimes her hair looks oily on top—"

She interrupts herself, like she's been possessed. Her hand is stopped over a piece of golden pomegranate decor.

"You will go to Explore Armenia," she whispers.

It takes me a second to realize she's talking about that big Armenian event that happens every three years, the one she was nagging me about yesterday. Must have been the pomegranate that reminded her—Armenians are obsessed with them, a symbol of fertility and abundance. We have five of them in our house, a modest number.

"Uh, yeah, we're going to that final event." I inwardly groan thinking about how my mom has signed me up for some overpriced, boring-as-nails banquet. But a small part of me rustles for attention, reminding me that Mom is finally going out again after Dad's passing, and I should be supportive of this.

Plus, the keynote speaker is going to be Congresswoman Susan Grove, who represents the fourteenth congressional district,

which is the one my newsroom covers. She's a quarter Armenian
and tends to champion Armenian causes, so somehow the Explore
Armenia committee ensnared her into showing up at their party.
Mark (evil Mark) usually sits in the press pit when she gives an-
nouncements, but I've never gotten to meet her. What if I could
cover the banquet? She might be willing to give a quote. Ugh,
that's stupid, though. I'm dreaming that I could land an exclusive
interview with a congresswoman. That's "out of my lane," as my
boss would say.

My mom is smiling now, a big optimistic grin. "You will go to
the other events, too. The men there, they're looking for Armenian women to marry. There is a reason they do the events all
through June. Very romantic."

Oh God. This is so like her: Five minutes after she finds out
I rejected Trevor's proposal she tries to set me up with Armenian guys. My body tightens in defense. "I hate to dash your
hopes, but I've barely processed what happened last night. Now's
not the time."

My tone doesn't register. I see it in her eyes, she's ready for
battle. "Now's the perfect time. I will call Nora Tereian and—"

She halts midsentence because the first guests have arrived,
thank God. They're family friends who she and I both adore but
who commit the terrible faux pas of arriving early at every event.
For Armenians, on time is early, thirty minutes late is on time,
and everything after two hours is late. Showing up before the
event's start time is borderline unforgivable. But we give them
huge smiles and hugs. The older woman compliments the room
and says to me, "Darosuh kezee." It means "May you have the
same luck," as in, "May you snag a good man soon." From her
expression I can tell it comes from a kind place, but all it does is

remind me that I had that luck, but I said no. I tell myself to stop thinking about that; it's time to play hostess.

The bridal shower is wrapping up, and everything has been going perfectly—on paper anyway—except for Diana's elementary school music teacher who's offended by her placement at the old ladies' table and made a rude comment to Diana's mom. Otherwise, technically flawless. I gave my speech—short and sweet (insert "Just like me!" joke here)—while transported outside my body, as if someone else inhabited me. That's how it's been the whole shower; I can joke around with Diana's and my absolute favorite cousins who came up from LA, make small talk with my old piano teacher, and buzz around doing host duties, but I might as well be some false Nar double doing a perfect imitation of me.

Not Diana. She—my perfect cousin who is three inches taller than me, slimmer, with thicker hair, and marrying an Armenian guy to boot—looked genuinely radiant all day. She feigned an unrushed demeanor while tearing open the ten thousand gifts she received as fast as she could while gushing over each and every single one and thanking the gift giver. There's something about Diana where she can actually exist in and appreciate the present moment. She doesn't immediately start planning for the future or bury herself in comforting past memories when things get tough. I envy her that.

After the last guest leaves, it's just me, my mom, Diana, and her mom on cleanup duty. And Nene, who straight up ignores the hubbub around her and seems relieved to be back into her novel of madeleine-induced stream of consciousness. Diana's fiancé, Remi—who appeared in the last fifteen minutes of the shower with a bouquet for Diana, to many squeals of delight—is also here, moving boxes of china and kitchen appliances into her car.

I'm spent and full, verging on sick, due to all the pistachio macarons and buttercream cake and crunchy Armenian pastries dripping in glossy rosewater. It might not be just the food, either. Something one of Diana's tantigs said keeps running through my head, not letting my brain rest (and no, it wasn't the time this same auntie informed me of my weight gain at a funeral. I was five). She was gushing to Diana about how her kids will go to the Armenian school (I mean, yes, tantigs make these assumptions if you get married) and how they'll help carry on our language. My mind immediately jumped to Trevor: how dismissive he's always been about my Armenianness; how while I was on the phone with Diana and said a couple of phrases in Armenian, he jokingly told me to "stop talking that devil language." There's a difference between marrying an odar who respects your culture and one who is . . . like Trevor. I can't help but think the branch of Armenianness would be snapped off with any children I had with Trevor. And suddenly that bothers me.

I wrap up one of the tablecloths, now stained with frosting smears and champagne spills, and toss it in the rentals bag. I try to feel how satisfying the takedown is, how I can clean and clear and put everything in the place it belongs.

But my brain won't stop. I keep hearing that phrase I heard directed at me so many times today: *Darosuh kezee.* Every single one felt like a cut. Because if I had said yes, would that be the kind of daros I want?

In the corner of the room Diana's mom has stopped working to pull Diana close in a hug and tell her how happy she is for her.

There's an immediate tug in my stomach that's sad, longing for the same. And as if the scene can't get any more sentimental, her fiancé strides up a moment later, pulling both of them into a hug and calling Diana's mom "mayrig," which means "mother" in Armenian. The two of them share a look of affection so sincere, it feels like I'm intruding. They are both completely synced and reveling in how lucky they got. I look away.

My stomach clenches with grief. I'm happy for Diana; this feeling has nothing to do with her. I just . . . Now that I see Diana and her fiancé and mom together, and now that I've gotten so close to being engaged myself, I feel how wide the gulf is between my scenario and hers. With Trevor, I will never have what she has. Maybe never with any odar.

My mother delicately places a cupcake stand into a box, then fills it with paper stuffing. I remember hearing her reverent whispering earlier about my going to that all-important Armenian extravaganza. It suddenly doesn't seem like the worst idea to check it out, sniff around the (likely) heavily cologne-scented edges of it. I step toward her but don't try hard to catch her eye.

"What would you say if I were . . ." I hesitate, realizing I'm about to say something bigger than casually attending Explore Armenia. And once I say the big thing, it'll be tough to take it back. But I'm feeling daring. I want a change. I want to try something, do something, at least give myself a chance for my mom to look into my fiancé's eyes with anything other than disappointment. A chance to not mute my culture for the rest of my life.

I restart. "What if I were to give dating Armenians another chance?" My mom's face snaps into focus. The cupcake stand is forgotten; a piece of stuffing flops halfway out of the box. I continue, talking fast, "Explore Armenia. Like you said, I can go to some events, meet some men—"

I stop because her hands are up in front of her, like this news is too perfect and she needs to repel it. "Vai Asdvadz," Mom says, then she dials it back because she can never accept that something is actually going her way without a catch. "You are not joking, right? Sometimes you make these jokes I do not understand . . ."

I'm all in now. I feel weirdly smooth, confident. "Nope, I mean it. And if there's any guy you want me to meet, no matter how hairy, I'll meet him."

A tiny voice in my head wishes I could say "guy or girl," but that's not the world we live in. I snuff out that thought immediately, which is easy to do because my mom is staring at me less like I said a normal sentence and more like I told her I'm beginning to think Gucci is a totally overrated designer. Then her face shifts to confusion, an eyebrow lowered.

"What about Trevor?"

I shrug, acting more casual about this than I feel. "We're basically over."

Diana walks over. "What's going on?" She must have seen my mom's face.

Mom trembles, and oh God, I hope she doesn't cry. I can't handle that. "She is going to Explore Armenia. To meet Armenian men."

Her voice gets small and high at the end, though she mostly keeps it in. She wipes a tear with the back of her hand. I shift my weight and look away.

Diana's eyes grow into concern. "Men . . . What about Trevor?"

Mom waves her hand in front of her face like she is so over this old news even though she asked me the same question ten seconds ago. "They're not together."

"Not right now anyway," I correct. I quickly tell Diana what happened last night, seeing the landscape of her face shift and burst at appropriate times. My mom stares in front of her, less in shock, more calculating.

"Enough about him," my mom interjects. "Hokees, why are you finally doing this? I've been telling you to marry an Armenian man your whole life. You never listen to me."

Diana is nodding at that a little too fervently. I say, "Can we not talk about the past? I'm telling you I'm going to do the thing you've always wanted me to. Because . . ." Now faced with the actuality of stamping out my Armenian culture, I'm terrified and clutching it like a lifeline. "Maybe you've had a point all these years."

Oh, my mom loves that. She's trying to tamp down an I-told-you-so smile and struggling to appear modest. "Well, they say mother knows best in America, that is true." She grabs her phone from a nearby table and starts tapping furiously. "Now, we need to start adding all the events to your calendar, and I will go to my network to find out—"

I interrupt her and gesture around the room. "Hold up. Can we finish here please?" Not because I'm particularly interested in cleaning, but because my mom's enthusiasm is starting to make me nervous about what I just agreed to. Like a tic, I glance down at my phone, which is exploding with love for the centerpiece photo I posted earlier. I breathe out.

Diana says, "Have to agree with her there, Tantig. They look ready to kick us out."

She nods toward a woman in a pencil skirt standing by the door holding a clipboard, thinly hiding her impatience. They know we're not members, just sponsored by one, so the club administration doesn't have to be polite to us.

"We'll review this at home."

3

You can't cook pilaf with big talk.

Խoսքով փիլաւ չեփուիր:

—*Armenian Proverb*

Back home, we've unloaded all the boxes of leftover food, serving dishes, and extra floral arrangements that weren't claimed. Mom seemed in a daze during the car ride, occasionally muttering Armenian men's names to herself, filing through her mental Rolodex of single guys.

I rush up the stairs to get undressed, past the dark sconces and candles and the mesh of traditional Armenian art and mediocre HomeGoods art. The style in our small but immodestly decorated home can be described as Tuscan villa–aspiring with a touch of goth. Not what I would go with personally, but it's Mom's house, and some dark Italo-Armenian mash-up is her muse, so who am I to tell her otherwise. One odd thing is that after Dad passed, she lugged all these Armenian rugs out of storage and unfurled them one by one around the house. I didn't know it was possible to amass so many rugs in a lifetime, but I guess my mom had been buying them, running them by my dad, getting vetoed, then secretly stashing them away.

In my room, I wiggle out of my dress, and I swear my rib cage expands about a foot. I take my first deep breath in hours. I shouldn't be judging my mom's design style since my room is sort of a shrine to my high school days, when I cared enough to decorate. Dad died a year and a half after I returned home from college, and I haven't been able to change anything. Yes, I'm pissed at him for drinking that night, and for taking out a second mortgage he never told my mom about, but so much of this room reminds me of him. There's a Love of Learning award I was given junior year that made the rich kids' parents mad because they thought their kids deserved one, too. Dad laughed so hard at them, at one father in particular, right in his face. "Turns out you can't buy everything," he said, and I was mortified but so proud at having such a brave dad. There's the desk he bought me in middle school, complete with heart cutouts for drawer handles, which we picked out together. My matching dresser is topped with organized clutter of makeup and perfumes from the last decade. Some of the smells remind me of him.

There's also a bevy of posters of Maroon 5 or *The OC* that don't have anything to do with him, which I should take down. I was obsessed with *The OC*'s Marissa in high school, her waify, doe-eyed beauty causing me to overpluck my eyebrows for years, which I so regret. I mean, what kind of self-respecting Armenian woman has to fill in her eyebrows?

A Chopin mazurka filters into the air from Nene's room. She has a repertoire of about a hundred or so songs she's been playing for the last couple of years, since she's been living here, so I'm basically a noted classical music genius now. Nene's a total introvert, and the way she's playing, with immediacy, feels like she is loving her me time after a social morning.

I pull on my UC Davis T-shirt and some ratty, pure-comfort shorts. I tug at my fake eyelashes. My eyelid skin stretches as I pry off one, then the other. I always forget how oppressive they are until my eyes are freed from those mini bushes. Just then Mom barges in. She's changed into a comfortable navy housedress and is holding her laptop. She's radiant with energy and cries, "Okay, Explore Armenia time."

That's fair. I did say I'd do this, and I knew the effect it would have on my mom once it sank in. So here we go.

Mom sits on my bed and opens her laptop. "There are fifteen events upcoming."

I join her. "That's way too much. I'm only going to go to the social events, not the 'learning stuff' ones. Can't meet people at those anyway." I lean to see her screen, and at the top there's Explore Armenia in red, thankfully in a font that's not Papyrus, the usual go-to for these types of things. I reach my hand over and scroll down. There's a whole calendar of events, and at the bottom of the page are the faces of seven people, the Explore Armenia board members. One woman's face stands out to me, distinct from the rest, with short curly hair, wide-set eyes, and modern (I might call it witchy) makeup. She appears younger than the rest of the board members.

Before I can read up on her, my mom scrolls back up to the events. She taps on something, smudging the screen. "The first social event is shourchbar."

Fan-freaking-tastic. Armenian dancing is my biggest insecurity, and—I look at the date—it's tonight. Shourchbar is Armenian line dancing where you have to know the moves. I can execute a single Armenian line dance, which happens to be the one they teach to preschoolers because the coordination required is unchallenging for floppy toddlers. No doubt they'll play it at some point so all the noobs can join in, but the rest of the night I'll be sitting on the sidelines. More time to schmooze it up with dudes, I guess.

I don't suppress my groan. "Can I skip this one? I'm tired."

But we peruse, and there are only four social events that make sense as places to stealthily pick up guys. The line dancing, an Armenian cooking class, Armenian brandy tasting (okay those last two sound pretty fun), and the big banquet at the end that we're already going to. There's also a live comedy show night, which would be fun, but going alone would feel weird, and going with my mom would mean no man hunting. There are also a bunch of history talks and Armenian genocide education events, which I am definitely skipping—total downers, and Armenians are so obsessed with the genocide, which I know sounds so horrible, but I feel like by virtue of growing up Armenian I've already heard it all. And a couple of classical and contemporary concerts, which are probably okay, but I have a life and can't be spending every spare moment doing Armenian stuff.

Part of me wishes my mom *could* come with me to these events. I mean, yeah, they're more for the younger crowd, and no, mothers aren't the best wing people (no matter how much they insist otherwise), but I want to see my mom out and happy. She used to do so much when Dad was alive. Now, as a widow, she feels like she's not allowed to. It's stupid, and I want to pull her out of it, but while her daughter is man hunting is not the perfect time to start.

My mom makes some noises of disappointment. "Perhaps you won't go to any after all."

At the very least, I can help her live vicariously through me.

"Fine." I sigh with great drama. "I'll go to the shourchbar thing tonight."

Then she claps, actually *claps*. "Now, how do we see who is attending? I can call up Nora Tereian—"

I need to shut that down fast. "Nope. We can do it all online." That's my cue to reach over and head to Facebook, where I find tonight's event and pull up the guest list.

I gesture to the screen. "Bon appétit."

She looks like I presented her with a lambskin Chanel purse. She begins scrolling and clicks on a name.

"Mom, open it in a new tab," I jam my arms into her space and show her.

"Esh chem! I can derive the Black-Scholes formula, don't treat me like I'm stupid," she argues, and shoves me away. Yeah, yeah, my bad. Lately, she can get defensive if I question her intelligence or abilities, and I suspect it's because she's retired after decades of being a high school math teacher—the highest level math they teach children, she always likes to remind me—and doesn't feel like she has *a thing*, so she needs me to know that she was once very impressive. But of course I know that.

And she's off. Scrolling, clicking, scrolling, clicking, with the occasional "Oooh" and "Eerav?" (meaning "Really?"). Then she stops.

"No."

I peer at the screen. "What?"

"Raffi Garabedian is going to be there."

"I'm supposed to know who that is?"

"Nareh! I've talked about his grandfather before. He was a high-ranking politician, and his brother owned the main newspaper in Beirut."

Lineage. Vocation. Connection. All required in vetting a man.

Sometimes I feel like all the Armenians my mom is impressed with were the folks in charge back in Lebanon. They carried their power over into the diaspora, at least in Armenian circles. But owning a newspaper is undoubtedly cool, even if that was your granduncle.

"Those two don't seem to mix well. Lotta corruption."

"It was Lebanon in the sixties, of course there was corruption. Anyway, his grandson, Raffi, I heard he's a doctor now. You will talk to him."

I check out his photo. It's hard to tell by the angle, but he appears to be what I can only describe as Abercrombie-model hot. There's this tilt to his chin that reads total arrogance. Hugo Boss aftershave and a pinch of, "Yeah, I do tweeze my unibrow on weekends." It could be my imagination, though, and I'm going to try not to be prejudiced by a possible conceitedness in a dark, angled photo. Or handsomeness.

"Done. Now let's see these other lucky men. Who else gets a rose . . . ?"

We dive in, Mom selecting a couple of choice suitors who pass her high standards, while I mentally prepare myself to get in the mood to go out tonight. Not just to go out, but to do work, in a way. To be on, be charming. I'm actually committing to this whole Armenian men thing, and I don't know, part of me feels like I'm jumping into this way too fast, and what about Trevor? But that side is quiet right now; I feel this mad impulse to dash into the woods and let adventure find me.

4

If you are afraid to wet your feet, you will never catch fish.

Ունք չթրջած, ձուկ չի բռնուիր:

—*Armenian Proverb*

I'm parked outside the Armenian school, which I didn't go to past pre-K because Dad didn't want me to. The fog on this side of town is so thick that you'd honestly think it was December.

I glance at the sparkly heels tossed on the passenger-side floor. When my mom saw me choose an adorable pair of gold ballet flats for tonight, she asked in her most scandalized tone, "You're wearing flats?!" Before I could answer, Nene recited in her proper Armenian, "Erekhan pan teer, heduh khnah." That translates to "If you send your child on an errand, go with them," which is such a sick burn I didn't even get offended. I consider wearing the heels, taking my five foot two to five-six, but if I'm actually going to be dancing, my back will not make it through the night. That is, if I go inside at all.

I stare at the event hall. Cute women dressed in cocktail dresses and shawls for the cold and men in business casual filter in. I'm wearing an indigo jersey dress that is fancy enough but also so soft and comfortable, and I swiped my mom's long gold necklace. How I look isn't the problem. Everyone seems to be here with people they know. It's not like they're all strangers to me, but so many of them are such far-removed acquaintances, and I always forget everyone's names, and I hate that game of "Should we say hi? Should we not? Can I just nod my head at you and smile?" My level of knowing them is almost more awkward than if I were a complete stranger. I am Boghos and Anahid's daughter. Haiganoush's granddaughter (my grandma's classical pianist days still hold clout, all these years later).

I know what they'll say about me. "Oh, now she shows up?" "She's alone? That's weird, but she was always weird. That's why she never comes to our events." "Her father was so snobbish." "Do you think she's gained weight?" "Who do you think is prettier? Her, her mom, or her grandmother? In their primes, of course. I've always said the grandma." "Doesn't she have a boyfriend?" And perhaps most prominently: "Why is she here?"

I'm so stupid. What was I thinking coming here, pretending to be part of this world? I've always felt outside it, even being full-flipping-Armenian. I should have begged Diana to come with me tonight, though I'm sure she's already in bed dreaming of her new seafoam-green KitchenAid mixer. Out of instinct I pull out my phone and start to text Trevor, then I remember he's on a plane and ignored my texts earlier today. I have no one. I feel so, so alone.

I drape my arms over the steering wheel, hang my head, and let out a long wailing groan. What the hell am I doing with my life? Why did I ruin such an easy, good thing?

Then there's a *rap-rap* on my window and I spring up.

A face is peering at me from outside, mostly obscured by curls, but I see one large inquisitive brown eye.

She says, voice muffled by the window, "Are you okay?"

Her presence, while shocking, is also having this warm, comforting effect on me. She seems so genuinely concerned. I put on a quick smile and say, "Yes, yes, all right." Then I make a motion toward the door, grab my purse, and step out. She backs up to give me space.

I'm outside, and the cold doesn't feel like an onslaught for once; if anything it's refreshing. We're wedged between my car and another black one, and it's feeling cozy over here. So this woman, my guardian angel—is that too dramatic? Whatever—is as tall as a palm and has this chic slouch. She's wearing a low-cut lacy black top with black pants and is sporting both a choker and a pendant around her neck. Her hair's incredible, with curls cut in an asymmetric bob. She's basically the coolest person I've ever talked to. I should probably say something.

I give the tiniest wave.

"Thanks for—I've got this headache." Something in her eyes, totally nonjudgmental, with a familiarity that I can't quite place, compels me to add, "And I'm a bit nervous to go in since I'm by myself."

She nods like she gets it. "I'm by myself, too."

When she speaks, it's like stepping into cool water. When she speaks, I lose all sense of what's around me.

And she's here by herself.

"Oh."

I am very smooth.

"Do you want to go in together?"

"Totally. Yes, thank you."

If I keep tacking words on to the end, maybe I'll find the right one. As we step out from the cars it dawns on me that my hair is going to be pummeled by the fog, so I throw away any last chance of seeming normal and set my purse on top of my scalp, hoping to at least preserve the top of my hair, which is the most important hair, as any blow-drying-straight woman knows. She smirks at me.

"The hair. Fog is its mortal enemy," I explain.

"I remember those days."

Oh right, she's au naturel. Hopefully she won't look down on me for making a big deal about my hair frizzing. Doesn't seem to be, but I can't tell. Who is this person? She looks vaguely familiar, but I definitely haven't met her before. I'd remember.

"I'm Nareh. Bedrossian. Thanks again for this, I already feel better."

"Erebuni."

Erebuni. I roll the letters around in my head. Not quite an Armenian name I've heard of, but familiar.

"Is that your last name?"

There's a calmness about her response that makes me think she's had to answer questions like this before. "Minassian's my last name. Erebuni's what my mom named me. Unusual, I know."

I've used the exact same word, *unusual*, to describe my name a hundred times, like over the phone—"I'll spell it for you, it's an unusual name"—or when someone is leaning in close, trying so hard to parse the word that came out of my mouth. Erebuni has to do that not only for all the Americans, but for Armenians, too. It gives my heart a little squeeze for her.

"No, I love it. Sounds familiar, but I can't place it."

We've reached the doors, and she pauses.

"It's the ancient name for Yerevan. When it was an Urartian fortress."

Okay, that's some level-ten niche academic Armenian knowledge right there. I wonder who her parents are—her mother, as she said.

My shoulders make a twitchy shrug as I try to make a joke but end up sounding more genuine than intended. "Can't believe I already met the coolest person at the party."

I'm regretting coming off like a clingy stalker, but she laughs, sweet with a little buzz to it, hummingbirds flitting by.

"Should we go in?" she asks. "You can sit with me and my friends if you like. There aren't table assignments, it's casual."

I tell her I'd like that, and I follow her lead.

5

Speech is silver, silence is golden.

Խոսքը արծաթ, լռութիւնն ոսկի:

—*Armenian Proverb*

Inside is another world. It's the large hall I've been in a dozen times—when there's only one Armenian school in all of NorCal, you attend most of your Armenian social events there. I'm instantly barraged with Armenian music, Euro-nineties style and heavy on this Armenian instrument, a zurna, that sounds like a buzzing electric clarinet. It instantly brings to mind a visual of a pleasantly red-faced man named something like Davo trilling his thick fingers on the instrument.

A ribbon of dancers, linked by pinkies, hop-skip to the music, twining themselves around the dance floor, growing and shrinking as they come and go. There's heat from sweat and lights and breathy laughs and conversation all around.

There's a bar right by the doors, and they're stocking all the usuals, your vodkas and tequilas and Johnnie Walker. A vague memory floats into my mind from when I was young: my dad and our family friends laughing and joking about "Johnnie walking."

I was too little to understand the joke, and time faded the rest. That whisky blend was always a staple at our social gatherings. I'm starting to think it was some kind of signaling, like my dad wanted to show he'd really made it in America if he always served Red Label.

Erebuni must catch me staring, because she asks, "Want a drink?"

Hell to the yes I do. I'm not dancing and meeting a bunch of strangers sober. I mean, I can, but I'd rather not.

I set my voice in a tone of mild surprise, like I hadn't considered the notion before she brought it up. "I guess so, yeah."

We step up, and the bartender's one of those people I vaguely recognize, whose name I should know. I'm flooded with how terrifying it is to be flying solo at an Armenian gathering. I'm usually under my mom's wing as she says everyone's name first or reminds me who people are, like, "This is Hera, your pre-K teacher's mom." Now all I can do is shyly say hello to the bartender. Erebuni's all over it, though. "Parev, Antranig."

Fresh on her heels I say, "Antranig." I ask how he is, and the three of us make the smallest of small talk before he asks me what I'd like to drink.

"One shot of Johnnie, please."

I'm going to drink to my dad's memory. I wonder what he'd think of me being here tonight. Mom would drag him (and let's be real, me) to the New Year's party here or the yearly fundraiser banquet. He'd go, be gregarious Boghos, the perfect husband, show off a little, and come home and complain about how exhausting it all is. How much he prefers the club. Less tashkhallah.

No, I can't imagine he would approve of this. If he were alive, I'd be with Trevor, celebrating our engagement. And even if I had broken it off with Trevor, he'd be setting me up with one of his club buddies' sons—a blond man of gigantic Swedish stock, a father in finance. I get a rotten feeling inside, dueling anger at myself and at him, then guilt for feeling this way about my departed father.

But there was a time when neither of us had to be persuaded or bribed to be in this hall. Diana and I were on this very stage twenty-three years ago for the Christmas pageant ("Hantes" in Armenian, which is important to add since Armenians are big on Hanteses). Dad moved into the aisle with his boulder of a video camera strapped to his shoulder, waving at me. The memory of him crouched down, positioned so he wouldn't miss a single second, tugs at my heart. I wasn't even the star—that was Diana, the Virgin Mary, cradling the Baby Jesus doll in her arms. I was assigned "fourth angel," wrapped in green satin with a tinsel halo on my head. I was deeply jealous of her leading role at the time, but Dad made me feel like my part was just as crucial. Plus, now look who's in the spotlight every afternoon on Channel 8. Kidding, kidding.

Erebuni gets a glass of pinot (classy) and we clink glasses. "Genatsut," she says, and it sends a thrill up my spine. There's something about a woman who looks like her—hip, I guess—who also has a fluent Armenian accent and whose first instinct is to speak in Armenian.

We drink, and I strain to not grimace as the alcohol burns its way down my throat. I threw the whole thing back like I was a freshman at a dorm party. It's embarrassing, but I feel like Erebuni gets my whole "I'm alone and feeling self-conscious about it" thing, so I'm not trying to hide it from her. Mostly.

Once the whisky passes, I feel my own breath for a moment, light and quick, wondering how I am standing here next to this

kind and stalwart woman. She motions for me to follow her toward the tables, arranged around the dance floor with simple
floral centerpieces and pomegranates.

In this room there are—if Facebook RSVPs are to be believed—
eight men I'm supposed to track and hunt. But when I glance into
the crowd, everything's a blur and no single face stands out.

I'm keeping close to Erebuni as she directs me to a table with
seven seats taken, only a couple free, and my heart seizes up because meeting new people, no matter how many times I do it, is
scary. But then I remember I'm like a mercenary here, on a job.
Plus, I can just reporter them; if all else fails, I'll ask them polite
and mildly probing questions about themselves. My brain starts
to prickle, like Johnnie and his cane are walking all over it.

"Hey," Erebuni says to what I assume are her friends, which is
only three of the people at the table (not seven, thank God). "This
is Nareh. Nareh, some of the best people I know." I shiver when I
hear the way she says my name, the tongue dancing in her mouth,
tap-tapping the syllables resolutely. My name is a fairly popular
Armenian one. She knows other Narehs; I'm sure there are other
ones at this party. But I love the way she says it, like I'm settled
into a boat, flowing down a tributary.

Erebuni motions to a woman wearing a dove-gray cocktail
dress, with narrow shoulders, large eyes, and a discerning, pride-
ful gaze. "Here's Janette." She pronounces the *Jan* not the American way but like the French *zhahn*. Janette and I shake hands, and
she reaches her arm over in such a dainty, royal fashion. I hope
my grip doesn't hurt her fingers. My dad taught me early on to
"shake like a man" so that people would take me seriously—oof,
a lot to unpack there—and I only modify it to spare limp-fish
shakers from physical pain.

"Parev, Nareh," she says in pristine Armenian, confident with a tinge of haughty. I "parev" her back and try to sail over the word and not let my American accent show. Understanding Armenian is one thing, but years and years of lack of use mean that American R's and harsher tones have crept in.

"And Vache," Erebuni continues.

Sitting next to Janette is Vache, who I recognize from Facebook stalking. I liked his seventies-style aviator dad glasses, which he is sporting now, along with a worn-looking purple-and-red-checkered shirt. He might have been one of the guys I asked my mom about, but she didn't know his family origins, so pass (for her anyway; doesn't mean I'm not potentially interested).

"Hey," he says, and waves. I give a small wave back, trying not to look eager.

Okay, I like this Vache guy. One *hey* and I'm already feeling chill vibes off him.

"And finally," Erebuni says, "Arek."

Oh God, this guy is on my mom's list. Arek, the engineer at some cloud tech company. He wasn't the hottest one—that distinction belongs to Raffi, my mom's favorite—but he is cute, despite not being my type. He's wearing a shiny black shirt and a gold chain with a cross that hangs around his neck. It's not, like, movie-prop huge, but it is prominent and statement-worthy. I do like that he's bucking convention of the type of people I usually see in our tech segments.

Seeing him in person, one of the potential suitors, makes it all real. I feel twin lightning bolts of energy, one a flash of excitement and the other anxiousness. Because I'm doing this—something new, starting fresh.

"Nareh jan, hello. Nice to meet you. Come sit."

He's got that typical Armenian American accent, and I swear he's going to drop a "bro" any second. But his friendliness feels genuine. I tell myself to relax. It's not like I have to kiss a prince before midnight or something. I'm just meeting people.

He stands and offers his seat to me, which I try to refuse, but he sits in the empty chair beside it, I suppose so I won't have to be stuck on the edge. Everyone is looking at me eagerly. I slide into his warmed chair, between Arek and Vache, and smile shyly.

"Barev, barev." Arek smiles back. He must speak Eastern Armenian, since his *P*'s aren't *P*'s at all, but sonorous *B*'s. It's a whole thing, but because the Armenian empire was once so large, and because we were fractured into so many diaspora communities, there are two dialects, eastern and western. My family, who originally lived in Turkey (historic Armenia), was forced out and landed in Lebanon. Armenians in that western area of the Middle East speak Western Armenian. Arek's family must be from modern-day Armenia, Iran, or Russia. Behind the pronunciation of one letter, you can start to intuit so much about the history of an Armenian person. I flush thinking about the concept. Or maybe the heat is coming from the whisky.

Erebuni slips into the open seat next to Janette, and I hold my breath because I feel like I interrupted their happy quartet and am bringing stranger energy into the mix. Also I wish I could be sitting next to Erebuni, who is the only person I "know," but no such luck. Then Arek grabs the wine bottle on the table and pours me a glass of red. He slides it right in front of me with a grin. I have to cool it after this drink because I am driving back, but I take it and thank him.

"Excuse me, Ere, what is the story behind this beautiful stranger you've brought into our presence?"

Thank goodness I reapplied my foundation, because I know I'm sporting tomato cheeks.

"I'm just . . . Nareh. Haven't been to events in a while. Thought I'd, uh, 'explore Armenia' again." They're smiling politely, but it's too polite, and I hate being boring. Punchline, what should I add? I armor up and say with false annoyance, "And my mom forced me."

That gets some chuckles, and Vache raises his glass. "With you on that. Armenian moms, the closest thing we have to Catholic guilt."

We all cheers, and the little hairs on my arm prickle with that alcoholic warmth. A group of new people, full of endless possibilities. This is going to be a good evening.

I continue, "Luckily she didn't make me go to any of the serious events. I mean, obviously they're important, but sometimes it feels like we're so obsessed with the genocide. Like I can't have one conversation with an Armenian person without them dragging in the genocide."

The music is still blasting loud as ever, but it feels dead silent in here. Vache and Arek are shifting in their seats, and Janette looks actually haughty now. Erebuni, though . . . curious? She's the only one looking right at me. My heart feels like it expanded into lung territory, and my entire upper body is one booming heartbeat. I reach to grab the rectangular pendant dangling from the end of my necklace and rub my fingers against the bumps of the jewels dotting the sides of it. See, this is why I never say what's on my mind. People don't want to hear what I think; they just want some sanitized version. I put on my most obsequious face and hope I sound sincere because I don't care about what I said, I just want to do damage control.

"I'm sorry, that sounded worse than I intended. What I mean is—"

Erebuni interrupts (and thank God, because I was about to invent everything after "what I mean"). "No, I understand. There's genocide fatigue. Year after year the same thing, no resolution, no change. Importantly, no recognition from Turkey or the US. But that's why there need to be some of us out there fighting, prodding both our people and odars, trying to help everyone understand that ancient history isn't just that. It has real damaging effects in the present."

I'm nodding so hard, mostly performatively, because let's face it, I've humiliated myself. I'm processing what she said, and some of it seems right. It's hard not to feel that fatigue she's talking about, but it was a horrible thing that happened in the past, and we as a culture need to move on and focus on the present. Still, I'm embarrassed as hell right now. My fingers haven't left the pendant, and the bumps on the side are digging into my thumb.

"And that's why I urge you to come out to the talk in two weeks, 'Genocide: Turkish Identity and American Liaisons.' Took a while for me to organize and convince Dr. Markarian to fly in for it. I'd love to have you there."

I freeze. I foolishly assumed my cheeks couldn't go redder than tomato, but I'm pretty sure they've been pulverized to ketchup. I turn to Arek. "I'm sorry, did she use the word *organize*, as in she organized it?"

He smirks. "Havadah."

Which means, "believe it." Not with attitude, but it's clear they're old friends and he's proud of her work. Also, neato. I've insulted her left and right, and now all I want to do is reverse-step into a bush Homer Simpson style and disappear.

She has taken a sip of wine and sets her glass down. "I'm on the planning committee. Mostly to set up the lecture series since my real job is at the Genocide Education Foundation."

This is getting better and better. How many times can a person die in one night? She organized the actual lectures I dissed a minute ago. Mertzur indzi, kill me now.

Oh my God, she's the woman from the website. An Explore Armenia board member. I never expected her to be so tall, so I didn't make the connection with the haircut and the mystical makeup. If only I had been taking ginseng supplements like my great-tantig Berjouhi had insisted were crucial for sharp memory, I wouldn't be in this mess. My eyes fix on the pomegranate centerpiece, hoping it will help me escape this rigamarole of embarrassment.

Her voice shifts, lighter. "But the rest of the committee lets me have a say on tablecloths and charger plates if I want to. Which I do. If I see anything gold at the banquet, heads are going to roll."

Arek laughs. "Who doesn't like gold? Especially us. We've got first and last names with 'Vosgi.' You're causing great offense to the Vosgis in our community."

The mood has noticeably leavened, everyone's postures more relaxed. The music filters back into my ears, sounding friendlier now, reminding me this is a party. Erebuni jokingly calls Arek a scoundrel in Armenian.

I ask if they've all known each other awhile and hope to God the question is innocuous and doesn't somehow lead to me spitting all over Erebuni's life's work.

Arek pipes up. "We grew up together in Fresno." He gestures to Erebuni. "Then these guys went to college together."

Vache adds, "Janette and I are from the South Bay originally." Ah, that's why I didn't see them around the occasional barahantes. They lived an hour south of San Francisco. Then Vache mentions something about how his freelance work would be better suited to LA.

"Freelance?"

He nods. "I write. Food journalism. Its native origins, how it ties to identity. Food subcultures." I'm gaping at him since that sounds absolutely amazing and I could talk to him all day about this. He must be reading the look on my face because he adds, "Don't look too impressed. I'm also a barista by day, out of necessity. Monocle Coffee, you know it?"

"Rings a bell. I'll check it out."

I glance at Erebuni to see if I can read whether or not she's annoyed with me, regretting bringing me to her table. But no, she's leaning back in her chair so contentedly, like she could close her eyes and drift off with a smile. Then she picks up her glass and takes a sip so slowly it's like she's beckoning the wine into her mouth. My heart jumps up to my throat and I immediately switch my gaze to Vache, who's been talking.

"Hipster grandmas?" he says, "Generous tippers."

"He's being modest. Our boy is basically a genius," Arek says, and reaches behind me, straining to clap Vache on the back.

"That word is terribly overused. I believe it should only be employed in extraordinary circumstances," Janette says, her voice pinched. Then I see a hint of a smirk. "Which is why, of course, we should apply it to Vache and his writing."

I chuckle. Well, I'm officially surrounded by a bunch of super-accomplished people, brought together by someone whose important work I belittled.

I ask, "And I'm guessing Janette works at the World Bank or the IMF?"

Erebuni and Vache smile, causing a warm neon-pink glow inside me, but Janette looks confused. "Why would I work in international finance? I'm an immigration lawyer."

She doesn't seem to get that that's not any less impressive (and, like, she deals with international stuff, so it's not a major stretch, and man, my intuition is spot-on). I guess it doesn't matter since I'm still equally intimidated by her.

Arek says, "Everyone here is trying to make the world a better place. But not me. Impossible to believe, but I didn't go into cloud computing for the social impact. It was the money, baby, and the money is good."

I laugh, then throw up my hands. "In that case I feel a bit better that all I have to contribute here is that I'm a lowly reporter. Local news for Redwood City. Fluff pieces mainly."

Arek looks stunned. "Whoa. Why haven't we seen you? An Armenian on the news?"

"Because no one under fifty turns on actual TV channels unless they're watching a game," Vache says. Then quickly adds, "Damn, I didn't mean that to be a dig. It's a demographic thing. I bet our parents know you, and I mean that in the best way possible."

Honestly, I'm smiling on both the outside and the inside since now that I'm not the only one making gaffes tonight.

Arek continues, "I don't care. Now I'm going to be looking for you. Gonna google you, Nar, and find those fluffers."

I do love that he called me Nar. This is a gift some people have, many Armenians in particular, to make you feel like one of them right away. I wonder if it's because there are so few of us in the world.

"Me, too," Erebuni says in a small voice.

Then something in her shifts, and she feels almost a little false, or desperate, as she asks, "Why isn't anyone dancing?"

"That's what I was saying," Arek says, like finally someone is seeing him. He turns to Vache, "Bro, getting you to dance is like trying to wrangle wild boars."

We got a *bro*! I knew it. Janette chimes in, "Mmm, boars are an aggressive species, Arek jan. Our Vache doesn't resemble anything boarish."

Vache is totally unfazed by their conversation. "I only dance if I drink too much, and I only drink too much if someone starts playing dancehall. Or Italo disco."

Arek shoots out of his chair. "Well, bro, it's shourchbar night, so take a shot and get up here with us. Ladies?"

I take stock of my inebriation, and I'm tiptoeing on a narrow beam in the direction of just drunk enough to dance. So I get up and tell Vache, "I'll take one with you. Let's do it."

He sighs and grabs a bottle of vodka from the middle of the table. "Fine, I'll dance, but only because Nareh wants me to." He pours us shots and offers me one. "For my new journalism friend."

"I'm dying to talk to you about that, by the way."

"Definitely. We will."

We clink glasses and throw them back, and neither of us disguises our disgust.

As our group makes its way toward the dance floor, the music gets louder, and I shout, "I don't know the moves to most of these songs, by the way. Just trying to set expectations here."

"No one does," Vache reassures me.

"I do," Janette says matter-of-factly. "So does Erebuni."

Arek is already pre-dancing and waving at people and shouting barevs and other niceties at them.

Erebuni appears beside me, and we share a smile. She's closer than she has been, and I can smell her perfume now, a rose musk, and something else woody. I like that it shows itself only when you're very near to her. I get protector vibes off her, and maybe it's the shot I just took, but my body feels cozy and warm all of a sudden.

We approach the dancers, and this is the fun/terrifying part, where to join in you have to catch a running train. Arek chases the tail and hooks pinkies with a cute woman in a skintight cobalt dress; they seem to know each other. Janette clips onto Arek, then Vache onto Janette, Erebuni next, which means, oh God, I'm on the end.

Scary because I'll stand out more. But the tail gets to wave a big-ass napkin around, which is a total thrill and kind of an honor, and I've rarely been in this position. Someone from the periphery hands it to me, white cloth ready to be swished, and simultaneously Erebuni hooks her pinkie into mine.

She smiles at me; her lips are lovely and her mouth is so wide. Then she jerks forward and we're off. I'm tracking the foot movements. There are, like, twenty complex moves to repeat, which means I am totally hopeless. I try to catch Erebuni's eye and attempt to convey "I have no idea what I'm doing and isn't it funny?" though that's been my flavor all night, so I assume she gets it. Like Janette said, Erebuni is a pro at the moves, and I keep looking down at her black snakeskin booties and try to emulate what she's doing. Her pinkie grips mine tight. I'm glad I came.

That's when I spot him across the room. Raffi Garabedian, the number one Armenian bachelor in the Bay Area. And wow, is he hot. He's got a sexy sharp jawline and these Old-World eyes, like Scheherazade was telling stories about him in *One Thousand and*

One Nights. He seems tall, too, the way he's leaning back in his chair, legs splayed like the ground in front of him doesn't afford enough space.

He's in conversation with two other dudes who seem familiar, and I could be wrong, but I get the feeling they're cliquey. They've got their crew and aren't looking for new members. And that's fine. If that is the case, I don't need anyone like that; I already found a group to befriend. My earlier blunders seem to have been forgotten.

I've given up on keeping up with the movements, but I am still having a ball out here. My temples and neck are gleefully feverish. Erebuni's pinkie and mine have become hot and slippery, sliding in and out of each other, but always finding a way to stay linked. Our dance chain winds its way toward Raffi, and though we're close, I can't get a real look at him since my back is turned toward him. I'm still brandishing that napkin like I'm a sabre fighter when it snaps in an unnatural way like it made contact with something. Then I hear a shatter of glass and a man yelling, "Vai!"

I turn around and see it. My napkin antics swiped a full glass off the table, into Raffi's lap, and it smashed all over the floor. And he's pissed, eyebrows knitted, like how could the universe have betrayed him in this way? Without hesitating, I detach from Erebuni and rush down to Raffi's feet.

Shattered glass and smoky scotch are dripping everywhere, liquid smothering Raffi's Gucci loafers. A total effing disaster. I can't look at him, but at least I came prepared with something to mop it up. I wipe at his velvet shoes. "I am so sorry. I got—I was a little overzealous with the napkin waving."

The frantic energy of the guys around me suddenly stills.

And then there's a hand under my chin, gently tilting my head up. I'm looking right into Raffi's eyes, stunned but delighted.

"What did I do to deserve a hot woman kneeling at my feet?"

His voice is a soft purr, and he's got a bit of that Armenian American accent. His beauty is honestly hypnotizing. When you look into a face like that, you realize you don't see too many drop-dead gorgeous people in your daily life. I mean, maybe in LA, but not really in San Francisco (sorry, SF).

Then all at once I realize how this must look, bad from angles both feminist and conservative—I'm pleasing no one down here but Raffi—so I jut up.

I try to arrange my voice into something confident. *Do not say anything about his wet pants, or I am marching you right out of here.* "Good news. Your shoes are going to make it."

He peers at them. "These old things?" Then he squints and sort of points at me. "Hey, I know you. Reporter girl."

"Y-you know me?"

And my occupation? I have one ridiculous thought where Raffi has a parallel-universe mom who's made him a list of eligible bachelorettes.

"Sure, at KTVA Nareh. It almost rhymes; easy to remember. Smart move."

Oh! He follows me on Instagram. Wow, first time that's ever happened. It feels both flattering and scary at the same time.

He says, "Loved the flower arrangements at your cousin's shower. But I loved that selfie you posted even more."

I'm blushing again, matching the pomegranates. I've never had someone so hot tell me they liked a photo of me, and it shows.

"Well, maybe you'll get to see more of them."

What. *What.* I can't believe I said that. This is my first flirtation outside Trevor in, like, five years. And it doesn't feel bad? Part of me can't believe I can just say things like this. The thrill of it makes me feel ten feet tall. Also, did I insinuate nudes just then? I might have. Oh God. This is not what my mom had in mind. But who's to say a legitimate relationship cannot be born from an exchange of nudes?

"I'll hit up your DMs."

He is looking like he swallowed something delicious.

"You better."

Then I turn around and walk away, swinging my hips for him.

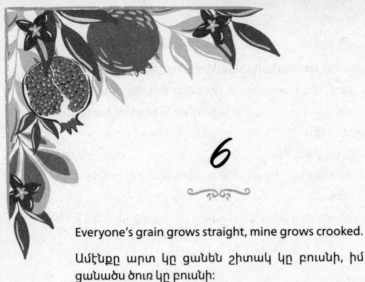

6

Everyone's grain grows straight, mine grows crooked.

Ամէնքը արտ կը ցանեն շիտակ կը բուսնի, իմ
ցանածս ծուռ կը բուսնի:

—*Armenian Proverb*

As I make my way to rejoin the group, I am feeling like hot shit, not going to lie. I might be strutting. I've got alcoholic armor on, telling me I can do no wrong. Yeah, I've been messing up left and right, but there must be some kind of guardian angel throwing my blunders into a blender and making whipped lemonade.

My new friends are in the center now that people have hooked themselves into the mix and others left the circle. I trot behind Erebuni as she's dancing, tap her on the shoulder, and entwine myself between her and another woman, who is another one of those specters of the past I sort of recognize. I give a little nod and a "Parev" and assume that will be sufficient since we're dancing. She reciprocates, then turns back to her friend, so, phew, that interaction is over. Guardian angel strikes again. I look to Erebuni, who cocks her eyebrow at me.

She shout-whispers. "Raffi G, eh?"

Oh. She knows him. And doesn't seem to like him? I try to

play it like I'm not that interested in him, and that the whole interaction meant nothing to me. And I'm not sure it does, other
than the feeling of getting attention from a hot guy. I think. "Does
he go by that? Raffi G?"

This foot movement is more complex than the one before, and
I've got no napkin to wave, so I'm trying to skip along as unas-
sumingly as possible, my only goal not to be an intrusion to the
rest of the dancers.

"That's how he introduced himself to me way back when. He
thinks it gives him some cachet, but it reminds me of Kenny G."

Definitely doesn't like him. I laugh because I doubt the Gucci-
wearing stud would be pleased to be likened to the crown-of-
curls king of sax.

"He does seem a bit conceited. But when you look like that,
it's slightly justified, ya know?"

The line stops and backs up, but I'm still walking forward,
yanking Erebuni and that other acquaintance with me, and the
latter shoots me a look, like, *WTF?*

"Want to take a breather?" Erebuni asks.

I do, more than anything. I detach immediately and shout
some smiling apology at the familiar woman for messing up her
moves. Erebuni, instead of heading toward the table like I thought
she might, strides toward the door. Soon we're outside, the music
now muffled behind us, and the icy-cold San Francisco night nip-
ping at our sweaty skin. There are little congregations of friends
smoking together, mostly men, and Erebuni leads us away from
them.

We sit on a bench side by side, and I can't believe that this
erudite woman is still paying me attention after I've continually
come off like such a vapid dum-dum. I sneak a look at her again.

She's very striking. She's got cosmic eyes, a pair of unexplored planets, alienesque with how wide they are.

"I know we've only just met, but I think you're a . . ." She pauses. "Quality person, Nareh. I hope we'll get to hang out more."

She's being so nice to me, and I don't want to miss my chance to apologize for earlier, so I blurt, "Me, too. And I am so, so sorry about my rudeness earlier. Like, I don't know what came over me. You're totally right about the Armenian genocide stuff. What you're doing, it's so impressive. You—you're impressive. I feel lucky we chanced into meeting each other. So hope I didn't ruin it by being a"—I search for a word more sophisticated than my first instinct, *asshole*—"dilettante, earlier."

"No. You're honest, I appreciate that."

Weird, because I don't normally think of honesty as my best quality. I could work on the whole white-lies-to-make-everyone-happy thing. I know I do that, but I can't stop. Looking back, I guess I did let the truth fly earlier tonight. About the damn genocide, no less. God, I'm such a tool sometimes.

The breeze picks up, and I get a scent of her rose perfume again. It's arresting, and I forget what I'm going to say. Or what we were talking about.

"What, uh, what scent do you wear? It's floral but foresty." That sounds creepy, doesn't it? Like I'm sniffing her. I try, "I'm into smells."

Ugh. As I said, a tool.

I wave my hands. "Sorry, sorry. I'm making it worse."

She seems entirely unfazed. "See? You're honest. And you're on the right track. It's called Trampled, like stomped roses on a forest floor. There's Bulgarian rose and, you know, agarwood?" I shake my head. But I *want* to know agarwood. And all the other things in her brain. "I dab one bit behind each ear." Her voice is smooth, flowing. My arms prickle. She smirks. "I'm into smells, too."

"Damn, Erebuni. Can we be friends?"

"I hope so. Let me give you my number."

Friendship sealed. We exchange numbers, and I give her my Instagram handle since that's the best way to keep in touch with me.

Then she asks, "So is Raffi the kind of guy you're into?"

She wants to talk boys? I didn't take her for that kind of woman.

"Not historically. I guess with his whole . . ." I'm about to give his entire family history in politics and newspapers and how that suggests to me he might be more than a couture-clad pretty boy, but I censor myself. "I mean no. I'm going with no."

She smiles, and it feels private, like it's just for herself and I caught sight of it.

"There you are!" Arek shouts, and he's trailed by Vache and Janette. Damn, I wanted to know where her line of inquiry was going. I don't want to assume anything, but the direction felt . . . intimate.

The men are sweaty, with glazed temples and damp shirts. Janette is unchanged. Arek has this look of childlike excitement, an earnestness in his eyes like someone's handed him an extra-large pack of gummy worms. "Special guest DJ Versace is in the house." He directs himself to Erebuni. "Did you know he was coming? You're so crafty. You know I love surprises."

They begin chatting, and I check the time. It's getting late, and I have work tomorrow. Oh yeah, I work Sundays. Every day of the week sometimes. The news doesn't sit around on weekends, which is a prospect that used to excite me, but now I mostly dread it. I'm not sure how it happened, how I got stuck as the reporter version of the whipping boy. But there's something about the optimism of this night, being lifted up by such good people, that I resolve right here, right now, to change my situation at work. Tonight, I'm going to put out calls for scoops, hit up my sources, and have a shiny polished gem of a serious pitch to deliver to Richard tomorrow morning. It's late, and I'm three drinks in, but I know I can do it.

"Afraid I'll have to miss DJ Versace. Gotta head home."

Erebuni asks, with a note of concern, "Are you driving back?"

"Uh, I was planning . . ."

I take stock of myself. My head's swimming, not like in a stormy current, but floating down a lazy river. Still, too much movement.

"Planning to take a Lyft back."

Erebuni places her hand on the back of my arm. Her voice is gentle. "Good."

I lose my breath. It's happening again, and I need to turn it off. It's been brewing, and I've been pretending it's not, but when her soft, cold hand sweeps against my arm, it's different than locking pinkies with her for a dance. My skin tightens and tingles and I can't keep deluding myself. Girl crush.

Ugh, I could wax so poetic on my girl crushes of days past. I get them way too often, and back when I was single they never led to anything except my own disappointment and the occasional ruined friendship. Sometimes it felt like every woman in the world was straight. Anyway, this is not the time; I'm man hunting. *So, Nareh, just stop.*

I excuse myself, jog back inside to shake her off, grab my purse, and call a car. I cringe at the fee, and my own stupidity for drinking too much to drive. The night before work. The daughter of a father killed in a drunk driving accident. Every time I get in a car I think about him, tell myself that I'm not invincible. But tonight my head was filled with too many happy things to leave room for me to think about the consequences of my driving. Maybe that's how Dad felt, too.

When I'm back with the group, I give a little goodbye wave.

"Don't be corny. Come here." And Arek wraps me in a big ole bear hug. Arek, one of my mom's suitors, crossed off the list. He's awesome—he is—but I have always been quick to know when I'm feeling attraction toward someone or have a chance at feeling attracted to someone (literally within seconds), and he is not one of them. Sorry, Mom.

Vache and I hug, and he's way more muscular than I would have expected.

"Mnak parov," Janette wishes me, and gives me two air kisses.

Erebuni leans in for a hug, and I'm in her curls, surrounded by dark roses and stepping on wood chips and snapping twigs in a forest. She's soft, but not frail like Janette; there's strength in her grip, and the way she holds me feels like she's giving me something to take home.

I settle into the car and stop myself from looking back at her. But I can't cut off my thoughts. Did she look at all? If so, how long did she linger? Why am I focusing on her and not who I'm supposed to focus on? I'm wasting my time getting lost in that perfume, in the wave of calm she exudes. Cool water. I close my eyes and think, *That's enough of Erebuni.* I force myself to wonder instead when Raffi might DM me.

1

Who is preferably heard? The rich and the handsome.

Ո՛րուն խոսքը անցուկ կ՚ըլլայ։—Հարուստին ու գեղեցկին։

—*Armenian Proverb*

It's nine a.m. and Diana's in my house. I'm hobbling down the stairs, and every step feels like my head is shrinking against its will. Three drinks and I'm hungover; that's twenty-seven going on twenty-eight for you. I was looking forward to a nice quiet sail out of the house and into a Lyft back to my car. The Sunday morning meeting isn't until ten a.m. today, and there's no breaking news, so I was supposed to have a calm morning. My mom tends to sleep in, and Nene, who was never one to chat it up anyway, says she's too old for idle chitchat. I was hoping to be alone with my thoughts, trying to process the carnival of last night. Right now the main feeling is *physically unwell* with a glowing undercurrent, a spark of optimism.

Diana is in the kitchen, comfy in yoga pants and a stretchy shirt, dropping ice cubes into two steaming Earl Grey glasses. Of course she looks impossibly chic in her most casual outfit.

"Nene," she whispers as she sets the tea down in front of our grandma, who is sitting primly in her white dressing gown. It makes her look older, and my heart cringes thinking of it. Nene nods curtly at Diana.

I walk into the room and hug Diana, about to ask her why she's here so early. She lives less than a ten-minute drive away, but she doesn't usually pop by until later in the day.

My mom rushes down the stairs. "Don't start without me!" And there it goes. Goodbye quiet morning.

I see what this is. The grand inquisition of Nareh Bedrossian and her luck with the suitors at the ball.

Diana is staring at me. "Tantig Anahid and I were texting last night. We have a *lot* to catch up on. You went to shourchbar night? God, you must be exhausted, doing that after the shower."

My mom waves her arms. "Exhaust, *psh*. Who did you meet?"

"Guys. I have to go to work. And, ugh, my car."

I explain to them about taking the Lyft back home, and Diana and my mom are more than happy to drive me to the Armenian school if it means more time to hear gossip about last night. Personally, I'm pleased to not have to pay for a ride again, but there's something in the conspiratorial energy between those two that's grating on me. Or that could just be the dull pulsing behind my eyelids. I sense a migraine brewing.

The three of us approach Diana's white Jeep, which she's had even longer than I've had my car. She's got her fading Delta Gamma sticker on the bumper and her Santa Clara University license plate frame. I reach for the back seat to sit with Nene, but my mom grabs the handle.

"Go sit with Diana. I don't want to crane my neck the whole drive." I begin to protest, but she interrupts, "I'm old, have some pity."

It is so not worth the argument. So I sit up front, and the second Diana starts the car, I shut off all the air vents blowing at me, because there is nothing worse than cold air on an already gloomy day. June right now across the country must feel so different than it does here. I long for the metropolitan heat, the warm blanket of humidity in Chicago, or DC, or New York. All the possibilities that a sizzling summer suggests, the whole population thrilled by the arrival of it—that's something I've never experienced, and I wish I could.

Diana backs out with a touch of careless abandon, and my mom is already starting with her requests for slow driving. "Gamats, hajees. You know I can't take it."

"I am, Tantig. Okay. Nar! So you're really doing it with this Armenian guy thing? Is Tantig Anahid exaggerating?"

"It's all true. I'm just . . ." How do I explain this? My brain is foggy, and I'm regretting not joining them for a glass of tea.

"Finally listening to her mother," my mom finishes, and I'm glad for it because it means I don't have to explain further.

Diana makes a daring left turn onto Nineteenth, the artery to the freeway; the Armenian school is off an exit right before it. We zoom past all of San Francisco's sidesitched homes while my mom makes a sound like she's sucked all the oxygen out of the car, and I can imagine her digging her nails into the handle.

I decide to open slowly. "So, I met Arek, the engineer guy. Also his friend named Vache, who's a food journalist. Isn't that cool?"

My mom retorts, "If you want to end up penniless, yes. What's his last name?"

"I didn't catch it."

My mom sighs dismissively.

Diana says, "Nareh always used to like the intellectuals."

Okay, past tense, diss on Trevor. I mean, it's true, though. I can tell you right now that being a lawyer and being an intellectual can be mutually exclusive. "We need to find you those East Coast Armenians. Darper en East Coastneruh. The ones who're more American because they've been here so long. You love that. Some Bostonian Watertown guys with checkered shirts who aren't afraid to wear bow ties and have jobs in, like, *finance*. Oh, I can totally see it."

My mom shoves off this idea. In one breath she says, "They don't come to our things, and we have plenty of men. Now, tell me about Arek Grigoryan."

I kind of love how all-business Mom can be about the prospect of dating (when it comes to Armenian guys). It's like she's a matchmaker in the old country, riffling her fingers through a hanging file. I explain, "He's super friendly, but he's like that with everyone."

"So you liked him?" Diana asks.

"Yeah, but he's not my type. Di, his shirt was so shiny I could have done my makeup in its reflection."

My mom and Diana laugh.

"Nareh-een ov guh portzess amousnatsnel? Kroghuh lav er." My grandma's got my back, wondering what kind of guy they're trying to marry me off to, and she's into Vache's journalism career, unlike my mom. Then again, Nene is an artist, and like recognizes like. But Vache, I don't know—he's awesome, but I felt only friendly toward him, and I'm sure he felt the same way, too. Ditto Arek. Yeah, Arek made a comment about my looks, but it seemed like a way to ingratiate himself with me, not flirt. And I'm happy with that. Two guy friends? Heck yeah. I don't have to date or ditch every man.

I tell Nene not to worry; I'm not marrying anyone yet.

Diana is speeding along a mostly empty street. My mom grabs Diana's seat and leans toward the front. "I see red lights. Gamats!"

Diana does a courtesy brake, probably slowing down two miles an hour.

I continue, "I made some other friends, too. A Janette, from the South Bay somewhere."

My mom chimes in, "Oh, Janette. Is she thin and small, reminds you of a bird? A pretty bird?"

"That's, yeah, dead-on."

"I know her. Yacoubians. Parents are both professors at San Jose State. Veeeeeeeery snobby." She draws out *very* for, like, ten seconds. "But you liked each other? That is good."

"More or less, we did. And there was also"—I brace myself and set my voice to almost bored—"another woman, Erebuni. Last name um, Mardirossian? No. Minassian! I think that's it. Do you know her? She's from Fresno."

"Erebuni? Strange name. Never heard of an Erebuni. Minassians, we know a couple, but none from Fresno. Who else?"

That's all I'm going to get on Erebuni. I'm simultaneously disappointed and relieved. What if my mom had known her family and, like, hated them or something? A modern-day Capulet-Montague rivalry. As soon as I think it, I'm struck with how I'm actually considering Erebuni as a prospect. I dunno, I'm tired, and my guard is down, and I want to see her again.

Also I realize how absurd it is to be worried about whether or not my mom dislikes her family. First, because that's assuming Erebuni has any interest in women whatsoever. Second, if she did, that she would like me. And finally, as if what my mom would object to would have anything to do with family ties and nothing

to do with Erebuni's gender. It's not like my mom is super prejudiced against gay people, unlike Tantig Sona, Dad's sister, who
has definitely liked antigay memes on Facebook, which she probably doesn't know are public. But my mom has lamented about
other people's kids being gay, because they'll have a harder life,
but good for their parents for accepting them, and it's so difficult
for everyone, etc. Not what you'd call progressive, but she doesn't
want to shut people up in closets, nor does she think being gay is
a choice, so that's a step in the right direction.

But what's holding her acceptance back is that it's not like the
Armenian community exactly welcomes LGBTQ+ people with
open arms. I don't know a single openly gay person who is strongly
involved in the community. It might be a symptom of my not being that involved in events in the first place. Like, there might be
some gay man on the committee for Armenian Young Profession-
als, but I wouldn't know about it. Instead, what I've grown up
hearing are whispers about such-and-such handsome man in his
forties with a good job who never married—Is he secretly gay?
Who cares? Leave the poor guy alone. And there are almost zero
mentions of lesbians, as if the notion does not exist at all. What
happened to all the Armenian lesbians? Either they get labeled
spinsters or they marry a man, I guess. The sense I get is that the
larger Armenian community is quietly hostile to anyone who is
gay. So even with my mom being more "tolerant," I never came out
to her or Dad.

Why would I? I know that it's not the modern way of thinking
about things, and Gen Z would roast me for saying it. But I've
only dated guys before. I've never mentioned being attracted to
women because I never dated any of them seriously, only messed
around, mostly in college. Hazy nights of us tranquilized by alco-

hol, enough to slip into actually doing the thing instead of just flirting around it, synapses sparking at the novelty of it all. Followed by them being annoyingly chill in the morning, straight girls having a bit of fun.

Telling my parents would basically have been saying, "I am having casual sex with women as well as with men." The very definition of TMI, in my mind. Now, if I gave dating women a fair shot, then that'd be different. So, for all my mom knows, I am as straight as Taylor Swift (my mortal enemy).

Diana knows, sort of, but it's not like I had a big coming out. Back in the day, we were discussing our exploits, as one does, and I brought up the women I hooked up with. She said she'd drunkenly kissed a girl or two but wasn't into it. I told her I *was* into it, and I think she almost views my sexuality as something I was experimenting with. Sort of like how I'm a reporter dipping into all kinds of stories. I could have pushed the point, but she is so straight and seems to have all straight friends, so I was scared if I drilled the point home, I'd seem weird to her. Plus, like my parents, she's only ever seen me with guys, so I can't blame her for thinking my bisexuality isn't a real thing.

Trevor knew, too, along with some college friends to whom I casually relayed my encounters. The friends, open-minded people, barely acknowledged it, like, "Oh, cool," perhaps not knowing what to say. Trevor thought it was hot and joked that we should have a threesome. At the time I was flattered, but now I'm not so sure.

Diana's pulled into the parking lot. "Back to the guys. Who else was there?"

Always back to the guys. Probably a good idea, anyway—I shouldn't press on Erebuni in case Mom starts to suspect (she's got a nose like a hound dog for anything I'm not "supposed" to be doing). Plus my mom has come alive in this conversation, a contrast to the general nagging droopiness she's settled into ever since Dad died.

She's become such a hermit, I'm almost thankful Diana is getting married solely to get Mom out of the house, helping her choose flatware or chiavari chairs. For years now, Mom hasn't visited friends for casual coffee like she used to. She'll talk to them on the phone but always declines invitations, saying she has to take care of Nene. I wonder if she doesn't want to visit their homes, rich with life, with husbands, to be reminded that she's a widow, that she's different. Mom does not like different.

But now she's sitting upright, attentive, and it's not just because of Diana's driving. I want to keep that going, and I know what she'll love to hear.

"I saved the best for last. I spilled a drink all over Raffi Garabedian."

"Vai, Asdvadz," my mom exclaims, crossing herself.

Diana is cracking up. She's heard about Raffi from my mom, I guess.

"But he didn't mind. In fact, he knew me from Instagram and said he'd slide into my DMs."

"He did not say 'slide'! Did he?" Diana shrieks.

"What is DM! Don't talk in riddles," my mom chides.

Somehow this whole conversation went from migraine-inducing to kind of fun. It's terrible to say, but I'm enjoying the attention. For almost a year all eyes have been focused on Diana and her Armenian bank-branch-manager fiancé, who looks like a handsome fox, all sharp features. Obviously, I'm happy for her, but it's nice to have my family hang on my every word, because I feel like they care about my future, too. It just sucks I had to finally date Armenian people for them to care. Armenian men, I should say.

"It means he's going to send me a private message on Instagram. Okay, I may have embellished, he didn't say 'slide.' But he more or less did. He loved the flowers at your shower, by the way."

"He saw my flowers?" I swear Diana blushes the tiniest bit rosy pink.

She pulls in next to my car, and I start to gather my purse and the bag of workout clothes I brought along.

My mom seems disturbed. "Don't be doing private things like that. Make sure he knows you're a woman worth something."

"Mom, I know. It's a saying. We were flirting a little, but he knows I'm a reporter. I'm not interested in a hookup." I pause, and ugh, I can't help myself. "I think."

"Nareh!" my mom shouts, and Diana is giggling.

"I'm kidding, I'm kidding," I reassure her.

Almost to herself she says, "Raffi Garabedian's eye is on my daughter. Who would have thought." Then, back to me, "When he messages you, show me. No, show Diana, too. Tserket togh chuh pakhi."

Such a vote of confidence. Mom insisting they'll help me so he doesn't slip from my fingers.

"Okay, I really have to go now. Di, thanks for the ride. Mom, I might be late tonight. I'm going to work out."

I'm halfway out the door while mom is saying, "Work out. What is always this work out? Some people aren't meant to work that hard. Focus on one thing."

My mom thinks Americans have an obsession with working out, and that no one worked out in Lebanon, and they were all fine. She and my dad would always squabble about his constant tennis matches and golf games, but it was nice that he and I had that in common. Dad taught me to be decent at both in case, ya know, I needed to show off my skills to land the big promotion. Too bad real life hasn't panned out like that, and my boss, Richard, is less interested in my killer backhand than my turning in a polished segment on time.

"I won't try too hard during the workout, how about that?"

She nods. "That is good."

I say goodbye to everyone and shut the door, taking care not to slam it. Diana hangs back a moment, waiting for me to get in and start my car. I hop in and turn on the engine so she knows I'm good to go.

Just then my phone pings with a text. It's from Erebuni, and I freeze. I don't feel foggy anymore. My body snaps into focus as I read.

> Raining links on you. In case you change your mind about going to Armenian genocide events, here's the link to the lecture

All right, I guess I sealed my fate yesterday and I'm going to have to go to that. Then again, Erebuni organizing it does make me a tad more interested in joining. There are dots as she's typing.

> A link to my favorite perfumery

I click, and it's a fancy New York atelier with a dark website and typewriter font. Definitely won't be able to buy any of those, but I'll read about them and imagine the scents. I imagine her tapping her finger against the bottle opening and pressing her wet finger against each side of her neck. More dots as she types.

And a hope we can link up again soon?

I cup my phone in my hand like I would a fallen petal, inspecting the message. Everything outside is grayish white with fog, washed over in one color, but here in the car I'm glowing.

8

I like him just as much as I like the smoke in my eyes.

Անպէս կը սիրեմ, որչափ աչքս մուխը կամ փոշին:

—*Armenian Proverb*

On my mercifully traffic-free drive to Redwood City (thank you, Sunday commute), somewhere near San Bruno, the fog lifts, revealing a crisp sunny day. People sometimes ask if my commute bothers me, and yeah, driving an hour in stop-and-go traffic isn't pleasurable, but I love traversing the Bay Area's microclimates, coming up for air from San Francisco's drab summer weather to a perfect seventy-five-degree day in Redwood City. Fun fact: The city's slogan is "Climate Best by Government Test," which is such a funny, twee mini-brag. It's *science!*

I waltz into the morning meeting on the heels of my text exchange with Erebuni. The rest of our texts weren't much. I thanked her for the links, assured her that I would go to the lecture, and let her know I'd be at the Armenian cooking class coming up in a couple of days. I read her reply when I parked my car, and she actually said, "Can't wait." I had to take a couple of meditative breaths not to get myself too excited. Not even the sight of evilly grinning Mark, who I haven't seen since I bodychecked him at Diekkengräber's, can ruin my mood.

"Nice to see you've recovered from your fainting spell," Mark says.

Okay, mood slightly ruined. Richard isn't here yet, so Mark can let his viciousness run rampant. Luckily Elaine, my work ally, is sitting right next to me, and I feel her body stiffen like a shield. She has no time for Mark's BS.

She turns toward me. "I know Mark's always been a dick, but is he losing his mind, too? Fainting?"

"I know, right?" I say, faking incredulity, mostly so I can see the veins in Mark's forearms start to pop and pulse. He's on the verge of a retort when Richard strides in.

Richard is in his late fifties, with a full head of reddish blond hair, mustache, and these eighties dad glasses that are accidentally back in fashion. He always stands for the length of the meeting and makes notes on the whiteboard in his incomprehensible handwriting.

It's a slow news day, which means the head desk (Richard and the lead producers) are asking us for pitches. After shourchbar night, true to my word, I stormed Twitter looking for tips and snagged a juicy one. I'm taking a bit of a risk with it, pitching a story outside my usual fluffy zone of coverage, but I hear my dad's voice telling his friends how his daughter covers the news, the real news, and it fuels me.

Everyone goes around the table, and when Richard gets to me, I start with, "I was hoping for a shot at a political story." There's a scoff from a few people in the room—Mark and the anchors. My cheeks flame. Deep inside, my tear ducts start to swell, at the ready in case I need them. God, why is that my first reaction? Keeping my voice as steady as possible—though it feels like I'm stepping along a wobbly plank—I continue, "I heard that Mayor Ortega is considering putting an emergency halt on the new salt marsh development, and a source close to the mayor's office is willing to talk to me."

The last part is sort of a fib, but I can get someone to talk to me, I know it. Richard turns to write down "salt marsh dev," and we're left staring at the sweat wrinkles striping the backside of his olive pants. "Is this true?" he asks. "Anyone got intel on it?"

Mark, with his disgustingly perfect hair, pipes up. "Yessir. I have reason to believe it is."

He's lying, but I can't fault him for the old move of pressing the buzzer on *Jeopardy!* first and making up the answer as you go. Richard says, "You should have brought this up earlier if you knew about it. But you've scored it, congratulations."

What the—? Mark looks like he won a Press Club award. Which he probably will one day, the bastard. But no, no way. He is not going to take my story. I want to jump onto the table and roar it to the room, but there's something in Mark's smug face and Richard's dismissiveness that turns my voice tiny. "Richard, respectfully, that's my lead and my source."

He barrels on. "And Mark's got the political beat. Would you try to steal a story about the latest exploding tech gadget fiasco away from Elaine?"

Steal? What the hell. But what can I say to that?

"No," I say, smiling, trying to look agreeable.

Because I can feel it, if I don't come up with something good quick, I'm going to be assigned another worthless story. But I've got nothing.

Except. Explore Armenia. A diaspora community in the Bay Area sharing various elements of their culture, targeting the younger crowd to keep traditions alive. Yeah, I can make it sexy. Screw it, I'm pitching.

"But I do have something else. This month, there's an event that only happens every three years."

"Bitconference is every two years," Mark interjects. "And Elaine's already covering it."

My eyes squint a little too hard with my fake smile. "Not Bitconference, Mark." God that feels good. I puff up my voice for the grand reveal. "Explore Armenia. It's an event whose importance extends beyond the Armenian diaspora community of the Bay Area. It's not only about preserving Armenian culture but sharing it with our local community. There's a cooking class coming up that could be very—"

"I'm going to stop you right there," Richard says. I'm not sure what I did wrong; that was sounding solid.

Richard appears some combination of bored and self-important. "Snoozefest. We don't get any bites on quote-unquote cultural stories." He spares me from doing those terrible air quotes to match the disdain in his voice.

But I dive back in, confident about my counterargument. "But food stories are always great for viewership. Last week you had me covering the food truck scene on Broadway—"

Richard barges into my sentence, voice calm but louder than mine. "Right. But those were about tacos. Everyone loves tacos. We've got a bunch of viewers, especially those white millennials we're trying to target, who love tacos. No one knows who Armenians are, can't find the place on a map, and they don't care to anyway."

I'm shell-shocked. I have a million responses to that, but they're all jumbled in my head, and the only one that comes out is like pure id, though I am reigning in my emotions as much as possible. "Richard, you know *I'm* Armenian, right?"

"And I'm a quarter French. If my boss told me not to run a story about France or, you know, croissants, I'm following that command."

Um, he thinks being French, from a huge colonizing nation that brutalized civilizations around the world, is like being Armenian. I shouldn't have brought it back to myself anyway. That's not my problem with what he said. I want to get in his face and say, "So you're saying I'm not allowed to report on an Armenian story because our culture isn't sexy enough for white millennials?" because no one can deny that sounds *bad*. But now it feels too late, and something in the energy has changed, like he's had the last word and lightened the mood with his pastry reference. I don't reply, and he examines his computer screen.

"Where's the slosh pot?" He types frantically. "Can anyone pull it up and project?"

Oh no, the viewer suggestions that come in through our website. They're always small, petty stories, and guess who always gets stuck with them.

Mark types and clicks furiously, and the comments page appears on the TV behind Richard. I don't bother reading it.

It could have been so perfect, the cooking class. I would have collaborated with Vache, an expert on Armenian food, and it would give Explore Armenia some press. And I'd get to strut my stuff in front of Erebuni. You know, totally platonically.

Richard runs his hand over his hair. "Why am I looking at the full list? Don't we have someone to curate this shit? Meredith!"

Mark is at the ready. "Sir, she's on vacation."

Richard shakes his head at the room. "You people and your

damn vacations." He briefly makes eye contact with me even though I haven't taken a real vacation in years.

Though. If Meredith is gone, that means no one on the head desk is going to be looking at the website. No one checks up on it but her and our intern. If I film the cooking class segment and upload it to the KTVA site without publishing it on the front page, Richard will never know. No one will see it unless I share the link with them.

It's not technically breaking any rules. Like, it's not illegal. Is it frowned upon and could it get me in some trouble? Yes.

But I'm going to do it anyway. I'm going to build my portfolio, help out my fellow Armenians, and stick it to Richard and show him—

Richard interrupts my reverie by assigning me a segment on a group of residents complaining about the excessive goose poop in their neighborhood.

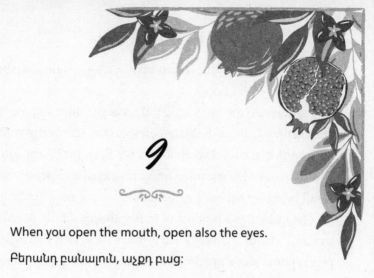

9

When you open the mouth, open also the eyes.

Բերանդ բանալուն, աչքդ բաց:

—*Armenian Proverb*

Three days later I'm at the Armenian school again. (I mean, where else are you going to get an industrial-size kitchen that allows for thirty people to be mixing and folding and stirring, all on the cheap?) But this time, when I park, I don't need to be rescued by Erebuni. Though I wouldn't say no to that, either.

I've been texting in a group chat with Erebuni and Vache to make sure everyone's on board with the details for today. The chat has been flowing surprisingly well and not been awkward considering I'm the new person in their group. Now I'm more at ease because I'm not walking into this place cold, wondering if they'll all want to speak to me again.

Plus I have a sense of purpose, like a wave billowing before me, clearing the way. I'm sticking to my promise to myself and reporting on the event today, Richard be damned. It's possible that someone at work will tell on me (*cough*, Mark) but chances are low. And Winnie the intern may be a sycophant, but she's not a snitch (at least, I hope).

I stride into the great hall and see signs directing me toward the kitchen. I almost hesitate—despite the number of times I've been to this school, I've almost never been inside the kitchens, and it feels like I'm sneaking into a restricted area. If only my pre-K self being served hot lunches could see me now. Hot shit.

The kitchen is a product of pure industry. Chilly. Metal counters and islands, no-nonsense eighties tiles, vats and ladles suspended from above or pinned to the walls. And it's brimming with people—mostly women, actually—inspecting the cooking accoutrement at their stations. People are picking up utensils, examining jars, drawing their fingers over the ingredient lists.

And there is Erebuni; I catch her profile. She's wearing a long black lace cardigan over a short dark purple dress and black tights. Gakhart. That means "witch" in Armenian, and it also happens to be her Instagram handle. *Intrigued* doesn't begin to cover how I feel about that, but her posts are private, and she hasn't accepted my request yet. She hasn't followed me, either, so I'm guessing (hoping) that means she's not a big Instagram person rather than just uninterested in me.

There's a moon ring on her index finger, and with her other hand she pinches the moon and twists the ring all the way around and back. I want to be that moon. Then I immediately tell myself to dial it back.

Arek is by her side, chatting with Janette and Vache. Judging by the lack of dudes, I wonder if Arek is here mostly to support Erebuni and her organizing or if he's into cooking. Vache, obviously, is here for the food and the stories behind them. As am I.

The event was actually sold out, super popular with only thirty spaces, but I wheedled my way in as press. Honestly, even better, because this one was expensive. Erebuni not only said she was fine with it, she used the word *thrilled* and said the story would be *in good hands*. I might have been running those words over in my mind for the last couple of days. And she welcomed the opportunity for Vache and me to coordinate.

I sidle up to them, suddenly shy again since they're all huddled together, these old friends.

"Hey, guys."

Arek gives me a sudden hug like it's a reflex. "Nar! I feel like we've been hanging out because we've been watching your clips. Damn, girl, you're a real reporter."

We've been watching? That sounds like they've been on some group chat analyzing my segments. I'm glad it's cold in here because that's the only thing helping me fight the spreading flush in my cheeks. "I—oh. I hope you were watching some of my best-ofs. I haven't always been given the greatest material to work with." You know, food trucks and goose droppings. None of my segments are what you'd call hard-hitting journalism, and I feel it so acutely in this moment, the shame of what they all must think of me, then of what my dad would think—oof, I snuff that one out immediately—but I try to fix my face to seem impassive.

"There's nothing to be embarrassed by, you sounded polished and professional in everything I saw," says Janette, and I just about want to die. How many is *everything*?

But Erebuni is reddening at the same rate I (probably) am. I thought I already liked her a whole bunch, but seeing her blush is like I caught her doing something she shouldn't. She hasn't exposed anything that's close to embarrassing, but now our conversation has her feeling that. And it has me hoping for something that probably isn't there.

Vache says, "I get it. I feel the same way when I find out someone has read my articles. There's a vulnerability to it, even if we're the ones who put it out there in the first place."

"Uh-huh." Then, hoping my change of subject gives them all whiplash, I say, "And speaking of which, Vache, are you ready to be interviewed? Erebuni, I'll get you later; you can tell me about how you and the group decided to organize this particular event. And if there's time I'd love to chat with Vartouhi."

Vartouhi is the master cook leading today's class. She's a consummate Armenian granny—roundish, clad in a plain dress just past the knees and a well-worn apron, short hair tied back, and olive skin dappled with sunspots from years of creating memories outside. She has the teacherly feel, which is perfect for this event. Commanding in the way she's walking around the room, getting people set up, but completely approachable.

Things are easy again. I set my tripod up in a corner, mic Vache, and have him tell me about some of the food and its origins. I read a bunch of his articles recently, and if he's as good on camera as he is on the page, this is sure to be excellent stuff.

And it is. After he shares background on the food, I ask him, "What would you say is the significance of an event like this one? Isn't it just a cooking class?"

Ah, I love a leading question. Vache and I talked ahead of time about what he wanted to cover, and this was a biggie.

Vache gives a knowing smile. "Right. On its face, it's just a cooking class. You can go to Sur La Table any day and learn how to make cioppino. But this event is more than following a series of steps. Armenian food isn't simply food, it's a testament to tradition passed on through the generations where our ancestors used ingredients they were cultivating and connected to. It's all about the shared tradition, people coming together to create and eat. Our food stands for survival and is a stand against cultural erasure. The fact that there are thirty young Armenians here, learning from an expert, means they are honoring their ancestors' survival. Armenians being together, learning, and continuing to pass on traditions is an act of resistance. We are using sacred recipes from our ancestral lands we cannot access."

Damn. I've got chills. I've heard some version of this before, but I don't know, coming from Vache right now it feels more immediate and important. Plus, this segment is going to be killer, and my whole body is buzzing with that adrenaline I get when I know I've got a good story. It's not breaking news, but in a way I like that better; it allows me to take my time with my interviews and think about the story as a whole instead of rushing something out based on gut reactions. I quiet down to listen to and record Vartouhi as she explains what we're making today.

In English, smattered with accidental Armenian (since not everyone speaks Armenian), she begins, "On the menu today is 'football' kufte, mutabel, and sarma." Her accent is strong, her words precise, each coming out with a point. "First, the football kuftes. They are so named because of their oblong diamond shape and color."

And they are absurdly delicious. If sini kufte is a pain to make, these are their feisty younger siblings. They're smaller, and it's wickedly tricky to keep their shape while baking or frying. No one in my family makes them; when they appear on the table at family gatherings, it's because they were purchased from an

Armenian caterer or market in LA. So it should be especially cool to learn any tricks from master Vartouhi.

"Mutabel is next. It is spicy, smoky eggplant dip. Usually appetizer."

My great-uncle Varouj's second wife used to make it for us, but since she passed on (RIP), neither her warm presence nor her excellent mutabel has appeared at any family functions.

"Next is sarma. We will be making a rrrrreal sarma." Her trill on her R is so long I get sucked into her words, like, hell yeah, it's going to be real. "In America they call sarma 'dolma,' from the Greek tradition. But ninety-nine percent of American dolma eaters have not tasted the deliciousness of the true sarma." Her finger is raised along with her voice, like she is sharing a great injustice in the world. Then she quiets. With a slyness, she says, "I teach you how to make."

It's true. The kinds I've gotten in stores are dry and unseasoned and make you feel like you're chewing cud. When an Armenian cook makes them, they are so limp from oil and lemon juice that they can fall apart in your hands. Authentic sarmas are stuffed full of complex sweet and savory spices. I'm stoked that I get to see this demonstration live.

The class begins and I roam the room, watching, taking photos, filming (always with permission of course). Vartouhi's commands are followed by the skittering of knives, participants' heads focused on their work or peeking at their neighbors. I ask Vartouhi if I can take a photo of her station and post a great colorful food shot to Instagram, the grape leaves being the centerpiece.

I get so swept up I forget I'm here to pick up guys. Uh, who was supposed to be here again? Mom wanted me to meet some PhD guy. The room is open, and there aren't too many men, so I

easily spot him. He's tall, with dark eyes and hair, pleasant looking. He has a look of kindness about him, but I can tell by the way
he's moving and talking, very loose and almost floppy, that I'm
probably not going to be physically attracted to him. I'll do a
drive-by and confirm.

He's mashing up smoked eggplant and chatting with a
cute woman next to him. "You know the eggplant emoji right?
Think about what I'm doing right now. Ouch. Ouch! I'm dying
by proxy."

He contorts his face into cartoonish pain, and I turn right
around and walk away. Besides, his companion is tittering at his
joke, so they seem well matched.

Wanting a conversational sorbet, I head back over to my
group. Feels a bit presumptuous to assume they're *my* group, but
none of them have made me feel otherwise. I'm putting away my
phone, aka my fancy news camera, for a break from filming when
I pick up on Arek saying to Erebuni, "Wait, Sheila works at Cloud-
base now? Your ex. The one who was always trying to sell us that
shit weed. I'm going to track her down and offer her a bag of
oregano."

Hold on. He's talking about Erebuni's ex? *Her? Sheila?*

Erebuni lifts the food processor full of the beige concoction
and scoops mutabel onto a plate. "Please don't. I haven't talked to
her in almost a decade. The news just popped up on LinkedIn."

Yes, *her.* I take a step back. She's not straight. She's not straight.
She's not straight. She's scraping the sides of the processor, flick-
ing every last drop of the food into the white ceramic bowl, which
makes me think she's a perfectionist, and also, wow, she's not
straight. She's rolled up the long sleeves of her lace cardigan so
they don't get dirty, and the plain beige apron she has on over her

witchy outfit makes her all the more darling, like she's brewing up a sweet charm. And part of me wants to step in and wave and say, "Me, too. I am also not straight, Erebuni." The second I think that, I know I need to cool it.

Then she turns to face me because, oh yeah, I've been hovering behind them for, like, thirty seconds. I smile in a way I hope conveys friendly, casual, and not as if world-shattering information has just been conveyed. As I inch closer, my neck aches like I pulled a minor muscle, because I've been standing so stick-straight trying to drown everything out and absorb their conversation.

Arek flashes me a smile, then continues, "Which team's she on? Customer happiness?"

Erebuni has a pinch of chopped parsley in her hand, and she dusts it over the mutabel. Erebuni's mouth twists. "Sales."

Arek chortles; he's practically choking. "Once a salesman always a salesman. At least she's got a better product now, if I can humbly say that."

I know Arek is just jibing her, but Erebuni looks a tad uncomfortable. Like, her complexion got wan, and I wonder if it's because I'm there and we're talking about specific inside jokes from the past, or if it's because she's not out (which, I mean, neither am I) and she's worried people will hear. Probably not that since Arek is one of her best friends and wouldn't do something so horrible. Or the worst option, which is that this woman is a gorgeous goddess who broke Erebuni's heart, and she's still in love with her after all these years. I instantly hate Sheila.

I step closer, "Ready for your close-up?"

She places a couple of pomegranate kernels atop the appetizer, and it looks super professional. Kind of rude of me since I just asked her a question, but I say, "That's beautiful. You're great at styling food. You should show off your skills on Instagram."

Yep. Planted the Instagram seed because she hasn't accepted my request and hasn't followed me, and I am dying to find out what's happening without being a creeper and asking, "Why aren't you following me yet?"

"I barely use it. Oh—" Her face shifts to something of remorse. "You gave me your info, right? Sorry, it slipped my mind."

That wave of shame washes right over me, like I am being so obvious about Instagram. Pathetic. It feels like she's saying I slipped her mind, though I know that's not true; she texted me the day after we met. I make some noises and words like "Oh, no, it's not . . . you know."

Erebuni lowers her voice. "And you're sure you want to interview me? Like I said, I didn't take the lead in organizing this event, it was mostly Kiki. I'm sure she'd love to be on camera." Erebuni tilts her head toward this Kiki.

Karoline Kassabian, aka Kiki, is the head of Explore Armenia. A handsome woman, she might be called, in her midforties with thick, banquet-ready hair and fingers fettered by diamonds. Today she's sporting a chartreuse blouse that I'd be nervous to get stained, but what does it matter to her? She's probably got another ten like it. She's around in the community, and I vaguely know of her, though not enough to say hi (thank God). She's sipping a glass of white wine and gesturing to one of her friends' mutabels and saying something that reads from across the room like a mean joke.

I also get the feeling, based on the way Erebuni spat Kiki, that the two of them do not get along. I wonder if it's more than just their different vibes.

"I'm sure," I say. "I prefer to interview people who aren't dying to be on camera. Gives it that touch of authenticity." And I almost wink but stop myself from being a cheesy flirt.

"Well then." She tucks a curly lock of hair behind her ear and smiles at me, and I'm wobbly, having trouble navigating her to the spot I've picked out for interviews. *She's not straight, oh my God, and you're about to interview her. Don't say anything stupid.* I bash my hip bone into a counter and pretend it doesn't hurt and isn't going to leave a bruise.

I hand her the little mic instead of clipping it to her dress because that's too close, and I'm afraid of being too close. I don't trust myself.

She's hovering, ready for me. I wish I had that type of devil-may-care vibe that'd let me ask, "So, the world wants to know, are you single?" and have it come off as charming instead of creepy.

The smells of roasted eggplant and chopped parsley pull me out of hypothetical fantasyland. Mustering up my confidence and nonregional diction, I ask, "Ms. Minassian, can you tell us about why you decided to put together this event?"

My first couple of words shock her into a smile, and I hope it's because she enjoyed hearing me turn on reporter-mode Nar. Or calling her by her last name. She clasps her hands together and leans slightly toward me. "We knew when we were organizing Explore Armenia that we needed to include an event centering around food. Food is a basic necessity, but it can also be art; identity. It can even be resistance. With the Armenian diaspora so fractured, Armenian food means different things to different people, but we wanted to share this slice of our food culture with the 'new generations,' so to speak."

The way she puts her words together, so collected and all with this chill twinkle, I know I am a goner. I ask her more, and she speaks, and every time I get to stand back and listen to her it feels like I'm invited into a private reception of two. The chatter of the kitchen is muffled, and I hear only her words and I wish we could go back and forth for many more hours. Honestly, I interview her a bit longer than I need to, and I'd normally say this would be a pain to review and edit, but somehow I don't think rewatching Erebuni is going to be a bad thing in my life.

I tell her I've got what I need. She says, "Are you sure? I don't mind redoing any of the questions. Whatever helps you. I may have slipped up when I was talking about Vartouhi's background. I slurred a couple words while I was trying to remember the name of her side business."

I shake my head. "No, you were perfect." And I wonder if she can hear the humming of my heart.

When she heads back to her station to catch up on the next dish, I figure it's a good time to shoot my stand-ups, essentially selfie interviews, which I wrote over the last couple of days. My tripod's already set up, and I tack the printed words to the stand. I click "Record," take my spot, and feel a light one-two tap on my shoulder. It's Kiki. Looking miffed with undertones of haughty.

"Are you the reporter?"

Okay, super rude. But I'll give her a chance, maybe she has a good reason to address me like an object. "Nareh Bedrossian." I extend my hand. "And yes, I'm from KTVA News."

She gives me a huge fake smile. "I'm not sure if you heard, but I'm the chairwoman of Explore Armenia. I'm ready to be interviewed."

"Oh, uh. Of course."

"I see you interviewed Erebuni."

That's definitely sniveling in her voice, and all that benefit of the doubt is gone; I am not a fan of Miss Kiki. "Yes." And I'm about to say, "Yes, because Erebuni is the whole reason this event is getting any press," but I feel like that would piss her off a tad too much and she might toss me out. So instead I say, "Right. She's been my contact and has helped me put together details for the story."

"Hmm. Next time you need details, come to me. She has strange ideas about some things, and I am afraid she might not always represent the Armenian community well."

My face is getting hot, and my peripheral vision is closing in. I'm feeling extremely possessive of my new friend. I want to say something rude to Kiki so, so badly, but I don't speak, hoping my anger can subside. I think, *Meditations, what did I learn?* I'm at the bottom of a deep ocean, watching this scene happening above the water. Yeah, and I want to drag this bitch down with me. *Nar, don't say bitch in that context; it's sexist.*

Kiki asks, "Did she say anything about . . . ?"

And leaves the question open and I'm not about to play fill in the blank with her, so I just stare, questioning her right back.

"I guess not." Then she snaps back into her rigid conceitedness. "All right. Ask me your questions."

I decide then and there I'm not including a second of what she says, unless I can find something to make her look bad so subtly she won't notice. When I ask her some of the same questions I asked Erebuni, Kiki spits back the insipid version of what Erebuni said. Worse, at one point she mentions how important it is for women in particular to learn this art so their children can eat Armenian food. I mean, yikes.

After Kiki is satisfied with the amount of blathering she's

done, she asks, "Are we done here?" I smile meanly and tell her she's free to go, which I hope annoys her.

I shake myself off from the haze of arrogance and stupidity Kiki left behind, then film my stand-ups. Once they're done, I head back over to see what the gang's up to.

Everyone's on kuftes now, rolling them and sliding their trays into the oven. Erebuni waves me over. "Do you want to help? I'm a little behind and could use an extra hand."

I suppress making dirty "extra hand" jokes, even in my mind (only somewhat successfully). "Definitely," I tell her.

Several groups of people have already popped their kuftes into various ovens, and the warm smell of spices is rising in the air. I wash my hands and sink my fingers into the kufte's outer layer, wet and squishy. Erebuni's fingers are long, stately. The way she rolls with tenderness . . . A hot jolt passes through me.

We don't talk for a bit, and I must be giving off weird vibes to her. Too stiff. Like, now that I know I might have a shot at something with Erebuni (I don't want to think too much about what that something is), that makes everything scary. Real. Plus, Erebuni doesn't know that I like women, too. I don't need to do a quick self-assessment to know that I read as super-duper straight. And, let's be real, a basic bitch. My hair is long past my shoulders, styled and sleek and very conventional. She's seen me in two dresses (and on the news, a million more dresses). My makeup is fairly heavy, not caked on, but I'm used to applying TV layers. I wear a lot of eyeliner. I have a variety of liquid matte lipsticks and berry lip glosses. I talk like a valley girl and drive a Honda Civic (at least it's not a white Jetta). I need a rainbow pin on my bag or something or she's never going to get the hint. I don't know why, but I want to immediately convey to her that we play for the same team (or at least that I play for both—no allegiances—and I'd be happy to play on hers any time).

It is June. I could mention . . . "June is Pride month," I blurt out. Erebuni's fingers stop moving. She's still.

Oh shit oh shit, why did I drop that? Where am I going with this? Think of something quick. I scramble out, "I wish I could cover the parade, but big events like that go to more seasoned reporters."

I'm lucky my voice didn't crack or I didn't gulp, and that was an okay save, but it's still super awkward to yank out of the clear blue sky; we're in an Armenian cooking class making football kuftes, and I'm talking about gay pride suddenly. Plus, it's a damn lie. I've never shown off my gay pride; I'm being as fake as Kiki's tan.

"Oh yeah?" Erebuni asks, and now she sounds nervous, probably because I'm making conversation like I'm baiting her or something weird. I attempt to beam waves of normalness at her, but I don't think life works like that. *Lord, please help me save this. I'm sorry about twenty years ago; I'm sorry I made Mrs. Nvart red in the face about the whole dinosaur thing.*

Then there's a movement to my right by the doors, and there's Raffi. Raffi G. He's leaning against the doorframe and generally addresses the room. "What'd I miss?" he says, and lends us all a smile that'd make Instagram models weep with envy. And I could be imagining it, but I swear I hear a couple of girly sighs from behind me.

Raffi wasn't on the RSVP list, but then again, who's that consistently on top of updating their attendance? Then, with a little lurch in my stomach, I realize he DMed me this afternoon and I never responded to his last message.

Referring to a matcha flat lay I posted earlier today, he said, Matcha lattes are nice, but vai jan, that selfie. More of those please.

He was aching with that "Vai jan." It's almost like saying, "Oh baby," and I'm not ashamed to say, it turned me on a little bit.

Still, though, I sent him a polite, arm's-length Thanks, there will be more. I'm not desperate. When he wrote back, better be 😉 I never responded. At the time, that seemed okay. Like, really, what am I going to say to that? But now seeing him in person makes me feel like I did something wrong.

Vartouhi hurries across the room, and I'm kind of excited to see the smackdown that only an old lady with no fucks left to give can dish, because he is super late and has interrupted the class. But instead she reaches up on her tiptoes and snatches his face in her hands and gives him two kisses.

"Tantig." He laughs through his squeezed face.

Then Vartouhi goes on to lovingly chide him about being a naughty boy (using the best word: "charageegee") for being late and then pinches his cheek and calls him her little beauty. I guess walking late into your great-aunt's—I assume, or family friend, since "tantig" can be used liberally—does earn you the type of castigation you'd give a mischievous puppy.

"Keedem, Tantig. I stayed late in the office helping my last patient. A little girl with juvenile arthritis," he tells her, but looks up and catches my eye. I smile nervously and glance down at the raw kufte. And he's a pediatrician too? A saint with a taste for Gucci.

While he's speaking, Kiki rushes forward, and she puts her hand on her heart when she hears Raffi mention his patient. She says, "So brave."

I feel Raffi's gaze on me again, and the whole awkward conversation with Erebuni, plus seeing Raffi and thinking about his insistence that I share more photos of myself with him, is a lot. I need to get out for a moment and regroup. I whisper out of the side of my mouth, "Bathroom. Be back." I hope she won't volunteer to come with me (though I do, a teeny bit, hope she'll come with me and I'll scoop her face in my hands and kiss her right on the mouth; ohhh, I love a bathroom tryst). But she just nods, and I sneak out the back so that I don't have to walk past Raffi.

I'm in the atrium right outside the kitchen. It's very unassuming when it's not decorated—just an old hardwood floor, cream walls, a couple of frames showcasing the school's donors, everything smelling mildly of bleach. One of the front doors is open, and San Francisco's fog is blasting through, making me realize I was like a frog being slowly boiled alive back in the kitchen, not noticing how hot it was in there.

As I pace, I'm giving myself a pep talk in my head. *Okay, Raffi is here, and he sort of likes you. That's fine. You owe him nothing. But you like Erebuni, and she's always super nice to you and including you in things, and you just mentioned pride, so hopefully she gets the hint? But she doesn't seem to like Raffi, and flirting with him will probably be bad if you want anything to start up with Erebuni. But. Do you? That would be a road uncharted, one that's certain to cause bumps. And you're still not certain she likes you in any way besides as a friend.*

I'm on the threshold of the bathroom's open door when a sly voice says, "Reporter girl."

Raffi's suddenly there, dangerously close to me, and I'm not sure how I didn't hear him sneaking up from behind. He's got this look in his eyes, like not only does he know he wants me, but he knows I want him. I don't think he should be so sure. His jawline is fucking breathtaking, though. And almost against my will I feel my arm hairs prickle with desire. I want to run my fingers along it, through his thick hair, want him to wrap his arms around me and tell me I'm beautiful. Because if someone that hot says it, it must be true.

"You caught me," I say, and I sound way too breathless.

He steps closer. We're in this small alcove, me backed against the women's bathroom and him against the men's. The smell of bleach is stronger. "You've been teasing me on Insta," he says, a light rebuke.

"Me? No I—I don't tease." I try to pull some strength out of the deep recesses of my body. "We don't really know each other, what's there to tease?"

He's got his flirty salesman voice on. "So let's get to know each other. A date. I bet you want a date, you old-fashioned girl."

"Uhhh," I say, and cough out a nervous laugh, buying time. This feels wrong. I mean, yeah, he's ridiculously hot and is clearly into me, and he's a savior doctor, and my mom and Diana would go nuts over me being with him. So I should say yes. This is the whole point: Raffi is the golden goose I need to take home. He's leaning in closer. His gum, it's spearmint. Unable to stand how little distance there is between us, I avert my eyes from him, that wolfish grin. There's a stain on the wall shaped like a mosquito; even the bleach couldn't get it off.

"I can't, I'm sorry, it's not you." It is, though, it's every alarm bell in my head screaming NO at me. His face turns. I see the sour disappointment and, afraid it's going to spread uncontrollably, I continue, "You're hot and charming and seriously, you could get any girl you want. I'm in a weird place right now." He looks confused, so the word vomit continues, "Honestly I sort of still have a boyfriend. I'm semi-engaged. Engaged. He proposed to me before he left on a trip to Germany."

His eyes soften, and he actually laughs. "Engaged. That makes sense. How else could you resist the charms of Raffi G?"

He confirmed what I suspected, that he'd respect another man having "claim" to me. Ugh. Something else is happening, too. Like, now that he's leaned in so close, breathed his gum breath on me, it's like he passed me the antibodies to his ferocious good looks, and I'm immune to them, which is rendering Raffi in a monstrously unflattering light. A narcissistic, sexist dull yellow.

"All right, reporter girl. I bid you adieu. Now, go on, powder your nose." He gestures toward the bathroom door.

"And you go and drain the lizard," I say, wanting to show in some tiny way that I can be subversive. Not exactly going to win an award for that one, but at least I didn't reply with a "tee-hee."

"No need, I came here for you," he says, and struts away, back toward the kitchen.

What the *faaaaack* just happened. I'm about to text Diana. *Wtf!! Raffi asked me out!*

But then I wonder how I can tell her that I turned him down. Mom and Diana, their smiles in the car, off fantasizing about me landing a catch like Raffi. No, they wouldn't understand.

Especially because part of my turning him down is because I know who I really want to pursue. But I blew it with Erebuni with that line about pride.

I need to get out of here. I'm feeling ill, like my stomach has disappeared. There's no way I'm going to enjoy any of the food now anyway. I head back to the kitchen.

It smells like comfort, with football kuftes browning, crisping at the edges. Pots full of the rice mixture for sarma. Some people are laying out grape leaves one by one, spreading the tips with care. And Erebuni is there, checking out Janette's sarma filling. They exchange a pleasant word or two, then Erebuni sees me. Her expression changes from warmth to something I can't read. Concern? I wonder if it's how I look. My mouth, my throat, feel hollow.

I make my way toward my tripod, disassemble it, and go to grab my purse, feeling Erebuni's eyes on me, wondering if I can get away with a brief goodbye.

Arek and Janette are absorbed in conversation. Arek is wafting the steam from Janette's pot toward his nose and sighing. "Just like Medzmama's. Uh, you know, like Medzmama's cooking, and my Medz was a master cook. Never mind." Janette looks on, stoic.

Vache nods his head toward my tripod. "Heading out?" he asks, a note of surprise coloring his voice. "You haven't gotten a chance to taste anything."

"I'm feeling unwell suddenly. I can't eat right now. Sucks." It's not a lie at all, so I'm convincing in my delivery.

Janette and Arek don't hear me since Arek is now wrapped up in trying to re-compliment Janette, and I feel like he'd lay himself at her feet just to get her to crack a smile. I'm glad they don't notice me leaving.

Erebuni says, "Let me carry this," and before I can protest, her hand touches the tripod, and I surrender it to her.

Vache puts on a smile tinged with disappointment. I wave to him. "Bye. Sorry again for leaving so quickly."

I step briskly, and Erebuni has no problem keeping pace.

Once we're out into the unremitting night mist, Erebuni asks, her voice welling with concern, "Are sure you're okay? Can you drive all right?"

"This kind of thing happens sometimes. I'll be fine. Wow, it's cold out here." I let out a violent shiver.

We reach my car, and I open it up using an actual key, like it's the year 2000 (which it was the year this vehicle was minted). I reach for the tripod, and Erebuni willingly hands it over and is looking at me as if wanting something. I don't say anything, and instead lay my equipment carefully across the back seat.

She says, "Well, I'll light a candle for you tonight. Stomach, you said?"

Somehow—maybe it's the adrenaline, maybe it's the ice-cold mist—I'm not feeling an ounce of compunction about asking weird questions, so I say, with a flicker of a joke, "Stomach, yeah. Hey, are you a witch or something?" I'm not sure it didn't come off accusingly, so I add, "Because that'd be pretty cool."

Her expression is at once pulled out from whatever tangle of pity she was caught up in before. The corner of her mouth quirks up. "I dabble in the Wiccan arts."

So hot. I knew it. Witches always held a certain type of fascination with me throughout childhood, but my interest was snuffed out at every angle. My mom never let me dress up as one for Halloween since it was bad luck to tempt the dark arts that way. We do not worship Sadana in this home, she'd say. Our Halloween decorations were gourd- and corn-filled displays, not so much the ghost and bat type. Dad allowed me to portray only the good type of magical—fairies, mostly. I would beg to watch witch movies and mostly be denied, and would read witch books under my covers after saying goodnight. In middle school I even drew a short-lived witch comic, *Sorcery Academy*. Then high school came along, and I stuffed that obsession into a back corner of my closet along with my well-loved stuffed animals and remaining dolls. The cool kids were not into witch stuff, and I was dying to be one of them. It sort of worked, and they let me hang around the edges of their friendships. Don't talk to a single one of them today. So of course Erebuni's a witch.

"Do you do curses-for-hire? 'Cause I have a bunch of people on my naughty list whose hairs I have access to."

She laughs, and the air fizzes around us. "You are a funny one, Nareh. If you're interested, I'd love to show you sometime."

"You have no idea," I say, and that felt good, saying exactly what I meant. And the possibility blooms that I didn't blow it with the weird pride line. She invited me to her house, I think. That's not something you say to someone you've assessed to be a weirdo. Hope wells in my chest.

A gust of wind growls by us, and my body spasms with the cold. I move to the driver's side of the car, grip the handle. Part of me wants to stay here, chatting with her about her witchiness until everyone has left, every car gone, all the lights out. But I already said I was sick, so I probably need to keep that up.

"I'll make it happen. I'm good at that," she says. Damn, why is it so sexy to hear her say that she's good at something, especially when that thing involves me possibly going to her place and seeing her magic (I can't believe that's a sentence I'm thinking in real life).

This time when I pull away, I do look back. She hasn't moved, and we lock eyes for a moment. I don't know if it's my wishfulness painting it the way I want, but what I see is obvious. Longing.

For an instant it lights me up, colors the dark streets in

splashes of electric reds and golds. Instead of driving, it feels like I'm running lightning fast.

What would that mean, though? If we liked each other. If something happened. Or would I stop myself from making anything happen because of how difficult it could become? I honestly don't know.

10

I have plenty of apples and pears, but my heart yearns for quince.

Տանձն ինձ, խնձորն ինձ, սերկեւիլն ալ սիրտը կուզի:

—*Armenian Proverb*

Thursday evening, the night after the Armenian cooking class, my mom says she has something very important to show me after dinner. We (me plus mom and Nene) have finished my absolute favorite Armenian dish, sini kufte (which basically means kufte in a pan). It's a meat-on-meat pie with a distinct diamond pattern cut into it: two outer layers of ground beef, plus bulgur, and inside is ground beef with onion, spices, and pine nut filling. It's criminally good, expensive because of all the meat, and a pain in the ass to make since you have to knead the meat forever.

Of course, I wouldn't know about the hard work part since I didn't make any of it tonight . . . or most nights. The Armenian cooking class, and specifically hearing Vache's and Erebuni's takes on the importance of our recipes, made me want to change my spoiled brat status, but between work and man hunting I'm not sure when I'll get to contribute.

Mom does it all now. Nene used to cook a lot back when my

grandfather was alive, but after he passed, she said, and I quote, "I spent fifty years being a servant to my husband and children. I am done." She's refused to so much as boil an egg since living with us. Power move. Luckily, my mom has always enjoyed cooking, and in her retirement has taken meals to a whole new level. Like a casual Tuesday-night sini kufte with a side of tabbouleh. Are you kidding me? Though I wonder if this meal is meant to butter me up so I am more amenable to whatever she's about to throw down.

I tried so hard not to overeat. Before I sat down, with the warm smell of roasted pine nuts and spiced meat in the kitchen, I told myself, *Now, Nareh, this time you will not gorge yourself. You will want to get thirds, but you will not indulge this notion.* All that talk is not from a "keep it tight" type of mindset, because I truly don't care when it comes to seriously good food. It's more that eating foods containing bulgur is a delicate dance; the bulgur sits in your stomach and expands until even your sweatpants don't recognize you.

In any case, I ignored that little voice in my head the second I tasted the first bite, so here I am, half-prostrate at the little wooden table in the kitchen nook. My mom's laptop is plunked down in front of me, and behind it is one of the flower arrangements from Diana's shower. It seems to be one I assembled, the giveaway being a hasty quality, with filler sticking out too high and not enough roses. Doesn't matter now anyway; the hydrangeas are weeping and the outer petals of the rose are crusting over. The filler's still in good shape, though, with hearty greens and teeny unopened buds pointing skyward.

"Why'd you have to make it so good?" I groan dramatically,

without a shred of restraint. I'm a five-year-old again, and it feels great to let it out.

She won't admit it, but she loves the compliment. I can tell by the lilt in her step. Next to me, she places a glass of Earl Grey with a piece of clove drifting over the surface. "For digestion. And it wasn't *that* good." Then she pauses, smiles. "Or maybe it was."

Mom jabs a finger into my shoulder, and I protest. She says, "Now, sit up better. Look at this."

She clicks on a tab that reveals a spreadsheet. She says, "Since you had no luck again at the cooking class, I make this to help you."

So . . . I didn't tell her about Raffi asking me out, or my turning him down. Pretending it never happened seems to be the best course of action, especially since Erebuni's been on my mind.

Erebuni accepted my follow request on Instagram the night of the cooking class. I was in the middle of following up on a lead, but dropped that and spent the next twenty minutes analyzing her profile. She hardly had any photos posted, only ten or so, but they were all witchy as hell, dark and moody still lifes, rich with detail. Red beeswax candles, crushed spices, lace doilies, amethyst crystals, engraved silver mirrors, dried lavender, the smoke from burning sage, and—not classic witch, but still a superstitious art—a dripping Armenian coffee cup. And they're skilled from a photography standpoint. Not ashamed to admit, I got a bit jealous. I've been busting my butt trying to understand how to take a good flat lay photo, studying other people's work, reading blog posts, trying different editing apps, and after a couple of years, my stuff is only okay. Or, it's good, but nothing about it stands out. I know it. And here she is; it looks like she barely cares about Instagram, and her photos are brimming with talent.

We texted a bit today, and I tried to hold back on how gaga her photos were making me, but I think she got the hint. Oh, and I got to show her how the cooking segment turned out. I didn't chicken out. I furiously edited this morning, watching Erebuni's portion a few too many times, seeing the way her lips moved, hearing that streetlight-in-the-rain voice over and over. At one point she said the word *stretching*. She pulled the word out and accidentally (or maybe not) pronounced it with a *stah*, and, like, it was so sexy I listened to it several times and became, uh, concupiscent.

I cut Kiki out, feeling that would be the greater insult. Between Erebuni's and Vache's interviews, and Vartouhi's instructing, the segment turned out to be the best I've created. This is what happens when I get to pick my own story. I'm only bummed I couldn't rub it in Richard's and Mark's faces. *See how I can craft a story?* Instead, I muttered, "Suck it, Mark," while the video and the accompanying article uploaded to the KTVA website.

I shared it on Instagram, which, even with my public profile, feels safe. It's my personal account, so only Elaine, my work confidant, and MacKenzie the anchor follow me. I told Elaine beforehand, and she supported it and swore herself to secrecy. MacKenzie, who is scary and self-absorbed, has never commented on or liked a single one of my posts. Mark's on Instagram, but his ass is blocked.

The post received mixed reactions. I mean, everyone who commented seemed to enjoy it, but a lot of my usual likers didn't respond at all. It was off-brand since I rarely post about my work. Doesn't matter. Erebuni saw it and thanked me a million times over for publicizing the event, and that meant more than strangers' comments. In the article on KTVA's site, I linked to Vache's site, which he said gave him a good boost in traffic, way more than he usually got. I know a day of traffic isn't game-changing but I was still glad to send people his way. The whole thing, even the deceiving Richard part, gave me a warm rosy feeling and made me wish I could choose my own stories more often.

But that glow of Erebuni's attention is slowly fading as I pore over my mom's spreadsheet. Along the rows I read the names of Mom-approved bachelors, and the columns are as follows: Age, Occupation, Family, City, Country of Origin, Height, Photo, and RSVPs.

Eight rows are entirely filled, with some question marks in the columns. I grab a quick sip of tea and instantly burn my tongue. Damn it, I always time it wrong, and the tea goes lukewarm before I'm brave enough to try it again. Though I'm terrified at my mom's meticulousness, I have to admit I'm a little impressed. Since my mom retired from her high school math position, she's seemed a bit bored, directionless. Could also be attributed to Dad being gone and Nene having to move in. When Dad was alive, no, they didn't always get along, but they were always *doing* things. Having people over, going out to the country club, organizing fundraisers, volunteering for this or that association. Now Mom feels trapped at home with Nene because Nene refuses to take care of herself, and I feel bad that my job keeps me away so much of the time, but it's more than that. Without Dad, Mom seems to think she isn't supposed to be out in society anymore, that her life is basically on pause until I produce some grandchildren. She's hinted as much.

So I guess it's not a terribly big surprise that she's poured so much effort into the creation of this document, which will hopefully be a stepping-stone to the end goal of a bunch of rug rats for her to chase after. I get it; every parent wants to be a grandparent (their reward for surviving parenthood), but I suspect my mom's just bored senseless. It's on me, I guess, to take this spreadsheet seriously and pull her out of the doldrums. Erebuni, though. She's *not* anywhere in "Mom's vision of Nareh's Life Plan."

I sit back. "Damn, Mom, you put a lot of effort into this."

"You like it?" She's smiling big. She knows she's done good. "Don't say your mayrig doesn't work hard."

"I don't say that."

"I know you think this."

I shake my head just a bit and scan the list. It appears not all these guys are going to be at all the events (at least according to Facebook RSVPs). At the top she's put Raffi and Arek. Of course Raffi gets top billing. Arek has a question mark by his country of origin. I point to that square. "Arek is either Barsgahye or Hyastansti. Also, he's from Fresno. But it doesn't matter, I told you I wasn't into him—we're just friends."

She pulls the laptop toward her and clacks the keyboard, filling the box with **Armenia?**; she says while typing, "Not that many Barsgahyes in Fresno. Anyway, you didn't give him a chance. Try again."

I tell her okay, though in my mind I'm like, *Bzzt, nope.*

On to the next. "Armen, getting his PhD at Stanford in chemical engineering."

Oh. The eggplant guy from the cooking class. There's a tug in my stomach as I'm transported back to that kitchen—the interview with Erebuni, the way she stared at me, anticipating, lips barely parted.

I shake myself. "I met him last night. He wasn't my type."

"Not your type? He is very good-looking! See his height? Six feet."

Damn. She is right on with that. "How do you know these heights?"

"For some, I have seen them, or I know their parents. You take weighted average, giving the father seventy percent more weight. If I haven't met them, I look at Facebook, see them next to others, and guess."

"That's very . . ." I try for euphemistic. "Well thought out."

I turn back to the spreadsheet and press on, hoping we can get through this quickly so I can head upstairs and daydream about making out with a witch. "Sako the real estate agent. From Syria. Okay, okay. He's fine-looking."

Mom annotates excitedly, "I've heard he's the number one agent in San Francisco. I got it from Angelina, who is also real estate."

I nod to let her know I'm listening, even though I am not feeling the same thrill about real estate sales. I wonder if it's because of Erebuni. God, I have no idea if she likes me like that; I wish I could shut down the Erebuni part of my brain. I squint at the spreadsheet, feigning interest. "Ara, an entrepreneur. That's a little vague. Oh, his mom was a seamstress, are you sure you want someone whose parents aren't Rhodes scholars who work at a think tank?"

"I don't discriminate!"

Says the mom who literally put a list together of men with promising careers and included their parents (aka family pedigree) in the spreadsheet. I don't fight it, don't quit now, though this is ridiculous, and it's all because my mom is having such a good time. I love seeing her this vibrant, her face rosier, eyes brighter than I've seen in years. I want to give her this. Let her be happy now, at least, because if by some chance I end up with a woman, it's going to crush her.

"Kevork the jeweler. Obviously, I was waiting for a jeweler to appear on this list. He's cute, too."

"His family owned it, now they passed it down to him. Very good at business, well respected in the community."

I've heard of him. He's always seemed nice from afar, but I don't know why any of these guys with their deep networks of friends would be interested in rubbing elbows with an almost stranger. I doubt they're all wife hunting, but then again, what do I know?

"Zareh, lawyer. Ugh not another lawyer." My mom has written "Lawyer, prosecutor" in the box. "Can I veto him? He looks like he takes pleasure in throwing innocent people behind bars."

My mom looks upward, considering. When she's ready with her judgment she says, "Okay. Only because I don't like his father so much. Two-faced type of man."

"See, knew it. And next Artur, who is a . . . Sargavak? Uh, doesn't that mean, like, a priest?"

"Yes, the apprentice."

"How am I supposed to marry someone who's married to God?"

My mom seems exasperated like it's so obvious. "Uffff, he's not a celibate priest. This kind gets married, and I heard he's looking for a wife."

I turn to her and try to arrange my face into normalness and not something that reads, "Are you serious?"

"Mom. Do you expect me, *me*—your daughter who art not heavenly at all, who got kicked out of Sunday school for insisting about dinosaurs and evolution—to be a priest's wife and live at the church? It'd be so hypocritical."

She is shaking her head defensively. "Things are different now with the church. More modern. Besides, he's very well educated.

And his mom's a caterer. You'd never have to lift a finger and have all the kuftes and sarmas you want."

"While that is tempting, I don't see myself there. Nene"—I switch to Armenian—"do you think I should marry a priest?"

But instead of Sargavak I use the word *Srpazan*, which is a celibate priest of a higher rank, almost like a bishop. I hope she'll smile.

To my delight, Nene starts to laugh, a joyous cackle. She says in Armenian to my mom, "Did you know, your uncle Varouj despised our Srpazan. At Nervant Boudikian's funeral, Varouj was spinning all these nasty stories about the man, who had come briefly to give the final blessings. Now, why do you think your uncle Varouj would hate the Srpazan?"

My mom is smirking because she knows the answer, and I am sort of dying to know what's tickled Nene so. Mom waits to let her continue.

"They had the same mistress!" Nene hoots and clutches herself with laughter. I join in because I definitely did not know that about my great-uncle or about Srpazans in general. My poor great-aunt, though. We weren't that close, but I was just thinking about her yesterday and her perfect mutabel. Uncle Varouj was always kind of a skeeze. I am so not surprised.

My mom is equally chuffed and adds, "A lady from Greece—not even Armenian. She had her condo all bought and paid for. By the Srpazan of course." She clucks and shakes her head. "All our tithings going to a seafront property overlooking the Aegean."

Just then my phone rings. It's Diana. I put her on speaker since I'm sure Mom will want to hear from Diana, too (and dominate the entire conversation).

She sounds breathless in anticipation of getting the Nar Armenian Man Setup update. "Nar! Tantig Anahid. Hi, Nene. Did I miss everything? Did you already go through the list?"

Wait. "How do you know about the list?"

Without hesitation, Diana answers, "I helped fill in some of the gaps."

These two. My mom's and cousin's names, Anahid and Diana, are near palindromes, and I'm starting to think Diana's mom is a psychic for naming her after my mom.

I make some sort of noise that implies annoyance, and it's ignored by both of them.

"We go through the list already. I hope now Nareh will make the most of the last two events," Mom says, throwing me a stern look.

Diana asks, "What about Raffi? Didn't he say he was going to DM you?"

Oh no. My stomach tightens. I never told them about our Instagram exchange. Not wanting to lie anymore—and maybe, let's be real, a small part of me wanting to show off that I can get attention from the hottest Armenian bachelor this side of the Mississippi—I answer that yes, we had a short exchange.

Instantly, there's a synchronous uproar from my mom and Diana, chiding me for not consulting them before responding and demanding to see the messages. I should have known.

I hesitate because I can imagine they're not going to be pleased with my lackluster response to Raffi's sexy message.

"Where my glasses?" my mom demands of the world while she runs off to search for them.

There's my opening. I can just make it up. Diana's not here to see. Raffi could have commended me for my cutting reporting on goose poop. I'm already entertaining puns about "fowl smells" when mom's back at my side, pushing the glasses up her nose. Damn it, opportunity squandered. Fine. I'll read his message.

I pull up the app and there is Gakhart—Erebuni's profile, a red beeswax candle dripping all over parchment paper covered in herbs. A slice of fear tears through me at the prospect of being found out, but my mom looks right through it, as if she doesn't see anything at all. Her non-reaction is instantly devastating to me, and I'm surprised by it. That's precisely how she views the prospect of me with a woman: nonexistent. But I should cheer up. If by some wild chance Erebuni is into me, it could be a fun hookup and Mom would never be the wiser.

If that was all I wanted.

Briskly, I tap to my direct messages and scroll down to Raffi's. His username is AlwaysHyeDoctor, with a sexy black-and-white photo of his face that looks professionally taken. Hye means "Armenian" in Armenian, and it sounds exactly like *high*, so you can imagine the cornucopia of puns it's produced among some groups in the diaspora. But in this case, hopefully Raffi, an actual medical doctor, is not always high.

I read Raffi's message out loud in a monotone voice, cringing at his "vai jan" because one, he no longer is the aspirational man I thought he was, and two, Mom and Nene are right here, and Diana's on the phone, and yuck. No.

"Oh my God, he's so into you," Diana croons.

Mom shouts into the phone, "Did I understand right? He wants her to take more selfie?" As if I couldn't answer.

"Ayo, Tantig, he thinks Nareh is beautiful and wants to see more photos of her."

Mom hugs me. "She is beautiful."

Diana asks, "Did you respond?"

I read the rest of the exchange, and Diana groans on the other end. "That's the most boring response possible, Nar. He set you right up. You could have said, 'What are you willing to do for one?' or 'What's your medical assessment of them, doctor?' but no."

I wish she could see the look on my face. "Gross. I'm your cousin, not a soap character."

She laughs and says, "I know, I know," right as my mom is saying, "That feels much inappropriate."

Before she can share another outrageous suggestion, I say, "I didn't want to come off desperate. Playing it cool is the way, trust me."

Then a gloss of shame licks at me. Raffi's already a dead end, and I'm giving them hope. Misdirecting them.

Diana begs me to tell her if he ever messages me again, and I promise her I will, knowing he's got nothing left to say to me. The squeals from her and my mom should be making me happy right now. I should be celebrating with them. I should have told them about being asked out and be puffing myself up about what an excellent flirt I am to have potentially bagged the ultimate prize man. I could be going on a date with him. Instead I'm some fake-cheery version of myself, and I am not proud. But what am I supposed to do?

We hang up, and I face my mom. "Can I go to bed now?"

"Yes, sleep nine hours and you will have nine men on your arm."

"There are only eight on the list."

"Sleep nine, and you'll find another one."

After getting myself ready for bed, I'm flopped down on my ruffled comforter doing some last-minute work on my phone. I glance up to give my eyes a break and I catch my *OC* poster with Marissa pouting down at me.

It reminds me of Trevor somehow. I do the time zone math in my head (Mom would be proud); it's about seven a.m. in Germany, which means he's already gone for his morning jog and is getting ready for work. The man's a machine. Probably doing everything he can to stop thinking about how his ex-girlfriend didn't say yes to his proposal.

Meanwhile, I've gone to two Armenian events already, declined a date, developed a crush, and been presented with a Facebook-stalked hit list of men. Am I terrible? It hasn't been that long since the combination proposal/breakup.

I wonder briefly if all these men and Erebuni are my way of distracting myself from the end of my relationship. If my agreement with my mom is a red-blue-and-orange Armenian flag Band-Aid over my Trevor wound.

Almost as soon as I think it, I shrug off the thought. No, it's over with Trevor, and not only that, I'm surprised by how the thought gives me this liquid warmth. Yes, I feel bad about how it ended, and I wish we had some better closure. And that ring, God, I hope he can return it. But this is all absolutely a good thing.

In one motion I spring up, climb on top of my desk, and rip the *OC* poster off the wall, not taking care to keep it intact. I'm done with her. I have better things to aspire to.

11

She is a very honest girl. How do you know it? Her mother affirms it.

Շատ լաւ աղջիկ է:—Ինչէ՞ն յայտնի է:—Մարը վկայեց:

—*Armenian Proverb*

A saleslady is clamping me into an ice-blue tulle dress while five of my family members look on: my mom, Nene, Diana, Diana's Mom (Tantig Emma), and my dad's sister (Tantig Sona, who likes to be involved). I was mostly nude in front of them seconds ago, and everyone pretended to be very modern and okay with it, including me, but we were all looking in different directions. There's a queue of thirty more maid-of-honor dresses lined up for me to climb into next, and the sweat's already building along my temples. I'm trying to smile for Diana's sake, but I want to rip off this itchy tulle-fest of a dress and bolt out the door.

It's Saturday, my day off, and I'm spending all day here before it's time to get ready for the Armenian brandy tasting, which I learned is at Kiki's house. And while a bunch of the guys on Mom's list have RSVP'd yes, it's not them I'm excited about seeing tonight.

"Diana, can my dress have a slit?" her teenage cousin calls from the room next door.

Before Diana can answer, the girl's mom yells, "Heesoos prgich! No slit, I tell you!"

We've taken up four dressing rooms, each crowded with Diana's relatives of all ages. I know I got mad when Trevor made those remarks about how loud my family can get, but, like, I'm sure the sales staff hates us right now. Then again, they're in the wedding business, so they're probably used to gaggles of women effusing over garments.

I can't help but think that if this was me trying on wedding dresses for my marriage with Trevor, it would be a quieter affair: both our moms, sitting outside the room, making awkward small talk about the dresses, not mentioning prices for fear of scaring Trevor's mom, who is, uh, thrifty. Right now, I'm not sure if I prefer that version to this.

My mom squints at my chest. "Will the bust look like that in the actual size? Or . . . more bust will show?"

She knows me. I'm wearing a strapless dress about seven sizes too large for me, but unfortunately it seems to be the correct size for my boobs. Welcome to my everyday clothing dilemma.

I catch the saleslady's eyes in the mirror, and she has an uncomfortable look like she doesn't want to give us the answer. "I have this style in her size but in a different color. We can see how it works."

There's the briefest moment of quiet as she exits the room, and I can hear Nene humming to the music. They're playing Mozart, which people think is relaxing, but his music is surprisingly energizing and, in today's case, only contributes to my nerves. It sounds like it's shouting, "Go! Go! Go!"

Nene is feeling the music, and seems to be grasping on to it like a lifeline. She is not a fan of being surrounded by loud voices.

I ask, "Nene, what's the name of this song?" Then quickly add, "I know it's Mozart of course," wishing to spare myself a lecture on why I can't identify my classical musicians. I played piano for five years, much to the disappointment of everyone. My mom wanted me to play the violin, and my dad wanted me to play the guitar, so piano was their splitting-the-baby deal since it could be both jazzy and classical. Nene just wanted me to be musical like her (she didn't live with us then, but she was highly invested in my progress). When, year after year, I made only marginal improvements, and then had one particularly disastrous recital where I played an off-tempo version of the "Turkish March" and forgot the notes halfway through (my mom said it was a cursed song because of the title), it was clear I had no talent, and I quit. Sixth grade was rough.

"'Eine Kleine Nachtmusik, Serenade Number Thirteen in G Major,'" she recites, sticking her finger up in the air; she's better than classical Shazam because I get to hear it in her heavy Armenian accent.

I remember that now, "A Little Night Music." And for some reason, that title reminds me of Erebuni, maybe because I've seen her only in the nighttime, or because she is like night music, the way she speaks and moves.

I feel myself in that glow for a moment until I'm pulled back to the fitting room by Tantig Sona. She shakes her head at me. "You are the most impossible size."

Uh, thanks? My Dad's sister never got married and never had kids, and who cares, right? Her choice. Well, she does. She blames a whole cadre of people for it (she probably has a point; I'm sure plenty of folks in the community were nasty to her about it), and she holds this bitterness about her sometimes. She's also hilarious, an awesome storyteller, and I love to have her around, but then she'll be mean out of nowhere. Plus, the damn Facebook antigay memes. Just like the memes, I pretend I didn't register her comment about my body.

"Size, mize," Tantig Emma says, shooing away the comment, and turns to Diana. "What about color? Hokees, are you sure you want blue in September? This light? It looks like icicles and snow."

Diana takes a breath and seems to stifle an eye roll. "I don't care about the season, we're getting married in September because it was the only open month at the Manor Hotel, and ice blue is what I want. There's also going to be a pale green."

"Green and blue together, akh akh," her mom quietly wails.

My mom has a handful of faults, but she's good about not butting into other people's business. As am I. We stay quiet but telepathically signal each other in agreement.

"I found it in orange," the saleslady says as she barges in with a hideous pumpkin version of the tulle dress. Almost reluctantly, I dip my legs in, and she zips me up, and sure enough, it fits great in the waist, then looks like a porno on top. Tantig Sona fans herself, and everyone is saying some version of "No, oh no."

"Told you guys," I say, trying hard to keep the satisfaction out of my voice. "I can't wear strapless."

"That eliminates more than half the dresses," the saleslady says, eyebrows raised.

Diana stands up, ready to battle the racks. "No problem, plenty more options."

I change back into my normal clothes and follow her. The spot is in downtown San Francisco, in a light-filled loft on the top floor of a ten-story building, giving us a view of Union Square and its hundreds of tourists bustling about.

Diana's fingers flit through hangers, each one smacking decisively as she moves on to the next. She pulls out a long chiffon
dress and drapes it over her arm. Some of the other tantigs are
roaming around the store, so now's my chance. I whisper, "I've
been meaning to tell you. Raffi asked me out. Uh, earlier this
week."

She yanks a dress out so hard, the hanger flies off and clatters
to the ground. "What?" she scream-whispers. "Why didn't you
tell me?"

No one seems to have noticed us. "Because I . . ."

*Am really into someone else, a woman, and Mom would never cheer
for that. And you? I'm not sure if you'd understand.* I bend to pick up
the hanger. "I didn't want you all to make a big deal out of it."

She huffs, and a lock of her hair flies. I continue, "And also
because I turned him down."

Diana's glare is like barbed wire. "Um, excuse me? Why would
you do that?"

Like he's a gem that can't possibly have any imperfections, so
if I turned him down, it's because of some fault of mine. I love my
family, but sometimes their lack of progressivism grates on me.
This is going to be an uphill battle, I feel it. I try for the facts. "He
was so sleazy, D. He leaned in way too close and called me an old-
fashioned girl, and he was too pushy, like he wouldn't accept no."

"Pushy?" Diana asks, disappointed.

See, I knew it. "Honestly if he wasn't hot, or a doctor, no one
would give him the time of day. He gives off bad vibes."

Diana examines an organza skirt and says, "That's nuts, everyone loves him."

As she lets it go, it flows back into place on its hanger, and she
stares at me. Diana and I usually like to keep things light even

when discussing tough topics. I don't know, it's like we shouldn't ever complain too much since we have loving families and that's made our lives good overall. So I don't see this concerned face of hers too often.

I alternate between looking at Diana and fixating on a mold-green dress. "He wasn't going to take no for an answer. So finally I told him I'm engaged."

Diana shakes her head. "That sucks. I mean, that he's out of the picture. Your mom was so into him, I feel like you should have at least given him a chance."

She doesn't get it. My family never will. Just like they probably would never accept my being with a woman. Grudgingly, if I'm lucky. That's the best I can hope for. "Yeah," I mutter, pinching a satiny dress between my fingers, hard.

Then, thinking about how Mom would react, perhaps less favorably still, I add, "Don't tell Mom."

Just then, my mom, holding a pile of dresses flopped over her arm, sidles up to me. I jump, but she doesn't seem to notice. "You are talking about tonight? This is one of your last chances. Remember your list. It's alcohol, so they're all going to be there. And in the mood to meet. You have a lot of work to do."

While it's lovely in here with the afternoon light and the stark white floors and ceilings, there's always something about lofts that spurs anxiety in me, deep in my stomach. I'm not sure if it's the high ceiling that feels impossibly tall or if it's the exposed pipes, like I'm seeing the guts of the building, which I'm not supposed to. Or it could be the conversation I had with Diana.

"I know, I know," I murmur. I'm trying not to let the guys feel like another to-do. Try on a thousand dresses, meet a bunch of Armenian dudes. There is only one thing right now that doesn't feel like I'm forced into it and that is hanging out with Erebuni tonight. Our texts last night ended so pleasantly, a mutual complimenting session that would probably nauseate any outsiders. It has me aching to see her, but it also doesn't make that anxious feeling go away.

And somehow I'm addicted to frying my nerves, so I mumble something about the bathroom, duck into the hallway, and pull out my phone.

To Erebuni I type, **Want to get dinner beforehand?** but don't send. *Dinner*, that sounds a little yikes. Then: **Want to get a bite to eat beforehand?** Sounds like I want to take a bite out of her. Which I do, but no. Finally I type, **Want to grab something to eat beforehand? Gotta soak up the booze lol.** And that's a masterpiece. I hit "Send."

Then I decide to actually go to the bathroom and make a point not to look at my phone. I put it on silent to stop the temptation to whip it out midstream. After I'm back out in the hall, hands washed and dried, I pull out my phone and sure enough, a reply from Erebuni.

> I wish. Have to help set everything up. Thanks
> for the offer though

Oof, it's like a gut punch. That's exactly what I'd say to someone I wasn't interested in romantically, someone I was trying to keep at arm's length. Well, damn. I should put more effort into the guys tonight if Erebuni isn't into me. I'm feeling irrationally mad at her, though obviously she's done nothing wrong. I know, I know, I shouldn't feel that way—like, it's a super-problematic guy thing to do—but I could have sworn I read desire in her face when she looked back at me. And all our texting, you wouldn't do that with someone you didn't like. Right?

Then another text pops in. **Could we hang out afterward?**

Oh hell yes. I trot down the aisle whisper-shouting, "Yasss!"

12

A wildflower on the mountaintop would not change places with a rose in the garden.

Սարին անհոտ ծաղիկն էլ իրան տեղը իրան փառքը վարդի հետ չի փոխել:

—*Armenian Proverb*

If someone would have asked me to guess what Kiki's house looked like, I could have told you room by room what to expect and would have been almost exactly dead-on. Imported Italian marble (my mom would be so jealous), a grand wrought-iron staircase in the foyer, a crystal chandelier, a giant entry table showcasing a flower arrangement that would have been tasteful if it were a fifth of the size. Honestly, everything is almost good, but falls short of it, swapping refinement for the whole be-impressed-all-ye-who-enter effect. Then again, maybe no mansion could be said to be tasteful; like, that's the point.

We're in Atherton, which is close to my work, but nothing like it. Let me stress: very different from the melting pot of Redwood City. It's this exclusive incorporated town, mostly flat, and you can buy a dump for six million dollars. Literally a tear-down. I'm shocked Kiki lives here, actually; the town is so white that Armenians are seen as highly ethnic. And how do I know so much about Atherton? Well, in a town of seven thousand ultrarich people, many of whom are old-money families with connections, when a group of them puts on a three-hundredth-birthday celebration for an oak tree on the single country club's grounds, they get their local news team to be there. And there's no better reporter to cover tree birthdays than me.

It's always an awkward affair, interviewing the moms of Atherton: six-foot-tall blondes, faces pinched and stretched and chemically buffed until they shine like the surfaces of the mirrors they spend so much time looking into. I wear my highest heels but still only scrape five-six, while they treat me like one of their purebred puppies and tell me how tiny and cute I am. Compared to that crew, Kiki is as reassuring to be around as my grandma (oh, she'd hate that analogy).

The party seems to be out back, and oops, I probably wasn't supposed to go through the house, but whatever, her bad for leaving the door open. I pass portraits of her brood of brats—I'm just kidding, the four of them are very cute, and I'm sure they are bright little creatures, still uncorrupted by the world. And I could have been too harsh on Kiki; it's hard to have four children, even with boundless wealth.

"Lost?" A man's voice calls. I swing around to try and ascertain where it's coming from, and my heart rate shoots up because I'm thinking about Raffi, and what if it's him catching me alone again, trying for round two. This place is so empty and marbly the voice bounces like we're in a circus fun house. Then I see him, strolling from a hallway I hadn't noticed.

He looks like a human thumb, a pleasant one. Cute roundish

face on top, sizable belly and thighs, thin calves. He's wearing a brown button-down shirt paired with darker brown slacks. I know exactly who he is. The priest.

"If you are looking for the bathroom, it is down this hallway, and the fourth door on your left. But the smell, uh, do not judge; it wasn't me. I would not swear on Jesus himself, because that is a sin, but let's imagine I did hypothetically." He winks, then makes the sign of the cross.

He has a mild Armenian accent, sort of like Arek and Raffi, but without the swagger of those two. There's something about his posture, the cut of his shirt, the downward cast of his chin that's giving off old-school vibes, like he's on the verge of giving me mildly condescending advice. He reminds me more of Armenian grandparents than of someone who is in his late twenties. I'm trying to meet him with an open mind, though, and not judge him by the fact that our introductory conversation involves a smelly dump someone left behind.

"Oh no, I'm good. I just got here, trying to figure out where this brandy party is happening."

And only then does it strike me that the priest is at an alcohol-tasting event. Is that all hunky-dory with the church? I mean, it's cool with me, but I didn't know the seventeen-hundred-year-old Orthodox church was down with its deacons socially sipping on a distillation of the blood of Christ.

He seems flustered, probably by the fact that he needlessly brought up the bathroom stank. "Well, may I take you there? I'm Artur." He extends his hand.

"Nareh," I say, and we shake. A decently firm grip, not a bone crusher, but one that shows his confidence. I know he and I are never going to happen. Like, the chance that I'll end up married to a priest is about the same chance that God himself will crash down upon the earth and command me to marry this priest. But he's a nice guy, and my mom wanted me to meet him, so there's no harm in being polite.

He makes a brief gesture indicating he's going to start walking, and then does. I follow him through the house. "Where are you from, Nareh?"

"Here—well, San Francisco. Born and raised as they say."

I always sort of hate myself when I say something cliché like that, but it's also so effortless when you don't care all that much about trying.

"Oh, very interesting, so you'll want to stay in San Francisco."

Is he trying to get new congregants? Kind of a weird question to ask. We pass through a dining room that is head to toe Baccarat crystal, the kind of display you see only on the furniture level of a Bloomingdale's (which I know because my mom, Diana, and I have often wistfully passed by the Baccarat display at Bloomie's). The table is stunning, actually, mirrored and gleaming, but the whole effect together is, as seems to be the norm, way too much.

"I—I guess so. I'm open to living somewhere else. But yeah, this is home."

"That's excellent. I'm the new Sargavak at Saint Anthony's Church."

Yep, I guess he's trying to recruit me as a follower. That's cool, he's always at work; I respect that ethic.

"Right, I thought I heard there was a new Sargavak. Great to meet you."

We alight to an atrium, like a conservatory, in white iron and glass, and it seems to be what juts us out into the garden. It's lovely here, verdant tropicals bursting from their planters, leaves as large as baking sheets. No one's here besides us and the plants, so this isn't the final destination, but man, I could settle down on one of these teak chaises and hang out all day.

I can't help it. I whisper, "Wow."

Artur pushes a door that leads to the backyard, and I'm sad we have to leave this spot. "Yes, God has graced them."

I am such an a-religious bastard, I don't know if that's a priest's way of saying, "They got lucky" or "They earned their wealth." Not about to ask. Besides, he has more on his mind, because he asks, "And what do you do, if I may ask? Do you have a profession?"

We're outside, and damn, a big house doesn't tickle me so much, but an outdoor area like this, yeah, my envy is turned straight on. There's an art deco–style pool, a copse of trees that seems to be hiding more backyard, an orange grove, a second house (literally, it's a normal-size house in their backyard), and a third sizable house in sort of a cottage style that has just a couple of tiny windows at the top. That's . . . eerie. We stand a moment while I take everything in. I almost forgot he asked me a question. "Uh, yeah, no problem. Ask away. I'm a reporter for a local station, close to here, actually. KTVA News."

He nods his head in bobbing surprise. "A reporter, wow. That must be demanding?"

"Yep, I work six days a week."

"Sundays off," he says matter-of-factly. He begins to walk toward the no-windows cottage. Our feet crunch under the white gravel path.

"Saturdays, actually," I say, matter-of-factly.

He sucks in his breath. Total sacrilege, I know it. "I see. You work very hard. Doesn't leave a lot of time for other activities?"

What the hell other activities is he getting at? Cross-stitching? I'm hoping he arrives at his point soon because this feels like a blind interview that I'm failing, though I don't give two powdery lokhums about the outcome. And that's just annoying and a tad rude. "It's fairly grueling."

We're getting close to the cottage, and there's a sign right outside it. EXPLORE ARMENIA: BRANDY TASTING. Artur asks, "And you like this, being a hard-working reporter? You want to continue?"

No point in giving him anything but the raw truth. Confession: "Definitely. If anything, I don't feel I'm doing enough. There's a lot of room for me to grow and get better. A lifetime's more work to be done. I can report forever, really."

As I say the words, I realize how stifled I am at my station. And that goal of improving? I'm not sure how possible it is. The joy of recording and editing the cooking class segment filters up in my mind, and I'm hit with simultaneous longing and worry. I want to do more of those, but Richard is going to keep being a huge blocker unless I change something.

We're by the door. Artur exposes a quick grimace, then turns it into a thin smile. "I see. Well, it was nice meeting you, Nareh. Have a good time here. God bless."

He opens the door to the dark interior cottage and walks in without looking back. I swear he's going to let it slam in my face, but he thinks better of it and holds it open with the tips of his ring and pinkie fingers. And finally people's voices filter through the opening. I made it.

But what the hell was that? Definitely an interview. Then my mom's words pop into my mind: *I heard he's looking for a wife.* Oh my God, that was my marital fitness interview. And I super failed it. I let out a gasp of a laugh as the ridiculousness of it washes over me. I step one foot into Kiki's house and get assessed for wife material by a priest. Life is good sometimes. I can't wait to tell Erebuni about it.

Also, now I know why there are only a couple of teensy windows. I'm in a wine cellar. Every wall is lined with barrels, and the ceilings are lit by more Baccarat chandeliers with yellow bulbs, and everything glints in brown and gold. In the middle of the large space is a series of tables set up with the amber bottles of brandy and etched glasses. There are two spiral staircases in the back that lead to a balcony area above, where there are still more bottles and glasses arranged along the counter. And it is buzzing with people, echoing; there's a thrill of energy in the air like everyone can't wait to get down to drinking.

I feel someone's eye on me, and gaze up to see Erebuni. She's in a bloodred satin shirt that ties in a bow on top, black jeans, and a black leather jacket. She's wearing low-heeled boots, making her even taller, a pillar among the crowd. Her cheek ticks up in a smile, and I feel mine doing the same.

She doesn't have to summon me. I wander past the crowds to the spiral staircase and climb, feeling the clank as each heel hits, the cold metal under my palm. She's there, right as I debark, having found a cozy spot in the corner. We hug, pressing ourselves against each other, and I'm in her flower garden again. I let go first, like I'm too scared of how long I'll stay if she lets me.

It's just us tonight. Janette doesn't drink, and Arek, who I'm getting the impression has a huge crush on Janette, is bowing out in solidarity. Vache is on assignment at an Armenian restaurant in LA that's going to not only show him secrets behind their two-hundred-year-old apricot cake recipe but also give him part of an apricot tree that originated in Armenia. If you've ever had an apricot from Armenia (which I haven't, but I've heard endless stories about Armenian fruit), this is apparently as good as gold. He was bummed to miss today's event, but he told me he would hitchhike to LA if it meant getting that apricot tree. It's going to be planted in his parents' backyard in San Jose; they already prepared the area for it.

"You look great," I say.

"So do you," she replies, looking me up and down. I feel a bit exposed, and it's not just the chilly air. I'm wearing a white dress that buttons up the front, tea length with flutter sleeves, a tight bodice, and a loose skirt. We could not look more opposite.

"Thought Atherton would be warmer than San Francisco. I didn't anticipate being in a fifty-degree wine cellar all evening."

"You can wear my jacket." She proceeds to slough it off as she speaks.

I protest, "No, it's fine. The alcohol will keep me warm."

"I can see your goose bumps," she says. I swear I shiver visibly at that because she's looking at my skin, pulled tight. She hands me the jacket. "I'm wearing long sleeves. We can share it back and forth if that helps you accept it."

The heft of her leather jacket is in my hands, and I feel a bit sheepish accepting this from her, but on the other hand . . . I slip it on, and it's warm from her body, perfumed by her scent, and heavy like she's hanging over me in a hug. I thank her, and my voice sounds shy.

I mentally clear my throat and say, "You will not believe what just happened to me. You know Artur, the Sargavak?"

"Oh yes, I do. Did he propose marriage to you?"

My breath catches in a laugh. How does she—? "I didn't pass the wife test. Too tied to my job. So no proposal. How'd you know?"

"He's on the prowl. He's already made three marriage offers as far as I know. He's never spoken to me, though, and I don't know whether to be relieved or offended."

I chuckle, and she reflects my smile. She continues. "He must have gotten his gossip about me from Kiki. I swear everything is so black-and-white with some people. Don't they know that just because you've dated women doesn't mean you only like women? Though that nuance likely doesn't matter for the wife of a Sarga-vak, at least not Artur. I heard he's more on the conservative side. I'm friends with our local Fresno Sargavak and Yeretsgeen—wonderful couple—and they've never made a big deal about my sexuality."

Holy shit, okay. So she's bi or pan, but she definitely, without a doubt, dates women. And is zero percent afraid to tell me to my face. Afraid, like I'm afraid. If I said it, it would be *admitting* it, like it's a bad thing. I've been so conditioned to believe that, I wonder if there'll ever be an escape from that type of thinking.

Also, I'm realizing that Erebuni isn't shunned by the community. There are people like Kiki who don't like her solely because of her sexuality, and the priest didn't hit on her, so clearly the rumor mill has done its work, but . . . she's in a leadership position in an Armenian organization and on the Explore Armenia board. Maybe the winds are changing after all. Then I remember she's from Fresno, and her parents aren't here. That makes a difference; she didn't grow up with these people. No one knows or has to see her family. Not like they would have to see mine. That thought is too terrifying to touch, so I walk away from it.

There's something else shiny to explore instead. She's left, intentionally or not, the perfect opening for me. And you know what? Screw it, I'm going to take it, because I don't want to be scared or ashamed of this part of myself. I won't be admitting it like a dark secret.

I attempt casualness, like I'm talking about the label of the brandy in front of us. "Or just because you've dated mostly men doesn't mean you're straight. Maybe I should whisper in Kiki's ear and get her to spread stuff about me."

She is welling in front of me, face blooming into joy. Her eyes grow larger, her mouth parts just slightly.

Her voice is low, a little smile forming. "There are benefits. Keeps away the chauvinists." Ho-ly shit. I don't know what to say to this, and I am certain I have a stupid smile on my face because I can't hide my delight.

But then a ringing sounds from below, and there's Kiki, clad in a pale gold dress, jingling a bell with a bow on the end. I have a vision of her using that bell to summon her kids to dinner. Hopefully not her staff to attend to her.

She's showing off all her veneers; even from all the way over here, I can see they're shiny with spit. "Ladies and gents, the Explore Armenia committee is proud to present our very first Armenian brandy tasting event." There's a semi-enthusiastic round of applause and some whistles. "I hope you all enjoy yourselves in my husband, Armen's, and my brand-new wine cellar. Tonight's event is put on courtesy of Zeli Winery, our new wine production company. If you'd like to try our wines, everyone today gets a coupon for five percent off your first case." She gestures to a stack of green flyers at a table near her.

Didn't take her for a winemonger, or being such a cheap-ass; Kiki continues to surprise. I give Erebuni a look like *Are you kidding me?* and she laughs, a couple of exhalations through her nose.

I spot Raffi. He's wearing a tan V-neck that matches his skin so well he looks topless, and he's whispering into the ear of a blond girl who looks like a cat. I realize he never said my name; I wonder if he even knows it. The woman he's with flips her hair, turns from him, and walks off, rolling her eyes. Guess I'm not the only one who can see past that jawline.

Kiki goes on to introduce the brandy expert, who is a shorter man with a goatee in a crisp shirt and tight slacks. He has a mic, so his voice bounces off the walls. "Welcome, all. It is my honor to share with you the elegant art of brandy tasting. According to some sources, Armenians have been distilling wine into brandy since the twelfth century, which means what you are about to imbibe today has most ancient roots." He pauses, and there are in fact a couple of *Ohs*.

"In Armenia, they say to drink brandy with your left hand, because it is closest to your heart."

For being a cynical bunch of survivors, Armenians can be blindingly sentimental. And I love it. Erebuni shifts her weight next to me, and I wish I could hear what she's thinking.

He continues, "First up we have Ararat, which is made by a company that's been around for a century and was the preferred brand of Winston Churchill. Please, pick up your bottle and drop a dash into . . ."

He goes on, but in my mind his voice fuzzes over like someone's covered his mic, because Erebuni and I, we're going to drink together. Partake, like he said, in this drink that's centuries old. She picks up the bottle, her dark purple nails wrapped tightly around its body. "How much?"

"One pinkie," I say, sticking mine out.

She nods, pours, and the brandy comes out fast, but she yanks the neck up in time. She hands me my glass and for a moment our fingers touch. Mine are so icy that though hers are likely cold, to me they have a hint of warmth to them. I readjust my hand to match exactly where her fingers were, like I'm trying to open a secret passageway by tracing my fingerprints over hers. The glass is etched with slivers of leaves, and I push my fingertips into the grooves. The glass balloons out at the bottom and is slim on top, just wide enough for your nose to peek through.

I've had not a drop of alcohol, but I'm already feeling reckless with my words, like wearing her jacket is some kind of permission. "Let's close our eyes and try to taste the fruit," I suggest. Communion in shutting out the world; I'm not sure why, but it feels like we're getting away with something.

We raise glasses, clink them, and the sound is unexpectedly lovely, not the usual crash of glass but the smooth pond ripples of crystal. I sip, and my lizard brain tastes stringent alcohol and a bit of sweetness, but when I swallow, the burning is pushed away, and that's when the promised flavors begin to appear.

We postulate about the apricots and figs, I pretend at tasting the toasted oak, and when she smiles again, I note to myself that another thing I like about Erebuni is that she finds all my silly jokes funny, or at least she is brilliant at pretending to be amused by them. I remember being goofy with an ex, way back, and he said to me point-blank, "You're not funny." In hindsight I can say, *Yeah, well screw you*. But I stuck with him for another two months. This, now—this is how a conversation should ebb and flow. It's comfortable but thrilling at the same time.

"I used to think this was BS," I say. "My dad loved wine tasting in Napa. We'd go with his buddies and their families, and they'd wax on about the notes of elderberry and the crème brûlée finishes. I was underage, but they still slipped me some."

Erebuni empties the rest of her glass, taking her time, exposing the skin of her throat to me. "Wine tasted like church for the longest time. We'd take communion at school once a month, and the taste of wine bread made me heave. I couldn't stand wine until my college roommates and I fashioned ourselves into intellectuals and threw Wine Wednesdays in our dorm with bottles of Two-Buck Chuck that we begged the transfer students to pick up for us."

She stares out toward the barrels, and I would love to see the slideshow running across her mind. "Communion, huh? A Christian witch?" I ask.

"Yes. Don't get me wrong, I have plenty of dissatisfaction with the church's views, but I'm a type of Armenian Orthodox. A Wiccan-Orthodox blend. I can imagine what you're thinking: heresy."

I raise my glass. "To heresy."

We taste a couple more brandies, one that's more chocolatey and nutty, one that's more woodsy (according to the guy, anyway). By the third tasting my palate is no longer anywhere near refined, and I can only detect, caveman-like, how badly the alcohol burns. Much burn or less burn. Now it's not only Erebuni's jacket keeping me warm. I feel the slow wave of alcohol spread over my body, shielding me from cold.

As I look around among the crowd, I remember my mission here and sort of groan about it. It's a bit hard to pick out the potential suitors, and do I have to actually do this? I want to tell her. My feeling of rashness from before has only grown. I feel like I can tell her anything. Even this. "So my mom sent me to Explore Armenia to find a future husband. I mean, I'm kind of kidding, but she has a list of eligible bachelors I'm supposed to meet."

An eyebrow arches. "Oh? And how do you feel about that?"

She is always so even, so curious. "I was into it at first, but then, uh, something changed." And seeing the way her eyes are getting big and not wanting to give her an outlet to ask me what changed, because I am so not ready for this (not as brash as I thought), I say, "But I should keep my promise to my mom and at least say hi to these guys. Can you help me make this fun? We can take notes on them, or, uh, rank them. Gamify the process." Her face is still unwavering, and I wish I could read her better. That power seems to be slipping from me the more I sip. I try to sound cheeky, because I am too afraid of being serious. "I prom- ise I won't end up liking any of them, if that helps."

She takes a mini step closer to me, and it wouldn't take much for me to lean over and kiss her. Her voice is low, so deliberate. "It does help." Oh my God, I want time to stop right now. But then she switches registers, the flirtiness gone. "Are you sure? You could just tell your mom you don't want to."

She's right, of course. But I feel like my mom and I have this understanding. And, like, what am I going to tell her? *Sorry, Mom, I fell for a woman instead.* No, nope, not ready for that. Let me make everyone happy, at least for now. Future Nareh can deal with everything else. "I—I know, but I already told her I would. The time for promises was before."

This seems to appease her—I mean, who doesn't want to keep promises to their mother? She scans the crowd below. "Okay, I've got you. Who's on this apparent list?"

I mentally fumble over it. Who the hell is on the list again? "Uh, Sako, this real estate guy."

She reaches for one of the bottles, and with her usual evenness, says, "I can save you some time there, he's not interested in women."

I guffaw. "Oh, huh. Are you sure?"

"One hundred percent. But please don't spread it around, he's not fully out."

I almost gulp. Like me. I try to read how she feels about it, and I'm sensing non-judgment. (I mean, why would she judge? But you never know; I'm still figuring her out.)

"In that case I won't tell my mom. She has a gossip posse."

Erebuni snickers. "Same with my mom, though she'd never admit it."

"Same!" I almost scream in delight. I do my mom-clutching-her-pearls impression. "Me? I do not gossip. Other people gossip and I hear things."

She laughs, then asks, "Who else do we have to size up?"

I reach back into my conversation with mom before I left tonight—she pulled up the spreadsheet again—and I try to visualize the rows. The engineer guy, no, he's out. Raffi's out. Arek's out. The Sargavak is out. And now Sako. Damn, so who . . . ? Oh yeah. "Only two more."

At this event, anyway. There's one final guy who's only going to be at the banquet. I continue, "This entrepreneur guy, maybe Ara? Berjian? And then Kevork from Vartanian Jewelers?"

She looks like she's holding her breath. I ask, "What, do you know them?"

"We've crossed paths a couple times. Why don't we meet them, for your mom's sake?"

"Sure," I say. I'm almost warm enough to take the jacket off now, but I want to keep this part of Erebuni on me. It spurs me to say, "But let's not spend too long on that. I'd rather get back to hanging out with you."

She buries her smile in her glass.

I follow Erebuni like she's my compass. She suggests that we meet Ara first, and as we approach, I begin to recognize him from his photo. His head is shaved bald, and he's slim but fit looking. He wears a pressed white oxford shirt unbuttoned one (or three) buttons too low, exposing dark chest hair, and cuffed sleeves with a monster of a watch adorning his wrist. He's chatting with the brandy expert guy, who looks wildly uncomfortable. No, *chatting* is not the right word. Evangelizing. Ara's raising both hands like he's preaching the good word.

"And that's why I'm saying there needs to be a bigger distributor to the US. This is liquid gold right here, and you only find it in specialty shops or the couple Persian and Arabic marts selling it to the same old customers who already know about it."

Erebuni moves into his line of sight, and when Ara takes a breath, she interjects, "Hi, Ara."

After a moment's surprise, he glows with a smile. "Erebuuunes. Parev. How's life treating you?"

He seems normal so far, a tad on the excitable side, but that's not bad. The brandy expert literally backs away slowly. I'm taking notes in case I need a similar exit.

"We were headed to get one of Kiki's valuable coupons and I thought I'd say hi." The way she speaks is so even, like she's sailing over a body of water without disturbing it at all. She turns toward me. "This is Nareh, by the way."

He shakes my hand, a real bone grinder. "Nareh, pleasure's mine." Then he looks at me quizzically. "Hey, you look familiar. Where've I seen you?" I open my mouth to speak but he blurts, "No, don't tell me, it'll come to me."

We wait there at his request, and I dare to glance at Erebuni and catch a little twitch of a smile.

He makes a guttural sound of annoyance. "Okay, I give up, where do I know you from?"

I'm not going to tell him how I know him, from seeing his face and stats on my mom's spreadsheet. And to answer his question, I have no idea. Though. "We haven't met, but I am on the news. I—"

"That's it. I saw you reporting on the cooking class. That was bombastic."

Did he mean bombtastic but try to make it fancy? He throws back a sip of the brandy and makes a short ah sound. "Knew it'd come to me. Reporter, huh? That's different. Sometimes feels like everyone you meet works in tech nowadays." And he huffs so hard I feel it on my face. Brandy breath.

It's true. I've been to parties with Trevor, and it's tech, tech, tech, tech. Thank goodness for my work, where my interviews generally are with non-techies. "Yep, we're the city of—"

He interjects, "What's a reporter make these days, anyway? You San Francisco or some smaller town?"

All right, here we go. Now I see why Erebuni didn't tell me anything. I feel like she wanted me to unwrap this egomaniacal present myself.

I ignore his question about my income and focus only on the second half of his question. "Redwood City."

He looks away a second, disappointed. "Damn, that's too

bad. I have a tip for you about the head of SF's planning department and how they're deciding on the random"—he air-quotes *random*—"lottery system for condo conversions. Not so random, turns out."

Really? That could be a story I could sell to Richard, if he'd ever let me tell it. Erebuni shifts next to me. I wonder if she sniffs BS or if she is starting to feel bad that she didn't just give me background on him first and let me decide for myself whether or not I wanted to meet him.

But in case it is legit, I say, "I could still use that even being in Redwood City. We cover San Francisco when it's a hot story."

He radiates. "You like that? I've got a dozen more. I got friends all over the city, people dropping off packages and fixing lighting. You'd be surprised the things they hear. No one ever takes me seriously, though. I've emailed tons of SF reporters."

Well, that's not good. If he's already tried reaching out and been cast off, there's probably a reason. Unsubstantiated rumor, probably. But still, I could use a little boost in my go-to sources.

"I'll listen. How about I give you my number? Text me tips anytime; we can talk more about them. Eventually I need to get statements on the record, though."

I give him my forwarding phone number that I use for tips, but I wonder if Erebuni thinks this is how I flirt with men. She hasn't moved in any way that's betraying jealousy or annoyance, but I need to make sure I check in with her afterward to let her know this phone number swap is purely business.

He whips out his phone. "I got you."

So we exchange numbers, and then I pretend like we have to go. Erebuni goes so far as to wave to someone in the crowd.

We squeeze through the patrons, who are getting rowdier

now. I hear a man shout, "Vor me dar, ara," which I'm fairly sure is a hilariously vulgar way to say, "Why do you care so much, bro?" There's something about hearing Armenian all around me that makes me feel simultaneously at home and like an outsider. Like, these people are so Armenian, they will swear casually in Armenian, and with perfect accents. I just don't hear it much in my own life. My mom speaks Armenian occasionally, mostly only with Nene, since she was coaxed out of it by Dad, who always spoke in English. Hell, he changed his name (not legally, but socially) from Boghos to the American translation, Paul. None of his American friends knew it. I grew up really, really American, but with this foundation of Armenianness that never left. I wonder what I missed out on. I wonder how Armenian the people in this room feel. Erebuni, specifically. Do they—does she—feel like me too? Never quite Armenian enough, always an American first? Or do they identify as Armenians first, and are enduring the Americanness around them, fighting off assimilation? I never thought someone telling someone else not to give a damn would stir up ruminations on identity.

Erebuni's arm brushes up against mine as we move through the crowd, and that wipes away all thoughts but the ones of her. Now I wish I had taken off the jacket. I want to feel the satin of her shirt against my bare arms, the press of her body.

We're safely away from the thick of the crowd, against the wall of wine barrels. She appears amused as she says, "That's got to be a record for getting someone's number." I'm about to be worried, but her voice hams it up, "And you told me you weren't interested in these guys."

She leans fully against the wine barrels. I step in, a tad closer than just friends. "Hey, he could be legit. You never know who's going to help you out in your career, especially with sources. That's my forwarding number, anyway. But yeah, I see why you didn't think we'd hit it off as soul mates. Anyone who 'has a guy' is probably not going to be a person I'm going to live with happily ever after. But hell if they won't prove useful in doling out information. So thanks for the intro."

She crosses her arms casually. "I knew that would happen. That's why I walked you down there."

She is being so cheeky, I love it. "Aha, so that's your witch power. You're like the Rumpelstiltskin of turning man hunting into career networking." I look around dramatically, like a nosy church auntie peeking over her glasses. "Who else can we hit before dawn?"

She chuckles, and I'm close enough to hear the little buzz above all this din. "No, I wanted to see what stories Ara would impose on you." Then she shifts, becoming mildly serious for a moment. "He's harmless," she reassures. "But also shameless. I'm surprised he didn't tell you how much his watch cost. He loves that thing. He might be saving it for your text conversation." She lowers her voice in mock confidentiality. "Five G's. He's told me three separate times."

I touch my hand to my chest and pretend to swoon. I am living to see her smile, her wide mouth, prominent teeth with incisors so sharp they look vampiric. I can imagine her dragging them across my neck, my arms . . .

"Should we meet Kevork?"

Ugh, yes, I guess so. *But then can we get back to us?* That's what I want to say. Instead: "Sure. Let's rip it off like a Band-Aid."

She pushes off from the barrels—springing up to her full height again—and ventures back into the swarm.

"Really? Not going to give me any hints this time before we meet him?"

I can hear her smile in her answer. "Nope, that's all you get."

A woman waves Erebuni down and gives her two cheek kisses. And because this woman is quite pretty in her little black dress, a flash of jealousy rises up in me. Then flickers out just as fast, because I know nothing about her, and Erebuni, after saying hello, keeps walking with *me* to our next destination.

"You know everyone, huh?"

"Just the same large group of people I see everywhere."

Makes sense. She plans these events. That's a whole other level of involvement.

She pauses, then taps the back of my shoulder, and again I'm swearing at this thick jacket denying me closer contact with her. I love the respectful insistency of her tap, though, from what I can feel. She leans in and whispers into my ear. I barely hear her say, "That's our guy."

Every inch of my skin prickles.

Please just keep your mouth there, or better yet, bring it closer, lips barely brushing my skin.

I realize my eyes have been closed, so I snap them open so I don't betray the private moment I was having. There's our next specimen, and sure enough, I recognize him from the sheet. Pale green eyes that tilt downward, olive skin like Erebuni's, an ill-fitting brown shirt, and frumpy slacks. His face is kind looking; I hope I'm judging right. He's standing alone at a two-person high-top table, tapping at his phone. And despite being a jeweler, he is not wearing a single piece of jewelry, not even a watch.

"Parev, Kevork," Erebuni says. Kevork looks up, a look of serene confusion on his face. She continues, "It's Erebuni, we met at the Heros Baghdassarian meet and greet a few months ago. This is my friend Nareh. We were passing by and thought we'd say hi."

The confusion lifts, but serenity mixed with ennui persists. "Oh. Parev."

And then no one is talking, and never has a room full of people shouting and laughing felt so silent.

"What do you think of the brandy tasting?" I ask, because this is my job, damn it. I can get anyone to talk. Open-ended questions for the win.

He shrugs. "It's okay."

Before the silence goes on too long, I jabber, "I wasn't all too familiar with Armenian brandies before, so this has been eye-opening." I pause a moment, thinking he might have something to say to that, but no. I'm trying to remember what my mom told me. He owns a jewelry business that he inherited from his parents, and supposedly he's good at it (probably not the customer service side). I try, "I heard, uh, someone saying that there needs to be a bigger brandy distributor to America. So these companies can get new customers rather than the same people who are buying them from specialty stores."

He shakes his head. "Who's saying that? That's never going to happen. You have to think about the competition, the huge corporations they're up against. Armenians dream so big sometimes. That's what lost us Cilicia."

Erebuni shifts her weight and clears her throat. I get the sense she's peeved by this. And unfortunately I have no stance on the subject because I never learned Armenian history beyond the genocide, so I have no clue what Kevork is talking about other than that Cilicia is definitely a place . . . some sort of land. Damn, when I admit it like that, it sounds awful. To save face I say, "Mmm."

He shrugs again. "Say what you will, it's true."

Erebuni seems to grow an inch taller. "Kevork, you might be interested in talking to Ara Berjian. Over there, bald guy."

Kevork looks over. "I know him. Always an opinion, that one."

Funny coming from a guy who just seemed to give a decisive opinion that irked my girl. *Nareh, no, she's not your girl.* Not yet.

Erebuni provokes him again. "He's saying brandy producers need to find better American distributors. You should share your knowledge with him."

I add, "Someone needs to be the voice of reason."

He nods, his mouth firm in a tight line. "You're right."

Without a glance back or a thanks or nice to meet you, he's off, ready to spew his dissent all over Ara. Poor Ara. Though something tells me they'll both have the time of their lives arguing over this.

As he walks away, I'm relieved that I'm done with the guy portion of the night. I've kept my promise—kind of—to my mom. There's only that one dude left at the banquet, a violinist, and I wonder if there's any chance I'm going to get to know him in good faith. This whole time, actually, have I been trying hard enough? No, I did. Raffi asked me out. And I'm kind of friends with Arek. I mean, he called me Nar.

The thing is, from the very beginning, it was always Erebuni who captured me. None of the guys stood a chance compared to her, and I see that clearer than ever. The only thing is that I can't think too far ahead about what that means for me. My mom. The goddamn banquet, where they're all going to be together. I mean, there's nothing going on between Erebuni and me, so it doesn't matter, right? Mom would never be able to detect my crush, not on a woman. Just like when she looked straight through Erebuni's

Instagram profile. Nothing to see here. *It's going to be fine,* I tell myself, and then my palms start to sweat.

Erebuni's standing next to me, head cocked like, "How'd you like that?"

My smile spreads into a toothy grin. "What just happened?"

"He's quite . . . pedantic. Doesn't like small talk. Can't blame him for that. He'd love to endlessly debate minutia is the impression I get from him."

I squeeze my face like I am super turned on. "Oof, my kind of guy."

She laughs softly, then appears pleased with herself. "I'm a matchmaker after all. Sparring partners."

"Congratulations," I say. My voice has taken on a much flirtier tone than I intended. My body seems to be leaping at the chance to show my cards.

And it continues to do so, this time with my mouth. "You know what I'd love right now? Some Haygagan sourj."

Requesting Armenian coffee after brandy is possibly the most Armenian thing I've ever said. But it feels right.

She's looking right at me with those elysian eyes, and I cannot get the image out of my head of them as planets, with winds whistling across craggy plains, full of life unknown. She says, "I know where you can get some of the best sourj in town."

Her voice is velvety, and I want it to run it all along my ears, my face.

"Where?" I ask. Barely. It comes out as a breath.

I swear she hasn't blinked. She says, almost a question, "My place."

Oh my God. My face prickles; I can feel it in my cheekbones. My mouth parts, and I can't hide it, I'm smiling with every excited nerve in my body, and I don't care. Let her know this is the thing I really, really want.

I can barely move right now, and I don't want to yet, because my whole body is buzzing with yes, yes, yes. So I give a tiny nod. "Please."

13

The heart of man and the ground of the sea are fathomless.

Հայ տղամարդու սիրտը, հայ ծովին անդունդը, երկուքն ալ համար չունեն:

—*Armenian Proverb*

I was a good citizen and took Caltrain down to the brandy tasting (it runs on weekends, thanks to the previously referenced Atherton moms who like to do their shopping in San Francisco), so Erebuni drives us.

I'm semi-shocked that she has a breathalyzer in her car and blows into it before so much as fitting her key into the ignition. If Dad had one that night, would he have used it? Would he have called Mom to pick him up instead? But there was no way he'd ever stick one in his car. He'd be too proud, saying he knew his limits. A pulse of sadness shakes through me, watching Erebuni blow into the tube, thinking how simply Dad's death could have been avoided.

Before I can ask, Erebuni explains that she's had too many friends get DUIs, some who didn't fully deserve it (two beers over two hours, barely a pinkie toe over the limit) and some who truly did (they apparently weren't hurt and neither was anyone else, but they quit drinking).

In telling me this she also mentions she's thirty-one, which, whoa, older woman. When I was a freshman in college, she would have just graduated. At this point, both our brains' risk centers have solidified, so I feel four years is an okay zone. *What a sexy thought, Nar.* Though I might be toning my thoughts down on purpose so I don't make a fool of my libidinous self.

The sun sets so late now, which I can especially feel on the Peninsula, where the afternoon light isn't blotted out by fog. The twilit skyline feels long and far and the good kind of melancholy. It's nine, and her car is hot, the air conditioning broken, so the windows are down, and my arms are sticky and hanging out getting wind-whipped.

She has the strangest music on, a haunted harp and a woman's voice that sounds like a plucked banjo string, and when I ask her who it is, she says Joanna Newsom. A far, far cry from the Top 40, but I think I like it.

We're in the moors of Belmont, a small city on the west side of the Peninsula, essentially one big hilly suburb. I would not have pegged her as a Belmont person; it's mostly families settling within the bounds of a decent school district. I tell her as much.

She has her eyes on the road. "I used to live in Russian Hill. Beautiful there, views of the Golden Gate Bridge from my rooftop, and the twenties architecture all over. But I'm from Fresno, and I missed the space. I got so lucky with this spot. You'll see."

We wind our way to the top of the hill—she's a great driver; I barely notice her driving, which is always a good sign—and at the end of a street she pulls into a long driveway surrounded by trees. It's getting dark out, but I can still see that there's a fairly sizable house up ahead, and I'm wondering if I'm in the wrong line of work. She parks away from the garage and simply says, "We're here."

I'm trying to decide which would be more impolite, being openly impressed by her big-ass house or pretending I'm unfazed by it. "Whoa, it's super remote," I say, pleased that this struck a good balance.

"That one's not mine," she says, gesturing to the home. "I rent their guesthouse, and it turns out they're gone most of the year. They come back around December. I've seen them for about a couple months total in the two years I've lived here."

That makes so much more sense. "Pretty sweet arrangement. They should just let you live in the big one."

I crunch on the gravel behind her. It's another microclimate here, so windy I can hear the cymbal thrum of all the trees around us.

"It's okay, I like the cottage. And while they're gone I can use their patio, which is the best part of their house, anyway. All the views."

Under the wind and the moonlight, I have the sudden urge to take her arm. I gave her jacket back as soon as we got in the car, what feels like years ago, so I'm bare-shouldered and trying not to shiver. But I'm a complete wimp, and I can't bring myself to hold her arm. We're silent, just the soughing of the wind and the crackling of rocks beneath our feet.

We reach a criminally adorable cottage that's backed up against a forest, with a tousled garden to the side of it. She unlocks the door and steps in. I follow.

She flicks on a light, and her home is thrown into a dark golden relief. She doesn't move to turn on any more lights, and I'm liking the dim vibe she's setting up. Makes me hopeful.

"Welcome," she says, not shy at all, like she's proud to share this. She sets her bag down and walks into her kitchen.

And, okay, this is not like anyone's home I've been in.

It's small, and that's normal, and there's stuff everywhere, but it's, like, intentional madness. There's art and photographs in various sizes all over her walls. Some occult stuff, some black-and-whites, some abstracts, some straight-up cheesy photos of her and (I assume) family or friends. Postcards, charcoal drawings, more photographs on a desk, leaning against the wall. Papers, pads, and candles all over her desk. Two tables completely covered, one with dried herbs (or dried flowers?) and bottles, droppers, more candles.

And then the other table, oh my God. There are amethyst crystals the size of my hand sculpted into Armenian khachkars, which are stylized carvings of crosses in stone. There are chiseling tools scattered nearby and shavings, and a lamp, suggesting she's creating these crystal khachkars. An Orthodox witch.

I'm drawn to it, walk up like I'm possessed, because I need to see more.

I speak, keeping my voice low with reverence, "I'm seeing this, right? Are these khachkars made of crystal?"

Now, suddenly, she seems shy. She ducks her cheek down into her shoulder and sneaks a glance at me. "I'm still working on them."

I want to pick one up so badly and feel both the smooth sides and jagged ends of crystal along my fingertips. "What more is there to do? These are incredible. Can I touch it?"

She's retreated to the kitchen, and I wonder if she's actually feeling embarrassed about her art. There's a clank from where she's standing, and she says, "Of course. Some of the edges might be sharp, though, so be careful."

I attempt to pick it up, and it almost slips from my grasp, it's so heavy. That's all I need, destroying her art. I handle it more carefully, the pricks of the crystal digging lightly into my fingertips. I've only ever seen khachkars in their traditional stone (hence the name, "cross stone"). Something about seeing a crystal carved into an Armenian cross feels both irreverent and reverent at the same time, and I'm no art critic, but that feels special.

"How much sugar do you like in yours?" she asks from the kitchen.

I should probably go over there and help. I set the khachkar back down gently on a piece of cut cloth. I think on her question and answer, "A little". The kitchen is right there, with a window cut out, so she was able to see me handling her art. I stand in the doorway. The kitchen has sage-green cabinets, and it's equally cluttered with appliances and spices and knives along a metallic rack.

She looks at home here, albeit a bit more dressed up than the true comfort of ratty-pajamas at-homeness. This outfit of hers. I want so badly to reach over and tug at the bow on her shirt, undoing it, revealing the skin of her chest underneath. But. Not now. She's holding a teaspoon heaping with finely ground coffee and plops it into the jezveh (a pot made specifically for Armenian coffee, with a long handle and a pouring lip) without spilling a single grain of it. Hers is a beautiful hammered copper one and the bent handle makes me wonder if she picked it up from the relic-filled Vernissage open air market in Yerevan I've heard so much about. She adds a dash of spice from a jar and says apologetically, "I know, cardamom isn't always traditional, but that flavor kick it adds is undeniable."

I wave my arms. "You're not dealing with a sourj purist. No complaints here."

She spoons a teaspoon of sugar into the pot and lights the stove. "You said you were in the mood for this? Does your family make it?"

They do. They did. Just like that, I'm knocked off my feet and thrown into a memory of Nene's house when we were younger. It's not one specific day I remember but a mash-up of a hundred days, a feeling. The *tap-tap* of my feet on the linoleum kitchen floor. Warm hues of greens and browns and ruby reds to contrast the cold of Twin Peaks. Pomegranate sculptures and the Armenian alphabet framed on the wall. And Nene sternly showing me how to ensure that the sourj does not boil over, to watch for the signs of agitation before they overtake the jezveh. Sitting in the kitchen nook on a rattly metallic chair, grasping my small Armenian coffee cup full of the dark, sweet sludge, and feeling that I was partaking in something very grown-up. I was always cold in that kitchen, and the nook furniture wasn't comfortable at all, but I would give anything to be back there in her house, which had to be sold.

Nene hasn't made it since then. My mom hasn't since her friend Nora doesn't come over anymore. "My Dad preferred American coffee, or at least he was enamored with the idea of American coffee. So Mom got used to making that. My father, uh, passed, five years ago."

Ugh. I did not come here to talk about my dad.

Erebuni sets down the spoon. "Oh, I'm so sorry," she says gently. I shrug, trying to not make her feel bad. Using the word *pass-*

ing, too, is a reflex, since I found using the word *died* makes people uncomfortable. Though Erebuni seems like she doesn't mind leaning into difficult spaces.

"It's okay. It was complicated. I mean, the death, no. He drank too much, he drove, he crashed into a brick wall and died before the paramedics arrived."

Her eyes are huge, as if she could make them big enough to absorb all my hurt.

"I didn't say it, but I appreciated your breathalyzer. He would never take a precaution like that. I loved him so much. We were always the close ones, teaming up against my mom. But since he passed, I've been seeing so much of the damage he left behind. It's weird, being angry at your dead father. He wasn't into anything Armenian, for one, which I always saw as a plus. God, I'm so embarrassed to say that."

Erebuni is listening with attentive little nods, her focus turning occasionally to the coffee, which makes her hair fall in front of her face like a curtain. She turns toward me, the curtain pulled back. "It's not embarrassing. We love what our parents love, especially a favorite parent."

She is so good; she truly does not make me feel like I'm burdening her. Even in the sadness of this conversation, she uplifts me.

"Well. I don't see eye to eye with him on that anymore. I get why he cast off so much of his identity, but he was wrong. You helped me see that."

She peers into the coffeepot. "I'm not sure I can take credit."

The kitchen fills with the heady scent of coffee and cardamom. It must be getting close.

"Thank you for listening to me. I feel like . . ." I pause, wanting to tell her how much she is starting to mean to me. I want her to know some part of it. I finish, "You really hear me."

We are looking at each other. Her voice is soft. "Everything you say fascinates me." I notice how close we are. How her lips are barely parted.

Then I hear bubbles humming against the copper pot, and she must, too, since she turns away, flipping the burner off. My chest heaves.

Too shy to acknowledge what happened, I break the moment further. I ask, lightheartedly, "How's it looking? No pressure of course."

She smirks. "I'm used to pressure. You can't make good sourj unless you've been lectured about it by your parent or grandparent at least five times. Lucky for you, I've been chided for years by all manner of relatives. My great-aunt Maroosh was especially picky. I hear her voice in my head repeating, 'hink ankam togh yera, verchuh mareh.'"

Erebuni examines the jezveh and barely sways her hips in what I think is a victory dance. Damn, I would like to see that again.

"Look at that ser." Her voice brims with pride.

Ser, the Armenian word for "coffee foam," also happens to mean "love." That's how important this process is to us. You can't make good coffee without love—ack, so cheesy. But it's also neat how that wove its way into our language. And I like to hear Erebuni say the word ser. Since it also kind of means "sex."

After pouring our coffee, alternating between the two cups to keep the consistency even for both of us (she's a master; that's a pro move I forgot about until I watched her do it), she hands me the cup and saucer and directs me to the main room. There's a low emerald velvet couch with some sun stains and worn areas that make me think this piece is old, and I brace for an uncomfortable seat, but it's surprisingly soft.

She pulls out a long matchbook, strikes a match, then flutters among various candles in the room, plunging the flame into the wicks one by one, a hummingbird collecting from flowers. She puffs out the match just before it licks her fingers, and a few moments later the air percolates with the smell of smoke (the Armenian word, *mokhr*, always sounded so mystical to me, like the people who invented it were in wonder of it). The walls dance with flickering light. Okay, she's clearly setting a mood. *It's on me not to screw this up,* I think, just as the back of my neck begins to get hot, a little damp.

When she sits, we're close enough that our knees could touch if we wanted them to. The bloodred of her shirt is striking against the worn green of the couch.

I take my first sip, and it's hot on my lips, but right up against that threshold. When the sweet cardamom hits, I close my eyes and look up. "That is so good." And I don't take pains to temper the lust in my voice.

"Thank you. Sometimes I think the best part is afterward, when you're alive with caffeine, and get your cup read. Anything seems possible. Reality shifts a bit when you're reading a cup; you open yourself to seeing what could be there."

So I'm a straight shooter when it comes to reality, but somehow, I like that she's not. Also, she's talking like she reads the coffee cup fortunes, which is usually a skill only the super-pro Armenian ladies can do, and even then, only select women choose to read. My mom never does, telling people's future's is way too much personal responsibility. If Erebuni does, I wonder how she learned. You need to have seen a hundred cups to know what a fox emerging from a waterfall means. I take another sip and ask, "Can you do it?"

"Oh, definitely. I've been trained in it." She gets that bit of shy confidence about her when she knows she's good at something. "It's a portal to intuition, similar to some of the Wiccan arts I follow. The art of sourj cup reading, similarly, has been passed on matrilineally. It's a practice from the past used to divine the future. Being from a people so tied to their pasts, the tradition was irresistible; I had to learn."

A reference again to Armenians' past, the genocide. She breathes it into everything she does, even coffee cup reading. There's a distant crackle of one of the candles, and I notice the room is filling with a second scent above the coffee, the candles ushering in nutmeg and orange. I make like I'm adjusting my dress and scoot the tiniest bit closer to her. When I look up I catch sight of her worktable again.

"Speaking of blending Wiccan and Armenian arts, can we talk about the khachkars? They are the most amazing things I've seen."

Her back stiffens a bit, and she pushes her cup back and forth on the saucer a couple of times so it fits perfectly in the center. "No, you're being too nice. My fear with them is that they feel like side-of-the-road tchotchkes. Do you know what I mean?"

My coffee is almost done, and I feel the hairs on the back of my arm standing straight up. This black gold is strong and hits fast. Excitement sparks in me all of a sudden, like I want to tell her everything and have her tell me everything, and that that would be the best thing ever. I say, "Like when you're on a long-ass road trip to Arizona to see the Grand Canyon and the Hoover Dam all in one, and you stop at some place selling turquoise and crystals and they're shaped like dolphins? Yeah, no, that's not what you have here."

She quirks out a smile, then sets her finished cup upside down on its saucer and places it on the table. Now the muddy dregs will spread down the sides of the cup and, in a couple of minutes, reveal her fortune. When she sits back, her leg brushes against mine, and I swallow my breath. She doesn't pull back all the way. Our legs are touching, and I feel the warmth of her against my knee. This is a permanent and intentional thing, and that means it's on. I have to tell myself to concentrate on my breathing because it's getting heavy now, audible.

She looks at the khachkars on the table. "Thank you. I'm intimidated. My mom's the real artist. And it's not my job; I haven't been giving it everything, enough attention. I dabble in too much stuff. That's plain to see." She motions to the room at large. "But I want these to be truly good. Meaningful and objectively excellent." I'm about to tell her they are, but she seems like she still wants to speak—she is suspended, waiting for something. Carefully, so as not to disturb her thoughts, I place my cup on the table in the same way. When I lean, our legs mash against each other still more for a moment, then are back where they were. She is as cool as ever, as if none of it is happening. But she doesn't take her leg away.

A moment later she says, "And once they get there, to that level—I mean if they get there—I want to make them big." Her voice grows with awe at this idea. "The size of real khachkars. Can you imagine what it'd feel like, seeing that in crystal?"

I can, and it's wild, and I love it, and I want one in my house, please. I tell her as much, in a tone that's clear to me that I'm still riding the roller-coaster high of caffeine. She smiles, and I'm afraid I'm coming off as if I'm just being polite or a suck-up with licentious motives. It's not true. I mean, not the sycophant part. She says, "It's an expensive project. To find the perfect size, a rare shallow depth. I'm not sure it's possible. But that's what I could make if I had true talent."

"Well, consider me a fan. And not to sound like I'm tooting my own horn, but I have a decent following on Instagram where I could promote it."

"I noticed."

I blush at the thought of her spending any amount of time gazing at my photos. "I could post your art anytime. You could create some kind of Kickstarter to fund your first project."

She shrugs. "I'm not good at asking people for money, but I like the idea. They're not ready yet in any case. Hopefully soon."

I want to tell her I'll set it up for her, I'll do anything for her. Luckily, I don't blather that, and she nods her head toward the cups and asks, "Should we do it? I'm not sure I should read my own, but I can read yours."

That voice, it's shimmering with promise.

"I'm in."

She peeks under my cup to make sure the dregs are set, dried enough. Appearing to deem them ready, she flips over the cup with care and sets it down in its pool of mud. The inside of the cup is a cascade of sludgy coffee grounds formed into branched patterns like veins. She inspects it and, with her free hand, traces something in the air above the cup as she thinks.

"I see a deer. I should say a stag, see the antlers?"

I do not, but that instantly reminds me of the deer head at

Diekkengräber's, and I'm suddenly stupidly nervous that she's going to see my engagement in the coffee cup, which makes me realize I never told her about it, but it's not even happening, so it doesn't really matter, right? There's time to share that story later. I make a noncommittal noise.

"It symbolizes protection. A protector could be another person, but it could also be yourself. Sometimes you're the one who steps in and defends yourself. The way he's half-formed, the catalyst, the thing you need protection from, hasn't happened yet, but it will." And seeing the look on my face, like, *What the hell, am I going to be mugged on my way home?* she adds, "Not to worry. Your protector will arrive."

I try not to sound scared when I say, "I'll keep that in mind." I know I make fun of my mom for her superstitions, but if you live in a house with a person spouting all manner of unfounded beliefs for a couple of decades, you're going to internalize some of that magical thinking. *A dream about getting your hair cut portends illness. Owls are the symbol of death. Don't tempt the spirits by showing your joy too openly. Naming your baby before it's born is bad luck. Dark ocean water in a dream means difficulty will come upon you. If you hand someone a knife, you will have a fight with them.* Now I'm shaking in my espadrilles because a witch told me I'm going to need protecting in the near future.

She squints, then sits upright, as if surprised. "There's something else." I edge over, peering into the cup and enjoying this shared space we're in. I'm in her bubble, but I feel completely invited. I smell roses again.

"I don't want you to think I'm making this up." She seems apologetic.

"What?"

She tilts the cup in my direction, points delicately, lovingly to the image. "What do you see?" she asks.

Eyes with lashes, a nose, the outline of a face, and curly brown hair. I see what she means. A little too on the nose, and still, there she is. "A woman?" It comes out as a whisper.

As if in response, she lowers her voice, too. It's slower now. "Yes. What do you think of her?"

I'll tell her. I want her to know. "She's very beautiful. Extraordinary."

"Oh?" There, she reddens again, the first sign that anything in her has been unsettled. I want to see more, knock her off the chair with nervousness. She feels so vulnerable when she lets the slightest feeling slip.

"Mmm," I say, like I'm sucking on candy. "Calm but powerful. Can I see her again?"

She hands it to me. My fingers wrap around hers, and that was why I asked for it, to feel the little chill of her skin. She lingers so long I don't think she's going to let go, but she does. I feel her gaze on me while I'm staring into the cup. We're so close now, the space between us has warmed. I feel the heat from her body.

My heart seems to be right up against the skin of my chest, pounding, raging to be let out. I'm too nervous to move. My eyes are open, looking at the grounds, but I'm not seeing anything now.

"What does a woman mean?" I ask. The most I can do is look at her, away from the cup. And this, facing her full-on, is itself an invitation, our faces already so close. She's breathing visibly now, her chest, her face, widening and blooming before me.

I feel her breath, soft and warm. "Can I show you?"

My yes is flutter-light, and we both lean in, her nose, then lips, silken-soft and slick with gloss, mine with velvet coating. She tastes of cardamom and sea salt. And my heart, it's so big, and it's radiating energy in waves and colors all around us, pulsing with every breath we sneak through our mouths. This, this, this is how it's supposed to feel. Flying through the city, catching every green light, headed exactly where you want to go.

Her fingers twine through my hair, and where they drag against my scalp they leave tingles in their wake. I don't know how long we kiss, but when she pulls away I almost cry out. It's a relief to have kissed her at last, to have plunged myself into this.

We were sitting so upright, clashing up against each other, so we both relax back into the couch, nose to nose so we can look right into each other's eyes. To see what's there now, what's changed. Her whites brighter, her irises darker. Her pupils are round and huge, sucking me in like a black hole. I reach for her hand, and it is cool like we're in outer space.

She speaks first, voice breathy. "I've been wanting to do that for some time. When I first noticed you in the car, I hadn't seen your face yet, but I was pulled to you. I had this immediate need to know you, this stranger, based on next to nothing at all."

It wasn't just an accident, then, her being a good Samaritan. There was more from the start. Her saying that, it lends weight to everything. Like we're not just taking out our lust on each other, the way every one of my hookups with women has gone.

"I thought you were the coolest person I'd ever seen and couldn't believe you were talking to me. I insulted you so many times that night." Briefly I cover my eyes in embarrassment, smiling through it, and I hear her low chuckle. She traces the edge of my cheekbone with her finger, and my whole body burns for her.

"They were accidental. I saw the core of you, all goodness."

"Mmm, I don't know about that."

"I do." And she reaches in to kiss me again.

After a while, when I'm partially blacked out, she releases me. She pulls back my hair, and her mouth creeps up to my ear. She pours her voice into it: "Do you want to see my bedroom?"

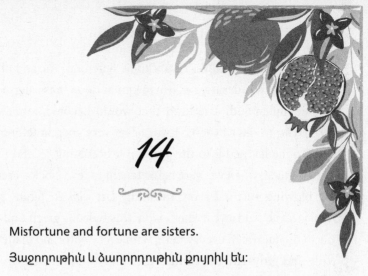

14

Misfortune and fortune are sisters.

Յաջողութիւն և ձախողդութիւն քոյրիկ են:

—*Armenian Proverb*

My breathing is clumsy. I'm foolhardy with joy and shock. I'm lying here, naked, her pewter sheets crumpled beneath me. My God. The way she gasped at the peak, like she was dying, I don't think I've ever made anyone feel that way. She's panting next to me, eyes covered by her arm, and I know the feeling, because I was there not too long ago. She's trying to hold on to it as long as possible.

And me. My whole body feels like a heartbeat. One flushed, pulsing being.

What. The hell. Have I been doing with guys this whole time? I curse myself for never letting an actual queer woman into my life before this. My God. Years of missing out. Not that men haven't been extremely pleasurable, because they have. But there was something different about what happened here, the attentiveness and attunement. It's wild. Maybe it's not women; maybe it's Erebuni.

I never want to move. I want to lie here until the end of time. My eyes are wandering, and there's an antique brass alarm clock on her nightstand. The kind that would become animate and *brrrrrrring* in old cartoons. I was never very good at telling time, never quite learned it to the point of it becoming second nature. In first grade, when we were being taught to read clocks, I remember blowing off the lesson, thinking, *Get with the future, people. Analog is out.* And a year later I wore this hideous green-and-black Casio digital watch everywhere, with every outfit, no matter how frilly and girly. Ah, the things that come to mind when you feel like you can melt into whatever surface you're lying on.

But that does look like it says eleven o'clock. My head's so airy, I could be wrong, but no, I'm sure it is well within the realm of "late." Which means, ugh, Mom. Some people can get away with living with their parents and never telling them where they are, but I sure as hell am not one of them. I texted my mom earlier but haven't let her know where I am lately, and I fear the missed calls and texts that must have piled up. And I don't know what I'm going to say to her now. I missed the last train home, just barely. Not that I want to be on the train alone at this hour, or in a shared ride for that matter. I guess I can call a Lyft at, like, six a.m. and sneak into the house and into bed? It's going to suck being so tired tomorrow, but this was worth it. Still, the thought of my mom is killing the mood fast.

I inch out of the bed and stand, feeling dizzy. Her room is, like, eighty percent bed, so I squeeze by, spot my underwear where she flung it, and pull it on.

Erebuni rolls over and asks languidly, "Where are you going and when will you be back?"

I open the door. With some hesitation, I ask, "You know how I live with my mom?"

She makes a face, lemon-pucker sour. "You'd think they'd understand we're full-grown adults. Happens to me every time I go back home."

So nice, so easy not to have to explain this part. All my friends, and Trevor, could never believe how my mom would keep tabs on me. One acquaintance actually didn't believe me when we were out in a big group once and I had thirty missed calls, and he was a real dick about it. So I showed him my phone, which finally quieted him.

I'm huddling around my phone because it's cold in the room, and I'm wearing almost nothing, puzzling over what to say to my mom, when I feel that Erebuni has stood up. She's getting dressed.

"Where do you live?" she calls, slipping her bra over her shoulder. Her breasts are small and stately, a nice contrast to mine. Huge ass, though. Perfect shape in my opinion.

"The city. I know, so far. At this hour I always make sure the driver has enough stars and enough ratings."

She's put on a worn black T-shirt. "You don't need to do that. I'm driving you."

I wave that off. "No, no way. That's like an hour drive round-trip, and it's so late, I couldn't ask that."

"You think after what just happened I'm going to make you take a cab home? Absolutely not. I am a gentleman." I laugh. It is very cute seeing her joke. But that's still a lot to ask of her. She continues, "I don't mind. I like going for night drives, and seeing you home safely is important to me."

I sigh. It is the best option. Home tonight, in time for—

hopefully—eight hours of sleep, and mom none the wiser, as long as she doesn't peer out the window. And more time spent with Erebuni.

"All right. Let's treasure hunt for our clothes."

We're in the car, and she does have a point: There's something calm about this late drive at the end of such a long day. We're on Interstate 280, which is flanked by foggy hills. At this hour there's just black vastness on either side of us, no city or suburban lights.

A new song starts. It's classical and familiar and—oh, I know it. "Is this Aram Khachaturian?" I ask.

She nods. "It is. The *Gayane* ballet."

Right, it's starting to take form. A memory of Nene in her old home, playing Khachaturian over the speakers and handing me the CD case to inspect, memorize. I make a sound of recognition.

"I watched the performance in Armenia," she says.

"The actual ballet?" It somehow never occurred to me that there is choreography, dancers, a set, attached to the music. And that if you popped over to Armenia, you could watch it.

"At their opera theater, a beautiful building in the middle of Yerevan. I need to go back; I feel the ache of it. There's always a part of me being pulled toward Armenia. Have you had the chance to go?"

I haven't. I tell her as much and leave it at that. My father never wanted to visit, claimed it was overrun with a Soviet mentality—lazy people looking for handouts. Our ancestors aren't from that region, anyway, he'd say. We're from historic Armenia, now southeastern Turkey. Now that Dad's gone, you'd think we'd be more likely to go. But the mental hurdle for Mom to get herself on a plane with Nene and me on a, what, twenty-hour trip counting the layover? There's no way. Mom doesn't think it's her place to change things up, travel, even have fun, in her widow status. So I don't see it happening unless something drastically changes.

Erebuni begins to tell me about her trips to Armenia, the views of Mount Ararat, the swallows swooping over the skyline, stopping for kookoorooz at roadside vendors, sipping espresso at midnight along Sayat-Nova where even children stay awake till one a.m. Everything she's telling me is making me yearn to go. A thought emerges—*I'll go with her one day.* But it is too perfect and precious an idea, so I shut it down. I listen to her voice, layered on top of the *Gayane* ballet, the swell of the orchestra taking deep breaths in and out, complementing our own.

A little while later, well into Millbrae, Erebuni asks, "You said you're into smells. What are some of your favorites?"

I honestly don't think I've ever been asked that question, but I am so eager to dive into my memories and think about it. It's like she knows; she finds exactly what I'm interested in. "That's a tough question. I mean, besides my new favorite one, which is your trampled rose garden, I love clean smells. Smells you'd describe as *blue*."

She nods, keeping her eyes on the road. She drives very comfortably, lounging back, with her left hand perching gently on the wheel. "I love that. I bet . . . white incense and saffron tea. You may have noticed back at the house, I sometimes tinker around with scent making."

So that's what they were, those stray petals and beads of lavender strewn over her table. She meant it; there are plenty of arts she dips her fingers into.

I make a sound of assent. Then it's quiet for a moment, and in the darkness, in my exhaustion, I'm plunged into another memory. I say, "There's another one. It's weird. I don't know if you've ever been to somewhere as pedestrian as Disney World, the one in Florida?"

She says she hasn't, but she has been to Disneyland in Southern California. I'm not surprised. My family went to both the OG one and the Florida one a handful of times, nice all-American vacations. I continue, "Well, at night, when it's time to go home, after hours and hours on your feet being zipped around on rides, you're in this cool and quiet air-conditioned monorail. Everything's dark but some neon streaks in the cabin and the fading lights of the park."

"I remember that."

"You're leaning against the wall and everything smells faintly wet, almost mildewy. Like, who knows the depth of all the rot behind the scenes? You can't contain Florida's humidity. But it doesn't matter. I love that smell."

She speaks, her voice a wave disappearing at the shoreline. "You associate that with a day's worth of fun. Family."

"I think so. Anyway, the smell of sweat on us now, and saltiness and stickiness, riding in the dark. This reminds me of that, but I guess the adult version."

"That's beautiful," she says. She reaches over, squeezes my hand lightly, sending prickles all along my spine.

She continues. "You're good at that—weaving a story. Like with Vartouhi's cooking class."

Miniature pride bombs explode in my chest, followed by that same longing pulling at me. Maybe if I can show Richard how serious I can be as a reporter, he'll allow me more freedom in my stories.

Then she pauses, and I wait, feeling she's about to say more. "I wonder, though, if I might ask . . ."

She sounds hesitant, and I feel like I know this: Someone is about to say something that could sting. I hold my breath. She says, "On your Instagram, you don't infuse it with that same level of storytelling. I mean, it seems to be working. You have tons of people adoring you. But for a reporter and for someone who notices the mildew at Disneyland, you don't capture that. I suppose that's what I'm saying."

A slow car appears up ahead, and Erebuni eases into and out of the left lane to pass it, still so constant. I am instantly hurt by her words, like I'm in a boxing ring without gloves, getting battered. I am so, so bad at taking criticism. I have two modes of response, shrink down and say they're right and apologize endlessly or ram back with still greater charges against the person (reserved mostly for Mom—sorry, Mom). And the thing is, Erebuni has a point, but . . .

I concentrate on not sounding terribly hurt. Only a little hurt. "That's not what people want to read, though. What's popular are flat lays of latte foam art on a white marble table with some loose flowers in the corner of the frame."

"Ah, so your goal is the most viewership."

"I . . . guess? That's—that's a good question."

I started posting almost as soon as the app came out. I used to write lengthy captions about single subjects—rediscovering my father's golf tournament trophy, the feelings behind Nene's Earl Grey—but none of that seemed to capture the public imagination like selfies and café flat lays, so I stopped with that type of story-telling. Once I felt the love, I kept giving people what they wanted, and the likes and comments kept growing. It makes me feel like at least I'm good at something. Worth something. But what is it that I'm good at? Not photography—I learned a couple of tricks, that's all; small accounts' photos are way better than mine. "People *like* me, damn it," is what I want to shout about my Instagram, to defend it. Then I remember Raffi's message, begging to see more selfies, and I wonder what exactly it is that I'm trying to get people to like about me.

"It does feel hollow after a while," I admit. "But I don't know what to do about that."

Her voice ticks up a notch. "I'm sorry if that upset you. That was rude of me, considering I'm a hack artist who's taken up a whole year on these crystal khachkars and still haven't gotten to where I want to be. You have a gift for this, and I just disrespected you over it. It's not my place."

I give her a couple of *No, it's okays*. She shakes her head. "That could have been me talking to myself. I am trying to push myself to be the best, to maintain artistic purity in my vision. Who the hell am I to slander someone who's made it?"

"I haven't made it. I only have thirty thousand followers or so."

"You have. I've seen the way people fawn over you in the com-ments." Then, a twitch at the corner of her mouth. "Got a little jealous of the ones under your selfies, to be honest."

I make a *tsk* sound (Armenians love to do that, the Greatest Generation is all about it). "Stop, you didn't."

"I did. Then had to talk myself down. *Ere, you have no idea if this woman is remotely interested in you. Though she did mention pride in a strange way, so that might have been her signal."*

I burst out laughing at the memory of my awkwardness. And we recount that evening from each of our perspectives, adding layers and layers to the memory.

We're in front of my home now. The road is thrown into an orange glow by the streetlamps and the mist slicking the streets.

"The family home," I say. It's true. I've lived in one house my whole life, with the exception of my four years at Davis. I can't imagine this building not being *home* to me forever. Even if I don't live here later (which, like, I hope I don't; I would like to get my own place at some point), with Mom and Nene living here, it'll always be home base. There are our treacherous stairs leading up to the front door—the eucalyptus tree's roots have been slowly pushing the steps around for years, so pieces of stone are coming apart or slanted. The roof has Mediterranean-style shingles and the architecture is what I'd call "boring late 1920s." We were too late for the ornate Victorian and Edwardian and iconic Marina-style homes and got a nondescript box with a few smaller boxes attached. But there is one unusual ornamentation—on the front face of the house, above the living room window, there's a keyhole surrounded by leaflike flourishes.

"I would have killed, as a teenager, to have grown up in the city. I hated Fresno then, the oppressive heat. I had a summer job cleaning cars at one point. The *interiors*. And every day was at least ninety, usually more like a hundred. And you got to grow up here, where at the height of summer your home is being hugged by the fog."

A hug—not how I would ever put it, but I like seeing the summer cold through her eyes.

She perks up. "Hey, speaking of, tomorrow is the summer solstice."

I marvel at how time passes so quickly once you leave school. I can't believe we've already almost hit the longest day of the year and I've hardly gotten to enjoy it.

"The solstice is a celebration of the Earth, and her lover, the Sun, being as close as possible. It's supposed to be the perfect day of creation. There's a bonfire at Ocean Beach with some of my Wiccan friends if you want to come."

I typically *haaaaaaate* San Francisco's beaches, because—you guessed it—freezing frickin' cold. Violent winds lashing your hair across your face. Like, even if you tie it, the winds pull it right out and whip the baby hairs all up in your eyes. And if you try to go in the water, God help you. Your feet will crack right off. I have shivered my ass off at Ocean Beach one too many times. But this is Erebuni asking, and a Wiccan bonfire does have my witch-hearted little-kid self dancing at the thought.

"I'm in."

"Bring something to burn. A sacrifice."

"Not a virgin, right? I don't know anyone left in that category. Though there is this one guy from editing who's a real incel jerk type—"

She smirks. "Something you want to let go of, clear out. Something to purify your creative process."

I'll have to think about that. I'm so easily into this, I'm not questioning the whole sacrifice thing. The idea of burning something that's getting in my way sounds like, I don't know, just what I need.

"I'll be there."

She leans in to kiss me, and I hesitate for a split second, because what if my mom is peeping out from the windows? I can't imagine how I'd explain this right now. I'm so not ready. But I don't want Erebuni to know how green I am with all this. So I dive in and kiss her as if the hesitation never happened.

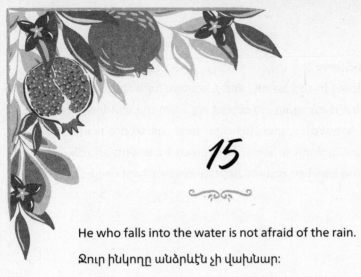

15

He who falls into the water is not afraid of the rain.

Ջուր ինկողը անձրևէն չի վախնար:

—*Armenian Proverb*

The following evening, I'm standing on the walking platform above Ocean Beach. It's June 21st, and it is, as expected, dreary as all hell. If it weren't for the prospect of more time with Erebuni, you'd never find me here. But I did come prepared. I'm wearing my thickest wool peacoat, thigh-high flat boots (because sand), and this cute woolen beret I never wear because it feels like a lot, but I figured the witches wouldn't mind my hat (witches being classically into hats) and I need something to keep the fog from sinking its humidity into my blowout.

Everything is gray, the sand is monochromatic, and the ocean's the color of dirty mop water, but I do admit I love watching the waves. Might be some weird human thing where we can sit and stare at the ocean ad nauseum. Seagulls, a permanent fixture on this side of San Francisco, cry out as they fly overhead. I've never trusted gulls, not since I was four years old. I was at the zoo when one swooped in and grabbed the toy my parents had just bought me. They didn't buy me a new one, and I've never forgiven the rats of the sky for their transgression.

This morning I tried to slip out of the house as early as possible to avoid Mom, but I was unsuccessful. At first I said so little, she sniffed out that something was up: "You always give detail. This time you are leaving too much out. Did you fall for that journalism man you mentioned? You don't want me to know?"

I had to assure her that no, Vache and I are just friends, and he wasn't even at the brandy tasting. Then I gave her the lowdown on Ara and Kevork; that kept her busy and away from asking me why I stayed so late if I didn't like any of them.

Besides, this relationship with Erebuni is in its infancy, and I need to see where it goes. Maybe this is just a hookup for her. Maybe she won't end up liking me if I embarrass her in front of her coven. If she dumps me like a rotten apple, there'll never have been a need to tell Mom. But I hope that's not the case.

I open my purse to take out my phone and see my chosen sacrificial object. Marissa's face from my *OC* poster. The poster was still sitting in the trash, and I cut her face from it and folded it up as my sacrifice. I don't want to be Marissa anymore, blond and button nosed, but also, after seeing Erebuni's place, I am finally motivated to redecorate my room. Maybe it does make a difference—your surroundings and what you can create. I'm living in a teenager's room, and I'm creating a teenager's content at work. And on Instagram (I remember Erebuni's words with a cringe).

I pull out my phone to let Erebuni know I'm here, but instead

I get a what-in-the-actual-HELL shock to the system, like I just stepped on a nail. A message from Trevor.

> Saw an affenpinscher puppy down by
> Gendarmenmarkt Square last night and thought
> of you. Can't stand not talking. I needed to say hi.

Goddamn it. Why now? The affenpinscher. Up until a few months ago, some nights when we were feeling hopeful for the future, Trevor and I would fantasize about what our lives would look like when we lived together. After Banana Joe, the cutest affenpinscher you've ever seen, took home the gold at Westminster in 2013, I've been obsessed with having that type of dog. Or we both kind of were, and it was always part of our made-up future home. Mid-century modern furniture and a little affenpinscher scrambling around. Honestly, he should have gotten me my very own Banana Joe as a proposal, and I might have said yes.

Ugh, I shake the thought away. Not now, not with the possibility of something so much—I don't know—richer in front of me. Yes, that's what it was like with Trevor. One-note. At most three. With Erebuni it's a whole damn mazurka.

I decide to use the same strategy I used on my mom. I respond, **Long live Banana Joe, forever may he reign.** Divert to the Westminster dog, not our hypothetical all-American dream dog. Hmm, that can't be all I say in my message. I need to respond to the second part. I type, **Nice to hear from you too. I hope you're having a good time over there.**

So bland. That should do it. I pray he doesn't get back to me now. If he does, screw it, I am not responding. This is Erebuni's night. I can't let Trevor dig his claws into it.

Turns out, I don't need to text Erebuni since there she is, rushing up the steps, waving. Oh my God, she's wearing a cape. She's gone full witch and I love it. No hat, but she does appear to be wearing a dress, and in a bright color for the first time since I've met her. It's burnt orange from what I can tell under the cape. And black Converse high tops. God, it's so cute.

She reaches me, and we hug, and I turn my face in so that my nose brushes against her neck, burrowing right into those roses, the smell that now thrills and comforts me. I need it, because I am still thinking about Trevor. What did he mean by *Can't stand not talking*? Did he mean that he's over the silent treatment and we're going to be all chatty now? He can't possibly mean that we're not broken up. Right?

"Hello, beautiful," Erebuni says to me. She pulls away and tugs gently on my hat. "You look like a Parisian ready for winter."

I flip my hair behind my head. "Sorry I didn't bring my cape. The formal one felt too dressy, and my casual one is at the dry cleaner's. I hoped you'd understand."

"I'll allow it this time." She nods solemnly, with a little smile peeking through.

I decide Trevor is finally feeling lonely and possibly horny in Germany, and that's why he texted me. It's nothing. So I'm going to treat it as nothing.

We start the descent to the beach, and I see her group from afar—about fifteen women, figures that are like flecks of color on the sand, reds and yellows—and for the first time I'm nervous. I have no idea what I'm doing, and apparently I look like a basic bitch on her first trip to France, and there is nothing spiritual or otherworldly about me.

I start to babble about how great Erebuni's outfit is. Like how

I joked about the cape but I really dig the look, and how I live, like, ten minutes from the beach and never come here and isn't that a crime?

Then Erebuni reaches over and clasps my hand. Our fingers are cold, but there's a hint of warmth in her palm that I'm sticking to. I'm here with her. I quiet. We're on the beach, bumping along with heavy steps as our feet get trapped by the weight of the sand. We knock into each other a couple of times, and I lean into it. She's so warm under the cape.

We walk up, and a small space opens for us. The fire feels exquisite, like a comfort in this damp, cold place. From the large flames, tiny embers escape and flicker into nothingness. Welcoming eyes meet ours.

Erebuni speaks. "Good solstice. Everyone, this is Nareh, a close friend of mine."

I wave to the group and hope they see that I am extremely open-minded and don't find any of this witch stuff weird. I mean, it is kind of weird, but I like it; there's a difference.

A couple wave back, some nod their heads. Everyone's in discussion as we're waiting for a few more women to arrive. Erebuni introduces me to Mabel, a woman in her fifties with mostly gray hair who calls herself a garden witch, dealing in healing herbs, essences, and tonics. Such a different life than mine. It almost makes me want to cast all my primary-color dresses into the sea and restart my career as an herbal witch.

"Would you like some telepathy oil for our journey tonight?"

I spoke too soon. I have enough on my hands communing with the alive spirits right here on earth. "Thanks, I'm okay. Not sure I'd know what to do, anyway. I'm new to this."

"It's all about intention, openness," she says. She whips out a roller-ball vial and dabs it on her forehead. "To open the third eye," she instructs. "You'll know about the third eye."

"Of course," I say, vaguely remembering something about chakras from watching *Fight Club* with Trevor and being completely obsessed with Helena Bonham Carter.

"I'm okay, too," Erebuni says. "Not going to engage in psychic work tonight; I have more of a self-focus."

Mabel digs into her cloak, and a small spray bottle appears. "Ylang-ylang and clove. To purify and reach your higher self."

"That sounds perfect," Erebuni says. She pushes up her sleeves and holds out her arms for Mabel—who seems delighted to help— then massages her wrists together.

"I love cloves," I murmur.

Before I have to make a decision about whether or not I need some wrist oil, the circle of women begins to tighten and quiet, so I do the same.

A woman—their leader, I guess, who looks about forty with long curly dark hair—begins to speak with the voice of a reverent librarian. She tells us what I'm sure everyone here already knows, about the bounty of the Sun and the Earth, how the fire represents the Sun and is warding off evil spirits (my mom would literally die if she saw me here), and how as the Sun descends beyond the horizon we can pull out our objects.

Even though everyone is quiet, there's enough ambient noise from the waves and other crowds that I breathe as silently as I can to Erebuni, "I have no idea what I'm doing."

She brings her mouth toward my ear, and I shiver. "It's all about focus. Think about what you want, tell yourself that, and that helps you make it happen."

Huh, manifesting. That sounds doable enough. Everyone is

reaching into their bags or capes and pulling out objects. I see folded-up letters, stones, fruit, and finally Erebuni gets her sacrifice out of her purse. She has a pamphlet of some kind, like you get at a community theater play or a funeral, which I'm dying to ask her about, but everyone is facing the fire now, so this doesn't seem the time for chitchat with your neighbor.

At the head witch's command, we raise our objects to the fire, and she begins to say a prayer of sorts. Okay, focus time. *Marissa, aka Mischa Barton, I used to read gossip blogs and save photos of you in a folder titled "thinspo," but that era is long past. I'm sorry I tore your poster off my wall and that I'm about to burn your face in a fire, but it's time. Nothing personal. It's just that I need to grow up, and I'm hoping this will help me. So thank you for all the good times. Hopefully this does something for me.*

As I watch others toss their objects into the fire, I throw in Marissa's face, holding my arm closer to the fire so she doesn't fly back at me with the wind. The fire curls the edges and eats at her face until the poster turns black. Gone. I'm free of that now, I guess. Time to keep that promise to myself.

Erebuni flicks hers in and takes a deep breath. Her hand reaches over and squeezes mine. I sneak a smile at her, which she returns, even fuller. The way she's looking at me, I have to wonder, do I have a girlfriend? *But Trevor is texting you,* a very annoying voice interjects. *Who cares about Trevor,* I insist to that voice, *when I've got Erebuni?*

Then the librarian-voiced leader starts singing this super-spooky song, like a female Gregorian chant, and all the women join in, Erebuni included, and I feel like I'm back in church on Easter Sunday, pretending to know the lyrics. It's both chilling and beautiful, and I feel like instead of on a beach I'm in a forest in Salem with wildflowers springing from the ground.

The song ends, and I'm doing my best to blend, like, *Yeah, guys, we hit those notes good.*

The head witch smiles. "Now we party."

Was super not expecting that, but I'm down. She bends to mess with something I can't see behind the firepit, but then EDM music starts playing, giving off a Burning Man vibe. Definitely serious about the partying.

Erebuni takes both of my hands and asks, "What'd you think of that?"

"Um, I loved it. I have to ask, though, what was your object?"

"I was actually meaning to ask about yours. Wasn't that some actress's face?"

I redden like I was caught doing something. "Mischa Barton, yeah, from *The OC*. I always wanted to be her, and it, uh, represents part of my life I want to leave behind."

As soon as I say it, I pray that she won't ask me what exactly it is about that life I'm trying to leave behind. Lucky for me, she seems to pick up on that. "That's fair," she says. "And to answer your question, that was a pamphlet from one of my mom's art shows."

Damn, that is brutal. I'm clearly not hiding my look of shock that well, because she adds, "No, not like I want my mom's art to burn down. I went to that show and thought, *I'll never be as good as her, so what's the point in trying?* But that's a counterproductive way of looking at the artistic process, at the point of art. I felt, for too long, like her success as an artist has been holding me back. So, into the fire. Don't worry, we have plenty of copies at home."

Huh, she mentioned in passing that her mother was an artist, but this is some interesting info. I can't imagine being into math and competing with my mom at it. Or piano with Nene. I'm suddenly thankful that I disappointed the women in my family by failing miserably at their passions.

Erebuni starts to dance, and she is *good*. So good that it turns me momentarily shy and I realize I'm just standing there watching her. It's one thing to know the steps to Armenian shourchbar, it's another to be intuitively talented at moving. I'm a conservative dancer—particularly while sober—relying on hip swaying more than any real moves. Erebuni grabs my hands and has me mirror some salsa-type moves, then twirls me around and pulls me tight. No one was watching before, but now there are a couple of whoops from the witchy women, and I'm totally embarrassed, except that Erebuni's guiding is working for me.

And then the mist turns to drizzle. Great, so much for my perfect hair, but at least the hat will cover up the top, which looks terrible when it's frizzy. Then the drizzle turns to rain. Not, like, a deluge, but undeniable water from the sky. The women shriek and seem to be enjoying it, Erebuni included. I wonder if it's good luck for it to rain on the solstice. I'm cringing at what my hair is going to look like, how it's going to ruin my whole look. Then Erebuni will see I'm just that dorky girl from middle school, and that'll be the end of us. My body shrinks into itself.

"This is incredible," Erebuni shouts, because over the music and the cheers it's harder to hear now.

She raises an eyebrow at me and my non-dancing body, and I can't help but tell her. "I'm not a huge fan of rain."

She looks up so the rain patters right across her face. What about her mascara? I could never. She says, "Why not? It's clean. This is the purification we've been waiting for."

A wind gusts so hard my beret flies off. God. All I need right now. I am chasing after it, sand swooshing up so high some of it gets in my eyes. And as I'm blinking furiously, trying to get that grinding sand out from under my eyelids, I close in on the hat, but a nearby seagull casually hops over, snatches my beret in its beak, and flies off. Mother-effing demon birds! I make some type of guttural noise of anger.

"Nar," Erebuni shouts behind me. "Did that just happen? I wish I had my camera out. I could have become as internet-famous as you."

The rain is pouring down, and my hair is slimy against my face, and I can feel the drops rolling down from my scalp, and I hate it, I hate it. I'm transforming into her again, my seventh-grade self with frizzy hair who's totally unsure of herself. I haven't changed one bit. Before I know it, I give a huge sniff and wipe my face. Erebuni approaches me, her eyes huge with concern. "Are you okay? Did you love that hat? I'm sorry I was insensitive about it."

She wraps me in a hug, and she is so warm, though she's wet, too, but instead of forgetting how upset I am, I at once feel her comfort because she's so kind about it. Still, I can't help but think what a catastrophe this is. I wanted my first witch get-together to be perfect. I can't handle a little rain; I turn straight into a baby. She's dumping me tonight, I know it. I sob a little more.

Through tears I manage, "That's not it. It's not the hat."

"What is it, then?" She gently pushes some hair out of my eyes. Her voice is soft.

I am aware I sound like a petulant child, and I'm trying to rein it in a little, but I say, "I know this is stupid, but my hair is all messed up. I never wear it natural. I haven't even seen it natural for years. I always blow-dry it immediately."

"Oh, Nar." She squeezes me. "I'm sorry you feel that way. I bet your natural hair is gorgeous, and I'm glad I get to see it."

I remember what Richard said that one time I wore it curly to work: that it was unprofessional, untamed. "It's not. It's wild. It makes me look like a lion."

She cocks her head. "And that's bad? Sounds inspiring to me. I want to be a lion." Despite myself, I laugh. She appears so earnest. She touches her curls, which are also sticky-slick with rain. "My hair's curly, too. I've learned it's all about the cut and how you feel in it. Trust me. I know it's easier with straight hair, and that people call it professional, but I'm sorry, that's just bullshit."

I realize I've never heard her swear before, and it yanks me out of this doom hole I fell into.

"Listen, you can be upset right now. Mourn it for a second."

My crying earlier seems to have mostly cleared out my sadness, so I joke, "My blowout. RIP."

"Excellent." She brings her face close to mine. "Let's see Nar the lion."

We rejoin the group just as the rain returns to a light drizzle. It's already happened; my hair is already not what I imagined, and Erebuni truly doesn't care. This is not eighth grade when I first got my hair straightened and everyone—including my parents—told me how amazing I looked and that I should do it all the time. This is me, as I am now, and this woman I am super into, and we're on the beach together. Also, didn't I say I don't want to be Marissa anymore? Huh, the pagan gods listened. I'm dancing on a rainy beach with a coven of witches, with my hair about as unflattering as it can be. It's been only a week and a half since Trevor left, and my life has turned upside down, but in a curious, inviting way. Wonderland.

A new song starts with a dirty buzz of bass that zips through my skin. I throw my hands out to the sides, lift my face to the sky, and sway, sway, sway to the rhythm.

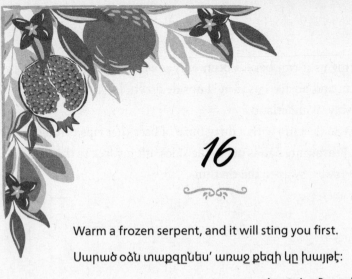

16

Warm a frozen serpent, and it will sting you first.

Սարած օձն տաքցրնես' առաջ քեզի կը խայթէ:

—*Armenian Proverb*

I'm late, duh, but that's because I made the harrowing journey from the Peninsula to the East Bay during rush hour. I know Southern California hoards all the infamy for its traffic, but they don't have bridges. Nine-mile-long bridges where you can be stuck. With no exit. A terrifying prospect if you've been chugging water all day without a bathroom.

It's the Wednesday night after the bonfire, and now I'm jogging along UC Berkeley's campus, approaching the building where Erebuni's genocide lecture is taking place. I had to stop and look at a map at one point because college campuses are the most confusing places in the world. I've had to do, like, ten news stories at Stanford, and I still don't understand where anything is or how you can get around that place; every building is made up of the exact same tan brick, every outlying street huge and winding, popping you onto an unknown corner.

I parked off campus, and while walking through a tunnel of

shops to get to Telegraph Avenue, I passed a dim sum place that
advertised sixty-cent bao. I was super tempted to stop and get
some but was already way too late, so now I have only the memory of hypothetical sticky buns in my head.

Berkeley's actual campus is very different from Telegraph's
head shops and white-kids-with-dreads vibe. It feels highly academic, and since it's a university, good job. As I'm on the cobble-
stone steps I can't help but wonder: Had I gotten into Berkeley,
would I be different now? I mean, of course I would be, but how
fundamentally? Would I have actually gone to their queer alliance
club and become a member? Would that have bolstered me to
come out, to be comfortable with that part of myself? Would I
have actually dated women?

The campus is mostly quiet at six p.m., but a group of blond
girls wearing sorority logos on their clothes pass me by, a couple
of them linking arms, giggling to themselves. Hmm. Who am I
kidding, I probably would have done exactly what I did at Davis.
Walk up to the club meeting, peer inside, see that everyone looks
much older and more confident in their gayness, and turn right
around and go back to the dorms. But who knows.

I enter the building I'm targeting, Dwinelle Hall, and my foot-
steps echo across the empty lobby. I wind my way through the
hallways, realizing I took the longest route possible, and finally
find room seventy-six, a lecture hall that holds about fifty people.
It's about three-quarters of the way full, which is good for a lecture on a topic as thrilling to the masses as the genocide of a race
no one cares about (William Saroyan's words, not mine).

There's a long table on the stage, where the speakers, including Erebuni, are sitting, mics in front of them. Erebuni is listening
intently to the woman on her left. I read her name tag—Dr. Seta

Markarian—and remember she's the professor Erebuni told me about the first day I met her. Erebuni doesn't notice me walking in, but as I slip into an aisle seat near the back, the chair, like an old movie theater chair with a velvet seat, squeaks under my weight. Her eyes dart up, and we see each other. She looks so serious—noble, even—and I feel this pride for her. *That's my girl,* I think.

Dr. Markarian is saying, "What many people don't realize about the continued denial of the first genocide of the twentieth century is that the very identity of modern Turkey hinges upon it. The political turmoil in Turkey during the First World War was the ideal backdrop for genocide. Armenians were classic scapegoats; we see it today. Everything in your life that is bad is due to the Armenians. They steal your jobs, they don't pay their fair share, et cetera."

Listen, it's interesting, but there's a part of me that doesn't want to examine it. Maybe because the horror is too big. That's been my family's line. Nene won't talk about it because her parents, survivors of the genocide, didn't talk about it. I don't know how they made it out. The tiny bit I got is that my mom once said their Turkish neighbors hid her grandparents in their basement. But then what? And how did they make it to Syria, then Lebanon eventually? It's possible Dad's parents knew about their history, but they died too long ago for me to ask them, and Dad *never* talked about it, always said that, yes, it was a tragedy, but Armenians need to move on. They should be more focused on being model citizens here in America.

A group of three people walks in, and I am relieved that I'm not the latest attendee. They sit in the same row as me, on the other side. I then spot the back of Janette's, Arek's, and Vache's heads (sleek, gelled, and fuzzy, respectively). I'd have to climb over four strangers to get to the empty seat near them, which does not feel worth it. I'm not trying to draw more attention to my lateness.

Dr. Markarian is speaking. "When a country is a true democracy, there's less ability to hide a sordid past. The mass killings and genocides of Native and aboriginal peoples in America and Australia, for instance, are not unknown by the general population."

Erebuni interrupts, "Though, the genocide of the Indigenous peoples of America isn't exactly taught in American schools, and it's rarely acknowledged that we are living on stolen land—we are on Muwekma Ohlone land here in Berkeley—but I understand your meaning. It's not a crime to mention it, unlike in Turkey, where it's the crime of 'insulting Turkishness.' In America, students may discover it later in their education. There are documentaries, books, et cetera."

"Precisely."

A hand shoots up from the group next to me, and a man is saying, "Excuse me," quite insistently. It sounds like he has an Armenian accent. Most of the audience turns back to look at him, and I'm thankful we're sitting at least six seats apart so no one thinks we're together.

Erebuni looks toward him; a shadow of annoyance passes over her face, then disappears. "Thank you, we are taking questions at the end," she says.

The young man, who appears to be in his early twenties, ignores the whole hell out of that. He stands up and says, "You are here discussing the so-called Armenian genocide when there are hundreds of documents proving that it ever existed. In fact, my

ancestors are from the Mardin region, where Armenians committed genocides against us. It's documented in my family that Armenians came in the night, murdered the men, raped the women,
beheaded—"

What in the actual hell? The energy in the room has abruptly
shifted, like the room itself is sitting straight up and is willing this
unwanted presence to please go away. That was definitely not an
Armenian accent, but a Turkish one. And, yes, cool, Turkish
people should come to these events, too, but, uh, not like this.
Like, holy hell, the things he's saying are chilling. That's what
we've been taught that the Turks did to *us*, and he's throwing it
right back. There are thousands of eyewitness accounts about the
atrocities that were committed beyond killing, and now he's saying *we* did it?

My eyes have been focused on the tan wood of the seat in
front of me, the fading veneer gloss chipped or rubbed off in areas. I wonder, suddenly, if it's safe for me, for all of us, in this
room. The audience seems to be mostly older, people in their fifties to seventies, and I'm worried for all of us. Did he and his
group show up armed with words, or something more violent?

Then I hear Erebuni. She is looking stern as all hell. When she
speaks it is still slow, a type of calm, but there is a rumble to it
that betrays her fury. "Pardon me. I assume, based on what you're
saying, that you—or your ancestors—are Turkish?"

He pipes up, "I'm a proud Turk, and—"

She interrupts, the boom of the mic no match for whatever he
was going to say next. "Thank you. I appreciate that you came
here, and I firmly believe there is a dialogue that can happen between the Armenian and Turkish people, but interrupting our
discourse midway with a string of fallacies is not the way to do it.

If you are willing to make a good faith attempt at a conversation, we'll happily accept it."

I am internally screaming. Goddamn, she is good. How can she possibly maintain her composure like that? I'm ready to tell them to get the hell out—you know, if I ever had the guts to do something like that.

Erebuni is flanked by a man on the panel who half stands, ready to take action. But Erebuni glances in his direction and gives him a quick shake of her head. He sits.

A woman in the Turkish group speaks up, seemingly made of calm and rage. "How you can say that when you create events to spread lies and propaganda? We know the truth: Armenians are the perpetrators, but you play victim to the whole world. You act so innocent, but you are the killers and the rapists—"

There are shouts from the audience, and I swear one of them is Arek, whose head is turned menacingly toward the intruders. Erebuni has taken a deep breath and then interrupts yet again. "Listen, this isn't a dialogue when you come with guns blazing. I understand why you're saying what you're saying—that's what this entire lecture series is about. Confronting the truth would be an existential crisis for the Turkish people, not to mention the possibility of reparations that the country would likely have to pay."

The group is scoffing and protesting, but Erebuni continues, voice louder than ever, "I understand where you are coming from. Listen to the words of Hrant Dink—a Turkish Armenian journalist assassinated for voicing his views."

She shuffles papers in front of her and pulls one out, and amid their objections, starts to read: "To the Armenians I say, try to see some honor in the Turks' position. They say, 'No, there was no genocide, because genocide is a goddamned thing that my ancestors never could have done.' And to the Turks I say, dwell for a moment on what the Armenians are saying and ask yourself why they insist so much." She looks up from the page. "So when I say I understand, I do understand, and I wish we would have—"

The Turkish guy is now standing while shouting, "Hrant Dink? You quote to us Hrant Dink? That traitor of a Turk—"

But now the man next to Erebuni stands—he is a hulking beast of a dude—and makes his way into the aisle, looking like he's ready to throw down. The crowd, too, has had it, and some of them are again shouting back at the Turkish lecture crashers. Arek is standing, but Janette is pulling on his jacket and seems to be imploring him to sit. Vache is shaking his head over and over. If there's an all-out brawl, I wonder if I'm small enough to hide under the seats. At least I can run like hell out of here, but it feels cowardly considering Erebuni is still sitting up there.

Erebuni says, "I'm very sorry for the interruption, everyone." But when it becomes clear that the group of three isn't leaving and that they brought muscle of their own (the only one who hasn't spoken is now standing up, blocking his friends), several members of the crowd panic and begin to disperse, fast.

"If you can please stay seated, I'm sure we can finish the end of our program," Erebuni requests, a strain in her voice. It's too late, and she knows it. More and more of the crowd is either leaving or forming a circle around the crashers, and Erebuni's face crumples.

We're sitting in the dim sum shop, each with two steaming pork buns in front of us. Gallantly, I paid for them, and as I handed over the cash, I mused that this is our first dinner date.

Not how either of us expected it to go, I imagine. Erebuni looks sunken, sitting across from me in the little wooden booth, like she's short at the wick. On our walk over she called the lecture a disaster and chided herself for not handling it better, but I told her there was nothing else she could do. We met up briefly with Janette, Arek, and Vache, but Arek was still so hotheaded that Janette steered him away. Vache seemed like he wanted to be alone and left without a substantial goodbye.

She's peeling the wrapper off her bao so slowly it's like she doesn't want to eat it at all. "I should have expected it, brought in security, at least had a check-in area."

It seems like she's being harsh on herself. Who expects their academic lecture to be crashed? "How could you have known, though?"

I take my first bite and I burn my tongue on the sizzling-hot pork. Even my teeth ache from it.

She shrugs. "It happens all the time."

I set my food down. "What?"

She's finally removed the bun from its wrapper but doesn't move to pick it up. "Consistently. Happened at Stanford recently, happened in San Francisco a few years ago, happened back when I was in undergrad."

That is wild. I had no idea. I mean, it's not like I'm going to genocide lectures constantly, so I don't have the opportunities to see this sort of thing, but I assumed what happened tonight was a fluke. Some weirdos who were bored on a Wednesday night. "Seriously?"

She looks straight at me now, and her fingers tap on the table occasionally as she talks, punctuating her words. "Nar, they will do anything not to confront the truth. That's what the lecture was supposed to be about, in a way. When denial is so wrapped up with identity, some people, usually extremists, will take any measure to protect their version of their identity. Every time we talk about the Armenian genocide, they take it as a personal affront, like we are pointing a finger at them personally, saying, 'You are a mass murderer.' But of course that's not true, and that's not why we talk about it. Our survival is still at stake, even today. We're bordering two nations that would rather we didn't exist. Turkey tried its best to eliminate us and denies it happened. And Azerbaijan, on the other side, claims we stole their land—us, the indigenous civilization that has lived there for three millennia. It's . . ."

She shakes her head and lets out a long breath. "I'm disappointed in myself, that's all. Genocide education is my lifeblood, and I should have known."

Damn. The self-imposed fog I've cast upon the topic of the Armenian genocide is beginning to lift, and I think I get it now, at least a little, what I couldn't see before. I always assumed the genocide was a static thing that happened, one tragic event covered in bubble wrap and placed on the shelf of historical archives. But after today I can see that it's still living and breathing, and the monster of it continues to claw its way into our lives. That's why she's so into this. Someone has to fight back.

I was sitting opposite her, but now I move out of my side of the booth and slide in next to her. I take her hand in mine. Her pulse ticks against my fingers, rapid and light, or maybe it's mine I'm feeling. I give her hand a small squeeze and lay my head on her shoulder. Roses, dark woods. She shifts, sitting back so she's not as hunched over. Almost like she's apologetic for being so down.

I tell her, "I'm sorry this happened. You are so passionate about our history, and this sounds corny, but it's honestly inspiring. You heard me before, I didn't care at all about the genocide. I was over it, as if it was something to get over, like a fad. But after today, I think I'm starting to get it."

She nestles her head against mine. "I'm glad you came. Even though it was ruined."

I pull away and face her. Her hand is still clasped in mine. "No, that's what made me get it. It wasn't some event encased in amber that we can look at in a museum. It's still alive."

"Yes," she whispers, and leans in and kisses me all at once. She tastes the slightest bit salty, like she's been swallowing tears. It slows everything down, and I'm lost in her and me, everything else slipping away.

When she pulls away, I see that part of my berry-pink lipstick has rubbed off on her, and I remember how I would wipe it off Trevor immediately (or sometimes not kiss him when I had lipstick on) since he got mad at me one time for not telling him. I doubt Erebuni would rail at me for getting rouge on her. I marvel that we can kiss here in a way that feels incredibly freeing. No one would look twice at us here in a little shop in Berkeley. After all that happened today, it's a little wrong to think that I couldn't do this elsewhere, but it's true.

Usually, shoddy fluorescent lights would grate on me, but tonight they don't. It's like they're shining a spotlight on us. I run my hand along her arm, sweatered in light cotton. "You made it your whole career."

She nods. "It started young for me. My great-grandparents were part of a group of survivors who recorded their accounts for a documentary. I watched it growing up. They lived remarkably long lives, into their nineties, so they had years of opportunity to impress upon me how real the horror was, how they did not want it to be forgotten. I see now that it was a bit rare, their willingness, their insistence, to talk about it. They were young teenagers— actually, my great-grandpa was ten when it started. Can you imagine?"

Ten. I was still secretly playing with Barbies. I can't imagine seeing my father and uncles rounded up and murdered in front of me. It's so far from anything I've experienced that even in my imagination it doesn't feel real. "Not at all," I say, my voice sounding small.

She takes a bite of her food finally, and I reach across the table and grab mine, now cooled. She says, "We can't feel guilty for it. They escaped and tried to create lives for their kids and grandkids, exactly so we wouldn't have to go through what they did. But I do feel it's our duty, at least mine, to do my part and push every day for recognition."

And what have I done? Less than nothing. I have two full-on platforms to talk to the public—Instagram and the local news— and I've squandered them. I remember the centennial of the Armenian genocide was this year, two months ago, on April 24, Remembrance Day, and I'm washed over in shame suddenly, thinking that I didn't bring it up at work. Even if Richard was going to shoot it down for not being newsworthy enough, I should have tried.

Erebuni is staring into the patterns on the linoleum floor, munching on her food. After my final bite, I wipe my mouth with a stiff paper napkin. I feel compelled to share my stunted attempt at airing an Armenian story, come clean about the whole thing. "Hey, I've been meaning to tell you. The cooking class story?"

She chews quickly, seeming to rush swallowing her food. "The one with your brilliant storytelling that I'm so thankful for?"

Gosh, she's sweet. After the horrible evening she's had, the event she's been putting together for months ruined, she still has kind words for me. As much as I enjoyed creating that piece, I don't feel I deserve her words. "When I pitched it . . ." I look skyward. There's a moth circling and audibly clinking against the light. Over and over. "My boss told me in so many words that no one cares about Armenians, and I couldn't do the story. 'Snoozefest,' I think he said. But I went for it anyway. I snuck it online, and technically my boss doesn't know the story's living on our website."

She sets her bao down, her eyes huge. "I'm appalled. By him. But also impressed by you. You did that?"

I shrug. There's something bothering me about it now. I was so proud of my subversiveness before, but hiding my story on the website doesn't feel like an accomplishment. "It was a quality story, and with you and Vache, you made it shine."

She shakes her head. "Thanks. But what your boss said, that's not okay. Does he think no Armenian stories are worth airing?"

"I'm not sure."

A flash of the Turkish nationalist's face pierces my vision, and the guilt I'm feeling reveals its full ragged jaw. Erebuni's entire livelihood is dedicated to sharing the message of our past, even when it puts her in danger. Meanwhile I snuck around Richard to get an Armenian story out, and only on our website. True, I shared it on Instagram, but to an audience less interested in ethnic culture than in selfies. It feels like such a half-assed attempt to be a voice for Armenians, and I want to do better. I never want to have to sneak around to get Armenians some coverage. I confess as much to Erebuni. She thinks for a moment, her eyes narrowing into a type of smile.

"I wonder if your boss would feel differently if you were to interview an Armenian congresswoman."

"What do you mean?"

The color is returning to Erebuni's cheeks, and I'm relieved that she can feel happy again after seeing her so crushed tonight. "The banquet. Yes, it's a fundraiser for the Armenian school, but it's also to bring attention to the bill Congresswoman Grove is cosponsoring. In short, it's to get the Armenian genocide officially recognized by Congress, which would not only be a major deal but it'd also include Armenian genocide education in schools. That's why I'm involved in it. My organization helped cowrite it. So I've been her contact, and I am betting I can get her to agree to be interviewed by our very own Bay Area Armenian reporter."

Well. I feel foolish for not looking into *why* Congresswoman Grove was attending the banquet. I assumed the committee had paid her a sizable speaking fee. But more important than my contrition is trying to piece together whether Erebuni just offered me an exclusive interview with a member of Congress. That would be truly badass. I would be the hero of the station. Erebuni continues to surprise me. Not only does she have this connection, she has so much faith in me that she'll use this very important social capital to try to help me. Me! I'm not even sure I can pull this off, but I know that if Congresswoman Grove agrees to the interview, I'll do everything in my power not to screw it up. Not just that, but to make this piece my chef d'oeuvre. I want to reach over and squeeze Erebuni's hand, feel her sticky fingers against mine.

But. Oh God. The banquet. The one my entire extended family has tickets to, including Mom. Erebuni and I, we've never talked about it. The moth has disappeared, and with it, so have the little plinks, but I feel no relief. Maybe it finally got zapped dry.

My face must have faltered, because Erebuni asks with tenderness, "Are you okay?"

Other than the fact that I have no idea how I'm going to juggle my secret girlfriend with my probably homophobic family, yeah. It's too big. A giant block of panic I can't begin to unpack. I want to focus on this beautiful gesture Erebuni is doing for me, not ruin it with the layers of shame and pressure that are building up around the implications of our relationship.

I brush away her concern. "My boss has been so negative about me lately anytime I try to rise from my position. I'm not the kind of person to stir up trouble."

I immediately feel like an asshole for saying it. She's presented me with a career-changing gift (at some cost to her, I'm sure), and I don't want to seem ungrateful, but I want to be realistic with her about how this might go down at work.

She peers at me with intent. She's not upset. "I never told you this, but I watched a lot of your segments." Then she instantly blushes, aware of what that means. I'm smiling. I can't help but think about her stalking my stories the way I peeped her Instagram. Her head gives a little wobble, and it's so endearing, her shyness. "I know," she waves me off. "I had a crush! But I wanted to tell you, I sensed a hesitance in some of your stories, like you were doubting yourself."

She noticed—? I never thought of myself that way, but at the same time, the moment she says it, the words ring of truth, and I know what she's talking about. Something always feels missing while I'm reviewing footage of myself. I was never sure what it was. I assumed it was my posture or lipstick or that I was plainly less talented than other reporters. I marvel at her eye, her ability to see what I couldn't about my own damn self.

She touches my arm, like, *Wait, I'm about to give you good news.* It's agony to not pull her closer to me, press myself against her. Not yet. I want to be a good listener. "But when you did the cooking class, that vanished. You were full of pride. When you posted about the class on Instagram, the same thing. Your writing was crisp. It came from a place of strength. I know you can be that person."

She is so sincere in her words, in the way she doesn't break eye contact, that I can't help but believe her. I need to believe her, that I can be more than the reporter who takes on the garbage no one else wants. I've been getting in my own way. Okay, that and probably some systemic sexism, but I haven't been helping my cause.

But what if breaking political news isn't what I want to cover? The cooking class, interviewing Congresswoman Grove at the banquet, these are slower stories. Slow doesn't mean worse, not by any means. But I'm seeing now how I prefer this type of storytelling. Part of me resists the thought; I should want to be a shark, pushing my way into the news like Mark, interviewing bereaved family members fresh in shock, pulling my camera out when conflict arises (instead of, *eep*, calculating whether I can fit under the audience chairs like I did today). What if that isn't me, though? The thought is too terrifying. No, the news is who I am. Dad's vision for me that I've been proud to fulfill. For now, I need to concern myself with convincing Richard to let me interview Congresswoman Grove if Erebuni can pull off her part. That's it.

Trying to sound more confident than I am, I say, "I'll do my best. Let me know if she'll agree to the interview, and if so, I'll put together the shiniest pitch so Richard won't be able to refuse."

She leans back, seems satisfied. Now I have more motivation to get this piece on air; I don't want to let Erebuni down. I hear her words again, *a place of strength*, and think, yes, I can tap into that. Okay, I'm doing it. Me. The reporter covering the annual Redwood City corgi parade no more.

We finish up, occasionally pressing up closer on each other. We walk to my car, holding hands under the muggy sky. Gaggles of students rush by us, drunk and shopping for records at Amoeba, and I marvel at how young they seem. Not sure when that happened, when I wasn't one of them. They listen to different music, have different inside jokes, have different heroes. And the most notable difference between us—or rather, between the me then and the me now—is that before, I had only myself on the line. As a student, I had an independence I didn't fully appreciate— whether or not I succeeded or failed impacted only me. There seems to be so much at stake now.

Erebuni's hand slides against mine, and though we're together now, I'm already planning the next time I can see her. We could go on a date, hopefully before the banquet this weekend. God, the whole family-at-the-party thing keeps cropping back up in my mind. But I'm here with Erebuni in this moment, and I refuse to let that ruin our time together. I have a lot of faith in future Nar. She'll come up with a brilliant plan that I wouldn't possibly be able to think up now.

We reach my car, parked on a tree-lined residential street quite a few blocks away from campus. It's a pretty street; there's a mur- mur of leaves in the wind. I don't want her to leave, but I also can't invite her over—my mom and all. I wonder if she'd . . . I unlock the car and motion toward the back seat. "Can I interest you in a car make-out session?"

She reaches for the handle. "Like teenagers in the high school parking lot."

Without a moment's hesitation, she climbs in, and I press in after her. "You speak from experience?"

"Perhaps," she says suggestively, impishly. I love when she's like this.

I drape my legs over her, and I want to kiss her and roll around back here and forget that there's anything bigger, but I can't leave it hanging. She's a badass woman—in her thirties for God's sake—and I'm giving her the seventeen-year-old treatment. "I'm sorry to make you have to throw it back to high school. My place isn't—it's awkward with my mom and all."

Her arm wraps around my back. "I understand." She hesitates for a moment. "But, Nar, I like you. I want you to know."

I'm totally frozen. She likes me. I mean, I know, after what happened in her home, that she doesn't dislike me, but the way she said it—there's more meaning behind this *like*. I can't move, because I want what she's saying to be real so badly, and I feel like one tweak and the spell will be broken. She continues, "I hope this isn't just a hookup for you. That's fine, of course, but I'd hope differently."

My whole soul grows bigger. This is—I mean, part of me figured, our texting, meeting all manner of her friends, inviting me to all kinds of events. It's not the trajectory you take for a casual hookup buddy. But hearing her say it, confirming that she wants this to be more, it fills me to bursting. I want it, too. Forget all the outside noise and the voices telling me, *This is a harder path. You're going to regret it and hurt your family.* Those voices aren't coming from a place of love. And I know, yes, we're in the goddamn back seat of my car right now because I can't take her home, but I wouldn't take anyone home this soon anyway. Let it be just us for a little while. Then the rest of the world.

I make sure she can see, in my eyes, my openness and seriousness. "No, it's not just a hookup for me. I like you, too. A lot. If you weren't sure of that, it's only because I'm holding back so I don't look like an obsessive fangirl. This means a lot to me. You do."

She speaks, her voice so breathy it sounds like she's writing in cursive, "I'm not the only one, then."

"You're not."

I kiss her, then lie back, inviting her to climb on top of me. She kisses my neck slowly, deliberately, and the ginkgo tree outside twinkles under the streetlamp. The heavy clouds give way to a light rain that dots the window, and I am transported; I'm in a beautiful place, inside a glowy pool at night with the woman I am falling for.

17

When a misfortune oppresses you, they will tell you it is a good sign.

Թշուառութեան չափին որ անցնի, կ՚ըսեն ադեկ նշան է:

—*Armenian Proverb*

It's Thursday morning. I'm the first one in the conference room, and I am ready to rock. I've claimed the best conference room chair, the plush swivel one that Mark usually plants his bony ass in. My laptop is open with my notes on my pitch—thanks to Erebuni and her confirmation that Congresswoman Grove has agreed to the interview. My water bottle is full to the brim, and my snack bar is unwrapped so I don't disturb the meeting with the crackles of opening it up.

After last night, I am feeling weirdly good. The prospect of landing an exclusive interview with a congresswoman—something not even Richard can deny is impressive—has given me a sense of purpose today.

Not to mention what happened in the car—oh my God. The necessity of keeping our clothes on sparked all kinds of creativity, I mean, really, I should quit my job and work in tech as an "ideas guy" because now I know I'm that good.

Erebuni and I have a proper date tonight, and I'm going to spend the night at her place. I only had to lie to my mom and tell her I'm working on an evening story with Elaine and that I might crash at her house. Wonder how many times I can get away with that.

Nothing has been able to bring down my mood in the last day, including Trevor texting me back that he misses me and hopes we can talk when he comes home. The reality is yes, we do have to talk. I still have his ring. And we dated for five whole years. We can't do the old ghost-each-other-and-move-on thing. We'll have to see each other and formally end things. Two weeks ago, before he left, the idea of that would have filled me with dread, but now it seems like the appropriate thing to do, and I have armor up to help me through it. It's probably Erebuni and the protective, joyful halo she casts around me. A little conversation with Trevor isn't going to bring me down.

As my colleagues shuffle in one by one, I can't help but be optimistic. I'm complimenting blouses, perfumes, drink choices. "I love a hard-boiled egg in the morning," I find myself gushing to one of the anchors. She raises her eyebrow but takes my awkward compliment, then throws back that I should consider her favorite brand of breakfast bars instead since they're lower in calories. Well, some things don't change. Though, when Richard walks in and clears his throat, she rolls her eyes in his direction, and I wonder if we might have more in common than I thought.

The meeting begins with the usual pitches and assignments, going around the room one by one. Then it's my turn. Puffed up like a bird, I begin, "I've scored an exclusive interview with Congresswoman Grove at a fundraising banquet she's going to be at this weekend."

Richard's mustache tweaks upward, which is his version of a smile. "Great work. It's confirmed?"

"It is," I say, inwardly beaming at how Erebuni pulled it off so quickly. Also, Richard said, *Great work*. I know I shouldn't want to hear that so badly, but it fills me with pride. And Mark looks personally offended. He's been in the pit at Congresswoman Grove's press conferences but never gotten to speak to her individually.

"Music to my ears," Richard replies. This is going to be excellent for my portfolio, leveling me up from National Soup Swap Day reels to exclusive federal politician interviews. I sweetly glance over at Mark, who is scratching at his notebook more aggressively than someone who is feeling chill. Man, it feels good.

Richard says, "Mark." And Mark snaps up from his work, ready for a command. "I want you to cover this story. You've got the know-how and the skills to pull it off."

Excuse me? Did he just take my work and hand it over to someone else? And effing Mark at that? Mark's shirt looks violently salmon all of a sudden, like it's mocking me. Matching his smug face. My peripheral vision begins to close in, and I know I'm not going to be able to keep the hurt out of my voice. While Mark is saying some kind of "Yes, of course, I'd love to—" I interrupt, "Richard, I'm confident I can do this story well. I'm not sure why you're assigning it to Mark? My source set me up with the Congresswoman. Besides, it's at an—"

I'm about to tell him about the Armenian banquet fundraiser, but Richard sighs, exasperated, like you would about a pesky fruit fly that zooms off every time you swat at it. "You aren't the right reporter for this."

I'm practically spitting now, and my mouth feels almost out of control. "Why not? I'm the one who tracked down this opportunity. It took my time and effort."

He waves me off. "Don't talk to me about effort. Everyone here puts in one hundred and ten percent, so that's not up for discussion."

My face is red-hot, there's no hiding it. My blood's pumping hard, and I'm afraid to speak, because if I say something rude, that might be it for me. But this is so monumentally not okay for him to do.

"Listen," he says, kindness returning to his voice. "We have a lovely lead on a five-year-old girl who wrote to Duchess Kate about her love of fancy hats, and she received a letter back. Well, from her lady's maid, but it was still a big deal to her. She's right here in Redwood City. The people need feel-good pieces, and you're our girl for that."

I'm their girl. For the little-kid fluff pieces. For God's sake, I don't even like kids all that much. I always get stuck reporting on them because Richard assumes that I'm nice and a pushover, so I must love kids. I'm never going to be taken seriously here, am I? Out of the corner of my eye, there's Winnie, our intern, whose face has gone gray and is biting her cuticles like she's tearing into a carcass. She, quiet and agreeable, is probably thinking this is going to be her fate at the station if she stays here any longer. Probably is. Unless I change things.

I blurt, "It's at the Armenian banquet. Congresswoman Grove only agreed to be interviewed about the Armenian Genocide Recognition Bill. As your only Armenian reporter, I'm a shoo-in for this interview."

At the words *Armenian Genocide* Richard rolls his eyes. "You should have mentioned that earlier. We, our local news team, are not in the business of reporting on hundred-year-old history. Mark, call her offices, see if you can get her to agree to talk about something else. Maybe the increase in crime downtown."

Again with this cruel indifference when it comes to my culture. He clearly knows about the genocide since he mentioned it's one hundred years old, so why can't he understand the impor—

Huh. It hits me fast: I used to think like him, too. *Enough with ancient history, let's talk about something new and hot.* It wasn't until I met Erebuni that I felt differently. I was able to change my mind— granted, my journey included falling for a gentle witchy woman who leaves my brain fuzzy and open to new ideas—but maybe I could help Richard change his, too.

I'm about to tell him that Congresswoman Grove is Armenian, that she authored this bill herself, and that because she's at the banquet to promote it, she clearly wants to discuss the bill in her interview. But I figure, first, I might as well let Mark waste his time on the phone with her staff. Second, I am going to that banquet, and I'm going to do that interview anyway. When I deliver Richard the exclusive story, then he can talk to me about what kind of reporter I am. And more importantly, maybe it will sway him to understand why these stories are newsworthy.

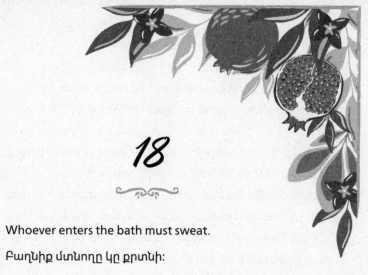

18

Whoever enters the bath must sweat.

Բաղնիք մտնողը կը քրտնի:

—*Armenian Proverb*

The next night, I'm researching Congresswoman Grove while surrounded by all the hallmarks of comfort. A mug of Earl Grey tea made British style (I'm only partially willing to admit that I was inspired by the little miss I interviewed yesterday), my favorite tattered sleep pants that were purchased back in eighth grade, and my portable heater stashed under my desk (the electricity bill is a classic fight catalyst in our home, so it must stay hidden). But none of it is working to put me at ease.

The banquet is tomorrow. The anticipation of the biggest interview in my career so far is causing some stress, but mostly, it's the list of attendees:

1. My mom and Nene
2. Diana and her fiancé and his family
3. Diana's parents
4. Tantig Emma's family

5. Tantig Sona
6. . . . Erebuni, who will be rather high-profile
   since I found out she's emceeing it

It's sort of an unspoken rule that most of the Explore Armenia events are for the younger crowd, but the banquet is for all ages. It's a major fundraiser for the Armenian school and other charities, so you can't exactly cut out the deep-pocketed baby boomers. Back when my mom signed us up for it, I was relieved she was getting herself back out there again (with a side dish of *groan* at having to attend some made-for-the-olds banquet). But now? The banquet has shot itself far out of boring territory.

I have no idea how I'm going to act around Erebuni, how to reconcile these two parts of myself. At dinner last night, and in Berkeley, we were PDA city, which felt so freeing and just exactly what I wanted. Unfortunately, it also means we set the precedent that we hold hands and kiss and whatever in public. Which I definitely can't do tomorrow. I'd be the outcast of the family, and my mom would be wailing and lamenting about her fate. *Everyone* would be talking about me, Anahid's gay daughter. And an only child—no backups, how unfortunate. I can't do that to my mom. At least, I can't throw her in like that. I have to help her dip one toe in at a time.

But I haven't even started. Up on my wall, where my high school poster used to be, is an abstract painting Erebuni created from Armenian coffee grounds. I spotted it on her worktable last night, and she mentioned she wasn't going to paint any more of them because it wasn't working for her creatively. But I was into it, both the shapes my mind started imagining and the fact that it reminded me of kissing her that first night, the taste of coffee still on our tongues. She said I could have it, so I hung it—my first attempt at adult decor in my room. When my mom asked where I got it, I told her it was for sale at the Armenian lecture. She praised me for supporting an Armenian artist. If she only knew.

My phone pings. It's Arek texting our new group chat with the five of us. He's sent two selfies of himself looking stern, first in a black button-down, then a navy one. The texts come in lightning fast.

Arek: Which look am I going for tmrw? A or B

Vache: Does it really matter when you're going to blind your audience with the sheen?

Arek: Sorry bro we can't all be mister rogers

Vache: I don't own a single zip up cardigan

Arek: Ur right, they have buttons

Vache: . . . they do have buttons

Janette: Everyone has their unique style of dressing that reflects their personality

Arek: But u like mine better right

Erebuni: Don't feed the ego, Janette. But to answer your question Arek jan, option B. Navy suits you

Janette: I must agree

This crew. My heart hurts at how much I adore them. This is so unfair. Right as I'm starting to get into my Armenianness and making some Armenian friends, and now that Mom and I are in such a good place, I'm risking destroying it all. Mom has been so cheerful. I want to keep that going as long as possible. But if I tell her about Erebuni and me, she'll freak out; her mind will immediately jump to what everyone else will think of us. From a regular, respectable family to something different.

See, this—this!—is why I never got too close. Skirt the lines of what is "normal" and you're labeled an outcast. This group wouldn't abandon me, obviously, but my family, the community at large, I'm not so sure.

I should tell Erebuni about my situation. That I'm not ready to be public because I'm not out yet. I never technically told Erebuni that I'm closeted. Or nontechnically. I skirted that topic altogether. But I did mention that I'm not ready to tell my mom about us, so hopefully when she sees or meets my mom (my heart pounds hard at that thought), she'll remember that. The thought of telling Erebuni I'm not out—it's terrifying to think my confession might ruin things. I mean, would I want to be in a relationship with someone who had to hide me from their parents? I wouldn't blame her for putting an end to this before we really got going.

There's this part of me, a tiny voice, going, *Hey, what the hell are you doing?* and I know I need to confront this all eventually. And by *confront* I mean either decide that dating a woman is too big for me and I can't do it and break up with Erebuni—and, really, is that an option for me now? It's not.—or somehow come out and hope I still have some family left afterward. Ugh, why do I have to make this choice? I wish I didn't like her so much, wish her whisper-soft voice didn't set every hair on my body on end, wish she wasn't so understanding and curious and ambitious so I could say, *Nah, not worth it*, and go back to dating only guys.

But I can't. So I'll have to make this decision after the banquet at some point. Besides, we're so early into this very new, budding relationship. I shouldn't have to make this choice now. I want to just revel in it.

Like how I woke up in Erebuni's bed this morning, the big Armenian tapestry tacked to the wall above us, her sleepy arms holding me close. We slept a decent amount after hours of tiring each other out. She is so expert at teasing—she is the teasiest tease—and that is maybe my only kink. Don't do the thing, don't touch the spot, but circle around and around and around it for hours, and then when I think I might die, plunge yourself in it. That whole time, it was like I was narrating exactly what I wanted her to do, except I wasn't, she just did it. Not that I would feel shy about telling her what I want. Very different from Trevor, who is efficient in all things and likes to get down to business (and finish said business) as quickly as possible. He called a BJ a "tune-up" once.

After an initial sleepy, half-awake period when it seemed like she was trying to go back to sleep and convince me to come with her, she jolted up, slipped on a black robe, and assured me that I didn't need to follow, and then a series of thumps and clangs sounded in the kitchen. She made me an Armenian breakfast. Foul (worst transliterated name ever; it's pronounced *fool*, but that looks just as bad in English) is one of my absolute favorites, and my mom occasionally makes it on weekends. It's fava beans topped with tomatoes, parsley, lemon, and olive oil. She busted out some Armenian string cheese and mint, and I felt like I was at a relative's house, but in the best way. With that feeling of home I could never quite obtain in my own home.

After some more deliberation about the shirt, a text catches my eye.

Arek: I think we all want to know what the MC is wearing tomorrow

Arek: Nar, did you get a special sneak peek?

My heart catches in my throat, and the sharp black strokes of Arek's message are thrown into focus. This is the first mention that anyone knows what's happening between Erebuni and me.

And honestly? The shock of it isn't great, but I'm relieved. I can actually tell someone about Erebuni and me and enjoy it.

Thinking fast, I text back, I'm not telling.

Then I text Erebuni, So they know, eh?

She replies, I should have mentioned that I told them. It slipped. Are you mad? You can be.

I'm not, at all, and I want her to know it.

I hate how messages can get misread over text, so I decide to call her up like it's 2005. Plus I want to hear those dusky tones.

She picks up. "You are mad," she says. And that voice, though anxious, does not disappoint. I'm transported to this morning, back in her bed, our post-breakfast dalliance. A wave of prickles rushes over the back of my head.

"Quite the opposite."

Trevor always hated when I said anything remotely British. *You're not British!* I hear him braying at me. But Trevor is not here, so I can *quite* all I want.

The group chat is going mad over my response, but I refuse to really read any of it and won't respond until I'm off the phone with Erebuni.

She sounds like she's been acquitted. "Oh thank goodness. Janette noticed us holding hands after the lecture when we all said goodbye and asked me about it. I didn't tell her not to tell anyone, so the word spread. They think it's cute, though. Everyone's happy for us."

"So am I."

Here—this is where I should tell her about the banquet tomorrow, that I'm not ready to come out to my family yet. In the distance, Nene begins to play piano, a pedal-heavy melody that brings to mind what it might feel like to walk in the countryside on the arm of your beloved. Some chaste ambling, chaperoned closely by your parents, or whatever weird stuff they used to do back then.

My mom shouts from downstairs, "No pedal! It's after ten. The neighbors will complain."

Erebuni doesn't seem to hear. She says, "Good," in that way that's a smile, that's a promise of every beautiful thing to come. During dinner last night, I learned so much about her. How her family would drive down to LA for her mother's art shows. Her father's local fencing business (*The classic duo of the artist and her husband, the fencing magnate,* Erebuni had joked). Her childhood dog, Garni, who was so beloved that when he passed, her heartbroken mother never allowed the family to have pets again. Her much younger sister—who was a surprise—who is still in high school and is obsessed with K-pop and was class president this past school year. Erebuni misses her most of all. She intimated that she'd love for me to meet her someday, and I am so down. Fresno always held this mythology to me, like it's this magical agricultural land in the center of California that's full of third-generation Armenians (and also plenty of first-generation Armenians). I have no idea what it looks like, what it feels like, because I imagine flatlands full of crops, but I know it's a sizable city. The important thing is that in my mind, any shop you walk into, you're likely to overhear someone speaking Armenian. I want to go there.

Erebuni will still care about you, I tell myself, *if you tell her you need a little more time to come out to your family.* I want to be courageous. I want to be the person who saves herself.

"The only thing," I start, and my heart pounds in my ears. I can't do it, I can't do it. My feet feel too hot suddenly, dry and burning. I yank them away from the heater, spin in my chair to face the bed. Then I will the words to appear. I clench my jaw like I'm physically extricating them. "Is that I'm not exactly out yet. And by not exactly, I mean not at all." Then I talk fast. "Oh God, I'm sorry, I've been keeping that from you because I'm so embarrassed and worried, but I had—I had to tell you."

Erebuni jumps in quickly. "Nar. Please don't. Don't be embarrassed at all. I know not everyone is in the same boat."

I didn't realize I'd been closing my eyes while speaking, but at Erebuni's words, I open them. My warm, familiar room; the frills of the comforter ripple like a beckoning pond. I stand up, my entire body sighing with the act, and plop on the bed.

"Thank you for understanding," I say, and it comes out more of a whisper.

She beams sympathy through the phone; I can feel how much she wants me to know she understands. "I figured as much when I dropped you off. Our kiss. You felt a little stiff—which is fine—so I assumed it might be a big deal if your family saw us."

Guess that's the downside of falling for someone intuitive. They always know.

"You assumed right," I say, some embarrassment tinging my voice.

"I'll be mindful of that tomorrow."

"Thank you," I say, imparting as much gratitude as I can with those two words.

Then the doorknob clicks, and my mom pushes through the doorway. I sit up too abruptly, bordering on suspicious. Mom's hair is wet with dye and covered in a clear shower cap. "Nareh jan, can you please text Di—oh."

In Armenian she whisper-asks, "Who are you talking to?"

Usually my mom uses Armenian to avoid the other person on

the line understanding what she's saying, but that's not going to work here. And I don't know what to do—tell Erebuni I'll call her back and risk seeming abrupt, like I'm hiding her (which I am, and which we just discussed, but it doesn't feel good, and I don't want to remind her of it) or ask my mom to leave and risk her getting suspicious about my phone call that I don't want her to overhear. The latter seems worse.

"Hey, mind if I call you back?"

"No worries. Sounds like your mom?"

I wish I didn't have to cut our conversation short like this. There was so much more I wanted to talk to her about. Actually make space in the conversation to see if she is ready for her emceeing gig tomorrow, how she's feeling, if she needs any help, and tell her how much I can't wait to see her all fancied up.

"Mm-hmm," I say, trying to sound casual for the benefit of both parties listening. It feels so lame.

She says to call her back anytime and gives me a flirty goodbye, which I unfortunately do not return. Mine sounds like I'm wishing a business acquaintance well.

My mom's eyes narrow. "Who was that? You never talk on the phone anymore, only to that boyfriend."

I sit up straight and correct her. "Or to interviewees for a story." I motion toward her hair. "You primping before the big party?"

My mom lightly touches her shower cap, rustling it. "Yes, the roots were getting very bad. Euffff, they're springing up like summer locusts."

A reference to the summers she used to spend in the mountains in Lebanon. She and Diana's mom have told us the story of being terrorized by bugs a hundred times.

"What were you asking me about Diana?"

She snaps into unofficial event coordinator mode. "Tomorrow she is going to pick the linens and needs your help. I think she called you."

Damn. Yeah, I do remember a missed call from Diana that I had to screen while I was deep in British hat history with that little girl. "I'll call her, but I suck at colors and linens. I honestly won't help at all."

"That's okay. You'll still go."

"Mom. It's my one day off, and the banquet's that night. I haven't had any rest for, like, a month. No, I'm not spending my one free morning debating tablecloths."

She seems confounded by my response, by my saying no to anything. "But you have to go. You're the maid of honor."

I'm not giving in. I've spent too much of my life discussing decorations with my mom, Diana, and my aunt, doling out pros and cons over which is a more tasteful way to go, which is worth the price and which isn't. I love them, but not the *stuff*. "Sorry, nope. Linens are not part of the job description."

Her face closes off to me a bit, and I know I've triggered defensive Mom. "You are being so stubborn. Does it have something to do with whoever you were talking to? He's a bad influence, whoever he is. Don't lie. You have someone new, I can see it in your eyes. You are excited about something."

I am surrounded by intuitive women. And Mom is the master. She can pick up on any subtle change, especially if I'm trying to hide something. Probably learned from years of my lying about not eating the kuftes, not finishing my math homework, not breaking the ceramic vase, not brushing my teeth. (What? My mom and dad would both flay me alive for any small transgression. A girl's got to learn to lie to save her skin.)

Also, I want so badly to tell her. Telling Erebuni was so free-ing, and I want to be free with Mom, too. I want to share with her the joy of a new relationship, the whole thrill of it. I haven't been able to do that with anyone in my life, and it's not like I don't want to. I'm dying to. I want her to read on my face, *Yes, you're right.* So I'm having a hard time tamping it down when I say, "Ugh, no, that's always your answer anytime I do something out of the or-dinary, like not going to an hours-long tablecloth conference. You think you see something that's not there."

She smirks, and I know my facial expression has betrayed my words. "Okay, Nareh, we can pretend there's no secret man in your life. He better be someone good, though."

He. Not even the thought that I could be with a woman.

I make a noncommittal noise. She changes tack, and excite-ment rushes back into her. "Oh! And guess who I got seated at our table? Garen. You know, the violinist."

Oops, I almost forgot about him. The last one, the hanging chad at the end of my mother's list.

"Oh!" I feign enthusiasm.

"Yes, he and his sister, a pianist, will be seated at our table, smack next to you."

I wonder what Erebuni will think of that. I mean, likely noth-ing. It's not like I'm going to be flirting with him.

"Good work, Mom."

She waves me off, though it's clear she's proud of her efforts. "It was nothing. I spoke with Vera, the mother of Lucine, who is very close with Hasmig on the planning committee, and she agreed it would be nice to seat them there since Nene is another cher-ished musician in our community. It is all set."

That is one good thing. Hopefully this violinist and his pianist sister won't be snobs and will talk to Nene about music. I know that'd make her happy, so I make a promise to myself to facilitate it.

I do want to prepare Mom for the very real possibility that I'm not going to fall madly in love with Garen, with any of them. That our little experiment has come to a close.

"Mom," I start, my voice soft and, I hope, conveying some level of vulnerability. "What if I don't like any of the guys? Is that, you know, okay?"

And while I don't *need* to ask my mom for permission for this, it still feels like something I want to do. Like that's still us and our relationship: I'm a kid always asking her for permission. I have to break out of it, but I can't.

Back, way back, one drunken night in Davis, I was out with the Armenian club—a rare bonding moment hours and hours past the event at someone's college apartment, everyone lulled nearly to sleep by alcohol but not wanting to leave the moment. I was lying back so deeply in a broken-down couch that I could feel the baseboards beneath me. One of the guys, Shant, was just about passed out on the floor right by my feet. He was wearing sunglasses indoors, and I remember he waved his glass like a drunken holy man and professed, "Your mother is the closest thing you'll ever have to God."

I remember falling into a hole then. The thought of mother and God dropped me right into feeling my head in a lap—my mom's. I couldn't remember why I dragged up that recollection or why I remembered her in a tight dress, legs packed into tights, and me, clinging to her. I just knew there was something to what he said.

Here in my room, Mom does sense something in me, since she

reaches over and touches my shoulder and makes a point of looking right at me. "Of course it is okay, janeegus. You don't have to like anyone."

This small relief washes over me, like I took an ice pick to the block of my anxiousness about Erebuni—telling her about Erebuni, specifically. I forgot, too, how understanding my mom can sometimes be when she strips away societal expectations. At her core, she wants me to be happy. I hope.

19

Two good fortunes never come together.

Երկու բախտ զիրար չի գտնայ:

—*Armenian Proverb*

For the third time this month, I'm back at the Armenian school, in their grand hall, but this time I'm flanked by my entourage. Mom is in Cleopatra mode, with elegant long eyeliner, wearing a black-and-silver dress. I've linked arms with Nene; I did her hair and makeup, and she looks so elegant. Diana is affixed to her fiancé, and they are both looking like the stunning picture of young love you'd see in a gold-framed painting. Their parents look on, proud and relieved that their kids have found each other. Dad's sister, Tantig Sona, is peacocking big time with her prom-queen hair and acrylic nails with a rhinestone dabbed on each index finger. Our extended family is also already here, some-where inside. I'm wearing a light gold dress that is, I daresay, super flattering on me, and I'm having such a good hair day that I already took an array of selfies. But I didn't post them. Instead, I sent the best one to Erebuni, letting her know I couldn't wait to see her.

Now that I'm here, though, my stomach is feeling less like happy butterflies and more like there's an oscillator whirring in it, sending acid bubbles all the way up my throat. I have to be four separate selves. One, I need to be the perfect daughter, niece, cousin, who is respectful and gregarious and attentive. Two, I need to be a reporter because I'm reporting on tonight's banquet since I've never felt more "screw Richard" in my life. Three, I need to be Erebuni's fledgling girlfriend and supporter since tonight's a big night for her. And four, I need to *not* be Erebuni's girlfriend but a straight woman interested in the guy she's going to be seated next to.

Cool.

We pass by the bathroom alcove where Raffi cornered me and asked me out. It was a week and a half ago, but why does it feel like a year ago? We check in and are given our name cards with little fish, cow, or carrot cutouts on them, and walk, our heels clicking, past the already-forming crowd and into the main hall.

Like on shourchbar night, the hall is buzzing with people. The decor is much swankier, with fabric draped dramatically across the ceilings and walls, flowers bursting out of tall vases everywhere you look. Light Armenian music is playing, and there's a massive mezze display in the center of the room, surrounded by an ever-steady flow of people picking up sesame-topped beuregs, football kuftes, sarmas, hummus, and toasted pita. There's a photo booth in the corner of the hall with a line snaking along the bottom of the stage. All around the center are tables for guests, and about half of them are currently occupied. I squint to read table numbers. I need to get to my seat soon so I don't miss my interview window. I cannot blow this. Just a tad more pressure to add to the mix.

Plus, there's someone else I'm hoping to catch on-camera. There's a major Armenian celebrity attending, an old B-lister named Alex Vanian. He's played the "ambiguously ethnic man" in plenty of major movies and shows, but he's most known for his role as Boris, the lovable curmudgeon neighbor, in a Coen brothers movie. The man's got a cult following. Armenians love to quote one of his lines to each other: "You're telling me there's a *rat* in here?" If I'm lucky, I might be able to get him to agree to be interviewed.

My gaze traipses over heads, trying to find Erebuni's, but it's too crowded and I'm too short to spot her. Ugh, I do see Raffi, though. He's got a glass of scotch in hand, palling around with his bros. They seem to be fawning over him. Just like at the brandy event, it feels good not to care. I pull out my phone and text Erebuni, Here! Where are you?

We're being interrupted every few steps now by acquaintances saying hi to us. My mom is cheek kissing some woman hello, and the woman says it's so nice to see her out, and only then do I realize what a big deal tonight is for my mom. Since Dad's been gone, she hasn't attended any sort of function like this, the kind she used to love and force us to go to. Seeing her now, beaming at people from her Armenian community, it's so obvious that she belongs here as much as anyone. I'm glad now that all of this, my whole strange instinct to agree to go to the Explore Armenia events, may have started bringing my mom out of her self-imposed shell.

After a million stop-and-chat detours, my family starts to settle into the two round tables assigned to us. Not bad seats— certainly not the seats of honor, but not tables smashed into the back corner. Diana goes and takes her seat with her family and her fiancé's family at the other table, and that suddenly makes me so sad, like this marriage is taking her away from me. I know it's kind of an irrational thought, because she'll always be my dearest cousin, but it's things like that, where she is joining with a new family and can't sit next to me anymore, that get to me. My heart aches for the old days when we were kids and things were simple, and at the same time, I wish for a future where I get to sit with my new partner and their family. I wonder if that would ever be possible with Erebuni as my person.

Shoving that thought away, I set my purse down next to an empty chair where the violinist guy is supposed to sit and hear, "Nar!" I flip around to see Arek, arms outstretched, already coming in for a hug, and Vache right behind him. Arek's indeed wearing his glitzy navy shirt and shoes so pointy they could stab someone. Vache looks like he strained to find something in his closet that comes close to black tie.

We chat briefly, and I ask them if their parents are around, but Arek's live in Fresno (like Erebuni's, who also aren't attending), and Vache says his parents aren't into the whole banquet scene.

"Janette's 'rents are here, though," Arek says, tenuously. "Not sure if she'll introduce us. I've never met them. Shouldn't be a big deal, though, right? But if she doesn't introduce us, I mean, what would that mean?" At some point it becomes clear he's talking to himself.

I reassure him that either way would be just fine, and that if he does get a chance to meet Janette's parents I'm sure he'll make a sterling impression.

"True that, yeah." He nods, bouncing up and down on his toes.

I realize I should do the same, too. Like, why not? I'll introduce them to my mom. Plus, that way, the more people I introduce her to, the less weird it will be when or if Erebuni comes by. *Just another friend I want you to meet, Mom.*

I usher them toward my table. "Mom, Nene, I want you to meet Arek and Vache."

My mom's smile is one of total innocence, like she has no idea who Arek is and not like she assiduously stalked him on Facebook.

"Parev, parev," she says, extending her hand. "Nareh's told me about her new friends. So nice to meet you," she says in Armenian.

"It's been a pleasure getting to know her," Arek says in his super-charming manner, buddying up close to my mom. It's like he loves being himself, the performance of every moment. For a split second, after the "aw, cute" wears off, I wonder, *Oh no, are Vache or Arek going to mention Erebuni and me?* They wouldn't, right?

Nene points to Vache. "Are you the writer?" she asks in Armenian, and I'm impressed she remembers our car conversation.

"I am," Vache replies in Armenian.

"My first love was a writer," Nene says with this devilish grin that I haven't seen in ages, that I even forgot she had.

Also, excuse me, what? Her first love?

"He was from my village, a talented poet of the Tumanyan style, just as depressing, you know. But beautiful."

The way she's speaking is enrapturing. I forgot how she can do this—she can, in her apparent frailty, command the room. I only wish Erebuni could be here.

"I love Tumanyan," Vache says.

"Yes, it was a shame. He was forced to give up his poetry and work his family's farm, and I was coaxed, perhaps you could also say forced, to marry a successful businessman in Beirut. 'You're our only hope,' my mother told me. How could a person say no to that?"

Oh, damn, Nene is laying it down. I did vaguely know this, as my mom loves recounting her past and how she came to be, and how she thinks deep down Nene was never that big of a fan of my grandfather. But to hear it from her—oof, feels rough.

But now my mom has her nervous smile on, too stretched. She wraps her arm over Nene's shoulders. "Mom, please, let's not tell stories about the Old Country right now."

I guess Mom is immune to Nene's charms. Maybe that's how it is with every mother and daughter. We've seen too much.

Nene completely ignores her. She picks up her wineglass and waves it at us. "Don't let that happen to any of you. Young people, you have so many possibilities."

For the first time, I get this sliver of hope, like Nene would understand that I have to chase the tougher path, that I don't want to go and marry the merchant from the city (uh, Trevor) either. Then, just as quickly, I feel hopeless because how the hell would Nene understand sapphic love as something normal? I don't think they had a word for gay back then. It was probably something like *unnatural*. And my stomach churns again.

After some more light chatting some people mention they want to grab some of the appetizers, and so do I, but I've got to get to work while I can. I'm supposed to meet Congresswoman Grove before the banquet kicks off.

Mark tried and failed to persuade Congresswoman Grove's team to change her mind on the interview topic, which I know because my new contact at her office called me, confused. I reassured Congresswoman Grove's aide that I was still going to be the reporter speaking on prearranged topics. When she asked if she should bother returning Mark's most recent calls, I replied simply: no.

If I were the banquet planners, I'd put her in the best spot, so I grab my tripod and walk toward the prime-location tables. Yep, good instincts; I see the navy skirt suit and sharply cropped and blown-out hair of the congresswoman. She's chatting with another woman wearing a gauzy, expensive-looking tunic-and-pant combination. My stomach's contents have not stopped their whirling.

As I sense a lull in the two women's conversation, I step into her line of sight, and man, there is something about politicians, especially ones at the top, that feels different than other people. There's this aura around her like she is exactly where she wants to be, talking to exactly whom she wants to be speaking with, and if you're lucky to step into her limelight, you will be blessed by it. So I'm feeling a combination of extra good and extra nervous when I introduce myself.

"Congresswoman Grove? I'm Nareh Bedrossian from KTVA News, a fellow Armenian American. Your aide Natalie Martín confirmed your availability for a quick interview. If you have a moment, I would love to hear about the Genocide Recognition Bill and why it's important to you."

She gives me such a warm smile I feel like we're old friends and says, "Of course. I came prepared. I have time to give a short statement now if you're ready."

"Extremely ready. Thank you so much," I say, as I whip my tripod into place as fast as I can without seeming desperate. Because oh my God, I'm going to get to do this—I'm getting an interview, a personalized chat, with an actual congresswoman. Ahhh!

While I'm setting up like my life depends on it, she says, "I saw your segment on the Explore Armenia cooking class. Very well done."

What? She *knows* me?

"Oh, thank you," I say, and I wish I didn't sound so lame or so shocked, but maybe she likes the effect her words can have on people.

"A friend of mine sent me the clip. My daughter is younger than you, still in high school, and in that rebellious stage, especially when it comes to her Armenian ancestry. She also happens to be big on cooking. I showed her your clip, and I have to say, it was like a little light went on in her mind. That weekend she asked if we had any old Armenian family recipes. I should be thanking *you*."

Uhhh, wow. So that cooking piece I did—which was a very nice and well-edited piece in my humble opinion, but didn't exactly break barriers in journalism—did have an impact. Something I created actually helped someone? Erebuni did say that piece came from a place of strength. *These are the types of pieces you're meant for,* a small voice in me urges. But I push it away, feeling the rapture of the compliment.

Then I tell myself to screw my head back on tight because I have a job to do. Still, I thank her graciously and start our interview.

As I shake Congresswoman Grove's hand goodbye, there's an insistent tap on my shoulder, one of thick fingers. I turn and find myself face to face with Alex Vanian, a short, staunch, balding man with thick, wiry eyebrows, who's radiating active energy. Oh my God. Okay, cool, not a big deal that this man has breathed the same air as Brad Pitt. That people have posters of him up in their dorm rooms. A legend. No, he's just a person. "You a reporter?" he asks with his New York accent.

"Sure am," I say.

He points one pudgy finger toward the tripod. "That the equipment they're using these days?"

My phone strapped to the top of the tripod is not the picture of professionalism, and I know it. I smirk. "We've got the big bucks over at KTVA."

His eyes lighten at my joke, the closest I might get to a smile. "It still rolling?"

I tap my phone's camera on. "It is now."

He presents himself smack in the middle of the frame and says, "Folks, it's about time we recognize the Armenian genocide. If you want to stop seeing my ugly mug repeating this over and over, just pass the stinking bill, and I'll be out of your hair." Oh wow, awesome. Alex Vanian coming out strong for the Genocide Recognition Bill. And he censored his swearing, thank God. Then he pauses, and the corner of his mouth twitches up, and he transforms before my eyes into Boris the neighbor. He squints. "You're telling me there's a *rat* in here?" Then, still in the frame, he winks at me and says, "Ya welcome."

Honestly, yep, I am damn welcome because I couldn't have asked for a better clip from Mr. Vanian.

Back at my seat, I quickly review the footage of Alex Vanian and Congresswoman Grove, and man, I am in awe of how well it turned out. This better make it to TV. *Please, Armenian ancestors, help me get Richard to see that this is worth airing. Help me share this with the world.*

Erebuni hasn't texted me back, but I'm guessing she's hard-core preparing right now, maybe in the back area behind the stage, so I'm not surprised. Still, hearing from her would make the start of this event complete. Breaking my reverie, a man sits down next to me. Oh no, the violinist, I almost forgot. Garen, that's his name. He's younger-looking than his photos, with a curly almost-mullet thing going on, and clothes a little too big for his thin frame. He looks sullen as hell, like he has no desire to be here. Kind of makes me like him more.

His older sister, who my mom informed me is a pianist, sits next to him like his protector, and I'm hesitant to begin a conversation, but then I catch my mom hawk-eyeing me, so I guess I need to do this.

"Hi, I'm Nareh," I say, giving him and his sister a short wave.

"Nice to meet you," he says in a voice thick with ennui. He barely looks in my direction.

I feel you, bud. His sister gives me a half smile, like, *Can we be done with this awkward intro and not have to pretend to be interested in speaking with each other?* Also get that.

There's a loud electronic tapping sound that reverberates through the hall, and when I look toward it, there's Erebuni, mic in hand at the podium, front and center. Saved by her. And wow, she is looking damn good in a black tailored suit. Not too witchy tonight except for her pendant-and-choker combination she always wears.

The crowd begins to quiet. "Hello, everyone," she tests, bringing the audience to a respectfully low volume.

"Congresswoman Grove, Alex Vanian, Very Reverend Father Pachikian, Principal Agopian, and all our honored guests," she begins.

Classic way of starting an Armenian speech. Diana and I used to joke that it's not Armenian unless you call every member of the audience out by name and title in order of their rank and importance. I'm impressed Erebuni was able to stop at four instead of the usual twenty.

Erebuni is discussing Explore Armenia. ". . . the deep importance to be reminded, to be reconnected with what it means to be Armenian."

I should be filming this. Standing up, I bump the table, and the silverware and glasses rattle, and one crashes, loudly. A few heads turn my way. God, this is embarrassing. I whisper "Sorry" to my family. Tripod in hand, I tiptoe to the sidelines, and start filming Erebuni's speech. At a pause, she looks my way and gives an almost imperceptible smile. I have that on camera, I think, her message to me right there in public: *Hello, my dear Nareh.*

"To that end, I'd like to welcome Congresswoman Susan Grove to give her remarks on this worthy cause she has championed. Congresswoman . . ."

The two shake hands and exchange a word at the podium, then Erebuni moves off, right in my direction. The congresswoman has begun speaking, but I don't hear any of it, just see Erebuni pacing toward me—light, unassuming steps as if this is, of course, the direction she would have chosen whether or not I was there. She takes care to not walk in the way of my shot, which I totally appreciate. But what is she going to do? How is she going to greet me? My heart pounds all the way up in my throat as she nears. And then she is next to me, and she takes me into a side hug, grasps my hand, and squeezes it once. Then she lets go.

I try not to exhale too hard, holding back my relief. That was it. She's taking what we chatted about yesterday seriously; I won't get outed to my entire family, not tonight.

I motion to my phone on the tripod, that I can't talk to her now because the film is rolling. She pulls out her phone, types, and shows it to me. You look stunning. How was the interview?

I point to her and mouth *Wow*, and am thankful my back is turned to my family. Then I give her a thumbs-up about the interviews. She types, then shows me.

Great. Is your family here?

I nod, widen my eyes, and spread my hands, hoping to convey, *Oh yes, all seventy of them.* She smiles, then types again.

Am I . . . going to meet them? As your friend of course. Hope that's not too forward to ask.

Oh God, yeah, we never talked about that part. I mentioned my family was coming but didn't offer up "And you should totally meet them!" and I hate that it has to be like this. I feel like that shady guy I dated back in college who didn't want me to tell anyone we were dating because we were in the same econ discussion section. With the benefit of hindsight and, like, growing up as a person, I realized he just didn't like me that much. Even though she knows I'm not out, I can't help but feel I'm doing the same thing to Erebuni.

I give her a thumbs-up and a smile that doesn't hide my nervousness, because even if it weren't for the whole closeted queer thing, I'd still be a little heart-poundy about a new partner meeting my family. That seems to thrill Erebuni, whose face lights up vividly at my response.

Throughout the next few speeches, we text and mime chat every time Erebuni walks off the stage after introducing each

speaker, and before I know it, Erebuni has given her closing remarks. They kept the speeches to twenty minutes total, which is
a relief because these heels are murdering the balls of my feet.
Plus it keeps the whole banquet in more of a celebratory mood
than the usual "You've unwittingly been held captive in an academic lecture–slash–timeshare presentation."

As I'm detaching my phone from the tripod, Erebuni rushes
from the stage toward me.

"That went perfectly," I tell her, and she wraps me in a surprise
hug. Her work for the night and for all of Explore Armenia is basically over, and she wants to share it with me. For the briefest moment I take in her perfume and revel in the tickle of her curls. The
urgent press of her body lights me up, and I wish we could continue this hug (and then some). But I pull away, thinking that I
don't want Mom to see. And I feel like a real asshole for doing it.

"Such a relief," she breathes. "How about you? You said the
interview went well?"

I nod. "Fantastic, actually. Thank you so much for setting the
stage. It feels like everything is going so perfectly."

She touches my hand, drips her fingertips over mine for one
shivering moment. "I know. I've got this giddiness coming over
me. I feel like this bill has a real chance of passing. Or maybe it's
you being here, getting to share it with me."

In any other moment I'd be taking full advantage of her mood,
like hopping on that rainbow wave and riding it along with her.
But I feel myself trying to dampen it instead. My posture, my en-
ergy, is saying, *That's great, but we need to be careful.* I actually say,
"Probably a combination of the two. What're you going to do next?
Climb Mount Ararat and plant an Armenian flag at the top?"

She smirks. "Not a bad idea. No, I'm thinking short-term. Need to eat some of that dinner I missed out on. Meet you afterward?"

We agree on that since I missed dinner, too. She heads to her table with the planning committee. The second she leaves I wish we were together again, especially since I have to sit back down and pretend to be into some guy. The only thing working in my favor is that he seems wholly uninterested in me.

As I head back to my table, I see that Nene has taken my seat and is waving her arms in discussion with Garen and his sister. I meander by and hear her voice, flinty, saying in Armenian, "You cannot believe that *Eroica* did not transform the meaning of the word *symphony*."

In her quiet fury she still carries herself like royalty. I slide into the empty seat by my mom, who has been watching this exchange and seems to be on the edge of her seat, like she's wondering whether or not to get up and stop it.

"Those two have many opinions on music," she whispers to me.

Nene's untouched plate of food sits in front of me—saffron chicken kebab with rice. Normally I'd be all over it, but my hunger seems to have dropped off completely; there's a trembling in my stomach. It's not good. I never feel human when I'm not hungry. It's a clear sign that something is off with me, and what will I do? Ignore it. "I can tell," I say to my mom.

She watches them closely. "I don't like the way he's not polite to an old woman. The way he dismisses her ideas. It reminds me of when your dad was at his worst, when he had been drinking. I want to pull Nene away, but tell me what you think. She seems to be enjoying the argument, no?"

Yikes, that mention of Dad is still reverberating through me. I know exactly the Dad she means. When we'd come home after a party and he would complain about my mom not sticking up for his side of some argument with his buddies, or would tell her next time they needed to bring a nicer wine to the party, didn't she know that? It was her job to know these things. I would run upstairs and pretend the conversation wasn't happening. Or much worse, I'm ashamed to admit, when I was mad about my mom for something unrelated, I'd sit around during the argument and feel like she was getting her just deserts. You didn't let me wear jeans to the party? Well, now someone's yelling at you. I regret ever feeling that way, and sometimes the ugliness of my past feelings consumes me. And Dad's not here; I'll never get a chance to defend Mom against him.

As to my mom's question, Nene doesn't seem to be fazed by Garen's mansplaining rudeness, and somehow she feels more alive now than usual. I say, "Let's keep an eye out. You're right, she has plenty to say and wants this schmuck to hear it."

I glance at Mom and catch her eye. I whisper, "So we can definitively say that Garen is out of the picture?"

She sighs. "Such a shame. He's world-renowned. You two could have been traveling from country to country." Then she shifts back to being probing. "You know the emcee? What was her name?"

My entire body tightens like I'm in an iron maiden and if I make one wrong move I'll be impaled. So she spotted us together. "Erebuni. I mentioned her before. Remember, she's friends with Janette, Vache, and Arek?"

Oh, that was a good one. Redirection for the win.

My mom glances behind her to where the guys are sitting. Her voice stays low, thankfully. "That Arek is a very cute one. I am so glad to finally meet him. Shnorkov dgha."

That means "proper boy," with all the implications that he works hard and respects his elders. Probably true, but I don't have time to recalibrate her hope about Arek and me shacking up, because I spot Erebuni crossing the hall, and I feel like I should intercept her so she doesn't feel like she needs to walk up here alone.

"Speaking of, I need to talk to Erebuni and, uh, Arek, about the segment," I say, hoping she won't ask questions about what exactly Arek has to do with the news.

In my haste, my ankle bends, and I nearly topple over, but I catch myself. God, I have to be more careful. I am starting to lose it. Weaving through the tables, Erebuni gives me a private smile.

Remember, I tell myself, *she knows she's being introduced as your friend.* Still, as I approach her, my body feels like it's been plugged into an outlet, nerves on fire.

My mouth is off and running. "Have you seen Arek and Vache yet? They're sitting right behind us. My grandma started telling Vache about how she fell in love with a writer back in Anjar but wasn't allowed to marry him and had to be shipped off to the city to marry my grandpa. Not awkward at all. I mean, just kidding, my Nene can say anything and somehow it's not weird. Like an old person superpower."

She touches my arm. "Are you nervous?"

I pretend to be offended, though I'm borderline shaking. The music's subdued, but there's a thick film of noise—chatter, voices high and low, forks scraping against plates, clinks and shrieking laughs—that is threatening to overwhelm me. "What would give you that impression? My ability to talk endlessly about nothing?

I'm good at that. I think years of pieces like 'Too Spooky for Trick-or-Treaters? Local Man's Halloween Decorations Send Children Screaming to Their Parents' have given me a nonstop arsenal of cotton candy dialogue I can spit up at any time. Anyway, I guess I am a little nervous."

I'm trying to shepherd her toward Arek and Vache's table, but she will not be steered. She takes the turn right toward my mom. She must have seen where I was sitting when she was making her way over.

"Don't be, it's me." She whispers in my ear, and for a moment the cacophony of the hall dies away. I have to fight with everything I've got to keep my eyes from lolling back into my head and allowing the shiver to pass all over my body. I am stoic, a statue. My mom's eyes flick up from Tantig Sona and Emma's conversation that she's half listening to.

"Hi, Mom. This is Erebuni. Amazing job, right?"

That was good, Nar. Simple and satisfying to both Erebuni and Mom. My mom extends her hand and gives a plastic smile. "Parev, Erebuni, nice to meet you. Nareh is right, you were excellent up there. You work for the Armenian Advancement Committee?"

Erebuni answers with her usual slick coolness. "Thank you. No, I work for the Genocide Education Foundation, not affiliated with the AAC."

My mom nods. "That is good." In a surprisingly uncharacteristic move, my mom is super not into the Armenian political organizations because she feels like they're too extreme and one-track. Like they don't allow for nuance. It gives me hope that she might understand the complexity of my situation. But it's also awkward that she straight up dissed the AAC, since most Armenians don't share her view and Erebuni could be one of them.

"I agree." Erebuni smirks, and it is so charming, how can my mom not love her, too? And lucky for my mom, her provocative opinion landed just fine with Erebuni.

"Erebuni helped get me an interview with Congresswoman Grove. It's going to be a great segment."

God, I sound as stiff as I feel. My mom actually reaches over and pats Erebuni's hand. "I'm glad you two met. This is what Explore Armenia is about. Armenians coming together. I always tell Nareh that. We treat each other like family right away."

The conversation is going well, but Mom's well-tuned intuition radar (I don't know if it extends to gaydar) worries me. I pray to the Armenian God (that I'm only partially sure exists) that our conversation keeps happening in this vague, openly interpretable space. Or that it ends soon.

And I guess the being upstairs listens, because the lights turn low and the music picks up, causing everyone to turn toward the speakers, where a DJ stands over his equipment. *Thank you, thank you, thank you.*

"Should we dance? Let's get Arek and Vache. Janette, too. I haven't seen her yet," I tell Erebuni.

"Ahnshoushd," Erebuni says, meaning "Of course." "Tantig, would you like to come, too?"

She's calling my mom Tantig, and it's so cute I wish I could tell her how sweet it is, but obviously I can't openly say that. My mom kindly waves Erebuni off. "Oh no, I do not dance anymore. I don't want to interrupt your young people's fun."

Then Tantig Sona perks up. "I want to dance. Anahid, don't act like you're too old to go up there with me. Maybe we can meet a nice pair of widowers." She cackles and yanks my mom up with her. Seeing that, Tantig Emma and her husband rise. Diana and her crew are already making their way toward the dance floor.

Erebuni waves over Arek and Vache. Arek bounds up, but Vache rolls his eyes, takes a massive gulp of his drink, and then joins us.

Okay, we're all doing this. Nene is still engaged in conversation, listening to Garen and spitting with disgust. I tap her on the shoulder and bend down since it's loud in here.

"Nene, do you want to come dance?" I ask her.

She looks straight ahead at Garen. "No, darling, I want to sit here and wash this boy head to toe of his frivolous opinions."

He scoffs, and the two go at it again. "Nene wants to stay and fight," I say to my mother, who's by my left side (Erebuni is on my right, and I don't know if I can handle this).

Our group and others like ours move like a tidal wave to our destination. We step onto the slightly raised white-tiled dance floor, which is brimming with people. I recognize the song but don't know the name, a classic Armenian electro track with a gregarious singer. My family groups themselves together, and I'm halfway between them and Erebuni, Vache, Arek, and Janette, who has now joined us. This is perfectly fine, dancing one hundred percent sober with my secret girlfriend, my new friends, and, like, my entire family.

But as song after song goes on, it *is* fine. I'm going to make it through tonight, then at some point I'll tell Mom, and it'll all be okay.

I'm starting to relax, and Erebuni must notice, because she gives me a playful shoulder bump, and then the best thing happens. A new song starts, and it's "Hey Jan Ghapama," which is one of my absolute favorite Armenian songs. It's a folk song (though

this version has all the electro-eighties treatment) about how excited the whole village is about this one pumpkin dish that's about
to be served. Everyone's in attendance—your parents and cousins
and aunties and in-laws—and goddamn, here it comes, a huge
heaping plate of sweet-smelling roasted pumpkin stuffed with rice
and walnuts and honey and cinnamon, ready to feed the masses.
The title and chorus are a group reverie that translates to "Hey,
bro, the pumpkin dish!" Basically, it's a total banger, and right now
I am feeling it.

Because that's sort of what's happening now, minus the delicious pumpkin snack. Everyone's here, and we're dancing, and
everything's okay. My mom is out and actually having a good time,
and Nene is over there by the table, laughing now, a genuine hearty
laugh. Diana is shrieking with joy as her fiancé does the airplane
move around her. Erebuni is so damn sexy, and she crushed it
today, and I got an exclusive interview with a congresswoman,
and everything's more than okay, I realize. It's awesome. I start to
really dance, and Erebuni answers that by flirtatiously facing me
and picking up the pace of her moves. I'm moving my feet, which
I rarely do because that requires actual skill, but I feel like I'm
nailing that, and Erebuni looks impressed. I lean over to her and
bury my face into her ear. "I'm so happy I met you."

She turns, pulling away from me slightly so we don't accidentally kiss. "Me, too," she says, her voice tangling with the music.
I wish I could sweep her up then, take her in for an actual kiss,
but we can't, not here. My eye catches the photo booth in the
corner of the room. That . . . could work.

I tap Erebuni and pitch my chin toward it, shouting to be
heard over the music, "Why don't we check out the photo booth?"
I try—hard—not to sound flirtatious because of the potential

overhearing audience, basically my entire family. I may have only half succeeded; I can practically feel the lust dripping off me.

Her eyes light with mischief, and this is where we should be holding hands, joyfully slinking away. Instead we briskly (and chastely) trot toward it, like we can't get behind closed doors—or a curtain in this case—fast enough. Since the dancing started not too long ago, there's no line. It's all ours.

Erebuni climbs in first, and I follow, savoring how immediately close we are to each other, legs and arms brushing. I yank the curtain closed, then adjust it to plug any gaps, ensuring nothing inside can be seen from the outside. Our feet are showing, that's it.

The screen is waiting for us to begin, to press the button to start the countdown, but instead, I grasp Erebuni's shoulder, pull her toward me, and kiss her. She responds quickly, cupping my face, drawing her hands down to my neck, into my hair. It escalates to ravenously making out, but I keep my leg posture mostly the same in case anyone is outside by now.

"I've been dying to do this all night," she groans into my ear.

My body flushes hot while I contemplate how much we can get away with in here. It shouldn't be, but it's so sexy that there's only a strip of cloth hiding us from the outside world. But when I find myself dipping my hands toward her blouse, squeezing the buttons in my hand, she gently withdraws.

"We should probably take the photos," she says. Her face sports reddish patches beneath her olive skin, her lips and eyes appear larger than ever.

"Right, we're here to take photos." I smirk.

I dab at my mouth to ensure no lipstick has smeared, and we

both adjust our hair. We share a look before Erebuni presses the button, and on my end, anyway, it says, *We got away with it, and God, I adore you.* Hers seems to express the same.

"Normal smiling one first?" she asks.

"Yes!" I say as the counter is already at three of the rather short five-second warning the screen gives us.

"Next has to be 'outrage,'" I direct, and she buys it. I love watching her face on the screen twist into a pearl-clutching tantig who's just heard a woman my age say she doesn't want kids.

"Pensive next," Erebuni suggests. We look off into opposite directions, pondering life's big questions, like how the hell did we get so lucky to run into each other that shourchbar night. Since I can't see her face, I'm excited to see the printout of this one.

The prompt for the fourth has started, and these last few minutes in the booth have been so lovely, I want to capture this moment, the entirety of it, exactly as it is. So I say, "I want to kiss you in this last one."

"You sure?" She appears concerned, though with a hint of hope, like maybe this relationship doesn't need to be hidden forever. And I feel that way, too. I want, one day, to be with her in front of my family, and there's this certainty that's come over me where I know it's going to happen.

"I'm sure. Besides, no one's going to see it. I can tuck it away in my purse."

The timer is at one and beeping loudly. No more waffling, so we lean in simultaneously and meet right in the middle. I'm not sure how great the photo is going to turn out since we rushed it, but still, we'll have this souvenir from our big night.

We're still locked, and we take a second there before pulling away.

"This was too much fun," she says, voice thick and slow.

"I wish we didn't have to go back outside."

"I know, but there'll be more," she says, smiling. A promise of our future, the one I promised her when I introduced her to my mom, danced with her alongside my family, kissed her in the photo booth.

"Yes, there will."

I pull the curtain aside, and the party is in full swing, the center of the room popping and bubbling with dancers like the pit of a volcano. But there's someone in line now. It's the nails I see first: acrylic magenta with a white rhinestone stamped on the forefinger. Tantig Sona is standing before us, holding a photo strip—our photo strip—staring at the very bottom one, hand clasped over her mouth. And directly behind her is my mother, squinting to make out what has Sona in such a state.

20

Better to lose an eye than your reputation.

Աչքդ ելէ անունդ չելէ:

—*Armenian Proverb*

As Mom studies the final photo pinched between Tantig Sona's fingers, her face morphs from confusion to horror to anger. Something hidden safe inside me begins to rupture, and there's no hope of saving it. I don't know what to do, and my usual defense of lying with my face or words doesn't come. Nothing but me staring back at her, my mouth partially open. I'm coming undone. Because I know, I know there is no taking this back.

Tantig Sona is about to say something when my mom instantly wipes her emotions away, like she realizes that she's in public, and an uneasy smile spreads over her face. She sidles up to me and links my arm in hers, tight as a vise, and whispers, "Come here with me."

I don't resist her and march where she drags me, but I do turn back once to Erebuni and try to convey *Sorry* to her. She is staring, dumbfounded. She looks like a broken stalk amid a thriving field.

To make things worse, I glimpse Tantig Sona looking disgusted and gleeful and obviously aching to share the evidence in her hands. This isn't going to stay between Mom and me, which is already a daunting prospect. The way she's walking—every step radiates electric fury. I can practically taste the metallic flavor in my mouth.

She leads me to the atrium, then to a hallway that leads to the school classrooms, quiet now on a Saturday evening. We're just out of earshot of the party.

"Mom, I can explain," I say, relying on movie and TV clichés, hoping that the age-old statement will help me out somehow. Do the explaining for me.

She releases my arm like she's shaking away a prisoner. She leans in close, a deep ferocity about her, and I am honestly a little scared. Of what, I don't know. Of seeing my own mother out of control, of knowing I made her this way.

"Are you crazy?" she angrily whispers. "You're kissing a girl at a banquet with our whole family present? With photo proof? You know that everyone will talk now—not *to* me, but *about* me. Has this been your secret the whole time? Is this why you've been so sneaky and so happy? That girl?"

I mean. Yes. *Yes.* She nailed it, what can I say? I don't want to deny it; I want to share with her that yes, this is who I am and what I've been doing. I've been wanting the whole world to know, too, but—it will damage my mom's social life, her standing as a respectable widow. Her whole gossip network will be turned against her. Any phone calls she gets will be to dig out information. Or she'll get women pretending to sympathize who are secretly congratulating themselves on having straight kids.

My throat feels hollow. I say, "I—It's been—It's not what it seems like," I say, solidifying my identity as a coward who wants to do the right thing but never does. I just need more time. I want to be with Erebuni, I do, but this was the wrong time to yank back the curtain.

Since I've been going to Explore Armenia events, but especially tonight, it feels like Mom's come back to life. She's among her people again; she's one of them. My kissing a woman threatens to drag her away.

If I stall right now, pretend it was a misunderstanding, I can lay the foundation to well and truly prep my mom, and ultimately my family, for my relationship when the time is right. That's all I'm doing, part of me thinks. I'm being rational about this, not a gutless craven who doesn't deserve her relationship with Erebuni.

"It seems like you have no regard for your family and are doing rash things to embarrass us."

God, I hate that. At least this I can rail against. Like, I have years of pent-up rage to unleash on that particular statement. "Is that all you care about? How we look to everyone else? You care more about them than about your own daughter?"

She gets more in my face and almost has a satisfaction about her. "You admit, then, that you have been with this woman?"

"No, we've been hanging out, but I didn't . . . I didn't mean for anything to happen."

The fissures and cracks that sprang up all over me as soon as I saw Tantig Sona with that photo of us feel like they're breaking off. Fragments of myself are crashing to the floor, the consequence of my lies.

But my mom's not buying it. She runs a hand through her hair, sending flyaways over her scalp. "I can't believe it. I cannot. You've been ignoring all the choice men I served to you on a platter, and you go for this woman instead. I had no idea you had this in you. I am—This is beyond me. I am going to cry." And her voice cracks at the end as she legitimately starts to tear up.

I instantly go into soothe mode because as much as my mom is in the wrong, she locks up and reserves those tears for special occasions, like when the weight of Dad's death hits her. Now, seeing her cry, I know it's real pain, and all I can think is that I want to make things better. I touch her shoulder, and she lets me. "Mom, listen, I'm sorry. It was a mistake. Hopefully it doesn't get out of hand."

She backs up in another burst of wrath, eyes still wet. "Oh, you know how Sona is. She is spreading to everyone what you did."

I feel this calm, rational ruthlessness take over. I want to protect my mom, first and foremost, from the venom of Tantig Sona. Erebuni isn't here, so I can feed my mom any message I want. Right now, family damage control. Later, the truth. "We'll deny it. We'll just deny it to everyone. It was supposed to be a cheek kiss, and we bumped mouths instead. That's all."

To save myself from ruin, I've stitched myself back together with poison thread. I am a fake type of whole again, held together while it seeps into my skin. But not yet.

My mom looks up, considering. "Perhaps she kissed you. You did not kiss her." She loosens her shoulders for the first time during this conversation. She's seeing the solution, and it makes me feel wretched inside, even though Erebuni won't ever know this is how I made it through behind her back. The balm for my transgression is that I'm pointing my finger at Erebuni and crying, "Witch, sorceress, temptress!" and everyone is going to buy it. A price she will never know about.

I nod. "Yes."

I can hear her exhale, and I can also hear the Armenian music again, the party chatter, sounds that my brain muted as it focused every synapse on surviving this conversation. And instead of feeling relieved, I. Feel. Sick. I survived, yes, but the cost feels high.

She eyes me suspiciously, because again, my mom is no dummy, and we both know that I am head over heels for Erebuni, but the fact that I so quickly gave her this explanation instead of battling her on it shows that I am on her side, and she sees that, too. But I'm not feeling that ease I was hoping for.

"I will go tell them before Sona's mouth gets out of control. You stay here for a few more minutes, then come back like nothing is wrong."

"Right, yes," I say.

I take a few steps out of the hallway to watch my mom leave, and standing right there, arms folded, with a look of betrayed disgust, one I've never seen on her face before, is Erebuni. Oh no. Please, please, God, let her not have heard any of that conversation. It was too loud out here, and my mom and I talked quietly. Right? *Right?*

My mom walks right by her, stepping slightly away, as if to avoid toxic fumes, and disappears into the banquet hall to do damage control.

We're alone, among strangers mostly, so I reach over to hold her hand, and she lets me. It is limp and lifeless. "I'm sorry, so sorry about all that," I say, hoping to keep it vague.

Her voice is layered with pain. "Did I hear correctly? Did you agree to tell your whole family that I came on to you out of nowhere?"

The poison's come to collect.

"N-No. I didn't." Someone behind us shouts, "Ara, aboush, hos yegur!" and it feels like the mood is getting rowdier. I cannot be having this conversation with party guests milling around. I go back into the argument hallway, as it will forever be known to me, and motion for Erebuni to join. Thank God, she does.

I take a deep breath hoping to convey to her how sorry I am, how I'm about to explain something. "I told her we've been getting to know each other and it's complicated—"

She appears less hurt, more confused by this. "That's not what it sounded like from what I heard."

"I know, but like I said yesterday, my family has no idea about my sexuality. Like, this is the first my family has any inkling at all about me being bi, and it's a shock, so, uh—"

"So you made me the bad guy?"

Yep, that is exactly what I did.

"I can and will undo this, but it's too much for them to handle right now. My mom, she's coming into herself again, and I couldn't tell her the truth, not yet. It was shitty of me to say what I did, I agree."

"How are we supposed to be together—out, one day—when your family thinks I'm this viper who's 'turned you'? There's no way."

She looks toward the atrium like she's about to leave. This could be it; she'll be gone, out of my life. And seeing her here . . . Erebuni, this woman who inspires me to be better, who herself is so brave, this woman who makes me feel funny and cherished. Right now I don't deserve any of her goodness, but I can't let her slip away. I say, "I will tell them the whole truth. I want to tell them, but I need to do that over time. I've made no effort toward it yet, so I—I've got to take it slow. And once I do, I'll tell them the truth about tonight."

She exhales audibly, looks toward the wooden floor. She presses the toe of her shoe into a crack, then pulls it out again. She doesn't talk, and I don't say a word because I feel like I will ruin it. Then, after what feels like five reincarnated lifetimes, she says, "You're right, sometimes I forget not every family is like mine." She straightens. "You'll do it eventually? You'll tell them what really happened tonight? I'm not asking for right away, but—someday?"

I nod, fervent as all hell. "Yes, yes I will."

Now she reaches for my hand, and it's reanimated, her touch forgiving. We're secluded over here, and I want to show her I'm not shrinking from her touch, so I move in and kiss her, and we linger there. I know this relationship, this fledgling thing, is completely worth it. I want to be with her.

Just then I hear a man's slurred voice. "Damn, girl, is this who you're engaged to? I thought you said it was some guy in Europe."

It's Raffi, holding a drink in his hand, slouched comfortably, drunkenly, with one of his buddies at his side snickering. The sight of him, hearing his words, makes me jump back like he's thrown a knife at me. I worry there are more coming.

Erebuni shakes her head. "What? No, she's not. This is Nareh." Oh, Erebuni, you think he has me pegged for someone else, but he's dead-on. I don't say a word, not sure how to talk myself out of this situation. I want to usher Erebuni away or snap my fingers and vanish. But we're in this damn hallway, and it would look suspect, like I was running, if I grabbed her arm and walked away from him.

And as if this couldn't be worse, Vache, Arek, and Janette appear behind Raffi in the atrium, no doubt looking for their friend who disappeared. More witnesses to my lying, I guess. I can't see any other way of getting out of this. They approach hesitantly, as if they're aware there's *something* happening.

Meanwhile Raffi is unflappable. "Yeah, reporter girl. I asked you out. You told me you were engaged to a European guy or something. Thought I had a mind like an elephant, but maybe you said it was a girl after all."

Erebuni seems mostly annoyed, like she wants me to swat this fly and move on. "Nar, what is he talking about?"

I should say I have no idea and walk away. And I know "It's not what you think" is a terrible idea, since that phrase has gotten me nowhere. Faced with the prospect of lying yet again, when moments ago I told Erebuni that she can trust me, I just—I don't want to lie to her. So I stammer, "It's complicated."

That's when her face closes off to me, like she's had one too many betrayals tonight, and that's it, she is utterly done.

"I need to get some air," she says.

She shuffles out of the hallway and edges past the crowd toward the doors outside. I don't care if it's desperate, I'm following her. I salvaged this once tonight, I can do it again. I won't lose her.

I give Vache, Arek, and Janette one look, an apology I hope they're able to read. *I am as bad as you think right now, and I'm sorry for it.*

"Wait, so who are you engaged to?" Raffi calls out after us, but I don't turn around for him.

The curls on the back of Erebuni's head bounce angrily over and over as she stalks toward the entrance, and I hear someone say hi to me, but I don't see them, and part of me can't believe how rude I'm being, but I don't care. I have to follow her.

I didn't realize how humid and sticky it had become inside until I take my first steps outside, and a flurry of cold night fog engulfs me. Erebuni is headed toward a secluded part of the school grounds, far from the banquet hall. The balls of my feet grind into my shoes as I jog behind her. Once we're well out of earshot of the smokers congregating just outside the doors of the hall, I whisper-yell, "Erebuni!"

Finally, she does turn, and my instant of relief at not being ignored fades when I see her face.

I catch up to her, and we're standing outside the principal's office. There are signs in the window advertising their end-of-year hantess, already three weeks old, not yet taken down. The tape is still tight, not even curled at the edges.

She crosses her arms. "You're engaged."

She is both matter-of-fact and outraged at once. It's the arch of her eyebrows, the tiny nods of her head, that tell me she is done. She sees me differently now.

I try so hard not to sound desperate, and instead cool, just explaining the facts. "No. I was—my boyfriend, ex-boyfriend, proposed to me a couple weeks ago, right before—"

"A couple weeks ago! You were engaged a couple weeks ago and never mentioned it?"

"It never seemed like the right time."

Lamest excuse in the book. It was more that I didn't want to ruin our brand-new relationship with a closet semi-engagement.

"You said, 'was.' So you're not engaged now?"

I never told Trevor no. I still have the ring. I mean, when he came back I was going to have some face time with him and break it off for good, in person, like a decent human would. But because I haven't had that chance yet, it's been this weird up-in-the-air thing. That's what I should tell Erebuni right now, or just say, "No, I'm not engaged," but instead I hesitate, because I'm trying to figure out how she would hear it, how her perception of me in this moment would color her understanding, and it doesn't sound flattering, to be honest.

A car pulls out of the lot, the mist thick in its lights, and exits the school. People are already leaving. I search for the right words and don't say anything.

Erebuni throws up her hands. "What am I supposed to think after all this? You're bi but not, you're engaged but not. Even at work, you want to confront your boss in theory but you don't do it head-on. I want to scream, 'Pick one!' You want everything and everyone, it seems. You can't play whatever side is most convenient at the moment."

This recognition passes over me, and I see at once how I haven't been able to give up any of my safety nets. I can't sacrifice any of it. I don't know how to be anything else. There's nothing I can do. I can't change decades of being like this. "I know, I know . . ." I'm saying.

She crosses her arms. "This is really—I wanted this to become something. I liked you a lot."

Liked, past tense. We're on the precipice now, and she is ready to jump. "Erebuni, please. I am so sorry. Have I said that yet? I mean it. I know I need to work on this part of myself, but it's tough for me. I feel the same way. I like you so much. This, us, it's special. You and I have something—"

With a brief shake of her head, she says, "Please don't. I'd prefer if we didn't talk."

Then she turns and leaves, the long walk back to the hall. Heavy clicks against the pavement. The tinier she becomes, the foggier, the more she's all around me. She's so huge, the ghost of her.

You had something so good, so real, I tell myself. Real, that was it. Erebuni called to all these dormant parts of myself, and in thanks I stomped all over her.

I have this idea that it's cold, but I don't feel it. I should be feverish and complaining and crying about my hair. I sit down on a bench by myself, and all at once my butt and thighs are wet from the condensation. I laugh at it, out loud, a thick, choked thing.

Left alone in the quiet, only the vague bass in the distance, I'm thrown to the bottom of the ocean, that image I always conjure during meditation because I imagine it as being quiet and peaceful. But now I'm in these depths, and it's suffocating, tons and tons of pressure, surrounded by a frenzy of deep, dangerous life. How could I have ever thought this was a calm place? I'm going to die down here.

My heart skips once, twice, and I gulp for a breath, desperate to try and find it again. My heart beats irregularly, a piano trill out of control, and I'm sure this is it: I'm having a heart attack, and I'm headed toward death right here. Without Erebuni and with that final horrible conversation with my mom, this is how I go. I gasp for more air. I put my hands over my face and bend over my lap. Then I hear it. *Ba-dum, ba-dum.* The beating of my heart, it's slowed, it's regular. Thank God. The hotness of my breath permeates through my dress to the tops of my thighs, and I let myself recognize that it feels good.

Deep breath in and long breath out. *My meditation app would be so proud,* I think bitterly. *The only one who cares*—God that sounds so pitying, I need to get a grip on myself.

Searching for reassurance, I look toward the night sky, but all I see is black-gray fog punctuated by bright spots of streetlights. When's the last time I saw the moon, I wonder. How am I expected to be a good person, make regular decisions, when there hasn't been a moon in the sky for weeks? I must be going nuts.

Especially because I have to go back in there and pretend everything is okay for the sake of my family.

And from their perspective, it probably is. When I walk back in there, I'll look just like the selfies on my Instagram page: I will be smiling, I will be alone, I will be straight again. *Wasn't that worth it?* I spit at myself.

21

Give a horse to him who tells the truth that he may escape after telling it.

Ճշմարիտ ասողի մի ձի, որ ասի ու փախչի:

—*Armenian Proverb*

It's the Sunday morning meeting at work, and after a night staying up poring over my computer, then attempting to sleep, drinking too much water, and getting up to pee over and over, I made it. You know, physically. Because I didn't arrive early, I'm sitting in one of the bad chairs, one that slants slightly downward and squeaks and complains with my every micromovement. I'm staring at the cheap white conference table, but layered on top are scenes from last night: Erebuni in the fog so wrecked from being lied to repeatedly. My mom basically saying that what people think of us is more important than who I am or what I want.

The AD part of the evening (after the death of my soul) was a travesty. My pretend smile must have been chilling, because Diana looked disturbed instead of sympathetic when she asked me if I was okay. I told her I was great. She told me Aunt Sona showed her that picture of me kissing the emcee. I told her no, that wasn't what it looked like. She's just my friend. Aunt Sona is looking to stir up trouble, I said.

We stayed just long enough that it didn't appear that we were escaping, but with the first wave of departing guests, Mom, Nene, and I wove ourselves among them and got the hell out of there. Thank God for Nene because she spent the entire (short) car ride home remonstrating and laughing at the gall of Garen the violinist. Mom and I did not say a word to each other directly.

We didn't this morning, either.

"Nareh?" Richard's voice grates in my ear. He usually avoids saying my name, and I remember why; it's because he says it like it's painful for him (and it's more painful for me hearing it as *Nahraye*). The whole conference room is staring at me like he's been trying to get my attention for some time.

"Yes?" I ask, my tone haughtier than expected.

"Your pitch?" he asks, matching me.

This is it. The moment I'm supposed to swoop in and display my colored feathers to the room, show them what I'm capable of. Though I painstakingly put together the piece last night instead of sleeping, I'm not in the mood to trumpet my achievements. I feel a dull beige. But it's my turn, and the entire room is staring at me.

"Last night was this big benefit for the Armenian school, and Congresswoman Grove was there promoting her Genocide Recognition Bill—"

"Eh," he interrupts. "Remember what I said last time?"

Instead of being intimidated as usual, something clicks in me—like I woke up—and in a flash, I remember what I need to be doing.

With more confidence I say, "Right, you said the Armenian genocide was a borefest."

"I didn't say exactly that," Richard says, scratching his head. "I said it didn't fit the brand of this station."

He didn't, but okay. "I got that exclusive interview with Congresswoman Grove," I say, straight-faced. Mark looks personally offended. Richard doesn't speak, considering.

I switch my laptop over to the video of my interview with her and show him the still. "Want me to play it?" I ask.

"That's not necessary," he says.

I quickly add. "I already edited the segment, I can set it live any time."

And it was hell. I strung together the interviews, my standups, and the other footage, including shots of Erebuni, which I cried to, especially when I reviewed the film where she smiled right at me, showing how she felt about me in that moment. I could only watch that one time.

His face reddens. "I'll have to review that footage."

"Why, Richard?" I ask, and man, I am sounding indignant again. But also, screw him. It's like he's getting off on belittling me in front of my colleagues.

"I don't know how many times I have to say this, but these are sensitive topics and you're a junior reporter. I have to vet your questions, her answers. We can't put just anything on the air."

Just anything. Nope, not today. I am so sick and tired of being treated like this, and I know I'm not the perfect employee, but he is the one behaving badly, and everyone needs to know. I'm done. He caught me on the wrong day. My face reddens and my body braces itself, as if preparing for battle. "I think you don't want me to be the face of your big story. Even though I'm the first reporter here, at least since I've been around, to get an exclusive interview with Congresswoman Grove, you don't want to air it because, one, you prefer me to be sniveling and submissive and take whatever crap story you shovel my way, and two, you refuse to see that an Armenian story has any merit. So you are both sex—"

"That's enough," he cracks. And though I should be relieved for the sake of my career that my boss stopped me short of calling him sexist and racist outright, I'm furious. My entire body is buzzing with adrenaline as he continues. "That's bullshit. Your ineptitude and bad attitude are too much. You're off chasing stories we didn't ask you to cover. I asked you multiple times to stay in your lane, and you keep crossing over."

Mark coughs. Richard turns to him, red-faced. "Yes, Mark?"

Mark has this look painted on, false humility. It spells danger. "Sir, I wasn't going to bring this up in public, but considering the conversation . . . I noticed that Nareh posted an unauthorized story on KTVA's website. A little cooking class, which you told her specifically not to—"

"I know what I told her. Thank you, Mark."

I gasp, out loud, like a character on a reality show. Except this is my life, and I have the sudden, horrible realization that I can't control it anymore. The wheel's slipped off the track, and it's grinding onto dirt, into the wild unknown.

I'm sputtering when Richard picks up. "I normally am not one to enable snitches," he says, glaring at Mark. That feels good, but my body feels like it's compressing, trying to shove itself away so no one can see, because it knows that what's coming next can't be good.

Richard plants himself to face me. There's no remorse in him. "Nareh, that's it. I want you out of here by the end of the day." He looks to the rest of the room as if remembering they're all there. "Sorry, everyone. You didn't need to see this."

Sorry, everyone? The room feels so stiff. My heart is pumping so fast that it's causing my body to shake, and I don't want anyone to see me like this. I stand up too fast, but I force myself not to show how dizzy I am, that I need to put a hand on the table to steady myself. A second later I fold my laptop and grab my water bottle, which clanks against the metal of my computer with every step, a mortifying auditory reminder that I'm leaving the room while everyone else is staying.

I can't believe I remember how to walk. Someone else seems to be carrying me. I'm on autopilot. I'm at my desk. I set down my stuff, ready to clear my workspace. I yank my bouquet of fake peonies by the neck and shove them into my bag. I'd always imagined packing my desk accoutrements joyfully, looking forward to my next gig. Me, quiet Nar, whatever-you-need-I'll-do-it Nar, fired for insubordination. Now I only wish I had been more rebellious. I could march back in there and scream at him, but the fuse has died out, and I feel myself shriveling, becoming even smaller than before.

Sometime later, maybe five minutes, maybe thirty, my coworkers—no, ex-coworkers—shuffle out of the conference room. I was hoping to have left before the meeting to spare myself further humiliation, but here we are. There's a presence behind me. Elaine, Winnie, and MacKenzie—the anchor who has never so much as acknowledged me—are at the threshold of my cubicle. I give them a wan smile.

"That was really messed up," MacKenzie says.

Winnie adds, "You might have a wrongful termination case on your hands."

A teeny part of my heart smiles at their sweetness. I'm not sure if that's true, anyway. I did post on the website without approval. I sigh at how I was pushed so far into a corner that I thought sneaking around Richard was my only option.

I thank them in a way that I hope is genuine yet dismissive of their ideas for further action, then wonder when everyone is going to go so I can finish clearing my desk.

Elaine stands up straighter. "Hey, the piece you pitched, it's all done?"

Oh, right. The other massive pit in my stomach: the banquet. I tell her it is.

Elaine looks alive with determination, and Winnie seems to have caught the enthusiasm, whatever this is about. Winnie says, "We can set it live in today's afternoon newscast!"

Um, that'd mean they'd have to get Editing to write MacKenzie's lines introducing my piece. Seems like it'd get shut down right away. I try to sound kind, but it doesn't come out right. "How're you going to do that?"

MacKenzie still has not cracked a smile, like always (seriously, she is the prettiest, angriest person I've met), but there is a glimmer about her face. "Editing owes me a favor. If I want this piece to get in, it's in. And I want it in, because Richard and his sexist ass can go to hell."

Amah Asdvadz, this team is the absolute best; I do not deserve their goodness. I had no idea I had so many allies. Then something I thought would never happen, ever again, happens: I am feeling the tiniest bit less horrible. Erebuni might see the broadcast, see my face on her TV or computer screen. She might reach out to me. The bubbles in my throat clear, and I manage, "You all. This is too much. But there are still roadblocks. So many potential points of failure—"

Elaine puts a hand on my shoulder and says, "There is no way we're letting you leave here without getting that on air for you."

That's when I cry.

22

Can a rose survive the sea or a violet the fire?

Կարո՛ղ է վարդը ծովը միջում, մանիշակը կրակին
առջին դիմանալ:

—*Armenian Proverb*

Telling Mom will be the worst. After I packed up my stuff and drove home, I flopped on the bed for a while. I guess she was out grabbing groceries. Then I find it in myself to get up and watch my final KTVA segment. I'm in the living room, squatting down beside the TV, flipping through the cable menu, mind utterly blank. Then our opening begins, "The Award-Winning Channel 8 News Team." Award-winning my ass. That was an award our parent network gave to the best afternoon news team in the Peninsula, and they sure as hell weren't going to give it to their competitors.

MacKenzie's face appears. "Good afternoon, I'm MacKenzie Vanderberg. Our feature story tonight is an exclusive look at a cause near to Congresswoman Susan Grove's heart. Nareh Bedrossian reports."

Oh my God, they gave me the lead. And she pronounced my name a tad better than usual. My heart surges with gratitude for my team for making this happen. Then my face looms on the screen, cheerful, radiant with the high of nailing a career-making interview. Of knowing your new girlfriend is going to be watching.

Hearing the din of the banquet hall in the background, I'm transported to that night. I smell the wine I drank, and phantom acidity tickles my throat. There's a flash of Erebuni as I introduce the banquet. I know there's more of her about to come. I can't bear to watch. Right now I can't stand to know if it ended up being a great segment or not. As soon as my standup finishes, I pause the TV, waiting for the live feed to run so I can fast-forward. Except I pause on Erebuni's face. She's about to explain the significance of the banquet, and it should be a straightforward intro, but the corners of her mouth are raised like she can't help the happiness running through her.

I wonder if Erebuni's going to watch this. Or if people will forward the segment to her saying they saw it. If there's any chance she'll get in touch with me. Then I remember how betrayed she was when she heard me talking to my mom, the slap of truth. Then, outside the school, the way she turned away from me, decisively. I didn't see her final expression when she decided it was over.

Then Mom walks in. "What are you doing?"

I quickly turn off the TV, as if that's going to make it better. She fully saw.

"Why you home? And watching her?"

Her. She might as well have added, *That evil woman.* I rub my eyes. "Mom. I got fired."

"You what?" In her anger, her *W* comes out like a *V—Vhat?*—and that *V* is sharp flint jabbing itself into my flesh.

"How could this be? My daughter, fired."

"I know."

"What are you going to do now? You know it is hard to come back from something like this. You must have done something very wrong. What was it?"

It feels like back in the day whenever I got a bad grade. But this time I'm not going to fight back. Something has bored deep, driving into me and leaving me hollow.

"You didn't get in friendly enough with your boss? No, you were not focused. You were too busy doing . . . doing . . ."

She glances up at the TV, now off, but the ghost of Erebuni's face is fresh in both our minds. I say, "Yes, it was my fault, but she's not why."

My mom viciously ignores that. "What are we going to tell the family?"

Always them, this very real and also false construct of people who are ready to shame us at any moment. She's embarrassed because of what they might think. And meanwhile, they're in the world acting to avoid shame from us. But I don't care what they do. I love my family. Wouldn't they feel the same way about me?

Tuesday afternoon, two days after my firing, there's been no word from Erebuni after the segment aired. Hours afterward, after some deliberation, I texted her a link to the clip online. All I said was, Here's the segment. You were perfect. I'm sorry. I'm so sorry.

But no response then, no response now.

I'm sitting in a scalding-hot bathtub full of bubbles. I lit a candle, one Diana got me that says MAID OF HONOR on the front. It smells like lemon and bergamot. This is the first nice thing I've done for myself, other than survival-mode eating, if you count that, because I have zero appetite. No showers, no sweets, only fitful sleep. And fifteen-year-old sweatpants with holey shirts. I don't know who I am without a job.

I dry my hand and pick up my phone, keeping it over the edge of the bath. Nothing from Erebuni still. I might have also called her once, right before I got into the bath. I close my eyes and try to feel her, stretch my hand across the universe to tap her on the shoulder and tell her how sorry I am. To feel her presence and send her loving warmth, but I can't quite get there.

Still, thank God for retreating into the water. I can't stand being in the house. My plight seems to physically pain my mom. Since the banquet, she's had horrible stomachaches and odd shooting pains in her legs and ribs. It's all because of me. So the last few days I've been lurching around the house thinking that I'm slowly killing my mom.

I never felt like living with my family was some kind of failure. But now? It feels so demoralizing. Once my severance runs out, I'll be the mooch daughter living off my mom's meager teacher's pension. It's four weeks long, so I'm going to use it well and apply to as many jobs as possible. As soon as I get out of this bath. Which might be never.

My phone pings, and I open my eyes, my heart singing with hope. Erebuni, it has to be.

Instead, it's Trevor. And it says, I miss you.

Without my willing, my eyes close. I set the phone down and sink into the water. My arm stings at first, though it also feels good.

To hear him say that . . . I didn't know how much I needed it. I didn't realize how utterly alone I was feeling until his message. I thought I had no one in the world, but now I have Trevor; it's late at night there and he's thinking of me. This is exactly him, swooping in at my lowest moment—there, dependable. How could I have forgotten that? Isn't that worth more than the extreme highs and lows of my short infatuation with Erebuni?

I go for my phone again. Same, I text back.

At once I feel wretched. The serotonin boost I got from his earlier text has vanished, and I'm drained. I feel like I'm cheating on Erebuni, though she made it clear she wants nothing to do with me.

He texts back, Germany hasn't been as fun as I hoped.

If I respond, if I tell him I want to see him, that'd be it, I couldn't go back to Erebuni. I shift, my body distorted under the water. The bath feels too cold suddenly, but instead of adding more hot water, I get out. I blow out the candle, sending lemony smoke curling up into the air before disappearing.

After drying myself and wrapping the towel about my steaming body, I text him back, but all I send is a sad face. Because it's not him I want to talk to, get together with. It's Erebuni. I am not giving up on her. Not yet.

I plumb the regions of my mind. How? How to get her back?

I am standing stock-still in the humid bathroom, eyes closed, pending inspiration. Her final words come to me. And there it is, a pilot light, sparking this energy in me I haven't felt in days. There might be another way.

23

The fly enters into the ear of the lion and conquers him.

Ծանծը առիւծին ականջը կը մտնէ, կը յաղթէ:

—*Armenian Proverb*

It's been a week and a half since my idea, and though I haven't heard a word from Erebuni, I've been busy. I channeled all my breakup energy into writing an essay titled, "Fired for Interviewing a Congresswoman and Other Stories from the Newsroom." Not only has it been written, it's been submitted to fifteen outlets. And has been rejected by thirteen of them so far.

Lucky number thirteen arrived this morning. The first thing I did when I woke up was grope for my phone and hit my e-mail app, and I was greeted with:

> Thank you for giving us the opportunity to read your piece. While the subject matter was intriguing, it does not fit our issue at this time. Please submit to us again in the future.

Well, at least that one was polite. I got one that basically said, "This drivel is not the kind of work we publish."

The only reason I'm still halfway confident about it is because Vache—yes, Vache—helped me edit it. I tentatively reached out to him over text, feeling that of all my new friends, I needed to apologize to him first (and suspected he might be the most receptive to it). He suggested I come meet him at his work, Monocle Coffee, and we chatted over lattes in cups so large they resembled soup bowls.

Turns out Erebuni didn't say much about the breakup to the friend group, and it was a strange relief to hear that she hasn't been going around bashing me to her closest friends. Vache seemed to think we broke up because of my being engaged. I cleared that up for him but also came clean and told him how badly I had lied to my mom to save face. And that I've been miserable because of it.

He seemed to understand how deeply I meant it, and I could feel there was something in him that really wanted to remain friends despite it all. So we kept on chatting, got to talking about writing, and I spilled my idea to him. Then, miraculously, he offered to take a look at it for me. And damn, he has an eye.

Now I'm lying on the floor of my bedroom, stretching my hamstrings after a luxurious hour-long workout because I have nothing else to do and I need to feel like I'm doing something. When I'm concentrating on the burn of my muscles, I don't have to concentrate on the fact that I have only two open submissions left, and most likely they'll follow the trend: "No, we don't want your essay."

It wasn't good enough. Or no one cares about sexism wrapped up in Armenian issues. Richard said it himself, and I'm starting to think he was right: They don't know who Armenians are, and they don't care.

I know it's a little out there, but I was hoping that if I got this article published I could send it to Erebuni (or, um, Vache could) and show her, *See? I'm not a total wishy-washy coward.* That with work, at least, I tried. I picked a side like she told me to do. And I paid for it, but I'm going to own it, write about it, make it mine. I kept imagining Erebuni reading the piece, what she might think. How it might turn into a second chance.

I twist to my other side, and my muscle yelps as I try to stretch it. *Pain is progress,* I tell myself, half believing it.

But no one's going to publish it, so it's just going to sit on my laptop unread. Nothing will change. She'll never forgive me. The thought of that makes me almost sick to my stomach, and I hold back a rolling tide of nausea. Ugh, I guess I worked out too hard. Mom would not approve.

I relax my neck muscles, and my face sinks deeper into the carpet. The threads tickle my nose. It's weird—this is the same carpet I grew up with, and while I know the shape of every stain from sodas or markers over the years, I can't remember a single incident that caused a stain. I'm sure they felt like such a big deal at the time; I'm sure Dad and Mom yelled at me about them.

My phone dings, and I assume it'll be Diana, who's been very sweet. She took me out for a manicure, and I complained about my ex-job and ex-boss, and she was super sympathetic, but I still didn't tell her about the real story behind Erebuni. I almost did, but my throat tightened and wouldn't let the words come out.

But the text is not from her, it's from Trevor. An actual text, not a WhatsApp message, which means he's back.

I untwist and sit up straight. I haven't heard from him since
our polite-with-notes-of-wistful texting exchange a week and a
half ago. He could be saying anything now. "It's over." "I want to
see you." "I'm outside your front door." I mean, probably not that
last one, but who knows, maybe he'd think it was romantic. I tap
to read it.

> Home in the U S of A. Finished unpacking. I'd
> love to see you, if you wanted. You can come by
> here.

Oh no. He'd *love* to see me. Went from some light I miss yous
to loving to see me. Sounds a touch more than polite. Part of me
feels like I need Trevor now, kind of like how I need to exercise to
do something and make progress. It's a balm for the thing I've
been trying not to think about for days. That at my core, right
now, I'm directionless and my future career has been derailed by
being fired. Not laid off but fired. That so much of my hope in the
last week has hinged upon my essay, and that it's clear by now that
it's never going to be published. The scary thought when I put all
this together is that I have nothing. But Trevor, he could be something. *Your safety net*, a voice tells me. And I tell it to shut up.

What would Dad think of me now? He loved that I was a reporter, that I was the face and the voice of American news. He
was always proud about my career when Mom wasn't, when she
mostly worried about the dangers and the physical stress of my
job. Disappointed wouldn't begin to cover how he'd feel; that's
clear. In a way, I'm glad he doesn't have to see me like this. There'd
be nothing tender in his feelings. He'd act like my getting fired
was an affront to him. My parents both have (or had) such high

expectations of me at all times and took everything personally, like I was an extension of themselves, not a separate person. Then he'd spring into action with a plan on how to get me back on my feet, perhaps a plan to sue Richard and the station. "John Casings is a lawyer. He can advise us," I imagine him saying. Or he'd ask me to get Trevor's advice, even though Trevor is a patent lawyer.

I feel, again, how much he adored Trevor. He met his parents only once before the crash, at a classic San Francisco steakhouse, and I remember how much he loved Trevor's dad in particular. Not surprising, I guess. Trevor's dad is exactly how I think cowboys back in the day were: tall, quiet, handsome, with a touch of misogyny. Dad would want me to jump back into the fold—he'd tell me that Trevor was my ticket back into a normal life.

But I don't know.

There's a knock at my door. I straighten.

Mom opens it. She's holding an armful of clothes, one fuzzy pink sock dangling from the bottom, threatening to fall. "Do you have any reds?"

It's been weird with her. She's assumed three modes around me: tiptoeing about my margins like I'm contagious, pestering me to look for jobs (though I told her I was writing, which according to her is not a job), or reverting to business as usual regarding the household chores and bills and the like. Not a word about Erebuni ever since that awkward moment she saw her face on our TV, and I haven't brought her up, either. I'm afraid of what I would say, that I might blame her for breaking us up, though it wasn't my mom's fault.

Mom may have a point about the job hunt, though. I am fully in favor of taking a mourning period after a shock, but this one feels bigger than I anticipated. The thought of going back to a news station makes me physically sick. That's why I've been writing my article and ignoring everything else—it's one thing that feels purposeful in my life. But there's a dread of realism that's lurking beneath it, because even if my article gets published, one piece isn't enough to start a new career. I hardly even know what's out there for me other than the news, and I'm too afraid to look, for fear that my hoped-for future—that someone would take a chance on my telling lovely cultural stories without a breaking news element—doesn't exist.

Now she's asking me about laundry. Then we'll be shopping for food. Cooking that food. Washing dishes. Cleaning the house. Mom has loved the extra help and piled more on to me. We've been making more complicated dishes, sorting through old clothes, and finishing tasks that have been long put off. But I'm not sure how much longer I can sit in this house cycling through a never-ending circle of chores.

"Mom, how do you do it day after day?"

"Laundry? I don't do it every day. That's the secret."

"No, I mean not working. How do you stand it? Aren't you bored? Don't you wish you were still teaching?"

She grimaces and waves dismissively. "Don't talk to me about this kind of thing."

But I want to push on this. I am honestly curious. "So you never want to think about it? I'm, like, a week and a half into unemployment, and I'm losing my mind. And you're way smarter than me; you must be dying. It's been years since you retired."

She shrugs. "You get used to it. What else am I supposed to do? I have no grandkids"—her voice darkens—"and apparently I'm never going to get them."

A reference to Erebuni, I'm guessing. It hits right at the center of me, sharp and ruthless in its carelessness. I want to hit back. "You can't just wait for me to do something to make your life more interesting—"

She interrupts, "Why not? I am your mother. A mother with an old daughter has expectations." Old! I'm literally so young by normal societal standards. Not by Armenian mom standards. "But life has been disappointing."

Nope, I'm not falling for her pity party. I feel like she's doing this purely for sympathy, and I have very little left for her after the banquet. Not to mention when I asked her where the photo strip of Erebuni and me was and she said she snatched it from Sona and destroyed it. I might have never wanted to see it again, that tiny photograph that caused so much trouble, but it wasn't the photo's fault. That photo strip contained the only pictures of Erebuni and me together, and even if I never see or speak to her again, I want to have it. A memory of when things were very, very good.

She looks back at me. "No, I will do the red laundry, then the whites, then the colors, do the vacuum and the mopping, and that will take up half the day. This is what I am reduced to."

Okay, that kind of does make me feel sorry for her, but she's still not owning up to her lack of responsibility and action, to relying on me to make things happen in her life. "But you have a choice in this. Just because you don't want to leave Nene home alone doesn't mean you can't create anything. Start a math tutoring business. Don't make it a business if you don't want to. Have kids come over here a couple times a week—"

She wrinkles her nose like I suggested she try leeching herself. "Why are you making work for me? Just have some baby, and that'll settle it."

I sigh. I don't feel like fighting. "I'm only twenty-seven and"—I raise my voice to preclude an interruption—"before you say you were twenty-seven when you had me, first of all, I know, and second, things were different back then."

She stares right into my eyes with a sardonic expression. "Yes, now days you can marry a woman."

I can't believe she actually referenced gay marriage and my sexuality so baldly. I'm a bit taken aback, and also want to share more about Erebuni with her. She's my mom; I want to tell her I'm hurting. But when I speak, it comes out wrong, defensive. "Yes, you can. Lucky for you, that woman doesn't want to talk to me anymore."

Her face closes off to me. "I don't want to know. You sort out your own affairs. I'm assuming no reds." She turns around, not shutting the door, and leaves. The pink sock falls to the floor.

I'm feeling wild and impulsive and angry and annoyed and so, so badly in need of love. You want grandkids? Fine. I'll give you grandkids. I lunge for my phone, and text Trevor back, I'd love to see you too.

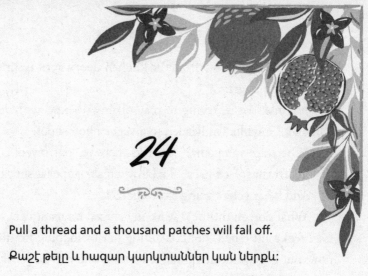

24

Pull a thread and a thousand patches will fall off.

Քաշէ թելը և հազար կարկտաններ կան ներքն:

—*Armenian Proverb*

A few hours later, I've showered, well and truly scrubbed myself, and taken my time blow-drying my hair and applying TV levels of makeup. I want to look good. After all, I'm headed to Trevor's to convince him I'm worth taking back.

I open the jewelry box where I've stashed away the ring this past month. I have to take the ring with me, obviously, but do I wear it? It seems so . . . final. I could just try it on, see how it feels? I slip on the ring, and the diamonds lining the band scratch at my skin. I haven't worn it since the day Trevor pushed it onto my finger. It's beautiful, no doubt about it, and it's the ring Dad would say I deserved. I suppose I'll just wear it. Dad would be proud of me now.

I slink downstairs hoping to avoid Mom. I hear the scrape of a pot on the stove and the sound of running water from the kitchen, so I'm extra quiet. As I kneel by the shoe rack at the front door, the heavy buckles on my sandaled heels clink when I pick them up. She peeps out from the kitchen doorway as if she's been on alert for danger.

"Just me," I say, trying to play off my unexpectedly leaving while looking like I'm headed to a *Vogue* photoshoot.

"Where are you going?" she asks, her eyes narrowed.

"To Trevor's. He's back," I add, when she appears shocked.

"And what you're going to do there?"

"What do you think?" I wave my ringed finger at her.

I feel a little bad, not consulting her or looping her in until now. But I've also kind of had it with my mom. This is what she wants. Well, the end result, anyway—marriage and babies. I fasten one of the shoes and work on the other.

"Oh," she says, considering. I guess she wasn't expecting that answer. She probably hasn't thought about Trevor for weeks.

Both shoes on, I stand up. I love that initial feeling of wearing high heels, when you feel so tall and see the same room from a new view. It makes me more confident about my decision. I'm literally towering over my mom. She looks like she's piecing together a puzzle, and she says, "Okay, then. Do what you think is best."

Hmm. She'd rather me be with Trevor, a guy she doesn't like all that much, than be with Erebuni, a woman who I'm sure, if she got to know her, she would adore. This is how the world works. This is who I have to be to make her happy. I grasp the keys in my hand so tightly the teeth dig into my skin, but I don't let go.

As I make to leave I say, without looking back, "I will."

After fifteen minutes of circling for parking, I wedge my car into an ultra-tight parallel parking spot on the left side of Trevor's one-way street (I'm a parking goddess and I demand praise for this).

He lives in the Marina, in a cream-and-gold early-1900s apartment building similar to all its identical siblings on the block. He's high up the hill, and you can see views of Alcatraz and the Golden Gate Bridge from his living room.

When I step out of the car, it hits me that it's sunny. And warm, even. There are a few watercolor-soft streaks of clouds in the sky. A nice day for a reconciliation. I leave my jacket in the car and check my phone. Two missed calls from Mom. Hmm. But no texts, so it can't have been urgent. She probably wanted to wrap up our earlier conversation in a way she found more suitable, where she had the upper hand. Mom likes to win arguments, especially with me. I'm not calling her back.

I head to Trevor's apartment building doors. I press the button for apartment number twelve, and a few seconds later comes the scraggly buzz of the door unlocking (which sounds more like something has gone horribly wrong than right, but I'm used to it after so many years). The last time I was here was a month and a half ago or so. The entryway smells the same, old wood with a touch of vacuum, yet the carpet on the stairs has had dirt stamped into it for what seems like five decades. I'm sure every resident can hear me as I creak my way up the steps, on the way to tell Trevor, "Yes, I will marry you. Let's live together and create a life."

I stand in front of his door and don't knock. I could just leave. Slip the ring under the door and bolt.

God, what am I thinking? No, I came here to be with Trevor. There's nothing wrong with him. He'll make a great life partner.

I raise my hand to knock, but the door swings open before I do. He must have heard me coming up the stairs.

Trevor is before me, light stubble covering his face. It makes him more handsome, which somehow annoys me. Without a word he takes me into a hug, and it's very sweet, but also my neck is squished uncomfortably, and if this lasts much longer I feel like I'm going to pull something. He feels so bony and hard compared to Erebuni. I squirm out and smile at him so he's not hurt that I pulled away.

"You look great," I say.

"So do you," he says, slipping his hand into mine and taking me in. "Heels and everything. God you're a sight. Those broads in Germany do not compare."

I cannot imagine Erebuni ever saying anything like that. Then I tell myself to stop it because Erebuni doesn't want me. He does.

He backs out of the way to let me into the apartment. It's the same, clean as a whistle as always. His TV takes up most of the main wall, but there are a couple of freestanding bookshelves with his old law school textbooks and a smattering of items like his massage gun, a Fitbit hooked up to its charger. His laptop and his productivity journal are on the table, so he must have been working right before I got here. Didn't take the day off, I guess.

I rest my hand against his black leather couch, briefly allow myself to enjoy the view of the Golden Gate, and half smile. "So you had a good time?"

His gaze meets my hand, the one with the large sparkling rock on it. Oh, right.

"You're wearing it," he mumbles, clearly touched.

I nod. Yep, this is it. I'm saying yes, this is what I wanted. I'm going to have a future with him. My throat feels tight.

"But you should know . . ." I trail off. I should tell him about Erebuni, that we had basically broken up so I hooked up with someone else. But it wasn't a hookup. How can I talk about her to him? I continue, "I lost my job. I got fired, actually. It's so shitty."

And surprising myself, I choke up, and God, there are tears in my eyes. He makes a long *aw* sound and wraps me in his arms again. My neck is more comfortable this time, but I feel like I'm in a vise.

This time he pulls away, and he looks me right in the eyes. "Schatzie, it's gonna be okay. I got promoted, plus a monster bonus. Honestly, you don't have to ever work again."

The way he says that last sentence. I doubt he meant it that way, but it feels like he took my entire career, shoved it into a box, and stomped on it. My voice sounds small. "Oh, that's good to— Congrats. I'm happy for you."

He looks me right in the eye and settles both his hands on my shoulders. "I missed you." He whispers it, like he's too scared to say the words out loud and show how vulnerable it makes him. Typing it is one thing, saying it out loud? No, don't show weakness. Then he brings his face closer and closer to mine and, oh no, he's going to kiss me. Why did I think this would be okay? He does it, his lips hit mine, and everything in me revolts. Every system in my body is rising together, shouting at me, *No, stop it.*

So I pull away and I'm about to tell him about Erebuni, but he lifts a finger, like, *Wait, I've got something.* He darts into the kitchen. I sink into the couch, wishing the leather were softer so that it would swallow me whole. I want to be brave, I want to tell him no, I can't keep this up. *Follow him, Nar. Tell him.*

Erebuni. I'm not done hoping, not done being sorry or wanting to make it up to her. Not done wanting to be with her. Even if my article never makes it, I can't give up on her.

Even if she never speaks to me again, I can't be with Trevor. I shouldn't have come here like this, I shouldn't have worn the ring.

I'm going to cut the net, setting myself up to potentially be alone forever. But free.

God, poor Trevor. *Sorry, bro*, I think, hearing Arek's voice in my head. The thought of Erebuni's friends lands gently on my shoulders, both sad and happy.

I stand up to follow Trevor, to tell him, but just then he waltzes in with a pep in his step, holding two champagne glasses and a bottle of Dom Perignon and of course he just has that lying around. He's always had a penchant for fancy champs. God, this is going to sting. Still, I know now more than ever it's the right thing to do. I'm going to start here with Trevor and keep doing the right thing over and over and over.

"I was seeing someone," I say. That wasn't . . . exactly what I wanted to say, but I can't bring myself to open with "We're over." There's a flare of anger on his face, the green of jealousy, then it smooths over into something else I can't quite read. Guilt?

He shrugs. "I can't be mad at you for that. I had a couple of hookups myself."

A couple? I'm having a hard time stifling the shock on my face because Trevor is not the type to casually hook up. At least that's what I thought. But mostly, I realize he doesn't get what I'm telling him at all, and he's about to do a "what happens in Munich stays in Munich" and say that we should forget each other's transgressions. But that's not what I'm trying to tell him.

He puts the bottle and glasses down on his dining table. "They were nothing, just girls at the club. One of those all-night parties where they almost didn't let me in because I was such a normie." He snorts at the memory. Then he gets serious again. "The girls meant nothing. One-night stands. They didn't have anything on you."

The way he says it, comparing me to one-night-stand club

girls, makes me feel like they perhaps did have something on me. But it doesn't matter.

"I wasn't—Mine wasn't—"

Why can't I just say the words? Fear of the unknown, of being truly alone, is holding me back, but I can't let it. *Get them out, or you'll end up making some excuse and end up with him out of convenience.* I can't do that, I won't. "I'm not sure we can be together."

That gets his attention. His eyes darken. "What? Is it because of this guy?" Then, accusingly, "Who is he? Someone I know? God, is it Dave? He always had a thing for you, I knew it—"

I interrupt him before that thought can go any further, "No, not Dave. Someone you've never met. I just met her recently myself."

His eyes bug out. "Her?"

I stay cool. "I told you I was bi. Is it so hard to believe?"

"Yeah, but I thought that was just for hooking up. Not, you know, for a relationship, for something you'd call 'meeting someone.'"

Typical Trevor. He's looking at the floor, shaking his head slightly. I reach for the ring and wedge it off, scraping my skin in the process. It sits in my hand.

"Trevor, I'm sorry, I don't want to get married. I think we should break up. Seriously, this time. Yes, it has to do with her, but let's look at us. We don't have that spark. Let's be honest, we've just been going through the motions lately."

I've kept myself calm, even agreeable. But he comes at me with fire. His face has shut out anything friendly in it, and I get a flash of him as his litigator persona. "Maybe you've been the one going through the motions. I haven't. I've been here. It's been real for me. How long have you felt this way? Years?"

I honestly don't know. My relationship with him has been a

flat line, always fine. Something easy in my life. So yes, it has been years, but I never realized it until being with Erebuni. My lack of answer is answer enough. He runs his hands through his hair, makes some kind of angry grunt. "You came in here wearing my ring."

"I hoped we could be together. I wanted to, but—it doesn't feel right. I'm sorry, Trevor. The ring is beautiful." Finally, I let it go, place it on his productivity journal.

He's shaking his head no, no. The day is too beautiful for this, almost mocking in its soft streaks of clouds, the periwinkle water of the bay. Tiny white sailboats look like birds settled upon the water. But I need to press on. "We'd be okay together, but don't you want to feel absolutely thrilled together?"

Trevor looks lost. No surprise. I've given him an entire jungle of surprises to get lost in. I figure, why not throw a couple more brambles his way. I say, "I've said it before, but I'll say it again. Katie is completely in love with you. She wants to jump your bones. You should, uh, give her a shot."

That rouses him into something resembling panic, which turns on my alarm sensors, too. He says, "Katie. Oops. I invited her over to celebrate."

I squint. "You. Invited. . . . Katie? To come to our reconciliation?" I don't know where to start. That he was so confident I'd come running to him (I mean, I did) that he invited someone over to party with us. And then instead of spending the afternoon with me, his back-together girlfriend, he was going to friend-zone me so that we all get to hang out together with his coworker who is in love with him? What about—

"Didn't you expect us to . . . you know?" I tilt my head suggestively. "Where was Katie going to factor into that?"

He has a hand out, defensively. "I mean, I don't know."

I am starting to think he does like her back. He's just been with me out of some misplaced loyalty. I want to tell him that, but right now he doesn't seem the most receptive to my ideas, like he might thrust it away just to contradict me.

He crosses his arms, then uncrosses them. "I wasn't thinking. Who cares? She'll be here soon." He lets out a short, frustrated breath. "You mean it? We're done?"

I nod. "We are."

Then I hear a tapping at the door, and Katie emerges. "Knock-knock. Hope everyone's ready to celebrate. I've got the Mt. Tam brie and a bucket of Hog Island oysters. Welcome home, mister!"

Katie, tall with long thick hair and black-framed glasses, wearing a quirky red-and-brown number that'd make Zooey Deschanel positively envious, enters with an air of euphoria. Trevor and I remain frozen in place. He was not kidding. He seriously invited her to come over at the same time as me. God, if I had any doubt in my mind that this was a bad idea (and I didn't), it's sure wiped away.

An instant later, Katie, shrewd as ever, reads our faces, and the smile on hers turns into a small O. "I forgot something in my car. The hot sauce, duh. Can't do oysters without it. I'll just . . . leave this—" And she places the goods on the coffee table and begins to back out, but before she can, I tell her, "No, it's okay. I was just leaving."

She cocks an eyebrow. "You were leaving." She says it as more of a statement.

I nod. Then turn toward Trevor. "Bye, Trevor," I say with an apologetic smile. He returns it with a capitulatory one, and we briefly hug. I can't get over how hard and angular his body feels, so different from Erebuni's, so clearly not what I want. Part of me is sad about our final hug—I mean, five years with him—but another part of me is so ready. Even if I never see Erebuni again, this is the right thing to do. Though I hope, so desperately, that's not the case.

I walk toward the door, where Katie is glued to her phone, but when I approach I see it's stuck on the lock screen. I lean toward her, and with a smirk, I whisper, "He's single." She gives me a look that's a mix of bossy and grateful and says, "'Bout time."

I shut the door behind me. It clicks, a slow, deliberate sound.

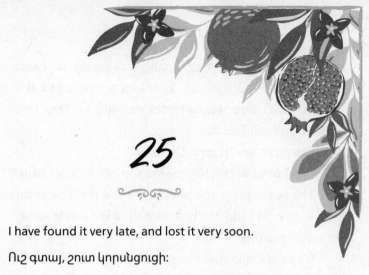

25

I have found it very late, and lost it very soon.

Ուշ գտայ, շուտ կորսնցուցի:

—*Armenian Proverb*

Outside Trevor's apartment, in the soft sunlight, a couple walks by hand in hand; she's holding a grocery bag, and he's resting a pack of sparkling water on his shoulder. They're in Ray-Bans and smiling, tall and blond and tan. An ideal I once wanted. Could have had just minutes ago. Their clear adoration for each other makes me certain they don't see me.

The Marina, for all its sweeping views and lovely old architecture, kind of sucks. It reeks of Trevor and his ilk; I need to get out of here.

I get in my car and close the door, waiting for the heat to become suffocatingly hot. Part of me wants to punish myself. I know I did the right thing, but I take stock of myself: I'm unemployed, broke off a five-year relationship, and worst of all, there's no Erebuni. I know I can't call her up and say, "Hey, guess what! I broke it off for real. I'm ready for you now!" I won't do that to her.

The still heat becomes cloying, making the air thick and hard to breathe. Enough of this. I turn on my car and roll down the windows, a warm Marina breeze tumbling in. Then I pick up my phone and call Diana.

She picks up. "Happy Thursday?"

"Di, I need to talk to you. Are you free by any chance?"

The fact that I'm able to even ask this question at this time of day—I am so lucky my best friend is a real estate agent.

"Are you okay?"

It's so uncomfortable to say the thing. *No, I'm not okay, I have no idea what I'm doing or what I've done or what I'm going to do. I need help.* I say, "Kind of. I need to talk out—talk out some issues."

"I'm guessing you don't want to meet at the house?"

I shake my head, though she can't see. I hadn't thought about it before now, but I know exactly where I want to go. "The beach. Ocean Beach."

I feel pulled toward the coastline, to see where the world ends. The way I miss Erebuni, it's been rising, but now it feels like a boil. I'm not sure if I have any chance of being with her again, but this feels like something I have to do. Some part of me hopes that being where Erebuni and I were, conjuring magic together, will help me find my voice to tell Diana what I've been scared to say. As I drive up, past Lands End, the view is magnificent: white foamy waves crashing for miles.

I choose the same location where the bonfire was and text Diana my spot. I rip off my heels and walk the beach barefoot. When the cold sand grips at my feet, I wonder if any of the grains are the same as they were those couple of weeks ago. If any of them still have Erebuni and me clinging to them. As if it would matter at all, but it feels important somehow.

Waves roar in at intervals, and though their crests are high, they're far enough away to be safe. Maybe that's one reason people like these cold Northern California beaches: the show of danger, but from a comfortable distance, like lions at the zoo. Diana waves from the parking lot not too long afterward. She is in her real estate agent costume, as I like to call it, pencil skirt and a sweater with pearls, and suddenly I feel a bit bad for dragging her out into the elements. At least her booties have a low heel.

"The beach, huh? I haven't been out here since I was trying to impress that guy Ben by pretending to like outdoorsy things."

If I'm not into nature, she's definitely not. To her, a meal on the back patio of a restaurant is roughing it.

"I came here recently, and . . ."

Today feels nothing like it did on the solstice. The sun is sharp, bouncing off sand and water; everything feels frenetic—the waves, the tiny crabs, and who knows whatever else under the sand, busy, busy to their next destination. Not that cool sense of calm Erebuni would wash over me. The courage I was hoping to glean from the environment seems nonexistent.

"Do you want to sit?"

Diana looks disgusted, like I asked her to lie in a pile of trash. "Hell no. I'm good here."

I smile at her, then it turns fake, strained, as I try to tell her what I dragged her out here for. *Just say it. Come right out and say it all at once. It'll hurt less.* I turn my face down, tickle my big toe into the sand. "This is awkward, but I have to tell you. Okay. Remember I used to hook up with the occasional woman in college? Turns out I do actually like women, too." The words jam together, coming out fast.

No way I'm looking at Diana's face now. The truth shouldn't feel so uncomfortable, but I guess I feel like I'm telling her about my sex life in some embarrassing way. I've been conditioned, I know, but there's no time to think about that now. I continue, a rush of words crashing into one another, "And at the banquet? I did kiss Erebuni, the emcee, and that super wasn't the first time. In fact, we were kind of dating and falling for each other, but because Mom saw Erebuni and me together, I freaked out and pretended Erebuni and I weren't together, and and then stupid Raffi told her I was engaged, and long story short, she dumped me. We might never get back together, but it's what I want more than anything. And if by some miracle she does give me another chance, what the hell am I going to say to the family? It could never work. Right?"

On my final word I gather the courage to look up at her. She's not shocked. She's almost impassive, like she's mulling it all over.

"I see why you took me all the way out to the ocean for this."

"You do?"

"I'm so worried about the wind turning my hair into knots, I barely care about anything else you're saying." She smiles. "I'm kidding. Nar, I always knew you liked girls. The way you talked about those hookups, it wasn't just for fun. I—I admit I didn't have the best response back then. Armenian school to Catholic school doesn't really prepare you for the variety of the world." She looks down. "I hope I never made you feel bad about it."

She always knew. "I mean, no. I didn't think you actually knew. I thought you just thought I was a little weirder than you."

She jibes me. "Well, that I can't deny." Then she turns serious again. "But not because of who you like. Though I can't believe you were dating that woman, Erebuni, and never told me! She's really pretty, and so poised. I told you, you always liked the intellectuals."

I can't help it, I blush. I love hearing her talk about Erebuni like this.

She continues, "I knew something was obviously up at the banquet when Tantig Sona was flapping around like a deranged bird, showing us the photo, but first of all, I didn't want to have anything to do with her gossip about you, and second, I wasn't sure what to make of it because I was so positive you'd have told me."

A touch of guilt comes over me for not trusting her before this. But I want to tell her the truth. "I was afraid you'd say I should focus on the guys and not get distracted by something with no future."

She pauses a moment. "I see why you would think that. I might have, at some point. But did you know Remi's brother is gay? Closeted. Even though his parents are open-minded, he feels like they'll never accept it, so he goes on the occasional sham date with a woman to keep up appearances. Breaks my heart. With you, I mean I admit I never thought it would come up. You were always dating guys, on track to marry Trevor . . ."

She comes closer to me, catches my eye meaningfully. "If this woman is who you want, or if it's not her, if it's someone else, I am with you one hundred percent. I want you to know that."

I haven't noticed until now that I've buried my feet completely in the sand, like hiding a part of myself in the warm and dark will help me get through this conversation somehow. Now I pull them out and rush up to hug Diana.

I whisper out to the ocean wind. "Thank you. I really, really need you."

We pull apart. She says, "I want to be a good cousin. You're my best friend, no matter what . . . even if you refuse to come linen shopping."

In the car, one door open, letting the ocean breeze in, I see I have a new e-mail notification on my phone. So I swipe to it, and see, oh boy, another e-mail from a magazine. Almost certainly another rejection. So far every time I've received a publisher's e-mail, I've experienced first this rush of hope, followed by an angry voice shouting that hope away because high expectations always lead to disappointment. Let's see if their rejection is a nice one or a mean one.

> Hi Nareh,
>
> Thanks for submitting your piece to us. I love your voice in this essay, and the way you balance the seriousness of the issue with notes of humor is refreshing.

Well, that's a nice detail, now let's get to the "but . . . we're not going to accept it at this time."

I read on.

> Your timing could not be better, as we're publishing a series on sexism in the workplace tomorrow. If you can get us an author photo and bio (third person) in

the next few hours, we can slide your piece in.
Otherwise, we may have to wait a month or two until
it's topical again. We can offer you $350 for this
piece, which is our standard rate for 1,500-word
essays.

Thank you! Mel

My body starts to shake, nervy, like I got a shot of caffeine
straight to the arm. I read it again to make sure. Holy shit, they
want it. To publish it. Tomorrow! I'm getting paid for it, too. A fair
rate. And they need something from me. I read again, and this
time the bio and photo solidify in my mind. Okay, okay, be calm.
No! Don't be calm. They need it from me ASAP, otherwise I'm not
going to make it into their issue. And I'd have to wait two months?
Hell no. I need Erebuni to see this now; it could be the difference
between us having a chance and never having a chance.

I shut the door, and allow the urgency to fill my body with
adrenaline. A bio and a photo. I'm mentally starting to write it,
mentally sorting through a bank of recent professional photos.
When I turn on my car, I smile inwardly. Years of navigating San
Francisco's worst traffic jams has prepared me for this moment. I
roll down the windows; I want to feel the wind on my teeth.

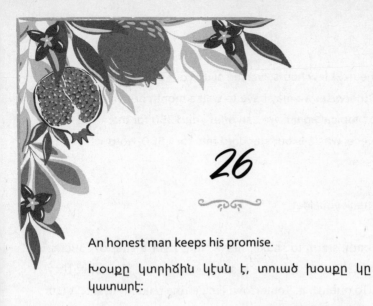

26

An honest man keeps his promise.

Խոսքը կորիճին կեան է, տուած խոսքը կը կատարէ:

—*Armenian Proverb*

I submit on time. True, I had to shout at my mom, over her protests to stop and tell her about what's happening, that everything was fine and that I needed some completely silent time to finish something important. I slammed and locked my door so I could concentrate. Then I altered my work bio so it was less about the news and more about me as a whole. All my work photos have a perky quality to them, but I found an outtake where I'm barely smiling and the angle doesn't make me look like a Miss America hopeful.

While I was holed up, Mom knocked on my door, which I didn't open, but she informed me she was going to her friend Nora's house to make pastries for her daughter's baby shower. That stopped me. Mom hasn't done a casual hangout like that with anyone but our family in a long time. This is a good thing, and I want to be happy for her, but there was bitterness in her voice, since Nora's daughter is only a year older than me and is married and having a kid. But I didn't say a word back except goodbye. I couldn't be thrown off from submitting my materials. And if it meant Mom would be gone for several hours, I could avoid talking to her tonight.

When I wake up the next morning, I play the refresh game. I brush my teeth and refresh. Wash my face, moisturize, and refresh. Bang out some pushups and refresh.

Then, as I bend into downward-facing dog, I lift up one hand to refresh, and I see the update, a massive banner advertising their series on the workplace. Oh my God. I collapse out of the pose, on all fours, staring at my phone. No, I need to savor this on the big screen. At my desk, I pull it up on my computer, and I scroll past fascinating, rage-inducing headlines. There's my article, Fired for Interviewing a Congresswoman and Other Stories from the Newsroom, against a tasteful backdrop of an abstract of Armenian flag colors (I have no idea where they got that, but I am loving it).

I speed-read it once and see they've printed it, unedited, in its entirety. This is wild. I mean, I've been on the air more times than I can count, and article versions of my segments have appeared online almost every day, but this feels different. This is a piece of my story I'm sharing with the world. I've shared my face, my body, my voice before, but never my opinions, never my history. It feels good. Scary, definitely, but good scary.

Then I read it again from the eyes of Erebuni and how she might feel if she reads it. I've done this a thousand times while drafting, but I need to do it again, in this font, with this spacing. She doesn't know I was fired, so I imagine her eyes getting huge when she reads the title. My brain also picks out the paragraph where I show pride in my home country (I may have called it the "motherland"), how Erebuni might feel proud of me. I know I need to send it to her.

But I can't, not directly. Silence since the banquet. She's sent a clear message that she doesn't want to hear from me. I should text Vache about it, and then there's a chance he'd send it to her? Should I ask him to send it to her? No, that's so desperate.

The articles on this site don't allow comments (praise Jesus), but I did link my personal Twitter. My Twitter got the full pre-article safety sweep. I removed all mention of my news station, rewrote my bio, changed my photo, and altered my name to be N. Bedrossian, matching my name in the article. I didn't want to bring too much scrutiny to Richard and the station specifically, though anyone who cared could dig into it. On the off chance the article went big, I didn't want people showing up at Richard's house, pelting rotten lettuce at him, or more likely, flooding his Twitter with hatred. I'm writing this for me, not for revenge.

People have started sharing. Nothing too extreme so far, a couple of "You've got to read this" and "Wow" comments on retweets. I decide to send it to some Armenian online outlets, wondering if there might be a potential collaboration with them down the line. Maybe I could be a freelancer. Leaning into the Armenian angle might be the way to go.

Once that's done, I know I can't keep procrastinating sending this to Vache, since he was instrumental in getting the article to this point. I won't mention forwarding it to Erebuni. If he sends it to her, great. If not, well . . . maybe I can ask him in a couple of days.

I scroll down to find Vache's name in my texts. I write, It's live. Thank you again for all your help with this.

I tap over to Instagram, wondering if I should post it there, too, but instead get sucked into my feed, peering into other people's perfectly curated homes and café flat lays.

Then my phone dings with a text. And I see her name: Erebuni. Just the name makes the entire room drop away, shoved out of my vision so that all I see are the letters that comprise her name, reaching out to me. Did she see the article? How in the world would she have known to look for it?

I open the text.

> This is an unexpected, excellent piece. Thank you for sending it to us.

Us. *Us?* I look at the top of my screen and see all their names: Arek, Janette, Erebuni, Vache.

I stifle a scream. I texted the group chat. Vache was the last one who texted—I knew I had scrolled too far down to find his name, but I wasn't thinking . . . Oh lord.

Then Arek texts, Not sure why ur thanking me but if u need someone with a shotgun for ur ex boss just let me know. I got u girl

Shit, shit, shit. Yes, Arek's message was sweet, and I'm relieved he's rallying to defend me after I broke his friend's heart by *lying* and being a horrible person. But. I need to not look like a weirdo, ASAP, so I text back. Sorry, I meant to text this to Vache. He helped me edit it. Direct all praise his way, the man is brilliant

Then I let out a primal groan. Erebuni's going to think I sent it to her on purpose, like the snake in the grass I've proved myself to be. I reread her message. *Unexpected.* I mean, right, it arrived in her texts out of the blue. But *excellent*, that word holds promise. You don't say *excellent* to someone you hate.

My phone announces another text, and while part of me wants to take my phone out back and shoot it, a stronger part is too curious about the new, looming message.

A text from Erebuni. A private text, not in the group chat (I double-check). It says, I'm proud of you, Nar. I'm glad you sent it, even if it wasn't meant for me.

I can hear my heart beating, it's running so fast. *Nar*, so familiar, it feels like she's leaning in close. She's proud of me, which means, first of all, I'm worth being proud of, and second, I did something, I took action, and she recognizes it. I have a chance. Or I might have a chance.

Before my brain has a chance to censor myself, my heart taps through my fingers, No, thank you for giving me the courage. And then, I know this is a lot to ask but would you by any chance be willing to meet?

Almost as soon as I send it, I think, *What have I done?* But then I burn with the risk of it, that it might actually pay off. The three dots appear, showing she's typing. *C'mon, c'mon, c'mon.*

Then, it comes. I don't think I'm ready yet. I'm still pretty hurt by our conversation.

Oh God, that feeling of shame, it hits like a fall to the floor, pain spreading almost instantly. I wonder briefly if I'll ever stop feeling this way. I can't believe I pinned so much expectation on this article. As if my being brave in one instance was enough for her to say, *Actually, yeah, forget all the lying and betrayal. I'm cool now.* It seems so obvious that it isn't enough.

Then the dots start again. A message arrives: But this article, I mean it, I am proud of you.

Just like that, a glint of hope is back. Her words are like a healing balm. *I know my truth stung, but here's something to make it a little less harsh.* She wouldn't give that attention and care if she were completely done with me, if the door were entirely shut.

It's on me. I need to act, and I have a hunch about what my next step could be. I've been hearing some words in my head since last night, urging me to examine them, tell them. When I closed my eyes, face resting on the pillow, they spiraled above me, calling out. I heard them again this morning but pushed them away, concentrating on the article drop. But I should pay them more attention, as hard as it's going to be.

First, I text Erebuni back. I understand. And thank you again for saying that. You helped me realize it needed to be written. There's going to be more. I'm choosing a side.

Then I decide that I am going to head downstairs and come out to my mom.

27

Every man has in his heart a lion that sleeps.

Ամէն մարդու սրտումը մի առիւծ է պառկած:

—*Armenian Proverb*

I will myself to walk down the stairs casually, which translates into an airy bop, like I'm a Fred Astaire wannabe. But I know that I can do this. I can tell Mom.

Nene is on the couch reading a French book about Beethoven. Her brow is furrowed, and I don't want to break her concentration. Mom's in the kitchen, wearing a flattering navy housedress. Stress cooking, by the looks of it. She's brushing the tops of phyllo dough pieces with egg yolk to make them crisp up and shine in the oven. There's also a pile of green beans ready to be trimmed. Beureg and fassoulia (a green bean, tomato, and ground beef stew) for lunch. So lucky.

"You finished your important work last night?" Her tone is somewhere between haughty and curious.

"I did. And you know what I can go for? Some sourj."

My mom sighs. "I'm busy here but afterward."

I open an upper cabinet, and there it is, the jezveh. Ours is cobalt blue with a long-trained peacock painted on it. "I'm going to make it," I say.

"You?" She stares inquisitively. I don't blame her, I've never made an impromptu Armenian coffee here at home.

"Where's the coffee?" I ask her in Armenian. I'm a bit embarrassed that I don't know where we keep it. She points to the freezer. "Top drawer," she replies.

I make the coffee just like Nene originally taught me and how Erebuni made it in her kitchen. No cardamom, though, since I'm certain we don't have it. My mom continues brushing the beuregs and pops them in the oven, stealing glances at my progress and finding nothing to criticize.

When I pour the coffee evenly between three cups, my mom puts her hands on her hips.

"Where did you learn to do this?"

This is it. This is where I tell her. "Where do you think?" I say. I end up sounding sadder than intended.

I hand her a cup of coffee, then dart out to place one on the table by Nene. She peers at me over the top of her book for a split second, makes a sound of thanks, then dives back in.

Back in the kitchen, I have my opening to talk about Erebuni. So I should. *Remember how Diana welcomed your coming out with open arms. Mom could do the same.* I'm trying to conjure the sea air, hoping it'll gift me some pluck. But the memory isn't sparking any bravery in me like I desperately need it to. I choke out something between a cough and clearing my throat. "Anyway," I say, "I broke up with Trevor for good. I gave him back the ring. It's over."

An amuse-bouche instead.

My mom lets out a long deep breath. She's . . . disappointed? Then she looks skyward, "Park Deroch! Thanks God."

Oh. "I knew you weren't a huge fan of him, but I thought you wanted me to settle down already and forget—forget, you know."

I still can't say her name in front of my mom. I tried, but the syllables are trapped in my mouth. How, if I can't speak her name, can I possibly tell my mom about who I am?

She rests a hand against the counter, like she can't hold herself up all the way. "That is why I called you so much. I wanted to tell you not to be with him, not to do anything, uh, what's the word?"

"Rash?"

"Yes! That one. So it is over for good?"

"Completely. This time there's no doubt about it."

She nods to herself. Then looks up at me, almost like she's afraid. "I want you to be happy," she says in a small voice.

Hope rears its optimistic head again. *Maybe she'll accept you after all,* it whispers. Just like Diana. I should tell her right now. There is no better time. She practically gave me an opening. But the hope scares me, things feel so okay between us in this moment that I'm not sure I could handle the crush of disappointment again.

It was such a beautiful thing for her to say. I should hug her, thank her. I don't. I take a sip of coffee, and realize I forgot to add sugar. It's bitter all the way down.

Mom ducks into the pantry to fish out cans of tomato sauce, then nods me toward the bag of green beans. Even though I want to leave and hole up in my misery, it appears my mom wants to split the work, and it'd be too selfish to decline.

Helping snap the ends off the green beans for fassoulia is one of my first memories of contributing to dinner. Here I am again, nothing more than a kid doing anything to please my mom. There have to be, like, seventy of these overgrown caterpillars in my pile, and while I'm not looking forward to the monotony of the task, at least it'll give me something to fixate on instead of my cowardliness.

We stand side by side, Mom's hands already flying over the beans, plucking the heads off like a decisive queen. Snap, snap. I fumble for my first one, get a group all tangled up in one another, and finally bend one until it breaks off. This is going to take forever.

The silence is all wrong. There's this urgency in me, a feeling that I'm on the precipice of something big if I can just muster up the courage to jump.

Mom's own words, that she wants me to be happy above all, are sparking hope in me. Plus, I already semi-confirmed that Erebuni and I were seeing each other with my comment about the coffee. Mom likes to be mentally prepared to accept new info. She hates surprises (hmm, kind of like me; I've never put that together). It's possible that enough time has passed.

"Have you been looking for a new job?" she says, more of an accusation than a question.

"Kind of." I get into a flow and rapidly pop off the ends of a couple of beans. It feels like I'm pulling myself apart instead of the legumes. I'm never going to say a word, am I?

She adds another couple of clean beans into the "done" bowl. "It is not going to be easy . . ." she begins, launching into her usual lecture about how my being fired means it's going to be ten times harder to find a new job. I can't listen to this again.

"Mom," I interrupt.

My stomach tightens. The words are in there. *Say it. Tell her. She already knows. You're just confirming.* It feels like the whole universe is whispering in my ear to tell her already, to get it out, stop holding it in.

I turn toward her. "I was lying to you before. I was with Ere-buni. We were seeing each other."

She steps back, and I swear her hand rises to her chest in shock. If I don't barrel forward it's never coming out. I find myself actually looking at her in the face. "It's true. We were, uh, starting to date. We liked each other so much. I can't help but think that she's actually the best person I've ever dated."

"Wha—You are telling me this now?" She's shaking her head. Not the best response, but it's not the worst. She's not screaming, she's not backing away or leaving the room. Her ears are wide open; she's listening to me.

"It's not a fluke. I've liked women, girls, for as long as I can remember. The same time I liked boys, I liked girls, too." My mind jumps to summer camp when I was seven years old, crushing on a beautiful blond girl several years older than me, the whip of her hair as she ran by during tag. "It's always been this way. And I know that might be hard to hear, but I couldn't keep it in any-more. It's just me."

I say the last sentence softly, and it seems to relax the panic in my mom's eyes. She lets out a choked laugh, and now I'm the surprised one.

"Ever since the banquet, I suspected," she says. "But you're so girly," she insists. "Are you sure?"

"Oh yeah," I say, and hope it didn't come out too lasciviously.

She covers her face in her hands and breathes out, then re-leases them. "Is there still a chance you will be with a man? You still like men? Or is that gone now?"

I try so hard not to be frustrated. I take a shallow breath. "I do like men, too, that hasn't changed. There's a possibility I might end up with a guy. But I'm telling you this because I might end up with a woman. And you have to know this about me."

She says, pleadingly, "It would be easier if you were with a man. For you and—I don't like to say this to put pressure on you—for me, too."

The whispers. I hate that this is part of the equation. I get the sense she would have almost no qualms if not for the outside intrusion, for the chorus of people yelling, "Oh the horror!" I feel for her. It's hard to say screw everyone else. I mean, it's what I've been having trouble with this whole time. I can't expect perfection from her when I can barely bring myself to buck convention.

"I know. And I'm sorry for all the pain this might cause you. I don't mean it to happen to us. But there's no helping it. This is who I am."

She shakes her head. "The community is so backward."

My face gets hot, my eyes fill. She gets it. I knew she'd get it. "It is."

Then her eyes well up with tears, and they don't seem happy. I want to groan because when my mom cries I capitulate to whatever she wants and turn my back on myself. I can handle her anger and hauteur, but never her genuine sadness. She takes a small step toward me. "Does this mean you will never have babies?"

I almost laugh. Of course that's what she's worried about. I shake my head emphatically. "No, it doesn't. I want kids, one day. There are ways to have kids without being married to a man." I switch to Armenian, "One day, you will become a grandmother."

She lets out a huge breath and crosses herself. "Then I can live with anyone you want to be with. Tantig Sona and her big mouth be damned."

I hope she'll do a whole lot more than just live with it, but this is huge. It feels like Tantig Sona is a stand-in for the rest of the bigotry of the community. Mom's on my side, and I can hardly believe it.

"Mom, it will be okay. I will make you proud," I say.

"Nareh, I am already proud," she replies. "Diana sent me your article. It was—I couldn't believe my daughter wrote such a thing. I felt I was there with you. And I wanted to strangle that man who did that to you."

She . . . she read it? "Why didn't you say anything?"

"I was about to tell you, then you interrupt me to tell me you are gay. Or not gay, I don't know the words for it." She huffs, then continues, "It was very good, that's what I'm saying. With that talent, I know you will find some new job."

My bottom lip shuts against the top one, trying to prevent a cry from bursting out. I can't get out the thank you, so I step over and hug my mom, and she hugs me back, and we're in it for a while, and I forgot how good it feels to just hold and be held by your mom. I'm a little kid again; she smells and feels the same as when I was five.

When we finally pull away my mom looks at me funny. "You know, there was an essay you had to write freshman year about a classmate. You wrote about your soccer teammate, what was her name, Jasmine? It was very descriptive of her body. I thought maybe you looked up to her a lot, but now maybe I think different?"

I know the exact assignment she's talking about. As a naive little freshman we had the weird prompt to write a descriptive essay about a classmate, and I took it as an opportunity to let my heart run free about my feelings for Jasmine on the page (not un- derstanding it was actually lust, though I had visions of us making out in the janitor's closet, not included in the essay). I can't believe Mom remembers it.

"Yep," I say, "That wasn't just friendly admiration. Full-on crush."

She shakes her head. "I would never see anything like that. Back home, everyone was either married or unmarried, there was no gay. You sometimes suspected, but a woman couldn't be walking down the street with a man you weren't married to, much less two men holding hands. They'd be murdered on the spot."

"That's horrible," I say.

She makes a sound of deep agreement. Then, her voice gets small, serious. "That stays in the mind forever. When I saw you kissing her—Erebuni—I thought, *They are going to kill my daughter.*"

Whoa. I never knew that. I could tell her don't worry, that's not going to happen. Her fear is unfounded. But she's sharing this part of herself with me, and I can tell she doesn't want to be reassured by facts. She wants me to know how scared she was. This is as close to an apology as I might get for the way she acted at the banquet.

"I'm sorry you felt that way."

Mom sighs. "I know it's stupid."

"No, it's not. That's how you grew up, that's what you saw and heard. I get it. I'm glad you can see past it now, though. Seriously, thank you for this. For everything."

She studies the yellow dish towel her hand is resting against, then waves me off. "Don't make it seem like I'm so prejudiced that was a hard thing for me."

I smirk. She always needs to be in the right. That's fine with me. "Okay, Mom."

Then Nene steps in, and she has this look on her face like she's about to share something big. Mom and I turn toward her. Nene lifts a finger. "Back in Anjar, there was a woman I knew, older than me."

I shift my weight. I love when Nene shares from her past, but I was kind of hoping to get more time with Mom to talk about my coming out, and Erebuni specifically. I'm afraid that if we get interrupted that's going to be it, no more returning to the awkward subject.

Nene continues, "She was a fierce fighter, from Musa Dagh originally. Photographs of her with bullets up and down from her neck to her waist. They say she killed fifty enemy soldiers while defending her home. She and her family finally left in 1939, I believe, when France annexed it to Turkey for good. I was nine years old then, and we met them soon after. Anjar was very small.

"She never married. She told me one time, after what she had seen and what she had done, she would never let a man be the boss of her. She was the most impressive woman I ever met, and when I married Hrant, I was sad that I couldn't be more like her."

Holy . . . so Nene was listening this whole time? She's definitely gleaned the same-sex thing. How much of the conversation did she understand? Also, between this conversation and the one at the banquet, it seems like Nene has some regrets about some of the actions she took, or rather didn't take. Her poet lover, the one she left behind to marry my grandfather. She's held them in for decades and is only now sharing them.

"So, I am telling you this because I think she is a little bit like your friend, Nar my dear. The tall one who spoke at the banquet, who you were joking around with every time she got off the stage. Those two women, they hold themselves the same way."

My mouth falls open. She was listening, not only now, but she saw Erebuni and me together at the banquet, miming and typing messages on her phone. My heart hurts thinking of how happy Erebuni and I were at that moment, not knowing what was coming our way only an hour or so later.

And that Erebuni reminds her of this fierce warrior lady from Musa Dagh.

"Bring her over for dinner. Let us get to know her better," Nene says.

My mom sucks in a breath, stealing all the oxygen from the room. One step at a time for her, and that's probably a bit much to jump into.

"She's, uh, a little mad at me now. Because I lied to her," I say.

Nene puts on that face like she has all the assurance in the world. She waves her hand. "You can make up. You're a very resourceful girl." She pats me on the arm and walks out of the kitchen like she didn't drop the biggest bomb on us.

I look at my mom. "Did you know about that?" I ask.

Mom seems both surprised and unfazed, like Nene doing these big reveals has been a regular part of her life. "Nene is a mystery to you and me," she replies.

She turns to the pile of beans and says, "Let's continue if we want to have any hope of eating fassoulia today." Then she adds in Armenian, "My daughter."

My window might have closed to expand on the details of all my feelings, but I'm already lighter. It's as if I've sloughed off an entire layer of skin, and I'm all shiny and soft underneath. I'm plucking beans, crushing garlic, and opening tomato cans like I'm not here. I keep replaying the scene from minutes ago over in my head.

There's something else. Now that I've told Mom and Nene, I

want to keep going, shout it to the world. I couldn't believe how freeing it felt to put the words down about what happened at KTVA with Richard, how badly I needed it. It helped me make sense of the whole thing. Now I need to do that again, and it's not like I don't have the perfect place to yell my sexuality to the world. The need to do it is tugging at me, urging me to look at it straight in the face.

It's almost ten a.m., and there is some light filtering in through the fog. I know where I need to go. I give the countertop one last sweep and tell my mom I need to head out for a bit. The way I say it, I don't ask for permission, I'm not apologetic. It surprises even me.

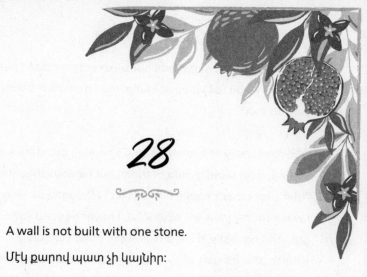

28

A wall is not built with one stone.

Մէկ քարով պատ չի կայնիր:

—*Armenian Proverb*

Back home, after putting the final dinner dish into the dishwasher, I'm back in my room, cozy with the heater on, reviewing the winning photo. I'm cupping the phone in my hands as if it were a precious gem and I'm in awe of its power. I scroll through the words I spent all day writing.

> This isn't going to be my usual type of Instagram post. It's the same smiling selfie, still Nareh who loves matcha lattes and spotting sidewalk blooms, but there's another layer about myself I've hidden too long, and I want to share it with you all.
>
> I'm bisexual. That's it, such a small thing, two words, but I've been terrified to openly say it. Afraid that people will think I'm oversharing, seeking attention, or getting explicit about my sex life. While I'm writing this I imagine

some readers waving their hands like ugh, we don't need to know. If you fall into that camp, the "Unfollow" button is easy to tap.

I'd occasionally see other people's coming out stories and be happy for them, proud of them, but I always thought, "that's for other people, not for you." I thought, as long as I was with my (now ex) boyfriend, I never needed to come out. And honestly, if I hadn't met the most incredible woman, there's part of me that thinks I would have never come out. The thought scares me, that I could have lived my entire life in the closet.

But now coming out is for me, too. Because I don't want to hide as if this is something shameful. Because I don't want to have to pretend someone is just a friend. Because I don't want to hurt people with lies just to bend to the norm. Because it's just life, and you can't help who you love.

Being open about who I am may make some aspects of my life harder (namely, community acceptance, because news flash, not everyone who lives in San Francisco is a bleeding-heart liberal), but even typing this, I already feel lighter. I'm hoping for the particular type of freedom that comes only when you shout about who you truly are. I'm hoping it will inspire others, too.

Thank you for being here with me and letting me share my story with you.

I've read and reread it a hundred times; it's ready. And the photo is perfect. I went back to Ocean Beach, my hair lashing around freely and a small surprised smile on my face, like the first blush at being tickled. And on my shirt, a new addition. I went to a tchotchke shop in West Portal and found a rainbow pin. I felt a little fake doing it, like, *Oh yeah, now you get a rainbow pin, Nar.* But then again, yes, exactly; this is the right time for me. The rainbow pin is peeking out from the corner of my shirt, where it still sits since I haven't taken it off. But I still haven't hit "Post."

Because even if I did come out to Mom, and no matter how confident I might sound in the post, it's still terrifying.

I'm megaphoning this to tens of thousands of people, some of whom I know. My cousins follow me, some of my mom's friends, too. It's their presence that makes me more nervous, not the strangers. Shoot, do I need to text my cousins one by one and come out to them first? No, that's not necessary. One post and done, spoken to the world.

I know what Dad would think. He would hate it. All those fears about attention seeking, oversharing, those are seeds planted by Dad. He wouldn't want the world to know that his daughter was into women, that she was not a perfect specimen of straight, white America. Well, screw that. A part of me is guilty for thinking badly about him, and also how I got off "easy," with him not being here to rage back at me.

A thought strikes me, and it's kooky, but I go for it anyway. "Dad," I say aloud. "This is who I am. I hope that you will be able to accept me."

I feel better then, like the last person I needed to tell has been told. Never thought my great sexuality reveal would include coming out to a ghost, but here we are.

On my wall, there's the abstract coffee art Erebuni gave me. I wonder if she remembers I have this, this piece of her in my home. The coffee spill looks like dirt at first glance. Then I see there's a shovel, a hoe. And possibly flowers trembling along the edges, dahlias and windflowers. I'm not sure if that's what Erebuni intended or if I'm the only person who can see these objects, but I feel they're a positive sign.

I really am turning into my mom with the superstition.

Well, here goes. I hover my finger over the button and tap it, quick, so that I can't undo it. "Post." It's done and out. I'm out. My heart jumps up to my throat. Oh God, what did I do? There could still be time to undo this. It feels big and terrifying to share, and it can't be undone once people see it.

Then the notifications begin. Heart. Heart. Heart. Heart. They flutter on-screen one after another like a pulse. Then some general comments come in, emojis of hearts with the flag. "Love you girl" from one of my cousins. Okay, maybe this . . . maybe it won't be so bad.

And let's be real, I did this in part so Erebuni could see my public coming out. It's for me, but in it, there's a strong message directly to her. It's a tad past nine, and while all I want to do is text Erebuni, I decide that one, it's too late to text someone who is still upset with you, and two, I should play it slightly cool instead of shouting, "Look what I did!" at her.

Instead, I lie in bed and soak up the comments of shocking kindness from strangers. I'm getting more specific ones now. Women saying they're bi, too, but haven't told anyone; women who are out and proud and proud of me, too; others who don't mention their sexuality who still thank me for the post, or say my hair looks cute like that. One guy who says, "Hot." Not the type of support I was looking for, but if he had to say something dumb, at least it wasn't hateful.

For a couple of years now I've generally tried not to let any comments get to me, the good and the bad, otherwise I'll fall into the trap of living my life by them, allowing a crowd to define me. I always imagine they're talking to a character, not to Nar, the real me. But today I slip off the veil and press my face directly into the comments, feeling their every texture. I am known to the world. I'm more me than I ever have been. That's the thought I fall asleep to.

The sunlight in my room wakes me. Judging by the slant of it against the wall, I'd say it's eight in the morning. It's . . . Saturday, yeah. It used to be my day off that I so looked forward to, but now I have a long docket of nothing waiting for me. At least I can read any new comments.

The thought rouses me enough to get my arm out of the covers and grab my phone. And yes, there are more than ninety-nine Instagram notifications, but those can all wait because there's a text from Erebuni. I prop myself up. Maybe she saw the post. And oh my God, she sent it just after eleven. A late-night text can only be a good thing. I think. I hope.

I swipe my phone open to read it. I read your post. My throat tightens. I'm stunned. That was a vulnerable and well-written post. It must not have been easy. How are you feeling after it?

Then a second one. You look very pretty in it, too.

An invitation to talk. And a physical compliment?! Yes, God, I might have a chance. I drag my face under the comforters and let out a happy groan. Then I pop back out for air and to read her text again.

Damn, it's still too early to respond. I think in half an hour, around 8:45, I can text back. I brush my teeth and gussy up while planning my reply, as if preparing myself physically is going to bring me some kind of divine inspiration, but it is useful to distract me from texting her back immediately.

Finally, I do. **Thanks, it feels great. I'm surprised by all the positive responses.** Keeping things cool, even though a more accurate response would be, "*You texted meeeeeeee! YESSSSS.*" In my politeness, I follow up with, **How are you doing?**

Shortly after, she responds. **I haven't been doing great but everything feels different this morning.** Hopeful? Would I be flattering myself to think I had anything to do with that?

Then, another comes in: **I understand if you don't because of how distant I've been, but would you want to meet up? I was going to go to the Conservatory of Flowers today. Would you like to meet me?**

I'd rather do that than anything in the goddamn world. Keeping myself somewhat restrained, I tell her yes, I would. She asks if I can be there in a couple of hours. I sure can.

29

From heart to heart there is a path.

Սրտէ ի սիրտ ճամբայ կայ:

—*Armenian Proverb*

I've never been to the Conservatory of Flowers. That's the tragedy of being raised in a city; you rarely visit the touristy spots, which are landmarks for a reason. We tried to go to Alcatraz once, my dad and me plus Diana and her dad. But when we got to the pier, tickets were sold out since apparently you have to plan these things in advance. I wish I had gotten to go with Dad, and I never attempted to see it again. But maybe I could with Mom and Nene; we could visit its craggy rocks and remember him.

I told both Mom and Nene that I was meeting Erebuni, and Mom gave me pointers on what to wear and how not to sound too desperate, which I will totally take. Nene told me to bring her home for dinner again.

The building looks like a massive white birdcage from the outside, and as I approach it, I can't help but feel like a sparrow hopping back into its home. It's eleven in the morning, still foggy over here and cool, but it's burning off, not as thick as earlier. I'm shivering in a white off-the-shoulder top over some blue jeans with a casual raw hem plus blush lace-up ballet flats. I am going for suggestive shoulder skin to tempt the mind in a look that otherwise says I'm not trying hard (I swear).

I glance around the vast park to see if there's a willowy witch among the groups of people, but I don't see Erebuni. She might be inside already, and I'm too nervous to text since it's eleven on the dot. Don't want to seem desperate. I press in alone.

Inside, it's a total contrast. Dark, tight spaces with plants groping for you with their ferned branches and waxy leaves. And the heat—you can practically smell the humidity. None of these tropical plants appear to be native to San Francisco, which makes sense considering the heat they need to thrive. I suck the air in through my nose and feel like I'm being cleansed somehow.

It's quiet in here, the couple of other patrons are speaking in hushed voices as if they're in a library. I feel like I was somewhere similar recently, and then I remember Kiki's conservatory, the glass entrance to her garden. Then I remember Erebuni in her bloodred top. Kissing her on the old velvet couch. Before me there's a long, tall plant, with soft furlike leaves at the end. The softness of the texture reminds me so much of that moment in Erebuni's cottage. Then there's a light tap on my shoulder, and a small "Hey."

I turn, and it's her. She's preened. She's wearing a plunge-cut black top over jeans and dark lipstick. The greenery surrounds her like an aura, which gives me a sense of her divinity. Then I feel this rush over me, an insanity where I'm questioning if it's really her or if my mind invented this figure. I realize I never expected to see her again. But it's actually Erebuni. Her micromovements, the side-smile (the world's friendliest snarl); I couldn't have invented that.

There's something about her, though, a tenseness that hasn't been there in any of our past encounters. Neither of us goes in for a hug. There doesn't seem to be any question that it's a no on that front.

"I like your top," I say, stupidly. "I could never wear anything like that."

Ten seconds in and I've gracefully drawn the conversation toward boobs. I am so goddam hopeless.

"Sure you could," she says.

It seems like she's about to speak again, but she stops. Instead, stillness surrounds us. If I don't say anything now, it'll be unbearably awkward. I gesture around us, "What a place."

She sounds her agreement. "Should we look around?"

"Definitely."

We both lead the way at once, in different directions, causing us to bump shoulders. I smile, rub at the spot where we touched.

"You go ahead," I say.

"No, you," she replies.

I take her up on it and steer us down a hallway where the plants on either side have grown into each other above us, forming an archway. There's an art deco metal grate along the floor, which my soles tap against.

In front of a delicate spider-shaped flower we both stop to admire, she says, "I didn't mean to ghost you after the banquet."

Thank God she pushed us into this conversation. My cowardly ass was not about to. But now that we're in, I might be able to steer through the currents. I make a couple of noises to indicate that it was understandable. She continues, "But I was so hurt.

And I thought if we talked, I'd get back with you and pretend it never happened but hold on to this resentment, let it poison our relationship. I didn't want that. I should have been more up-front. But I was pained and shocked by the engagement news. By what you said to your mom."

That night hits me all over again, the way she looked at me, utterly betrayed. And she wasn't wrong. To push the memory away, I focus on a waxy lily, a green so light it's almost yellow, so shiny it could be fake, like they stuck a decoy in here and there to make the place look more lush. But I know that's not the case. Everything here is real.

I find myself unable to articulate how sorry I am, and I'm certainly not able to look at her. At least we keep walking. My eyes straight ahead, I say, "I know. I can't blame you. Not that I'd blame you, it's just an expression. I mean, it was a lot, that night, and I'm sorry for it."

She takes a breath, like she's bracing herself. "People's word, it's important to me. I like to trust, be full of abandon in relationships. Friendships, too. And while of course, of course I understand people's situations in coming out are different, it'd be very hard for me to be the hidden girlfriend. I can do that for a bit, but I need there to be some trust that it wouldn't be forever. And after that night I wasn't sure I'd ever get it."

I nod, eyes downcast. "I can see why you thought that."

She stops walking. "But I've been a wreck, Nar."

What? I always assumed she angrily moved on. That she had her private rage against me and then popped right back into her daily routine. I can finally look at her. She appears actually distraught. Hands clasped together, like she's afraid to separate them.

"I missed you. We barely . . . we were together a couple weeks, but it felt much longer. I convinced myself you went back to your fiancé and I shouldn't reach out."

I have to say something here. If I wait, my timing might feel too late, an afterthought. I want to be up-front with her.

"I did—"

She interrupts. "What? But your post . . . You mentioned me in a way that made me think you couldn't be with him."

Her tone is a lot more alarmed than I expected. We were speaking like in a song, everything leading up a crescendo, and now it feels like I shut it off. And wait. Did she just imply that she wanted to meet up because she was certain that Trevor and I had broken up? I didn't want to hope that's what this was, her wanting to get back together, but of course I desperately wished it. And I may have just trampled over my chance.

"No, no. I did, but only briefly. After we talked, after you left me, I was feeling low, alone. I'd never felt so alone. So when he came back from his trip and seemed interested in wanting to meet up, I didn't want to pass up the chance at feeling like anyone in the world cared about me. I know, it sounds so bad, but that's the real reason I went. And when I got there"—oh God, let me find the courage to say it because I know this could ruin everything, but I want to be honest with her—"I did kiss him."

"Oh," she says, voice small. Her face shades with disappointment, her lips shrinking into a pucker. Then she's on the move, as if she doesn't realize she's walking.

I keep up after her as we enter a new room, this one hotter and more humid than the last. The plants get bigger, their leaves fan out impressively. The wetness in the air must be making my hair curl, I realize for the first time, and don't mind it.

I try to catch her eye. "It felt so wrong. You and I were broken up, had been for a week, but I still felt like I was cheating on you somehow."

An older couple in purple and blue windbreakers approaches us from the opposite direction. Erebuni slows to a stop, and I quiet and give them a polite half smile. As they walk away, my voice stays hushed. "I also weirdly felt like I was cheating on myself, like I was betraying myself. So I broke everything off with him for good, like, immediately after that."

I can hear her exhale. It doesn't sound like relief, though, more like thinking.

I step toward her, catching her reluctant stare. "I thought I'd never see you again, but I still cut it off with him."

Her eyes appear distant. "But you did try to go back to him. Tried him on for size."

I give an apologetic shrug. I'm not done, I need her to see the full picture. At least she's listening. I haven't lost her ear yet. "I mean, in a way, yes. It wasn't good of me. We had five years together. I had to see him in person no matter what since we ended things so . . . unclearly. I was in a bad place when I went there. Part of me assumed we'd just reconcile and fall into place. That this was what I should be doing. Like, I thought my mom might want me to be with him."

"Ah right, your mom." She doesn't say it with vitriol or sarcasm. It's plain, like an immovable object.

That sparks something in me. I, too, thought that was the biggest obstacle. I mean, it was, but it turns out it wasn't rooted into place forever. I try to hide a smile. "Not anymore. You saw the post. I didn't just come out to the anonymous world. Before I wrote that, I told my cousin Diana, then my mom. Even my grandma."

Erebuni stops walking again just as we enter a new room, the most open one we've been in so far, with massive lily pads shaped like tart pans dotting a pond like stepping stones.

"You told them? I hoped but I didn't believe . . ." Her voice has a desperate edge to it.

"Yes." I don't say anything else because I'm too busy enjoying the transformation of her face. There's a leavening of every feature.

"What did they say?" She's sounding expectant, hopeful. She wants to believe this will work, and the feeling she's giving me, I absorb it into my skin like sunshine.

I speak fast. "Diana knew, basically. She was so kind and supportive. And my mom was okay. She's had some time to digest it, so once I told her outright, it wasn't such a shock. She understood that this is me." I smile at her, "It's going to be okay." The last part comes out thickly, and when I feel a tear hot on my cheek, I realize I'm saying it as much for me as for her. I haven't fully admitted it to myself yet. It's going to be okay, and that's the baseline. It might be more than okay. Much more.

Then I feel it. Her hand is in mine, a serenity in her touch. I'm tranquilized by it, my whole body rippling and unable, unwilling, to move. The world, perhaps from my wet eyes or the shaking inside me, takes on a grosgrain texture. And the way she's looking at me is entirely new. Her cheeks have reddened. She's open, suddenly.

"Nar," she says.

I wipe the tear with my other hand, not daring to remove the one she's cradling. I never want us unclasped.

"Yes?" My voice is heavy from the tears I'm trying to hold back.

"You did it." It's not a question, but I still answer.

"I did." It comes out a whisper.

She steps closer. "Can I kiss you?"

I nod, and draw my face toward hers. The downy softness of her cheek rubs against mine, then she kisses me, lips as yielding and strong as rushing water. The smell of her rose perfume mingles with the humidity, turning it so heady I lose myself in it and know that no matter what happens, I will never forget this.

She pulls away gently. There's a flush to her face, deeper than before, the etching in her irises more distinct. There is nothing hidden, no secret fears. Every line in her face is open. I set to memory her cheekbones, the width of her eyes. But I don't want to have to only remember it.

I need to tell her that; it's as important as breathing. "I want to be with you. Really. You're so special to me, and I want to give you and me a real chance."

She strums her thumb over the top of my hand. "I'd like that very much."

I can't help it, I almost launch myself at her with another kiss, and she takes a couple of steps backward. We land against a wall of plants, without crushing them, and vines curl around our hair like garden snakes.

We laugh at the near fall.

"This is actually happening, right?"

"It is," she says. Then, confessionally, she says, "I couldn't bear to be away from you. Everything I did had a little less luster in it, even the things I've always cared most about. Your article, then your post, I knew they were a turning point. You made such strong, difficult decisions. I feel bad for ever doubting that you could. I'm sorry I didn't have more faith."

I'm still not over the thought of her missing me during the last couple of weeks. How she must have felt when she saw my article, then my coming out post. Part of me knew, though, that it wasn't entirely over with Erebuni. That silver thread that connects us over the ether, it was stretched taut but wasn't broken. She must have felt it, too.

"No, no, I'm the one who's sorry. That night at the banquet, let's face it: total shitshow."

She laughs. "Total." She pulls a small white petal out of my hair. "But you more than made up for it."

She reaches for her bag. "And," she says, pulling something out, a bookmark maybe. "Speaking of the banquet . . ."

She hands it to me. Our photo strip from that night. "I'm not embarrassed to say I've been carrying it around in here. Just in case."

Every one of these photos, even the two silly ones, is radiating our joy at being with each other, with ourselves. They capture us entirely as we were, and, as I allow myself to hope, as we will be.

"I can't believe it. Mom said she'd thrown it away, and I was so angry at her."

"Two copies," she says with a contented grin.

I hold it in my hands like a precious piece of jewelry I thought I'd lost.

"They're beautiful," I say.

Being here with her, like this, is exactly what I've wanted. Her Cheshire smile and the knowledge that she's been thinking about me this whole time. Her forgiveness. But I'm also starting to get self-conscious. I haven't felt like much these past few weeks. I've been a pajama-wearing, chore-doing shell of a person, wishing for better things. "If you want to give this another shot, I'm not sure how much I have to offer as a girlfriend. I'm unemployed, and who knows when I'm ever going to get work again. I was fired. I mean, you read the article. You sure you want to date me?"

I'm half joking, but also mean it, and I hope she sees that.

"I did see that. I thought it was very Armenian of you. Die in honor of the cause, up against bigger enemies." She smiles at her little joke, then says, "You're full of potential. In fact, last week I was talking to a friend of mine who's started up a Vice News–like media company focusing on Armenian issues—longer form, more storytelling. Of course I thought of you, but at the time I assumed you were still working at your station. I didn't put two and two together until now."

I force myself to tune in to what she's saying because there's a full-on parade with a drumline and sparklers going off in my head. This could be it.

She continues, "If you're interested, I'll connect you. He's looking for reporters."

My guardian angel. That would be a dream, the perfect outlet, the one I didn't let myself hope for. It sounds better than any other job that's passed through my mind these past few weeks, and I find myself already thinking about stories I could report on. It's not a sure thing, and I'm not sure if a company like this would hire me since all my segments are, well, cotton candy, light and sugary. But I do have my article. The Armenian cooking class. The Armenian banquet piece with Congresswoman Grove. I can show them just how badly I want this.

I haven't said anything yet, and Erebuni adds, "Only if you're interested. I didn't mean to barge in on your career."

"No," I stop her. "It's incredible. I would love it." I feel possessed by something, the immenseness of possibilities, a pure rush of optimism that nothing can shake. I want to share it with her, beam it in her direction.

I say, "I would love to tell you all about why. I want to tell you so much more, and hear everything about what you've been doing. Can I be super forward and ask, can we spend the whole day together? Do you have any plans?"

She doesn't seem surprised at all by this, and is as even as ever when she brings my face close to hers. "I have no plans but you."

I take hold of her hand, kiss it, but don't let go. We continue walking around the conservatory, noticing plants we walked by but didn't see before. Even if we spent the entire day in here, we'd keep discovering something new.

We walk slowly, stopping to breathe in the magic of these plants. We pause sometimes to kiss, to rest a head on a shoulder. We do exactly what we want.

Epilogue

It's better to go into captivity with the whole village
than to go to a wedding alone.

նախընտրելի է բանտարկվիլ բոլոր գիւղին հետ
քան թէ հարսնիքի երթալ մինակ:

—*Armenian Proverb*

"*Now we'd like* to invite everyone on the dance floor to join the
happy couple." The DJ's voice booms over the speakers, the lights
turn neon blush. *The happy couple.* The words take root in my
mind, that crashing recognition once again that this is the wedding of my dearest cousin, my friend from birth. And what a
venue, the Manor Hotel, one hundred years old with sky-high
ceilings and turn-of-the-century gilded detailing ornamenting every inch of wall. I'm sitting in some fancy tufted chair, all of Diana's (and a smidge of my) hard work with her dream linens and
silverware and flowers—from a professional florist this time, thank
goodness—surrounding me. My place is at the king's table, with
the other bridesmaids and their dates. And Erebuni at my side.

She's wearing a dark purple cold-shoulder dress with sheer
puffy sleeves and her layers of necklaces. On her eyes, a stroke of
metallic purple shadow. Dark matte lipstick. She's radiant, my date.

I stand, feeling my fullness after the steak and veggies (which were only okay, because it's hard to feed three hundred people, and hard to compete with the Armenian appetizers the hotel agreed to let us serve). I'm in a floor-length ice-blue dress with sheer tulle wrapped around my chest and neck like a halter. It ended up looking cute, for a bridesmaid's dress. No strapless, no complaints.

I reach for Erebuni's hand, an Armenian cross ring on one finger, a moon ring on another. "Dance?" I ask.

She smiles and rises. We start to ease our way out of the space we're in, but then Erebuni stops and directs my gaze toward my mom's table. My mom is sitting there, puzzling over something held in her hands, just under the table. Strange that she's not getting up to dance since she was all over the dance floor during the entrance numbers. And Nene's leaned back with her arms crossed.

"Should we see if your mom and Nene want to come, too?"

Nene has insisted that Erebuni call her Nene, which she's gladly adopted. It is so goddamn sweet that Erebuni is looking out for my mom. I agree and we change course, toward my mom. The DJ is blasting "Uptown Funk," which Diana and her giant princess-cake dress are twisting along with. Not sure how she can bend her torso like that in a corset, but there she is, defying physics. Her fiancé—wait, *husband*—Remi, is dancing alongside her, holding her hand and staring at her like her hotness is about to scorch the earth. Which it is. A crowd has loosely formed around them and is growing in size as guests are beckoned toward the dance floor by Bruno Mars.

As we approach my mom and Nene's table, Tantig Sona, who was sitting a few seats down from my mom, spots Erebuni and me, lifts her nose right into the air, and sashays past us with palpable disdain. For a moment I'm steeped in it, my very real fear that my family would reject me, that I would be alone. That Tantig Sona has rejected me. Then I remember: Erebuni is right beside me, casting me in protective strength, and Mom told me not to worry about Tantig Sona for one second. Her opinion does not matter, she told me.

Standing now, just ten feet away from us, Tantig Sona whispers into one of Diana's tantig's ears and nods her head toward Erebuni and me. The fear climbs again. A pain heaves inside me, that my own aunt, my dad's sister, would see me as someone worthy of contempt, kindling for the gossip fire. I've known her my whole life. Laughed at her jokes, eaten her food. It hurts, though I know she's wrong. It may never stop hurting. Diana's tantig whose ear was being poisoned by Tantig Sona doesn't so much as turn toward us, and she gives Sona a curt smile, then walks in the opposite direction. And that, that's been the balm. I am filled again with the remembrance, the feeling of a bright, warm light, remembering that the rest of my family is behind me. I have been so impressed by them and their refusal to indulge in Sona's need to spread gossip. Not seeing my and Erebuni's relationship as a piece of gossip at all. Welcoming us and my new relationship with the same enthusiasm as they'd share for any new couple. Mom led the charge, led by example, and for that I am forever grateful.

Erebuni sees Tantig Sona's gesture. She takes my hand in hers—cool and soft—and gives it a light squeeze. "It's okay," I whisper to her. I hope she can read in my words that while it's not okay of Tantig Sona, and no, it doesn't bounce right off me, I'm not at all going to let my aunt's actions get me down.

We approach my mom, who is clutching a piece of paper in one hand and a blue pen in the other. She finally looks up when we're right on top of her; Mom's always had a knack for focus.

"Aghchiknerus," she says with the smile of recognition, welcoming us with the Armenian phrase for "my girls." There it is again, that marvelous feeling of acceptance, that mom has grouped Erebuni and me together.

"Are you taking a quiz?" I ask, because that's what it looks like from here, questions spaced along a page.

A little boy of seven or eight runs up to her then, a curly mop on his head, and says, "Oreort Anahid, eenchbes uhree?" Everything instantly pieces together as soon as I hear him use the name "teacher." My mom is straight-up correcting math homework at Diana's wedding. Now that she's back in the math business (as a tutor this time), she seems to be having trouble letting go of it. Not even her niece's wedding can pry her away from fractions.

She turns to him, pleased by his presence. "Perfect score. I could see you weren't sure about number five, but you worked out a solution. Excellent." Then to Erebuni and me, "Antranig is my best student."

The little boy beams. She hands him the paper and waves him away. "Tell your mom that's an extra twenty dollars. Okay, thank you."

I smirk. "I love the enthusiasm, but we should probably hit the dance floor. Support Diana?"

My mom waves me off. "Don't be hard on me, I am bringing in good money now." She rises carefully.

"Have to appreciate your dedication to your craft, Tantig," Erebuni says.

My mom reaches for her drink and takes a large gulp. "Vodka," she says, pronouncing the V as a W. "You know of craft. Everyone is talking about your khachkar."

She nods her head in the direction of the gift table, where Erebuni has placed one of her amethyst khachkars. It sits with a simple ribbon and gift tag around it. There are three guests surrounding the table, eyes locked on her art. She finished, at last, and the first one went to Diana.

My mom leans into Erebuni. "But don't tell Diana it's stealing the thunder."

Erebuni and I laugh. Then I ask Nene if she'd like to join us, already knowing the basic answer I'm about to receive.

Nene is wearing sage green, her hair done up in a stately bun. She leans back in her chair. "I'm content to watch all you young people. I've danced at enough weddings. I'm only going to two more," she says, pointing at Erebuni and me. She's said this before, yesterday in the car on the way to the rehearsal dinner and back. "My other two granddaughters'. Karine's, and yours, Nareh jan. So hurry up, I don't want to die before I see you and Erebuni get married."

Mom lets out one quick sigh, like here we go again, and also because it is a lot. I mean it is for me, too. Erebuni and I are still in the early days, but . . . I can hope. I laugh, I bend over and kiss her on the cheek. I sneak a glance at Erebuni to see how she's reacting, and I believe I detect a pink flush that wasn't there before.

Mom, Erebuni, and I teeter in heels toward the dance floor. There's suddenly a buzz in my pocket—oh yeah, the dress comes with pockets—and I pull out my phone.

It's from Vache: Hotel rez confirmed, emailed you the info.

A charge of excitement zips through me, thinking about our upcoming trip to Washington, DC. We'll be covering the Armenian Genocide Recognition Bill for Pom Media, the new Armenian news outlet Erebuni told us about. Vache and I are also going to collaborate on covering the human-interest pieces at the Capitol, with the descendants of genocide survivors who will be there. And of course Erebuni is coming, too, since her organization helped write the part of the bill concerning genocide education. It'll be our first trip together. I can't believe this is my life.

I quickly type back, **Perfect**, and pocket the phone again. "We're all set with the hotel," I tell Erebuni.

"I wish you did not have to travel so much," my mom whines. "Planes are very dangerous."

"I promise we'll take care," Erebuni replies.

"I believe. You're more careful than this one," mom jabs me lightly.

"Hey!" But there's only lightness in my voice. Mom can roast me all she wants when she's propping up Erebuni.

We've reached the dance floor and we politely weave toward Diana. Her face beams, sunflower-like, when she sees us.

There is a collection of tantigs and uncles and cousins and family friends, some close and others vaguely familiar to me, and we are all surrounding Diana and Remi in one radiating circle, dancing to the bass thump of the music.

I'm not wound up tight about it. Not walking myself off the ledge of anxiety about people seeing Erebuni and me together. Instead, I want to grab hold of our group's collective energy, sink my fingers into it, swing from its rafters, celebrate how lucky I am.

In this case, that's doing an exemplary rendition of "YMCA." Erebuni gave an elegant shrug and launched right into it beside me.

The unmistakable synthesizer version of "Lady in Red" begins, among whoops of recognition from the guests. It isn't a Californian Armenian wedding unless "Lady in Red" plays. As couples begin to find each other, Erebuni makes like she's about to move away from the floor. She leans in close. "We can sit this out if you want. I want you to feel comfortable."

When she pulls away, her face is all placation. She means it, she wouldn't be offended. I hold her petal-soft hand. "Thank you, but I feel great. About you, us, all of it."

There's a moment of surprise in her posture, a tiny jolt, but then it softens, and the beginnings of a smile appear. "Come," I say, and usher her back toward the center of the dance floor. We put our arms around each other, bodies press tight. I hope I'll always feel this, the thrill that slaloms through my veins every time we're close.

She's glossy from dancing, and I swear her wide eyes are brighter. Under the press of her sheer sleeves, I feel her warm skin. I lean my head toward her, tilt it up, and kiss her. And this time, it's intentional, it's open, and it contains all the wild happiness that can come only with freedom.

I'm at my cousin's wedding, in Erebuni's arms, which is right where I want to be.

Acknowledgments

First, a great big thank-you to Katelyn Detweiler. Thank you for taking that chance on me, for your tireless advocacy, and for elevating my story with your astute vision. Every email from you is a joy, and I am so grateful for all that you do (which is . . . so much). I thank my lucky stars every day that you are my agent.

Thank you also to Denise Page and Sophia Seidner and the rest of the team at Jill Grinberg Literary Management; it's a pleasure working with you all!

And where would I be without Cindy Hwang and Angela Kim? Thank you both so much for making my dreams come true. Yes, my call with you was one of my life highlights but every interaction since then has been such a pleasure. Thank you for your keen eyes and your direction—you saw deeply into Nar's psyche and helped pull so much more out of the story. Thank you also for your unwavering kindness throughout the process.

The team at Berkley has been such a joy to work with. Thank

you to Kristin Cipolla and Elisha Katz for your expert help in getting the word out about this book. Thank you Abby Graves for your copyediting sorcery—truly magic. Thank you Katie Zaborsky for lending your eagle eyes to this book. Thank you Christine Legon and Alaina Christensen for helping bring this story into the world.

To Liza Rusalskaya and Katie Anderson, thank you for creating such a gorgeous cover. You captured Nareh and Erebuni's essences and infused this cover scene with so much romance. I am so thankful for all the Armenian elements you deftly included.

A huge thank you to Jesse Q. Sutanto for choosing my story to mentor, for being the absolute best, all the time. Thank you for helping me believe in *Sorry, Bro* and making it shine, and for your endless generosity. Without your guidance I would not have made it here.

A mega-thanks to Heather Ezell, who was the very first reader of *Sorry, Bro*, who guided me with both kindness and cunning. I wouldn't have been able to finish my first draft without you, Heather, so thank you a million for being the best book coach ever.

Thank you to all the Author Mentor Match volunteers for creating such a valuable community. And shoutout to my AMM crew, absolutely lovely people and talented writers, all of you: Elizabeth Reed, Elle Gonzalez Rose, Po Bhattacharyya, Alice Y. Chao, Hadley Leggett, Tiara Blue, Zufishan Shah, Jenna Yun, Kalie Holford, Hannah Bahn, and Trang Thanh Tran. And shoutout to Trang for those wild two weeks during the query process where we were all exclamation points in the DMs.

Speaking of queries, big thank you to Dahlia Adler for generously giving your time in reviewing my query and list, and for all your kind words about *Sorry, Bro*. I am forever appreciative of your help.

To Leanne Yong, thank you for your sharp eye and hugely helpful edits on my query!

To Tim Ditlow, thank you for your querying advice and enthusiastic support. It means so much to me.

Nona Melkonian, thank you for answering my many questions about journalism and reporting!

A big thank you to Mary Antoinette Chua for helping me with your brilliant IG ideas and for all your cheeriness along the way!

Thank you so much to the all-star authors who generously took the time to read and blurb this book!

Thank you to Nancy Kricorian for posting Armenian proverbs on Twitter, sparking my interest in them, and for referring me to the Armenian proverbs book, *Seven Bites From a Raisin*.

Thank you to the Berkletes—such a dynamic group!—for being there for me the many times I came running to our chat for help. A treasure trove of generosity and support.

To the Word Cave crew who hasn't already been mentioned, thank you for your friendship and support during the tough sub process. I am rooting for us all! Taylor, Kayvon, Kyla, Jeff, Kamilah, Miranda, Sarah, Andy, you're all the loveliest people and writers I look up to.

To Elyse Moretti Forbes, my goodness, thank you for being there with me every step of the way. Thank you for letting me scream my good news, for commiserating with me with the bad, and for your multiple avenues of support. Any time I doubt myself, I go back and reread the email you sent me after reading *Sorry, Bro*. You are a superwoman, and I am lucky to be your friend.

Amy Kazandjian, I am so thankful you agreed to be my Armenian cultural reader. You've been such an enthusiastic supporter, and your keen eye for Armenian humor added another layer of depth to *Sorry, Bro*. And your audio and video responses to my writing? Seerdus letsoun eh.

To Lisa Weinstein, thank you for your unending support of my writing and my book. It makes my heart light up when you introduce me as a writer or tell your friends about my book. And the fact that you hosted the very first book club for *Sorry, Bro* will always be one of my most special memories. Truly, having your "in real life" support means so much.

To Jen Corrigan, thank you for your consistent championship of my words. I've learned so much from you and strive to reach the level of brilliant vulnerability in your writing. I'm so thankful for your friendship!

Irving Ruan, you are a master of humor writing and I am so grateful you took the time to help me learn how to make my words funny. So, people, if you don't find this book funny, it's Irving's fault. Jk, please know that I am eternally grateful, Irving!

To Robert James Russell and K.C. Mead-Brewer, thank you for teaching me how to write. RJR, for helping me understand for the first time ever how important setting is, and why. K.C., for helping me learn to hone beauty and love in my writing. Thank you for being such patient, kind supporters, even though my writing pales in comparison to your talent. You're both top individuals.

It's been decades but I think of you often—Dr. Jane Healey, my high school sophomore English teacher, thank you for being the first person to tell me I'm a writer. That moment, and your teachings have stayed with me forever.

To KZV, my Armenian school, and the many educators within your walls: you were my whole world for over a decade. Thank you for the family-like community and for connecting me so deeply to my heritage. I hope I honored you in the pages of this book.

A very big thank you to Cindy, Tom, and Alex for watching my kiddo many weekends and weekdays so that I could write. Many deadlines were met only because of your help. Thank you, my dear family, for always being so supportive of my writing; it means the world.

To my little ones, my loves, thank you for teaching me how to stop being so precious about my writing time. No longer do I need to be at a café, exactly at seventy-four degrees, the correct level of caffeinated, the perfect song. Thank you, also, for growing my heart, and helping me empathize with mothers everywhere. This book could not exist until I became a mother. I love you.

To my Armenian family: thank you for being you. The times we get together are some of the most cherished memories of my heart. I could finally channel some of this into my writing, and I hope, if you read this book, you feel how much I love you all.

Dad, thank you for always finding ways to encourage me with my writing. First, always fueling my love of books with our many visits to comic book stores or gifting me books for Christmas, and since then, always asking how my writing is going, and even mentioning my writing in your speech at my wedding. I've always felt you know how important writing is to me, and I am so grateful to have your support.

Tamara, my sister soulmate and my first critique partner, thank you for your effusions of love for this book. I said it before, I'll say it again: The fact that you loved *Sorry, Bro* is enough for me. When I was writing, I still felt that part of myself, when we were 10 and 8 years old again, on the floor drawing stories side by side to share with each other. Thank you for always letting me tell you anything about this book, about the process, and for cheering and commiserating with me. I look up to your writing skill and hope I can write anything as well-plotted and hilarious as you. (I am still laughing about your Banana Republic sweater joke).

To Mom—the mom in this book is not you, of course, but I could have never written her without knowing you. I think she steals the show, personally. Thank you for your contributions to my book, in helping me with translations and Armenian spelling. And mostly, thank you for being the number one influence in my life, for always pushing me to be the best I can, surrounding me with resources, and for teaching me to concentrate on the important things. I love you, I'm grateful to you for this beautiful life.

Ryan, thank you. You were there every step of the way while I drafted and edited this book, while I moped and celebrated. When I shrieked early mornings that I had an idea I had to draft, you took over. When we went months without our nightly Netflix hangouts so I could write, you always understood. I can talk to you about my writing any time and you'll be genuinely interested and completely supportive; it truly means so much to me. And thank you for the title. Who knew a joke over dinner could make its way onto the front cover of an actual published book?

If I missed anyone, please know that I am absolutely mortified and will spend the rest of my life occasionally reliving my shame, usually when I am just about to fall asleep.

One last group to mention. Thank you to readers everywhere, especially Armenian and queer Armenian readers. I hope this story with a happy ending resonated with you, gave you hope or at least a little light. There aren't nearly enough Armenian stories, and it's been a goal of mine to add another (and another and another and another, if I get my way) narrative to the Armenian cultural collective, to share our ancient and beautiful traditions with the world. Thank you for picking it up and reading.

Keep reading for an excerpt from

Lavash at First Sight

The next Berkley romantic comedy by Taleen Voskuni.

I open the conference room door, balancing my laptop (Air, for efficiency) and water bottle (navy blue, for subliminal "I'm not a girly girl" vibes) and am happily surprised to find my boyfriend, Taylor, sitting in a swivel chair, concentrating on his screen.

"Early for my meeting? I'm honored," I say, sliding next to him. *My good luck charm*, I think, right before the biggest presentation of my career.

God, he's hot. I never thought I'd be with a guy like this; he has the look of a tennis player: tall with thin, toned limbs and thick, almost-wavy, almost-blond hair. He looks perilously handsome in his blue oxford button-down. I've idolized men like this since back in high school, and none of them would ever look at me. Me, the perfectly average in every way swarthy Armenian girl. But guess what—thick eyebrows and big butts are in now, and I bagged one. He's mine.

I rest my hand on his knee, and he instantly sloughs it off. Ugh, his stupid rules, I forgot. But we're in the room without any windows facing the office, plus an opaque door. Seems safe to me.

"Not at work, Ellie," he chides.

Our dating is a secret even though we're in lateral positions, so it's technically allowed. We don't even report to the same boss! Taylor goes to such great lengths to hide it at work—and outside work—that sometimes I worry he's lost interest in me. Since he's not from the Bay Area and moved out here for this job, most of his buddies are his coworkers, so he'll be out with them, and I'm not allowed. But then he'll text me late Friday evening and come over, and he'll grab my waist and lift me up to kiss me like we're the only two people in the world.

The thought of it stirs me, and I whisper into his ear, "Right, I'll have to wait until after work to give you the present I've been working on."

He pushes his swivel chair away and, damn, it looks like I've gone too far. I'll have to be in damage control mode. "I'm sorry, I'm sorry," I say before he speaks.

Then he does. "I'm not sure we should keep doing this."

He's serious. The way he looks at me isn't with any of his Friday-night desire. It's the way he looks at one of our coworkers when he's rejecting their idea for being "too out of scope."

The blue of his eyes that has always been a source of pride for me—my ocean-eyed boyfriend—now feels empty and vast. His sharp features, which I've always imagined gently pricking me in the most enticing ways, morph into ice picks.

"I can be more subtle, I promise. I lost myself there, that wasn't me."

I need this, I need him. It's been only a few months, but he's the one for me. I could see us working our way up the ranks, a power couple now at Abilify and then beyond. Two Fortune 500 CEOs, married. Think of the Bloomberg profiles. Hell, he's so hot we might even make *Vanity Fair*.

His voice is almost even, except for a pluck of disgust in it. "I've been wanting to tell you. This isn't working. I feel like I'm living two lives. I hate it."

He hates it. He hates being with me. He hates *me*. The logic is simple, sound, and I'm not talking myself out of it. He's doing it, he's breaking up with me now, four minutes before the chairs fill up with our company's most important directors and VPs, in the fucking Wallaby conference room (all of them are named after Australian creatures because of where Jack, Abilify's cofounder, is from).

I need this account. I practiced my slides more than twenty times and got feedback from all my reports. It was supposed to be perfect. Now I can't even remember the title.

Instead, images from the weekend fill my head: curled up beside him under his tartan duvet, the hour far too late, abandoned glasses of scotch on the nightstand.

"We were getting so close. I thought we were going to start"— I'm almost too embarrassed to say it—"dating. For real, and I would be your actual girlfriend. You told me all those things about your brother—"

"Stop. It's done. I'm sorry I had to do it here, but I've been holding it in for days."

The shock of him wanting to break up with me for days is interrupted by the Tremendous Trio—the three women I manage— pushing open the conference door. The first of them, Nina, stops short when she spots Taylor and me. "We can . . . come back?"

They know. Taylor and I are supposed to be a secret, but it's what he wanted, not me, so I couldn't help but tell my crew anyway. Not like it came as a surprise. Abby was all over it with her intuition and had been dropping hint-y comments for weeks. I felt slightly uncomfortable sharing information about my love life with my reports, but I tried to keep it as quick and professional as possible. No comments about a certain penchant for reverse cowgirl, for instance.

I wave her off. "Meeting's starting in a few, come in." I am doing my best impression of a normal, happy person. I rush over to their side of the conference table. Taylor loses himself in his computer.

"You all feeling ready with your sections?" I ask them.

"Entirely. I committed it to memory and have written out and answered all possible questions that may be fielded." That's Jasmine, the quant star of the group.

"Are . . . you ready?" Abby asks me, voice uneasy.

Never show weakness as the leader. I need to turn these feelings to anger and then channel it into dominating this presentation and landing Operation Wolf for my team. Screw Taylor and his sneaking around with me. He thinks he's better than me? He's a nobody from some podunk town. And, admittedly, it is pretty cool that he made it all the way out here on his own. No! He's the worst.

"Totally," I tell her as bile rises in my throat.

It's then that the CEO pushes in. Reid Erikson is one of the only people in the company who scares the shit out of me with his bald head and missile eyes, his targeted commands, and his whole lack-of-smiling thing. The man wears a Patagonia vest daily, without fail, except on the one or two hundred-degree days when he removes it, revealing a Patagonia-branded T-shirt underneath. I did not know he would be attending. He was not on the invite list, but Operation Wolf is a big deal. The cold of the conference room settles over me, like he brought the Nordic winds in with him.

He's trailed by the cofounder and president, Jack, who plants himself in a corner and asks in his Australian accent, "Youse mind if I do some squats in here?" No one minds, and Jack begins bending his ass toward the window, up and down.

Then rush in the VPs and directors, including my boss, Jamie, the marketing VP. Jamie's . . . okay. I don't feel like she's necessarily rooting for my success, but her insistence on perfection, especially with slides, has pushed my abilities to the next level. She's an odd one. Always has her nails perfectly manicured and sports well-curated minimalist jewelry but also is really buff, loves hiking and skiing, and never eats. Well, not true; she seems to subsist on the Oreo snack packs stashed in her purse. I nod to her briefly (Jamie likes brief), and she acknowledges me with a blink.

The whole reason we're here is because we're in the process of wooing what could potentially be Abilify's biggest client—Zarek's, the world's largest international coffee chain, whose logo is a wolf (hence the code name)—to join our performance management platform.

That's right, we do performance review software. Like, keeping track of how good or crappy your employees are. Not exactly the most inspiring product of all time, but it's a solid group of people, and we're growing fast. They call us a "unicorn" in Silicon Valley, meaning we're already worth a billion dollars. The founders (including the terrifying Reid) took a chance on me when I was no one, and now look where I am: senior product marketing manager. Just one tiny hop-step away from director, which is practically within smelling distance. All I need to do is land Operation Wolf.

I peer at Taylor, who has not looked up and is angry-typing, which at this company is a show of deep focus and revered by all. Don't bother someone who is angry-typing.

I step to the front of the room and flawlessly transfer my slides to the conference room's screen (which is saying something because every room transfers differently, and all of them require multistep and often buggy processes, but I made it my mission when we got the new tech installed to never be that person who can't figure out how to get her slides up on the screen and have to ask for—ugh—*help*).

But when I scan the room—through the window I see the morning light breaking through the fog—even Reid's presence doesn't bother me as much as Taylor's, and he still hasn't looked up from his damn computer. Last week we changed up our routine, and instead of hiding at one of our houses, we went out to Emerald Eyes (a clubby club full of young twentysomethings), which I took as a sign that things were going well. When I realized on the way out that I lost my phone, he ran back in and made a huge point of searching the dance floor, finding the manager, and yelling at some unhelpful people. That was it, I thought, he obviously cared about me. Now I'm wondering if he's just a power-tripping sadist.

I keep vacillating between hatred toward him and self-pity toward myself. I want to jump onto the table and point at Taylor and yell, "We were together, I was falling in love with him, and he broke my heart five freaking minutes ago," then kneel down and burst into tears. Those imaginary tears are feeling very tempting, and a little too real, like it could happen.

Jamie clears her throat, breaking my reverie. I read the title slide in my head, "Operation Wolf: Taming the Beast / Customized Portal for Prospective Client / May 2017." But I cannot speak.

Something is happening to my eyes, they're getting hot, wet. My throat is tightening. And I know if I say one word it's all going to come spilling out, fountains of tears and choked cries.

But everyone is going to think it's because I'm nervous about this presentation, which is not the case. So I use that feeling in my throat and let out a couple closed-mouth coughs bordering on chokes, put up a finger and crease my eyes into seriousness, as if there's an involuntary physical battle being waged inside me (which there is), and then, to a bevy of stunned and concerned faces, I step out of the conference room, run up two flights of stairs until I get away from the Abilify offices, fly into the bathroom, and let everything out. Then I pray I haven't ruined it all.

I really don't deserve my team. In my stead, Nina stepped up and began presenting my slides as well as hers, and she, Abby, and Jasmine switched off until I walked back in four minutes later as if nothing had happened. As I've learned from watching leaders, I simply said, "Excuse me. Thanks for taking over, team," and then jumped in where they left off. I resolved not to look anywhere near Taylor, and that tactic seemed to work.

Jamie has seen the presentation before but still takes notes in her immaculate handwriting in her millennial-pink notebook (even though she's a Gen Xer). She swears by writing everything down by hand and has got me in the habit of it, too. She makes a couple of new points she's never brought up before, so I have to gracefully concede to them, but it doesn't bother me too much.

Reid asks a couple of questions that aren't difficult to answer—if you understand a CEO's mindset, which luckily, I do—and I give concise, confident replies to them. He nods shortly and settles back in his seat. Normally he'd put his feet up on the table, but there are too many people in the conference room for that.

And after the final slide and some brief discussion, the magic words come from Jamie. "It sounds like we're all in agreement here. Ellie, your team can proceed with this portal vision. Please stay in close sync with tech and sales as you build it out. We'll need it done in three weeks."

I should feel elated—again with the jumping up on the table, but this time in joy—but I don't. I feel dry, unwanted, like Jamie has ripped a page out of her notebook, crumpled it up, and tossed it.

"Thank you," I say, a lot more coolly than I would have if my heart hadn't recently been trampled over. I wonder if that makes me more of a boss, not showing excitement. Then I wonder if that's really who I want to be, and immediately shove that thought away. Of course it is.

At my desk, after a congratulatory huddle with the Tremendous Trio, I tell them we're all going out to a celebratory lunch at Zorba's on me. They deserve so much more, but I will be sure, as always, to make that clear in their performance reviews. I check my phone. A missed call from my mom plus a text.

How are you Nazeli jan? Give me call to say hi.

My family refuses to call me by my nickname, Ellie, and sticks to my real name, Nazeli. It sounds beautiful in Armenian but awful translated into English, like a hybrid of "nauseating" and "mausoleum-y." So professionally I go by Ellie. Mom called minutes after Taylor dumped me (a lump rises in my throat thinking of that). The woman has a sixth sense, though she never knew Taylor and I were dating. I knew she'd lament yet another white boyfriend, so I planned to keep him hidden unless things started to progress. Which, of course . . . I guess my instinct was right.

I hole up in the phone booth Abilify has purchased—not, like, a red British phone booth, but a sleek modern one, sort of like a sexy coffin with a window, plunked down in the corner of the office. There's a decent view of all the desks, including Taylor's, though he's not here yet. Probably in some other meeting, probably completely over me.

It still smells new in here, that freshly manufactured plastic scent that hits you hard as soon as the door shuts. I dial my mom, and she picks up after several rings.

"Nazig jan," she starts (the diminutive of Nazeli), "You haven't called. Are you okay?"

We didn't talk for one day, which is enough for an Armenian parent to file a missing persons report. I'm twenty-seven, unmarried, and live away from home, which is a cardinal sin, and believe me, the tears and stomps were aplenty when at age twenty-five I announced that I was moving out to an apartment in the city with a *roommate*. They're over it now, though.

"I'm fine," I say.

"You don't sound very happy. Are you eating okay?"

"Oh yeah."

I haven't been. Cooking is usually one of my most favorite things to do, but with all the prep for Operation Wolf, plus all my weekend nights devoted to Taylor (my throat tightens), I've stopped cooking. It's been takeout and the Whole Foods hot bar when I'm too hungry to wait. What I wouldn't give right now for a sini kufte: the ultimate comfort food, a meat-on-meat pie spiced with cumin and pine nuts. Kneading the meat like bread sounds like the most relaxing thing in the world right about now.

"You are lying, but that's okay. I make you harisseh and bring to you tonight."

"No, Mom, it's okay. I'm fine. It's a half-hour drive."

"It's no problem. Rima makes every meal for her son. He has not cooked once since he left the home. Did you hear," she says, then launches into a five-minute monologue about Rima's son, which I have to interrupt, otherwise I'd be sitting in this phone booth all day listening to stories about people I hardly know.

"How's the business going?" I ask, even though I know it's going just fine, same as always. My parents own Hagop's Fine Armenian Foods, a packaged-food company that makes lavash bread, falafel packs, manti, and dolmas and used to make hummus until the market got too crowded. They mostly sell in Middle Eastern stores throughout California and at two local San Francisco grocery co-ops.

"Is going okay. We are preparing for the Chicago conference. You know Ned Richardson is going to be there, and Bab was able to set up a meeting with him. If it's successful, we can be in True Food grocery chain, can you believe?"

Huh. That would be a huge deal, major growth for the company. Before I can respond, she goes on. "You would be very good at that meeting. You know all the business talk and how to be around these people. Bab and I"—here she hesitates a moment—"we want you to come to Chicago. Help us. We are getting old now. This year, is harder for us to carry all the tables and food everywhere. You know Bab's knee, not getting any better. And I am afraid what the Chicago trees will do to my allergies. I don't know those trees."

The conference is next week, and with Project Wolf, there's no way. Plus, I hate to say it, but my parents' business isn't exactly sexy. Packaged foods? And their branding is awful—it looks so old-school. The name alone. I've tried to get them to update their brand a million times, but they haven't listened. We've gone through this song and dance of "Please, we need your help" but "don't change a single thing we're doing" way too often. So I've been a hard no when it comes to Hagop's Fine Armenian Foods. I do feel for them lugging all their stuff around, though. But I say, "I can't just take off work like that."

Mom is undeterred. "Only three days of work to take off. Wednesday, Thursday, Friday. Then the Saturday, Sunday, you don't have to take off. You telling me you can't take three days?"

Outside the booth, twenty feet away or so, Taylor is returning to his desk. He glances in my direction, probably feeling my gaze, then, face utterly blank, turns away. The phone booth seems to contract, the air sucked out, the sound a pure void. I'm convinced the door isn't going to open, that I'm going to die in here.

"Hold on, Bab wants to say hi."

My father's sonorous voice comes on the line, shaking me from my claustrophobia. "Nazeli? Listen, today I learn that there are approximately one sextillion—that's one with twenty-one zeroes—stars in the universe. And the scientists think there are more planets than stars, if you believe this. But!" he shouts. "We are the only planet we know of with life. This is God's miracle," he says reverently.

"Yeah, that's pretty amazing," I say.

"This is why you must come to Chicago with us."

Oh my God, these two. They are unbearable in how well they team up.

"We have one beautiful life, and we want you to come spend it with family. Help us."

"Why can't Edmond go?"

My much younger brother is still in college, but it's summer break now. I don't see why he can't join, especially since it seems their primary need is brawn.

"He is beginning his summer training, didn't we tell you? He's going to Pebble Beach for almost a month."

The pride in my father's voice is clear. Baby bro happens to be a gifted golfer and got into Stanford on a golf scholarship. I'll still never forgive him for besting me in the ranking of schools, since I'm supposed to be the brainy one, but at least I know I got into Berkeley on a Regents' scholarship, which only one percent of students receive.

"Okay, okay, I'll think about it," I say, knowing there's no way I'm going to go.

We hang up shortly afterward, and before I can make it back to my desk, I'm ambushed by Jamie, who looks more serious than usual. Probably wants to talk about some Project Wolf details.

"Have a minute? I booked Dingo for us," she motions toward a nearby glass conference room.

"Of course," I say, wondering when I'm going to get any work done today.

We sit on the same side of the table, facing each other. She clicks a pink-tipped index finger against the table.

"Listen," she says, and a part of me irrationally flares up, fearing I'm about to get fired. "I'm trying so hard with you."

Oh shit, am I? But no, my performance reviews are excellent—mostly excellent, though Jamie always manages to find plenty of room for growth. Still, I would need to be on a performance improvement plan (aka, a "your ass is about to be fired, so shape up" plan) before they could fire me. It's in the company handbook.

"The beginning of that presentation. You walking out? That was unacceptable."

"I had a medical—"

"No, you were nervous, I could tell. Listen, we all get nervous. I bet even Reid gets nervous. But do you think when he has to deliver bad news to the board he walks out of the room and throws up, then comes back?"

"I wasn't—"

"Whatever feeling you were having, you need to murder it on the spot and move on. If you can't kill it completely, lock it in a box to come back to later. Therapy's great for that. I have the number of a fantastic lady who does therapy for corporate leaders."

"Oh, thanks. That'd be great." There is no way that therapist takes insurance.

Jamie leans back in her chair as if gabbing with a girlfriend. "You're so close to being perfect, but there are things like that that make me question whether or not you are upper-management material."

"Things?"

She straightens. "There's something else I've been meaning to talk to you about."

Oh God, I honestly have no clue what she is about to say. Wait, maybe she knows about Taylor. Should I preempt this? Jump in and say it's over? No, never admit to wrongdoing. Not that hooking up with Taylor is wrong, because neither of us is each other's report or in the same growth chain, but lateral office relationships are still looked down upon.

"I've got an unbeatable deal to sign up at Equinox, where I work out, that includes ten private trainer sessions for only—brace yourself because this number is nuts—seven hundred dollars. Can you believe that?"

I am staring, deer-like, because I'm not sure if she wants me to agree that this number is wildly high (my take) or wildly low. I give a "Wow" that I hope can be interpreted either way.

"I'll forward you the details. I get a little discount off my membership too. Everyone wins."

So she doesn't know about Taylor and me, she's just MLM-ing her gym membership. Wait. That's not all it is. She prefaced this saying this is preventing me from being upper-management material. My body is?

I mean, it's true that I've gained a little weight recently, but I thought it suited me. *Love weight*, I called it, from being with Taylor. Ugh.

She flexes her bicep. "Gotta keep up with all the macho BS in this office, be one of them. No better way to do that than muscle tone. Got it?"

I am mentally gluing my mouth shut, otherwise my jaw would plummet to the ground. Forget the $200 a month that the gym costs. Add in the personal training sessions and that'll take me up to almost $1,000. I'm still trying to wrap my head around my boss telling me to get in shape in order to be considered for a promotion. Is that real?

I would talk to HR about this, but I know what happens to people who talk to HR. Fired. Not right away, but eventually. You're labeled a "problem person." Besides, Melissa, the head of HR, is Jamie's best work friend. So I nod along.

"Totally," I say.

When Jamie opens her mouth, I wonder what fresh hell is coming for me. "Hiking is fantastic, too. We're so lucky to live in a place where we're surrounded by breathtaking trails," she continues, and I'm wondering when the hell this conversation is going to end.

You know what? On top of her delirious overstepping in this conversation, I hate exercise. There, I said it. Nothing about it ever has or ever will appeal to me. I don't mind casual strolls; I can walk for hours through the city if there are interesting things to look at, places to go. But being yelled at by a perfectly toned fitness instructor with fake lashes to "embrace the burn" is not my idea of a good time. Armenians, as a whole, aren't big exercisers. My parents don't work out, my relatives and cousins don't, my grandparents didn't, and my great-grandparents were marched by Ottoman Turks through the Syrian desert with no food or water and left to die. So yeah, the survivors didn't go on fucking hikes after that.

Mercifully, Jamie ends the conversation shortly thereafter.

I walk back to my desk and stare blankly at the screen in front of me.

Taylor, a couple of rows in front, stands up and goes to another meeting without looking my way.

My phone buzzes with a text, a group chat with my parents. **We are so happy you are coming to Chicago!**

And I decide yes, screw this place, I am going to Chicago.

Taleen Voskuni is an Armenian American writer who grew up in the Bay Area diaspora surrounded by a rich Armenian community and her ebullient family. She graduated from UC Berkeley with a BA in English and currently lives in San Francisco, working in tech. Other than a newfound obsession with writing romcoms, she spends her free time cultivating her kids, her garden, and her dark chocolate addiction. *Sorry, Bro* is her first published novel.

CONNECT ONLINE

TaleenVoskuni.com

🐦 TaleenVoskuni

📷 TaleenAuthor

Ready to find
your next great read?

Let us help.

Visit prh.com/nextread

Penguin
Random
House